CITY IN MY HANDS
MANNAHATTA SERIES
BOOK 2

THOMAS MORE

Mannahatta Press
HISTORY REWRITTEN

NYC DREAMS
PUBLISHING HOUSE

To Kristen. Without you, no words, no books, no life.

CONTENTS

PART ONE
THE END'S BEGINNING

CHAPTER 1

"No, no—not like that, girls!" Sakima sighed as she gazed at the arrows scattered on the well-trampled field around her. Small feet running in every direction had crushed the yellow, brown, and green grasses down to the ground, giving the surface the look of a thatched rug.

"Please stop trying to split other student's arrows. And please, use only one arrow at a time." Sakima held her hand flat above her brow and stared up for a quick glance at the crystal blue sky above Mannahatta. "I am serious, ladies; none of this double-arrow nonsense!" she said, looking back at her students.

The crisp smell of drying autumn grasses filled her nostrils, while a cool breeze rippled through the target practice field. Sakima studied the sight in front of her and noted with disappointment that not a single arrow had ended up in any of the dozen targets, let alone in the bullseye.

"You need to concentrate," she called out to her students, doing her best to hide her frustration. "Remember what I've taught you and—"

A young girl spoke up, interrupting Sakima's message. The girl had a temporary tattoo on her little arm that looked almost a lot like Sakima's "monster killer" tattoo. She tugged at Sakima's top. "But Sakima, that's how *you*—"

"*Miss Tamanend*, please," Sakima corrected her.

"But Miss Tamanend, that's how *you* did it when you saved *Mënatink Ohëlëmi*—the Land Below! Rescued all the people there. That's when you became a Mannahatta warrior and the true legend!"

"You killed Yakwahe by splitting your mother's arrow, remember?" another student chimed in.

"Of course I remember, but I did not kill that monstrosity." Sakima's brow furrowed as she remembered the day. "I only sent it back to—"

"So why can't we do that, too, Miss Tamanend? And be legends too, like you? Why? *Why?*"

Sakima shook her head. She appreciated the enthusiasm, but not so much the hero worship.

"Look. First of all," she said, a bit of exasperation in her voice. She exhaled hard to calm herself. "That was a long time ago," she said, waving her hand downward in a dismissive gesture.

"No it wasn't, Sakima! I mean Miss T," a young boy said, the only male child in the group. He was a Two Spirit, and he sometimes dressed as a girl and played with the girls, which was what he was doing today. A perfectly reasonable thing to do for those Mannahatta boys who wanted to do it. "It was only a year and a half ago!" he corrected her.

"Was it?" Sakima said, looking back up at the distant blue sky with its dazzling autumn sun for a second or two. She couldn't remember when the sky had last looked this beautiful and magical. *It's a good sign*, she decided. *The future looks bright.* "Seems like a lifetime ago..." she said in a hushed tone. She breathed in deeply, collecting herself and concentrating her energy on the lessons again. "Let's get back to work, all of you—silly time is over. And please, please, stop with that legend stuff!"

"But you made all of Mannahatta safe. Forever!" said a small girl in pigtails, a little green feather in her hair, which her auntie had dyed to imitate Sakima's legendary and quite powerful feather. The girl jumped up and down with excitement.

"Forever is a long time, Tangetta," Sakima said ruefully. But she gave her kid sister a cheerful, encouraging smile and gently rubbed the top of Tangetta's head.

Sakima clapped her hands together and raised her voice so that all the children could hear. "All right, that is enough time-wasting from all of you. Get back in line, at your spot in front of your—and *only* your—target. Let's try it again. One arrow. And in case you have forgotten, the objective is to at least hit the target. The closer to the center, the better."

"Show us, Miss Tamanend! Show us!"

Eager young students leaped about, some with joy and others with silly coaxing. Sakima was legendary, and watching her shoot arrows was a rare treat, like a private concert with a swift, superstar musician.

"Okay, okay," Sakima said, waving her hand at her squad of archery students to settle them down. "Just one shot, then you all get back to work. Agreed?"

"*Yaa-ay!*" the group screamed with enthusiasm, jumping and running around like baby mechbears, *mechmàxkwi*.

With a shrug, Sakima nocked her bow with a standard arrow—nothing too special this time, no homing devices or other technological enhancements.

She aimed and fired without hesitation.

Bullseye.

She nocked and loosed another arrow in virtually one flowing motion, more a dancer than a warrior.

Another bullseye, splitting her first arrow perfectly in two—right down the middle.

The children roared in approval, some of the littler ones attempting to do somersaults.

Sakima deliberately and slowly turned her head to gaze behind her and away from the target. She made a show of it, causing many of her students to giggle and cry out things like, "No way!" "She can't!" "Impossible!" with joyous, nervous expectation.

Then, without looking, like a magician completing the best trick for the final act of the night, Sakima loaded, fired, and hit.

Three arrows, all bullseyes. The third arrow splitting the previous two apart.

The aspiring archers around her whooped and yelled with glee. A group of high-energy kids chased each other around in circles.

"Sakima is the best!" one of them shouted.

"No one can beat Sakima!"

"Our Sakima is the greatest in the universe!"

"Whoo-hoo, Sakima!"

"*Eluwiwulik*—the best!"

"Okay, everyone, demonstration over," Sakima said, unable to hide her pride behind a big grin. She had to acknowledge that, as much as she knew it might jinx her down the road, she *was* pretty remarkable. Her ability to hit a target less than half an inch across—the base of the arrow twenty-five feet away—was actually quite extraordinary, if she thought so herself.

She smiled, but her face also turned a bit pink. Being praised was still so new to Sakima after years of being told she was wrong and different. Not years, though—virtually her whole life. Now to be so accepted, and even, frankly, exalted—well, she didn't yet have the emotional tools to deal with it. It all made her feel a bit giddy.

Sakima dismissed her smile and returned to her more comfortable, serious demeanor.

"Okay, let's get back to work. Let's all line up again in the same squads, one behind the other at each of the target lines. But this time..." Sakima hesitated for a second. It was not the best way to learn, but with this group of students, she felt it was necessary. "This time, we will shoot from five feet closer. Each of you at the start of your line: pull up the marker from the grass. Take five paces toward the targets and push it back in."

She walked backward to retrieve her arrows embedded through each other in the target, keeping an eye on the young people. And they were somewhat obeying what she had commanded. Students vied for the front portion, and two or three wrestled to pull out the marker from the ground. It was a rubber rectangle held into the earth by two plastic spikes about eight inches long, but it seemed beyond most of her young charges' abilities to get the things out of the soft dirt.

"Okay, okay. People, get organized! I said *one* of you pick up the marker..." Sakima rolled her eyes. She yanked her broken arrows out of the target and tossed the pieces on the grass. She jogged over to the first group, which had managed to extract the marker free.

"Here," she said. "Push it in right here." She indicated the correct spot with the tip of her foot.

Before she could move to the next line of eager students and show them the proper location, Sakima sensed a strange rumbling in the sky. She glanced up, expecting to see dark thunderclouds. But the sky was blue with only a few small, puffy white clouds drifting calmly by. Besides, the weather report for all this week was clear skies, no rain, no storms.

Sakima shrugged her shoulders and approached the next line. "Really?" she said. "Does that really seem to you to be five feet away from the initial spot?" She shook her head with feigned annoyance. She tapped her foot on the ground and then pointed from where they'd stuck the marker—nearly ten feet closer to the target—and back at where her foot was.

With a dissatisfied moan, the students plucked the marker where they had put it in the hope of making great bullseyes from such a vantage point. They then walked it back to Sakima, where she stood with a raised eyebrow of disapproval.

Again, Sakima heard and felt that same rumble, the sound of thunder in the distance. And once again, she peered up at the sky, tilting her head slightly in confusion. But the sky was still robin's egg blue and as calm and still as a meditation pool. Not a storm cloud in sight as far as her eyes could see.

Sakima was bothered by this but didn't know why. It was strange, and she thought, frankly, that she'd been imagining things. Although she strongly believed in portents and signs, she figured her senses were off track today. That her intuition was picking up signals that just weren't there.

With an amused smile on her face, she proceeded to the third line of students. This one was led by her little sister, Tangetta. Her sister's line was straight, nobody pushing or jockeying for the front position. And the marker was exactly in the correct spot.

Sakima tapped her foot on the marker and nodded at Tangetta in approval. *She's got some good leadership skills. Just like her big sister.*

"Good job here," she said, looking up to address the entire line of young archers, who immediately began high-fiving each other.

Sakima stepped away and moved backwards so she was looking at all three groups of students. But before she had a chance to talk to them and tell them about their next lesson, she felt the ground quake beneath her feet. Sakima wobbled a bit before she shot one leg behind her for stability. She watched as her archers reacted the same way, some falling onto the grass, others shouting and talking.

"*Ekee-ay! Èchei!*" many of them yelled. "*Wow!* What is going on, Miss T?"

Sakima stared back up at the sky. She couldn't shake the strong sense of foreboding filling her subconscious. Something wasn't right, and it bothered her.

This gut feeling she had was suddenly confirmed by what she next witnessed in the highest parts of the sky. The beautiful blue had turned an almost sickening yellow-green. Slim black clouds infected the horizon, and all the white clouds had disappeared, destroyed by the incoming—*incoming what?* It didn't look like any storm Sakima had ever seen.

Instead, it looked like what Sakima thought would be how another event would appear: the strong, sharp winds, the strange noise that had just started—like the screech of metal misaligned against metal—the smell of, of... Sakima couldn't place it. But it smelled how blood in your mouth tasted.

No, this scenario was frightening and never before seen or discussed. But it matched the prophesies, and Sakima recognized it for what it was.

It was *Ekhokiike*.

The End of the World.

CHAPTER 2

The skies above the peaceful world of Mannahatta continued to fill with dark, ominous clouds—the kind that arrive before the worst hurricanes or the strongest tornadoes. The blackness began to eat up the yellow-green, puke-like color into which the blue skies had so recently morphed.

The previously soft autumn breeze shifted from northeasterly to southwesterly, increasing to a strong gale-force wind. The temperature dropped more than ten degrees in less than five minutes.

Then the ground began to shudder. Sakima rushed her charges —some yelling, some crying, and a few nervously laughing— toward the shelters at the other end of the field closer to town. "Go, go, go!" Once they were safe and secure, she returned to the unfolding scene at the sporting fields.

A blackened shadow within the dark gray clouds started to emerge. After a few minutes, the shadow revealed itself to be a massive interstellar ship. Sakima wasn't sure if she was seeing a mirage or something real. The entire ship was as wide as a *pahsahëman*—a Mannahatta soccer field—is long. It was much bigger than the alien ship on the mountain, the one which had brought the People Who Fell from the Sky—the *Alànawènik*—to Mannahatta.

The shaking caused people nearest to the lowering machine to tumble to the ground. The sound it made echoed like a violent screech, and painful to hear.

Faded and battered lines of crimson crisscrossed on two sections of the front of the spaceship. This red cross appeared to be made up of both metal pieces—with some kind of sensors embedded in each section of the metal—and paint.

The alien spaceship, a destroyer-class ship of a type Sakima had learned about from her new friends in the Mannahatta military, had the name *Ästra Ån Ima* emblazoned across the side. The ship's engines only made a low humming sound now, as if the ship itself were waiting patiently for something to happen.

Another ship, about half the size of the first one, appeared next. It also had two large crimson crosses across its front section. Another minute passed, and a third ship appeared from out of the gloom. This one was smaller still, about half the size of the second spacecraft. It too was marked with red crosses. The lines of the crosses on all three ships got wider toward the end, flaring out significantly.

A few of the Mannahatta dignitaries, Sakima's father included, had arrived during the brief time Sakima was away making sure the children under her care were safe. The officials moved now in single file toward the newly arrived ship, which was only a few feet from touching down on Mannahatta soil.

The officials strode up bravely to what they must have assumed to be the front of the ship. The large red crosses appeared on either side of the main entryway, based on the square edges all around it, which outlined a massive metal panel. The Mannahatta leaders were ready to greet their visitors, as well as assess the danger they might present. There had been no time to put on official garments, so everyone—including her father, the Sachem Takachsin—arrived in whatever they had been wearing when the skies went sick and the ground trembled. Some wore shorts, some pants. Her father had on what he always preferred to wear when he wasn't doing anything sachem-related: his running suit.

Despite their casualness and their apparent hope for a friendly meeting, in Sakima's mind the danger was clear and present. She wished the warriors, the Mannahatta *ilaok*, would start to prepare themselves for the worst: an invasion. Because for Sakima, that was plainly what this was. At least that's how she saw it, what her instincts told her. Her hand gripped her bow more tightly, and she felt her muscles tense. She didn't like the fact that, instead of going back for weapons, the *ilaok*—many her friends and compatriots— stood in rows of ceremonial lines, hands at their sides, weapons- free.

The Mannahatta dignitaries' smiles revealed that they all were hoping for the best—that is, that these new visitors had come in peace—as had their last visitors, the *Alànawènik*, who had arrived on Mannahatta almost a half a millennium ago. But those with friendly intent do not show such military might or make such a loud, terrifying, and intent-to-intimidate entrance.

And yet, Sakima hoped she was wrong this one time. She wanted these aliens to be peace-loving and that they had only trav- eled in such threatening ships as a deterrent to any nation or civi- lization that might think them weak. Because no sane person would interpret this armada as anything but an aggressive show of force meant to terrify on sight.

The Mannahatta dignitaries glanced back and forth at each other from discomfort, displaying an awkward feeling of not knowing what to do. Perhaps they were thinking, Should we shout? Wave the Mannahatta flags? Or maybe even play some welcoming, nationalistic-style music?

Her father, Takachsin, turned right at that moment to look back at the military musicians along the last row of the unarmed Manna-hatta warriors in the open field. Sakima guessed that he had asked them at some point to run and get their instruments and meet him in the fields when he'd first left his office. Because he now made a motion for them to start playing with a vigorous upward wave of his hands. Within seconds, the drumming began, slow and soft at first, but gradually louder and faster until it reached a strong, steady beat. Some of the *ilaok* began to break ranks and dance and sing, mesmerized by the positive, rhythmic tribal beat.

Then a low rumbling emerged from the largest of the spacecraft, as if in response to the sound of the dramatic drumbeats. This was followed by the deep sound of powerful engines producing signifi-cant torque. Then the front, covered by the blood-red cross design, began to open. It did so bit by bit, showing that the door was of an immense weight, as if it were reluctant to disclose those who hid in there, protected behind its safe and sturdy metal structure.

Sakima fought her way to get closer to the front of the warriors and nearer to the dignitaries of the tribe. Something wasn't right, but she hoped it was she who was wrong. As she made her way along, she waved to a couple of her friends among the group of the *ilaok* warriors. These were of the "protection" class, similar to the New York City Police Department (NYPD) she saw when she was down in *Mënatink Ohëlëmi*, the Land Below. Other warriors were of different classes, akin to the armed forces of most nations. And then she saw him.

Her eyes froze as if there were a light shining upon the man. She stayed still, although her legs were bent in preparation for walking or running. Unsure what to do and why she felt so strange, Sakima absentmindedly stroked the back of her neck to appear to be lost in thought when, in fact, she was in a complete panic.

The reason for her sudden hyper-nervous spell was the appear-ance of a particular young warrior, Private Lèke Gischileu. He stood tall as an oak, his long black hair pulled back in a braid that ended halfway down his back. He had what could only be called chiseled features, with broad cheeks, a strong nose, and a sharp chin. His dark brown eyes sparkled, and he flashed her a big smile, showing straight and dazzling white teeth.

Sakima took a deep breath and forced herself to give Lèke a small wave, and then she started moving again. *You fool,* she admonished herself. *Why do you act like an idiot every time you see him?*

She had feelings of affection for when they were both in high school, although never in the same classroom or anywhere else close enough to chat. He was a bit overweight then, and his hair was not quite shoulder-length. And he was shy, more shy than Sakima by far. But today, here and now, in the middle of a world changing moment of potential danger and death, she acted more shy than she'd ever felt in her life. She was embarrassed that she felt like a smitten school girl and not the warrior she most certainly was.

Sakima stood up straight, her jaw locked, and regained her focus on the moment. Looking around to finish assessing the situation prior to Lèke's arrival, she noticed a crowd of curious civilians and reacted right away. Sakima pointed at these people who hadn't yet moved back and made a chopping symbol with her hands. The warriors who were watching her for instructions responded right away by running over to the storage shed on the far left side of the field. They returned in less than a minute, carrying black and yellow sawhorse barriers.

They set these up along the perimeter, about a hundred yards from the ship. They signaled the crowd to move back, and when the people did, the warriors moved the barriers further back. They repeated this procedure two more times. Then, satisfied with the distance that the populace were from the events that were about to transpire—good or bad—they stationed themselves every five *shaèk* along the barriers. Most turned to face back toward the ships and the dignitaries, while some kept their eyes on the crowd, especially the well-known troublemakers among the Mannahatta people.

Sakima marched up to the group of officials and gave the sign of respect: tapping her closed fist against her chest and nodding her head. Most returned the respect, but one did not: her own father.

"Sakima," he said in a gruff near-shout, "you are not to be up here with the officials of the tribe. As great as your contribution has been to the tribe's safety and to its history, you are not a dignitary, and this is a moment for tribal dignitaries only."

With swift precision, Sakima snapped her fist back to her side, gave her father an angry stare, and stomped back to the front of the first line of warriors. When she turned to face the ship again, the door was more than halfway open. In another half minute, it was all the way up, exposing a dark, cavern-like depth of the ship.

What she saw gave her no comfort. Lines of alien warriors, clad in metallic armor and helmets and carrying weapons of a type she'd never seen, lined both sides of the ship near the open door. The bands of fighters ran back into the ship as far as she could see until they disappeared into the shadows.

There were at least a hundred of them. Mannahatta warriors presently in the field numbered barely fifty, and that included the musicians and other non-fighting "warriors." If this was to be a battle, they were already outnumbered. *And that's just this one enemy ship. I mean alien ship. Visitors' ship. Ho tamwe, oh my, I don't know!*

She set her jaw as her eyes narrowed. If there would be a fight here today on her beloved island planet of Mannahatta, she was determined that it would not go well for the other side, regardless of the numbers or the odds.

Sakima patted her knife, Chessi, reassuringly, while she could feel herself tightening her stomach muscles. She switched her bow to the proper hand and gripped it tightly, causing her small bicep to stiffen and bulge.

And then she waited, hoping for peace but expecting war. She did not have to wait long, however. She could hear the pounding of boots on the hollow metal floor. A congregation of shadows emerged from the interior darkness. There now stood a group of five men out on the ramp that had automatically emerged as the door raised upward.

Two men on each side took a protective stance next to the man in the middle. This man was at least a foot taller than the tallest of the guards at his side. And they all had the same strange, almost ghostly-white complexion. Sakima had only seen people like this when she had visited the Land Below. This man, obviously their leader, wore a burgundy hat on his head that matched his red cheeks and nose. Out of the top of his floppy hat emerged a white feather from a bird Sakima had never seen. The feather was like a cloud: fluffy, puffy and enormous.

The ostentatiousness of the hat matched the fur-topped cape that descended from his shoulders down his back. Strapped to the man's waist were two glittery and showy swords, one huge and the other even more massive. They were attached to each hip, left and right, their handles at the same level of his hands at his side. The sheaths for the swords were shiny silver and covered with many jewels. The handles were also bejeweled, but with even bigger gems.

The men who had accompanied the leader were soldiers, and high-ranking ones based on the medals and other accessories attached to their chest plates. The man with the red hat also wore a chest plate, but his more resembled a king's tunic. While it was clearly armor, it was designed with so much gold filigree and blue-and-white design elements that it was almost distracting, taking attention away from the man wearing it. Sakima wondered if that was intentional: While your adversary was fixated on the beautiful, ornate armor, they would never see you coming until the instant before you sliced their head off.

If not noble, the man appeared very proud, arrogant perhaps, in his stance. Shoulders thrown back, posture perfectly upright, eyes straight ahead, a faint scowl on his face. When he started to speak, Sakima noticed that as he did so his hands balled up into fists, and the men at his side formed a strategic flank around him that seemed more like aggression than protection.

"People of Mannahatta! Behold, your God has arrived! Rejoice!"

Oh, Kishelë! Not this again. Sakima rolled her eyes. *Another pathological jackass with a god complex. It's everything Machto wished he could be, times ten.*

CHAPTER 3

The man waved his hand over the crowd in a gesture that Sakima knew he must no doubt think would be interpreted as benevolent.

"You have nothing to fear; I will provide all that you need. Your primitive culture will be respected, of course it will. But more importantly, it will be improved. We will bring you savages into our better, modern world. And I will be here as your new god to lead you every step of the way."

He waited uselessly for the applause he expected but which never showed up. The man glared at the soldiers by his side. This was clearly an individual used to canned, predictable responses. Clearly a leader who only spoke to and at crowds of his base, his most ardent followers, or at least people forced or paid to be in that role and to applaud on cue. By all appearances, a non-responsive crowd was not something this man was familiar with, ever.

But the crowd was not quiet for much longer. A grumbling started across the field, growing louder by the second. Sakima could sense the negative wave before it crashed around her and right at these strange, unknown visitors.

"Go back to where you came from!"

"Buzz off!"

"We don't need your 'help,' *kèpchat*!"

"*Booo-oooo*!"

Some of the language used was a bit too coarse even for Sakima's ears, as familiar as she was with it nowadays. This was due to her having been part of the Mannahatta Warrior Armed Forces and other Mannahatta defense teams for the past year.

Sakima tensed up even more. *This yelling and cursing is not good. Not good at all.* She hoped her father would do something, and she was not disappointed.

"People of Mannahatta!" her father yelled, his hands raised high. "Please, let us hear more of what our visitors have to say."

A few people in the crowd continued to boo and swear loudly. But after a short while, the chanting and the volume of the crowd noises noticeably decreased. Sachem Takachsin continued, lowering his hands with deliberate slowness, like a conductor controlling an orchestra. As if he was seeking the correct pianissimo tone for the next passage of the piece being performed.

"That's better. Thank you, my friends; *wanìshi*." He then turned back to the tall man on the ramp. "Please excuse our language and reaction. In my people's defense, you used incendiary language—'primitive' and 'savages' being the two worst of the…"

The large pale man with the floppy burgundy hat held out his hand to silence Takachsin, which naturally angered the Mannahatta leader.

"What?" Takachsin yelled out, incredulous. "How dare you—"

Pahòke put his hand out and rested it on Takachsin's shoulder. "Go slow, my friend. They perhaps have different ways of communicating that strike us as rude, but which—" Before he could finish, the man on the gangplank of the spaceship returned to his oration.

"Surrender now, unto your new god who stands before you, and I promise none of you shall come to harm. Resist me and resist my fellow explorers—who all come in peace—and I can also promise you that such a simpleminded act will initiate your doom!"

As the man raised his hand up high above his head, gesturing to the sky, additional squads of Mannahatta warriors arrived, distributing weapons and ammunition. "And doom shall rain down upon you heathens," the man continued, "with such force you could not survive for even a minute! Do not try to go against me, for it is foretold that I would one day come here, and you would supplicate yourselves unto me."

"This is patently ridiculous," Takachsin whispered harshly between his teeth to his friend. Then he turned around and raised his arm up at his side at eye level, bent at the elbow, his palm facing his face, and waved his hand back and forth.

Immediately, the Mannahatta warriors behind him closed ranks. They formed a phalanx of men instead of the parallel rows in which they stood, assembling themselves into the shape of an arrow. The men toward the point of the arrow then knelt down and loaded their weapons. The men toward the back, who had delivered the weapons, turned and jogged off down the hill.

In mere minutes they had returned, riding inside and on top of small hovertanks—*pèmitàn sëkahsën mpàki*. The hovertanks bobbed gently in the air like rowboats on a river. Though small by tank standards, the hovertanks, painted green and red and blue, held three warriors each. One the driver, another who controlled the tanks' top guns, and a third who was in charge of communication, as well as the smaller machine gun mounted in the rear. Twelve such hovertanks waited at the back of the ranks of warriors like *ulusàk*—wasps—hesitating before the sting. They moved with care into two rows of six, each tank offset from the one before it, and all with a clean view of the invaders' ships.

Though not blatantly aggressive, and perhaps even only defensive, the move nonetheless prompted the large man to turn to the military people at his side. He conducted a brief consultation, prompting three of the men to dash back into the belly of the spaceship.

"Let me tell you why we're here," the man who had humbly referred to himself as god went on. "It's not to subjugate the weak, although that we will do. It's not to destroy your lands, though if provoked we shall do that as well. No. Our main purpose for being here, the reason we have arrived, is to take back our technologies which we discovered had been given to you by our sworn enemy, the people from the planet Eldëror. They are a crass, grotesque people who knew not what they had when they gave it to you, you mere Eldians.

"Yes, Eldians. It is the name I give you now, even though this is not Eldëror, it shall hence forward be your most accurate name. You will forego whatever strange, unpronounceable name you've given yourselves and use this name, 'Eldian.' A name that my people and I can pronounce and understand with great ease and associate with your savage-level of thinking and living and the murderous betrayal we know exists in your hearts—each and every one of you." All the while he was pontificating, he took a few steps forward, which went unnoticed by those enthralled or horrified by his speech.

He advanced the last few steps quickly while removing the heavy sword that hung at his left side out of its sheath. He stepped forward in one fast, powerful move, one that happened too swiftly for even the best warrior to respond. With brutal accuracy, he made the blade do its natural work. The light that shone along the edge of the blade revealed it was made from mpoaolonium (Mp). And the sight of Pahòke falling to the ground revealed its murderous intent.

"Now you know what a *god* can do!" he shouted. "Now you know that I must be both feared and loved!" He turned and ran back as fast as he could into the safety of the ship as the door closed behind him with extreme force. It crashed down at many times the speed it had taken to initially raise up. The steel and mpoaolonium embedded in the door deflected all of the arrows that had instantly shot at it. The door stood impervious to Mannahatta's powerful exploding arrowheads.

Takachsin dropped to his knees in anguish and held his best friend's lifeless body in his arms. He cried out in pain. Then a look of pure rage turned his face into a contorted mask of vengeance. "Destroy this horrific ship! All of these vessels! And every single monster in them!"

However, even before he could stand and lead his men in a counterattack, gigantic cannons along the sides of all three of the ships fired. The blasts sprayed the Mannahatta warriors, as well as the crowds of onlookers, with laser-like beams of deadly mpoaolonium.

Warriors fell to the ground, dead instantly, with their bodies in flames, screaming their last words.

CHAPTER 4

The full force of the *ilaok*—Mannahatta warriors—responded in an instant, firing back with every weapon they had. Numbering only about fifty or so, the *ilaok* rapidly lined themselves up in three columns of attack. The first group continued firing directly at the main ship, the *Ästra Ån Ima*. The other two columns flanked along the left and the right, as their training dictated, and as their military knowledge commanded.

But it was far too little and much too late. Sakima's year-long warrior training made it easy to identify the other two spaceships: the *Ästra Ån Pit* and the *Ästra Ån Ni*. The *Ästra Ån Pit*, a medium-sized gunship. The *Ästra Ån Ni*, a destroyer escort-class ship and the smallest of the three. Now both ships joined the fray, opening fire on the crowds of warriors and non-warriors alike.

Sakima saw her father dragging Pahòke out of the way from both enemy fire and "friendly" fire. A contingent of warriors had already joined him and were escorting their Sachem away from danger. But Sakima saw her father freeze and then turn and ask for a spear from the warrior who had rushed to his aid. The warrior handed it over, a worried expression on his face. She saw her father hold up his hand toward the warrior while he shook his head in defiance. Then Takachsin turned back toward the ships and started running.

With no time to put on his war clothes or paint his face for battle, Takachsin sprinted directly at the ship, crouching and weaving as he ran to avoid being hit by the many beams of mpoaolonium. Once at the front of the biggest ship, he hacked away with the spear at the ship as if desperately trying to find a way in through the metal sheathing of the spacecraft.

Sakima continued to observe her father with growing alarm as Takachsin lowered his head and intently reset some switches on the spear. She saw the spear now begin to glow with that telltale cyan blue—mpoaolonium, Mp. Takachsin aimed the weapon back at the ship, and the spear gave off a rippling glow of many shades of the original blue color, like a radar pulsing. The spear was doing the searching now, Sakima realized. A wave of blue light swept across the front of the ship—seeking, calculating, analyzing, penetrating.

Suddenly, the light coming from the spear shut off and a spearhead shot out from the spear with no apparent prompting or action by her father. In the blink of an eye, the spearhead hit a small area of the ship about three feet from the ground. It appeared to be either a small window or a large controller. Sakima had no idea which and didn't understand why either would provide any kind of advantage. She only wanted her father to leave, get away from the invaders' ships and get to safety.

But he still stood his ground, exposed to danger, holding the spear against the front metal skin of the alien mothership, the *Ästra Ån Ima*. She watched as the spearhead drilled its way into the front of the ship. Smoke cascaded from where the spear drilled, followed by an unexpected explosion.

Her father took a few steps back from the concussive wave of energy. Sakima saw his shoulders fall as he stepped forward again, hand extended, and examined the metal plates of the ship in front of him. He'd failed to make a dent in the surface, let alone create an opening, a way to get in.

Meanwhile, two larger tanks, different from the floating type that had arrived previously, rolled into the field as bullets and lasers scattered bodies everywhere. The huge, imposing tanks—*chitanësit sëkahsën mpàki*—were on opposite sides of the alien ships. But these two tanks—as impressive a sight that they made—were, at best, only about a tenth of the size of the smallest of the three ships. But unintimidated, the warriors in two Mannahatta tanks began firing Mp missiles at the biggest ship almost immediately.

The bombs exploded against the hull making no apparent impression. Over and over the big guns boomed. Over and over they met their target. And again and again they caused no damage at all.

A crashing noise came from the middle ship, the *Ästra Ån Pit*. The cacophony echoed like electric feedback from the biggest amplifiers and speakers at a concert. Next, a cannon-like device close to the size of Mannahatta's largest tanks—but all weapon and no wheels—appeared from out of the top of the mothership. A beam of Mp the size of which Sakima had never seen before in her life, almost like a river of cyan light, blasted through the air.

One of the tanks vanished in a tenth of a second. It vanished without a trace, erased from existence and history. No explosion, no debris. Not like earlier, with the flames and the shattering. Then, an instant later, the second tank met a similar fate, shuddering, wavering like a mirage, and then disappearing.

A similar device emerged from the smaller ship. In choreographed tandem, both initiated their synchronized assault on the Mannahatta fighters and their fighting equipment. None of the Mannahatta warriors' weaponry were protected by any kind of Mp-deflecting shield. Like a tidal wave of murderous light, the weapons began destroying and disappearing vast groups of warriors. Sakima looked on in horror, tears flooding her eyes.

Then Sakima screamed. Not a scream of fear or disgust, but one of pure anger. She gritted her teeth in her down-turned mouth, her eyes narrow slits of rage. Burned grass and fallen compatriots were everywhere as the piercing sound of the cutting, laser-like Mp beams filled her ears, to the point of blocking the sound of her own screaming.

Sakima ran forward, hyperaware of the warriors in her view who were also sprinting into battle. She noticed how many fell, how their weapons caused no damage to their adversary. How they were being mowed down without any ability to wreak some damage of their own on this deadly new enemy. As she held her bow and knife, her confident run decreased to an unsure trot.

What could I possibly do that any other warrior has not already tried? She wept at the full realization of her own impotence as it firmly planted itself in her mind. *What can I do? How can I help? How can I save my people? Other than also throwing myself headlong into the fray and to certain death.*

Then Sakima had a sudden thought flash into her mind. The mechSuit suit—the *mechakgilik!* It was still in an experimental state and not ready for battle, certainly. Maybe it would be dangerous to use at all, even outside the theater of war. Maybe, in fact, just as useless as every other weapon and plan of attack the Mannahatta warriors had tried so far on this day of death and remorse. On this beginning of the end.

CHAPTER 5

A deafening blast returned Sakima to the situation at hand. A third *chitanësit sëkahsën mpàki* tank had arrived, shot its missiles, and had actually found a vulnerable spot on the smallest ship.

Could this be possible? Sakima studied the smoke billowing up from the side of the ship. She noted the position of the hit: to the left and slightly above the doorway ramp mechanism. There was a circular symbol in gold there, imprinted with the image of a lion wearing a crown. The symbol sat just above where the attack had created the recent wound. *It is practically an ideal target.* She scrutinized the other two ships. They both had the same marking in exactly the same place. The lion-like creature symbol faced in two opposite directions: one faced left, the other right.

There is nothing I can do here, Sakima decided. But then it registered deep in her brain that there *was* a way she could make a difference elsewhere.

Without pausing or thinking about the consequences, a still-stunned Sakima bolted in the direction of *Puhùntèk Mahtakeyëwakàn*, the Mannahatta War Room, where the tribe kept—among digital and paper maps, physical and digital "war games" tables, and multiple technological evaluation systems—an arsenal of weapons.

Sakima tried not to glance at all the destruction and death and horror on all sides of her as she ran. She knew she wasn't retreating, but recognizing that it might look to others that she was. She tried not to weep as she sprinted through the field of smoke and fire and blood. Tried not to let her emotions overpower her as she witnessed the falling bodies of the innocent shot down in their prime. The senseless gore, the meaningless murdering of innocent people. People who were, just minutes ago, living their lives, going about their business as ordinary people. Harming no one, living in harmony and joy.

I am going to personally kill every single one of these scum-sucking bastards—taonkëlàxàm! As she ran, her eyes filled with tears. *Kill every. Single. One.*

Sakima forced herself to look anyway. All her fallen comrades, too many to count, their flags and feathers rippling in the wind that had kicked up. She studied the storm clouds blackening the skies like mad flocks of crows. It was still a few miles off, and she wondered when it would reach them and if it would bring heavy rains and lightning or more pain, more devastation, more death.

Finally, Sakima broke into a sprint away from the battlefield and toward the magnetic car railway. She jumped into the next available *pèmitàn mpàki*, which slowed down just enough to let her hop in. *How is this still running? How has anything kept working while hell descended on Mannahatta?*

She punched in the coordinates for *Lëpweichik Èlikhatink Mannahatta*, where the War Room, *Puhùntèk Mahtakeyëwakàn*, was located —in the exact center of the building, protected by a series of walls and sensors.

The hovercar whooshed along the track. Normally, the car made various other noises, but right now it proceeded amid the chaos barely making a sound, at least to her ears. Within just a handful of minutes, Sakima had arrived at the Mannahatta Technology & Research Center. She leaped out and charged toward the building.

The entranceway now used a combination of facial recognition AI, which the doors here always used, and the newly introduced technology of odor recognition. No two people, even if wearing the identical amount of the exact same cologne, smelled the same. This identifying combination—unlike the retina scan—could not easily be duplicated, if at all. Security teams developed and installed the new device to prevent any future traitors or psychotics—or both, based on Machto's treachery—to be able to enter the building. To prevent anyone from breaking in old-school style, they reinforced all the weak areas. And Machto's uncle—who had taught Machto how to break in, how to use the portal, and more—had been arrested, tried, and was currently serving his second year of a life sentence.

Both of these input checks processed in milliseconds, allowing Sakima to enter the building with hardly a pause. Once inside, she knew just where to go. She raced forward and then right to enter the large atrium room filled with *Alànëmëskat* technologies and weapons. She strode right up to the table where she had stored her cuff and where it was on display for others to see and learn about. There had been no reason to wear it since she returned from the Land Below over a year ago. No other creatures of mythology had escaped—not even come close—and there was no further sign of Machto these past many, many months. He was presumed dead, and that was that.

Sakima slipped the cuff onto her left forearm. Despite the carnage and mayhem only a few miles away, this familiar action made Sakima release a long sigh. It felt good and right that she was wearing the cuff again. It relieved her intense feelings of stress and instantly filled her with confidence.

Next, from the adjacent table, she grabbed the swirling laser device. She wanted to give the device a quick test. But she decided instead to trust that the 500-year-old weapon, which had worked so perfectly on her accidentally arming it a while back, would work fine just over a year or so later. Maybe she would get a chance to use it, maybe not. But having it with her pumped up her confidence.

With this weapon in hand and her cuff firmly in place, Sakima moved down the corridor. She let herself into the prison area after waiting for the giant, heavy doors to scrape open. Once she entered, the doors closed with an echoing thud.

Here, Sakima sighed again. It had been quite a while since she'd stepped into this place of dangerous memories. On either side of her, behind the murky glass, lay terrible evil in the form of mythological monsters. Or, more correctly, they were once thought of as only myths, but that idea was surrendered centuries ago. Now everyone knew better and had learned the hard way just how terrible these beings were, the real damage they could cause and how nearly unstoppable they actually were. Yakwahe had only been defeated by a combination of pure luck, prophecy, Mannahatta mysticism, and perfect arrow shooting by both her and her mother.

She shuddered and shook her head to release herself from the memories of her adventures in the Land Below over a year ago. How she'd almost lost her little sister, Tangetta. And how her dear mother had walked on that day to join the *awèninkahke*, the departed. Sakima stopped in her tracks, deep in thought.

Her mother…

CHAPTER 6

"Shoot, Sakima. Shoot that arrow I gifted you, the arrow you hate so!" Sakima's mother had yelled out to her, using the last of her strength on that fateful day in the Land Below.

Tears filled Sakima's eyes as she thought about her mother, Wùnita. *Miss you, Mom.* She wiped at her tears and thought of that stupid arrow. The most ridiculous thing she had ever seen. She had wondered how such a "girly" arrow could do anything at all. Other than attracting derision from all who laid eyes on it.

Sakima remembered the day her mother had handed it to her, in what she realized now was her mother's solemn ceremony.

The shaft of the arrow was a transparent pink color. You could see the pink mostly where the sun hit it, though. Otherwise, the shaft appeared to be a shimmering white. Then there was the rainbow, each feather dyed a different color of the rainbow: blue, yellow, green, orange, and purple. The arrowhead itself was sparkly pink-gold.

Her mother had been right: Sakima hated it. But the memory of that arrow brought a soft smile to Sakima's face.

Sakima realized that today, when she could very much use her mother's guidance, and just maybe, another magic, love-infused arrow. But she was on her own, once again, in what might only end in tragedy. A battle she was too aware that, this time, she might not win.

She shook her head again, shaking off the fear and the bad memories, the good with the bad, and continued around the corner. Past the portal—*Skontay Chìpilësu*—past the engineering workstations, to the back of the farthest corner of the space. The entrance that would take her into the War Room, the *Puhùntèk Mahtakeyëwakàn*.

After a quick fingerprint scan—*that is old-fashioned, right there*—the hefty door slid open to reveal a long hallway. At the farthest end of the hallway yet another door stood. This one required voiceprint confirmation. Again, Sakima passed through with no trouble.

Then she stood still, breathing softly, in an amazing, large circular room.

The big room was about seventy feet in diameter, with ceilings that rose to twenty feet high. Bulletproof skylights guided the sun down into the enormous chamber.

Decorating the room were Mannahatta drawings and craftwork, including leather and beads and shellwork. The walls had been constructed of aged walnut with hand-carved Mannahatta symbols everywhere, both small and large. Symbols of the sun, wolf, moon, man, woman, turtle, turkey, bear, mountain lion, eagle, hawk, cornstalks, and more.

The builders had weaved with sweetgrass and spruce bio-identical materials that were made to never decay or rot into the cathedral ceilings. They appeared as fresh today as Sakima gazed upon them as they did two hundred years ago, at the time of the construction of the *Puhùntèk Mahtakeyëwakàn* longhouse-style room.

In the middle of the vast room was a massive oak table about seven *shaèk* in length—roughly fifteen feet across. Sixteen chairs had been neatly arranged around the big table, equidistant from each other.

All Sakima could smell was the delicious scent of the pine and grasses above her head. The room was dark and peaceful, giving no indication of its serious purpose. She strode over to the far wall and flipped up some of the switches there. The wooden sheathing of walnut on a number of the walls raised up quickly, revealing double rows of large one-hundred-inch monitors. The monitors flickered on, one after another.

Sakima watched as the center of her village appeared on three of the monitors, from different angles. Another set of monitors displayed the village centers of other tribes. Still others showed the military fortifications of these tribes—those who were friends, and those who were not.

Six monitors showed the sky above Mannahatta. Another three showed the grounds surrounding the building. And finally, the last to come to life, were four monitors showing the game fields, each displaying a different quadrant of that outdoor area.

Sakima gasped as, in an instant, she was reminded of the destruction going on there, the Mannahatta losses. *So many bodies!* Flames and destruction everywhere. From what she could see, the invading ships had still taken only minor damage during the battle.

She slammed her fist on the small console in front of the monitors where she stood. Then, jaw clenched, she marched over to another panel in the wall. This one was twelve feet tall by four feet wide and covered in the same walnut veneer as the other parts of the room. She tapped on the wood three times, and it slid up and away, as had the panels in front of the banks of monitors. Sakima took a deep breath.

There in front of her, a large door stood locked and fortified. It was big enough to fit a tank in terms of height, but only a fragment wider than two warriors standing side by side. Sakima held her eye toward the ires-reader. There followed a sharp beep and the door quickly sweeping aside with a loud "whoosh."

And there it stood.

The battle armor that Sakima had helped design. More than helped design—it was her idea almost entirely, especially the functionality of the thing. She didn't engineer any of it, but provided multiple sketches and reams of notes, which the engineering team used as the basis of its own work. The engineers that brought it to life had to solve an extraordinary number of quantum puzzles to make it happen. Matter versus antimatter. Dark matter; strange matter; even enchanted matter. Mpoaolonium incorporated into a metal suit as both weapon and protection. A feat thought impossible, the stuff of science fiction, really, and not solid, practical science.

But the *mechakgilik* was real and science-based. Painted with symbolic colors of the Mannahatta—red, yellow, green, and blue—the suit, more of a giant robot, stood in the bay in shadows. In another second, the lights flickered on, covering the mechSuit armor in soft bluish light.

Sakima smiled at how perfect the suit looked in those colors. She recalled how she'd decided that this colorful paint job was required—despite her joking about it at first. Because she understood how that color scheme was a spectacular way to present the suit in battle. The engineers had painted the suit a dark, metallic black, with parts highlighted in yellow, green, and red. All the lights and visors shown a light blue.

Sakima pressed the *tulpe* button on her cuff twice. The giant armor with its robot shape took a few mechanical steps forward. The scent of oil and grease filled the air as whirring sounds and metallic noises echoed about the small cabinet-like room.

When the machine of mecharmor reached Sakima, it stopped and waited. Sakima gave it a good once-over. She couldn't help but notice a burnt odor. *That ain't right.*

There was also an odd, inconsistent sound, like an engine misfiring. *Needs a tune up,* Sakima noted. *Among many other things...* She smiled anyway, feeling a sense of pride that she'd been able to guide a team to bring this dream to life. The team's amazing feat filled her with pride.

I am just going to ignore the hundreds of failed attempts that ended up in the recycling piles, she thought. *Just going to concentrate on this beautiful thing in front of me right at this moment. Now: time to go!*

Sakima tapped the blue wolf *xinkwtëme* option on her cuff in the correct pattern. First, she held it down for two seconds. Then she released it and tapped it again twice. Finally, she held it in place for one more second and eased off.

The top and a good portion of the front chest piece of the mechSuit—the hatch—opened. It revealed a metal ladder leading up to a leather seat at just about Sakima's eye height. The seat was crafted of soft, lab-leather in a buttery color, stitched with Mannahatta symbols and with tiny beads made from clam and oyster shells outlining its top and sides. Sakima climbed up the ladder and positioned herself in the driver's seat. Although she was more standing than sitting, she found it surprisingly comfortable. She slapped on her seatbelt harness into position, and with a loud clack, locked it in place. Sakima then pressed the wolf button again, just once and fast. The mechSuit's hatch closed, securing her safely inside.

Sakima adjusted the viewfinder, giving herself wide angle views on her left and right peripheral vision locations. Straight ahead, she added zoom view to the normal view. Sakima then tested the heat vision, movement vision, and night-vision options. All appeared to work as expected. She smiled.

Then she checked the weapon levels. While mpoaolonium lasts almost forever, overuse could cause the equivalent of an empty tank until the substance reloaded itself. Sakima reminded herself to ease up on the trigger once she was back in battle to be sure the mpoaolonium had time to regenerate.

The mechSuit existed as a flawed but beautiful thing. Capable of so much, but the full potential—if any at all—had yet to be determined. This would be the first time the *mechakgilik* suit would be tested on the fields of battle. And this immense and horrible battle, which raged just a short distance away from where Sakima now stood—ensconced in the most incredible fighting suit ever created—might be its last. Certainly its worst.

Sakima pressed the red turkey *tschikenum* gem on her cuff, and the machine moved again, stuttering a bit at first as the hydraulic fluids filled the relay tubes and made their way to where force was needed.

Sakima guided each leg raise and footstep with the controls in her hands and the pedals at her feet. Once free of the storage and maintenance cabinet, she guided her way through the War Room and past the engineering workstations, speeding the machine up as she went. It was now walking at a fast clip, but not quite jogging.

She guided it down the hall and back into the portal area and off around the corner into the large space that held the beasts' cages. Now she pressed forward even faster. The large door ahead was closed, and Sakima had no intention of blasting her way through—although she certainly could have done so. As she and her machine raced as one toward the door, Sakima frantically worked the jewels on her cuff. *Which combination is it?* she thought, nervously trying combo after combo. *Not the right time to forget this.* Distraught, she accidentally pressed the accelerator handle, pushing the machine into a sprint.

Oh, my Kishelë! I'm going to crash into that thick, bomb-proof door and kill myself!

CHAPTER 7

Sakima, inside her protective *mechakgilik*, smashed into the door with such force that the thick, ballistic hatch crumpled like paper where she hit it. The *mechakgilik* bounced back and fell to the floor with a crash, sparks flying and smoke drifting from her suit, destroyed beyond repair.

"Ouch," Sakima said, more from embarrassment than from any pain caused by the collision itself. The suit worked, that's for sure. It gave her complete protection from serious injuries and, ideally, death. "Okay," she said, unsnapping herself from her harness and crawling up out of the undamaged top of the mechSuit.

She landed on the cement floor as softly as she could. Then with care, she straightened herself up, checking for injuries as she did so. The strong design of the *mechakgilik* meant she had no bruises or cuts and suffered no soreness of any significance.

Sakima noticed on the floor that the back of the *mechakgilik* had popped off because of the collision with the giant doors. She knelt down to decipher the writing on the interior of the back panel. Once she was close enough, she read what was there. Part of the label on the panel contained preprinted prompts. Next to each prompt appeared handwritten notes and initials.

Test Run 1: Alpha: PASS
Test Run 2: Beta: FAIL
Final Run: Ready Test:

The "Ready Test" field was, unfortunately, blank.

Next to each result were the initials, "PL." Dr. Pahòke Lippoe. Her father's best friend. She stood up, shaking her head. So this was a defective, or at least, a "not ready for use" model. She wouldn't make the same mistake twice.

She trudged back to the storage area to select another suit. Returning to the cabinet area in the back of the large conference room, Sakima pressed the necessary buttons on her cuff to make the next mechSuit march toward her.

She climbed up and in as she'd done with the first mechSuit, started it up, and went on her way again. At the giant exit doors, she passed through without issue because the doors responded as intended along with the *mechakgilik* behaving as designed—that is, safely. Sakima managed this time to get the code right, half from memory and half from luck: *tulpe* for strong, *xinkwtëme* for action. Sakima pressed both the turtle and wolf jewels together. As the mechSuit sprinted forward only a *shaèk* or two away from collision, the door scraped open like the gates of a medieval fortress, and Sakima inside her machine of wonder sprinted through it at near top speed, past the alien artifacts, and out into the courtyard.

And that's when Sakima put the *mechakgilik* into overdrive. The mechanical super-warrior transitioned from a sprint to something more like jet-speed, the landscape flashing by Sakima in a blur, pulling her cheeks back as it jetted through the space. She'd be on the battlefield in seconds now—and she couldn't wait to fight back.

At least, that was her plan.

This mechSuit stopped abruptly, tumbling to the dirt below, where it shut down with a sad whine.

"Kishelë!" Sakima called out, staring at the earth on the other side of her visor. She watched as a pill bug dug itself deeper into the soil. With a sigh, she reached over and slapped the emergency eject switch and was shot away from the mechSuit. She landed in a well-balanced squat but with a look of disgust on her face. Her lips flat and one eyebrow raised as she watched as the suit burst into flames.

There existed one last suit, one final chance to save her people. Her grand design, her brilliant military suit, must prove itself now. Or else all she would have accomplished by running off the field of battle was to make herself unavailable and useless at a critical point.

Sakima returned to the War Room, the *Puhùntèk Mahtakeyëwakàn*, limping a bit as she made her way back. Fortunately, she hadn't gotten far with the second suit.

Back at the storage cabinet, she popped open the rear panel—not that seeing the testing results mattered now, as this was the only *mechakgilik* left—because she just wanted to know whether this suit was likely to fail her as the other two mechSuits had done.

A grin grew on Sakima's face as she read inside the back panel. What she saw was the best she could have hoped for:

Test Run 1: α (ALPHA): PASS
Test Run 2: β (BETA): PASS
Final Run (READY UP): PASS

And again, they were all signed, "LP." *Thank you, Uncle Pahòke,* she thought with a smile. A smile which turned into a frown as the sadness of his fate hit her again.

She climbed in one last time and started the suit. Soon she was once again outside, heading for the conflict. In less than a minute, she was back at the battlefield, entering the wide expanse only to see the last of the Mannahatta tanks disappear into nothingness. The killing fields were almost too horrifying for her to view. She peered away from the bodies strewn about everywhere, in order to keep her resolve and not fall apart at the sheer impossibility of the task that lay before her.

A profound anger deep inside her welled up and grew large and overpowering. Sakima navigated her mechSuit so that it pointed at the alien ships.

Then, as she kicked her *mechakgilik* into overdrive to charge at the invaders, she screamed at the top of her lungs.

"Die, you—"

Wait, she thought. *What was the word Blue, and Curly, and MJ, and Janie Jones were always using back on the Land Below? Oh, yeah, I remember now...*

"Die, you muthah-*fukahs!* Die!"

CHAPTER 8

Sakima stepped carefully around ruined machines and fallen bodies and medics chugging past it all in her mech-Suit suit. She was relieved to see that many *ilaok* were not actually killed, only wounded, and some not wounded too badly, and others unhurt. This brought her no joy, but a bit of solace knowing things were bad, but not as dire as she first thought.

Sakima focused her viewfinder ahead of her and zoomed in on the biggest ship, the one named *Ästra Ån Ima*. She used the focus to examine the whole spacecraft closely, seeking other areas of vulnerability. But she found none—at least no obvious point of attack, anyway.

She switched to the heat-sensor mode. While the ship's skin was clearly thick and had a force-field in operation, with her machine suit's built-in technologies, she was able to make an interesting observation. A large contingent of the enemy's forces hunkered down right by the main door, as well as at two other locations at the front of the ship.

So, Sakima thought, *if I can get through the outer materials at those three locations, I might cause some significant damage. And possibly a casualty rate that might make these alien aggressors rethink this attack.*

She knew the two points of weakness on either side of the great door would act as the best initial targets. She kicked her *mechakgilik* into high gear again, leaping over the wounded men scattered in the field in front of her in great bounds. She safely crossed over groups of fallen *ilaok* with ease and grace. Sakima wished she could help her colleagues, but she had no medical training, not even in military field dressing. Yet, she knew she could help by providing them comfort, especially as a warrior and an empathetic person.

But stopping even for a few seconds for each *ila* would add up to minutes or even hours—time she did not have. She based this on the number of bodies of warriors scattered and suffering around the battlefield. Time that would give her enemies more room for more destruction and death-dealing.

Sakima had to make a difficult, cold-blooded, but absolutely necessary decision: to keep moving, to keep attacking, as she was trained. She knew deep in her heart it was the right thing to do. She swiftly traveled almost ten *shaèk* (roughly 30 feet) with each leap. The mechSuit had been designed not just for swift travel with its ability to move at high speeds, but also for jumping ability. Leaps that would enable the warrior to move quickly vertically as well. This allowed the machine and its rider/driver to ascend up the sides of hills, buildings—and maybe, based on today's events, enemy spaceships—with ease. Leaping as she was, over and over, in just a few seconds, Sakima now stood less than twenty-five *shaèk* from the main ship.

Sakima flipped two switches on the left side of the console in front of her inside her *mechakgilik*. This caused both guns, one on each side of her machine, to rise up into position. Then she lifted the protective hood that covered a bright red button and clicked that button down. The weapons—which AI aimed at the enemy guns above and directly in front of where she stood—began pulses of bright blue mpoaolonium light rays. The guns of the invaders, which were controlled both by living operators and AI, responded without much of a pause with a barrage of their own. Directed at Sakima in her protective battle suit, who stood exposed and vulnerable on the field all by herself.

This onslaught would be the ultimate test of the antimatter technologies built into the suit, and Sakima knew it. Testing had been disastrous in the early stages of creating the antimatter panels for the suit. But over time, Mannahatta engineers designed the suit to react with perfect timing and accuracy. One molecule of incoming, targeted mpoaolonium met with the exact amount of anti-mpoaolonium. The result being that the incoming Mp received by the mechSuit was instantaneously and completely neutralized, as if it never existed.

Over the weeks and months of development, the scientists led by Pahòke could stream more and more Mp particles at the shield-like antimatter panels for the suit. Eventually, the Mannahatta scientists pushed the operational effect up to the nanomole level, at speeds that were almost immeasurable by their technologies.

They created custom panels to fit on the mechSuit suit that could defend—via both the anti-Mp nanoparticles and AI—a deadly onslaught of military-grade Mp. And the metal could protect a warrior being shot at for a full ten minutes at the highest force.

The panels received no damage at all. Not a scratch. Not a burn mark. They didn't even heat up. It was the complete neutralization of Mp in a battle-level scenario; the negating of Mp at the nanomole level, almost like time had stopped. More like the incoming, military-grade Mp were transported at the speed of light to another dimension where they could cause no harm. Sakima had been thrilled. And so had her dad and Pahòke, and all of the engineering team.

The impossible, they all sensed, had been achieved.

On the battlefield now, inside the suit not studying the blast shields in isolation, Sakima felt the incoming Mp waves like fire and rocks, pummeling against the front and side of Sakima's protective suit. Though subatomic level in size, the force of the blasts hit her like a million bits of ice in a hailstorm, with roughly the same level of noise.

But the suit didn't crumple, didn't fall apart, didn't dent. In fact, it didn't move, and Sakima never felt the *mechakgilik* even put a foot back for stability. Sakima felt as if she were in a giant metal box being buffeted by a mighty wind. But that was the all and the entirety of it. So far, the blasts from the enemy's greatest weapon did not affect Sakima's special mechanical suit too badly. The antimatter built into the suit at the molecular level did its job precisely as Sakima had envisioned. Every atom of Mp was met with the equal but opposite amount of antimatter Mp, dismissing the barrage as if it were just a search light shined on it. Sakima smiled. She felt like a god, like a superhero.

My turn now, you këlulël kèpchats, you damn idiots!

Sakima switched off the AI. It had managed to do a yeoman's work responding to the blasts from the weapons on the alien ship with a nonstop, wave-after-wave, counter-firing of Mp toward the enemy. And the damage was as Sakima had hoped. She'd prayed to *Kishelë* that these nasty visitors had not yet developed their own antimatter defense against Mp, and it was clear they hadn't. All six guns along the face of the big craft, as well as the three on the side nearest Sakima, were destroyed. Or, in some cases, not as much destroyed as made to vanish.

With the heat vision option still active, Sakima noticed a considerable commotion within the bowels of the ship. It occurred to her that the enemy seemed unprepared for an Mp-antimatter defense. They also probably did not expect the Mannahatta here on Mannahatta to have developed Mp into a weapon, as they themselves had done.

Sakima took this moment to go on the offensive. *I don't know what they have brewing right now,* she thought, *or what big surprise they might have which may put an end to me and my mechakgilik. But I'll do all the damage I can until and if such a countermove by my enemies is revealed.*

And with that, she began blasting the known weak points of the biggest of the three ships like a dentist drilling out the biggest cavity in giant teeth. She squeezed the trigger bit by bit, increasing the intensity of her attack for a full minute. Then she remembered to let the trigger off and then turn it back on, in a pumping rhythm instead of nonstop. This technique kept the Mp from wearing out and gave it time to regenerate, as she and the engineers had discussed during the suit's creation and testing.

The target she was aiming at—the left side vulnerability near the top of the large door—exploded with a loud boom, sending giant pieces of metal into the air and across the field. Sakima took no particular notice.

Destroying the weak spots had never been her ultimate goal. Destroying the entire ship, however, was. Pumping the triggers like a pro, she kept drilling deeper and deeper with her Mp laser into the hole her weapons had initially created. Until, at last, she heard a loud, groaning bang of metal against metal. Without hesitating to revel in her victory, Sakima swiveled her position so she faced the second weak spot and began the same surgical procedure there.

When she heard the next great groaning bang after exploding her way through the spaceship's skin, the gigantic main door of the *Ästra Ån Ima* collapsed to the ground. It was as if the front of the ship—in fact, the door was nearly that large—had fallen off impotently. The door thundered into the earth beneath it, sending dust and smoke through the air like a sudden brown fog.

Taking three long, graceful bounds, Sakima positioned herself directly in front of the smallest ship. With now well-practiced precision, she made short work of all the spacecraft's external weapons. She soon had that ship's main door crashing to the ground as well.

She continued on to the third, mid-sized ship, inflicting injury on both the alien fighters and the alien defenses. Soon this ship too was laid bare, its personnel—like those in the other two enemy ships—fleeing for cover.

As the final door slammed into the ground, throwing dirt clouds high around it, Sakima turned around and headed back to her original target: the main spaceship, the *Ästra Ån Ima*. She ignored the dust and the noise in order to concentrate on what was happening in this one, the largest of the enemy ships.

Sakima's machine identified heat-shapes fleeing toward the back of the structure. She kicked the mechSuit into fast-forward and stomped closer to the opening.

There, with the courage of a thousand *mechkwèn'shùkwënay*—a thousand cougars—Sakima propelled herself within her Mp-powered mechanized suit through the cavernous and defeated opening of the big ship.

Directly into the the darkness and the unknown dangers within the large alien craft.

CHAPTER 9

Nine-year-old Sakima Tamanend felt the sun's heat on the back of her neck, despite hiding in the shadow of the brush in the *Tèkëne* forest. She felt her heart beat fast at the excitement of discovery. In all her exploring in the *Tèkëne* forest, she'd never discovered anything like this before. The darkness, the implied danger. The thrill of exploration into unknown territory.

Kneeling next to the craggy opening of what appeared to be a cave, the smell of the underground space caused young Sakima to pause. The odors weren't what she had expected, although she had no idea what she thought it might smell like. Sakima thought it was strange that what she was smelling had the musty, scent of dead leaves. Even though, at the same time, the air was so cold and fresh it reminded her of the best days of winter.

She laid down on her stomach, her legs stretched out behind her, to study the opening. She pushed her face down into the chilly space—it felt so different from the summer heat all around her. In fact, her face was now feeling chilled while the rest of her body, even the back of her head remained toasty warm.

It seems possible. Maybe I just might fit!

Turning her head a bit, Sakima peered down with one eye to try to see what it was like down there. It looked to her absolutely thrilling. She lifted her head up and examined the opening. Yes, it was quite narrow, with jagged edges. But as she examined it from side to side, it struck Sakima that the opening could be just wide enough for her to fit through. Her brother made fun of her for being so skinny. *He should talk; he's even skinnier than me.* But her thin body could well be an asset in this instance.

Sakima pressed her face back down again, but this time into the widest part of the opening. She could see a bright spot in the darkness down below. The sun had made its way in, around the shape of her own head. But it was enough for Sakima to conclude that the space below appeared to be more than large enough for her to stand in and even walk around in a bit. If, of course, she was able to get down there.

This is so exciting, she thought. *This could be my new fort. No more making do with hiding in bushes and beneath branches and always being discovered. No, no one would ever, ever find me down there. It would be my underground longhouse, hidden from the world.*

She wedged herself into the widest section of the crack. She could sense that this spot itself was not much wider than a foot. The sun started to set and Sakima knew she should really be heading home. Over an hour ago, she had promised her mother that she'd be back in a few minutes. She had something important to do, and she told her mother that she'd be happy with what her daughter did as soon as Sakima got back.

Sakima's mother, Wùnita, had laughed cheerfully and had told Sakima, "Okay, but if even fifteen minutes go by and you are not back, consider yourself in serious trouble." Sakima had instructed her mother not to be so picky about the time—fifteen, sixteen, seventeen—it was all the same, really.

Despite her promise, Sakima knew that this discovery of hers was much more important than any arbitrary timeline. She started to force herself into the opening, knowing in her heart that she would fit and that she'd make it down into this amazing, secret place with no issues. She climbed down bit by bit into the tight space, inching her right leg first, then her left, then—gingerly and slowly—her midsection. Sakima had to squish her body in tight, sucking in her stomach and holding her breath in order to contort it around the pointy stone outcrops. Finally, she eased her shoulders through.

Now all that remained was the ultimate challenge: her head. It got stuck right away and she was worried that it might stay that way. But she found that if she pointed her chin up toward the setting sun, it would fit at that unique angle, with her neck stretched and twisted to one side.

At last, Sakima got to the point where she was more inside the cave than out of it and found her tippy toes barely in contact with a narrow ledge. Beneath her, she could see the original spot she'd noticed earlier when the setting sun illuminated the cave. Right now, it struck Sakima that the area was looking like an excellent place to land: the dirt there seemed soft and there wasn't a single rock in the whole space she was targeting. She took a deep breath, closed her eyes, and then—with one leg leading the way—plunged toward the flat and what she hoped was a soft surface six feet below.

She hit the ground and involuntarily, but fortunately, rolled, taking all the impact pressure from her ankles and knees into her backside, distributing it throughout her body. The roll reduced the impact to a tolerable level, and the soft dirt and sand, which had never been stood on, yielded almost like a cushion.

Sakima laid there for a moment, a huge smile sweeping over her face, surprised that she had executed the landing so well. *I did it. I got in!* She stood up and noticed immediately that the area was much bigger than she could have realized. She gazed back up to where she had jumped down from and determined that she wouldn't be able to get back up there now, even if she wanted to. The opening was too high for her to reach, and there was nothing to stand on to get her any closer. Even the ledge which she had managed to touch with her toes was too far above her.

Further, Sakima realized, while that little opening seemed somewhat manageable coming down through it—although a bit trickier than she'd calculated—it now appeared impossibly narrow. From the clear perspective of being down below, peering up at the now illuminated passageway, she saw it quite differently. The opening was actually insanely narrow and with a hundred knife-sharp protrusions of stone everywhere. Somehow, her luck was good enough today and she hadn't gotten cut or hurt on the way in. And she would not be getting back out the same way, for all the reasons. She knew this for sure.

Sakima glanced around the space in which she found herself. She wouldn't say she was trapped here. But she had to admit, though, that she was committed to finding another way out, if there even was one. The filtered light from outside gave the gloomy space a blue haze, as if lit by one of the moons and not the waning sun. Sakima felt almost as if she were on a moon!

In the far distance, she heard the sound of water dripping, one single droplet at a time, with a long gap between each little *plop*. In the other direction—for the way in front of her was a fork separated by only a minute section of rock and dirt—Sakima heard a mysterious wind. The air was damp in the direction of the sounds of water. Not pleasantly damp, though—more like a rotten, moldy smell. From the other side, the wind side, the air felt fresh and not old or stale.

Sakima didn't know what to make of this, which direction to take. Or perhaps she should just stay put and wait for someone— her daddy most likely—to find her. Then she made an instantaneous decision, having considered all of her rather limited options. She decided to proceed in the direction of the wind. While it whipped through the alleys of the compact cavern, it made a raspy sound that indicated the danger ahead. Yet she figured it might actually be safer than going toward the water.

Because if the dripping was the start of a pond in the cave, she might well be trapped underwater if she were to fall into it in the blackness. Sakima understood that the light from the slight crevice above would fade soon, maybe within a few steps, and then she'd be quickly enveloped in total darkness. She'd proceed away from the water then, so as not to add the threat of drowning to her overall, already quite dangerous predicament.

Sakima journeyed on, taking the left route toward the wind. Thinking that maybe where there is a fresh breeze, there might be another opening that was letting that air in. Perhaps one she could reach, perhaps wider than the one above her right now. Maybe even a passage out that she could simply walk through and back into the *Tèkëne* forest.

Her eyes adjusted as she moved along, stepping carefully so as not to trip. The last thing she needed was to be lost in a cave with a broken foot or bloody knees. It was bad enough that not a single person in her family nor any of her friends knew she was down here. Her fault, but it hadn't been her intention.

She hadn't meant to find a cave today. Certainly hadn't intended to climb down through a crevice in the earth, as delighted as she'd been to actually find the same and make the climb. No, she'd been skipping through the forest as she did almost every day. On a sunny, warm afternoon, filled with such a sense of happiness, she could barely contain herself. She'd only wanted to pick some berries and some wild flowers and take them home to her mother as a surprise gift. A few minutes in to get the berries, a few minutes to get back out. Fifteen minutes proved to be a good estimate, in fact. But now both berries and flowers lay in a miniature heap at the mouth of the opening to the cave she was in, like an offering left at a tombstone of a beloved.

Sakima was cheered to see that what little light entered the cave through the crevice at ground level revealed enough. Sufficient to enable her to at least see shapes and outlines and the edges of things. Everything looked like a shadow, light and dark ones, large and small ones, scattered in the blackness in front of her. The fading sunlight beaming in only able to highlight some of the black shapes grayer than black. She noticed as she made her way along the path she'd chosen that the light was fading faster than she'd have thought, based on the distance she'd traveled so far, which was basically only a few feet. She realized then that the sun had nearly set, shrinking in the sky, and not hitting the crevice at the same angle anymore. She'd have to hurry if she was going to find a way out with the aid of any light at all, even as weakly fading as this one was.

The bloodcurdling howl she heard next as she stood frozen in total darkness partway down the "wind" path filled Sakima with such terror that she spontaneously began to whimper, tears streaming down her face, her hands shaking like tiny leaves in a violent storm.

"Mommy…" she whispered.

CHAPTER 10

Inside the ship, *Ästra Ån Ima*, Sakima switched on night-vision mode for her viewfinder. Because either her direct attack destroyed all of the initial lights in the interior of the enemy spacecraft, or the plan by the invaders was always to shut them off under certain attack situations. Sakima's destructive siege which led to her gaining entry inside their largest ship had to be pretty high up there in their worst-case scenarios.

The interior of the area directly off the giant gang-plank door was as wide as five Mannahatta tanks sitting side by side. And this was the narrowest passage in the entire ship. Sakima glanced about in all directions, spying for trouble, but the area had been completely cleared out. The fallen alien soldiers, if there were any, had been taken away as well—dragged out of sight or perhaps thrown into some hidden room belowdecks.

Night vision revealed such little extra information—that is, nothing at all—that Sakima could've seen with her own unaided eyes here in the relative darkness that this part of the ship was empty of life.

Sakima quickly stomped her mechSuit to the far end of the wide space and entered an even larger area where she could see that there were multiple levels going up. She counted at least three before she returned to surveying the room itself.

Surrounding her were vast metal-and-plastic consoles and equipment in an area as big as a half a dozen Mannahatta football fields, nearly 2,000 *shaèk*. The floor was made of thick metal, as were the walls. All the machines and consoles except one had lights flashing in what Sakima took to be an alarm pattern. The machines, not flashing alarms, appeared to be dead. And again, Sakima didn't detect a single alien fighter.

What is happening?

Sakima reached up and switched on the heat vision sensors. Looking up at the stories above her, she made out a few heat prints showing life forms up there behind walls. Scanning the floor she was on, however, she saw no such life form evidence.

Where do I go now? Left, right, up, back the way I came?

While she pondered this puzzle, the motion indicators on the dash of her *mechakgilik* showed the floor was vibrating. She couldn't feel it yet, so she tapped the indicator panel to test its accuracy, to be sure it wasn't an artifact of some kind in the readout. But even after she'd tapped a few times, the waveforms and numeric read-outs continued to display detected motion. In fact, it was now increasing, both the waveform and the count.

And then Sakima finally felt it herself. An unmistakable tremor that grew stronger by the second. At first, she thought that the ship had been set to self-destruct. With trepidation, she turned to peer back at the exit. She did a quick mental calculation of her escape route and the time it would take her to get out of the ship and free from danger. If this was, in fact, a self-destruct countdown, she'd have ten seconds and maybe less to get off the ship before it exploded. And unfortunately, at least another ten to stride in her machine far enough away to avoid the blast fallout. *Let's hope this is at least a thirty-second countdown,* she thought as she operated the mechSuit to turn 180 degrees and point it at the room she'd just left.

The rumbling and shuddering continued, equipment on the walls shaking with insane speed. She looked at the readouts on her dashboard: they were off the charts, the numbers spinning so rapidly she couldn't read them. The waveform skimmed up to the top of the readout panel, where it disappeared. Now Sakima worried the ship would explode before she got out of the room, or maybe even when she returned to the next room. Let alone off the vessel and far enough away from the explosion to avoid the worst of the shrapnel. *Okay, okay. I'm out of here now. Please, Kishelë, watch over me.*

But before she could finish her thoughts and take any action, Sakima and the *mechakgilik* she was inside of and controlling were plunged to the ground. The ship wasn't self-destructing.

It was taking off.

Sakima slid into the first room, which wasn't what she'd hoped for right now. Back when it was the way to freedom and off the ship, yes. But at this moment, to be anywhere near the opening of the ship as they flew into space was the worst place to find herself. Sakima knew enough about physics to know that she'd be sucked into the silence of space before she even knew it had happened.

As if she was clairvoyant, the ship tilted up a few degrees for takeoff, and then a few more, propelling Sakima in her mechSuit toward the wide-open hole where the door to the spacecraft had once been, before she had blasted it to bits.

Sakima slid helplessly toward the opening, almost imperceptibly at first. Then the slick metal suit in contact with the metal floor caused her to skate with increasing swiftness toward the entryway as the ship left the ground, headed for space with increased velocity.

Inside the mechSuit Sakima could see the field below her as she slid on her back toward the opening where the door she'd blown off its hinges should have been to protect her from being ejected out of the ship. She could just make out the shadowy shapes of the bodies of the warriors still waiting for rescue spotted about. She watched the billowing smoke of the damaged buildings and so many trees on fire. Then she saw all that shrink to mere dots as the *Ästra Ån Ima* hurled into space, higher and higher in the atmosphere up toward the black nothingness of space.

She watched as all of Mannahatta—the greenness of it, the blues of the rivers and lakes—the entire country that she loved, shrink away. And then clouds, layer after layer of clouds, clouds which grew thinner and more transparent as the ship bolted toward the vastness of outer space. The invaders' craft now traveled at phenomenal speed as it prepared to break free of Mannahatta's gravity.

The mechSuit—in which Sakima found herself effectively trapped within—slid closer toward the opening and to certain death with parallel speed.

Sakima knew the suit had not been designed to grab anything. It didn't even have external, passive hooks that she could try to notch into some part of the ship's metallic skin. No, it was made for warfare, for shooting, for toppling, for crushing—and for speed. Not for jumping up from a lying-on-its-back position. Not for grabbing at passing poles or braces or any kind of handhold. Because the machine did not have hands, just weapons, lots of weapons.

Sakima was all too aware of this design flaw now. If only she had included a grappling hook or a hook of any kind in her original design. She watched with horror and wide open eyes as she sped toward the opening and certain death. This explained why no one was on this floor, in this area.

There would soon be no oxygen, and soon anything not nailed down would be sucked into outer space. And at that exact moment when she had this realization, she saw that the land and clouds had been replaced by a deep blackness and near-nothingness. And silence, empty haunted silence.

Below, Mannahatta spun slowly and gracefully, like a ballerina near the end of her award-winning career. Tears filled Sakima's eyes as she gazed down upon her shrinking home, the land she loved with all her heart. It appeared so tiny then, surrounded by space, like a small canoe in the middle of a mighty ocean. She wondered how the land of her people had been able to exist for this long.

It appeared so small and defenseless, probably the view the Taturåkee had when they first arrived in her universe. How these bastard invaders had even able to find her island planet among billions of stars and suns seemed impossible. A tiny world, easy to beat, simple to defeat. They counted on that, as much as they hadn't predicted that Sakima would be among its defenders.

But what did that matter now? We have lost—I have lost—lost it all. In hours. Everything gone now, as far as she could tell. And now, a silent ending in space awaited her. A cold death in space to be her final reward for bravery. *Oh, my Kishelë. This really is the end for me.*

The beeping inside her mechSuit boomed so loud that Sakima finally snapped out of her self-involved reverie. She shook her head and clenched her jaw. Her eyes narrowed and her eyebrows became cinched on her forehead.

Sakima closed her eyes to help her concentrate in the few seconds she had left before reaching the opening and being flung out into space.

Think, Sakima, think! They must have done something. You must have thought of this—of a fail-safe! Of something like a panic button that would, I don't know, seal the mechakgilik into a life-giving encasement complete with oxygen generators. Right? Maybe?

Sakima frantically searched her memory of the unit's design for any kind of solution that might save her life, any emergency lever or special survival system. Anything she might be able to use in any way to rescue herself.

She searched and probed and found absolutely, positively, nothing.

Nothing at all to save her life.

CHAPTER 11

Hunkered against the damp wall of the cave, the young, frightened Sakima tried her best to get her bearings, tried her hardest to be brave. But it wasn't easy.

The howling had stopped, but the effect it had on her nine-and-a-half-year-old psyche lingered on. It drained her bravery right out of her body. She lost the joy and certainty that she'd experienced when she first squirmed down into the narrow cave. But now her confidence, what little there was, had gone as well. The confidence which had told her she would get out of this predicament. Get home to her family for dinner. Eagerly tell them all fantastic stories about this.

But now she experienced something she'd never felt before in her young life, at least not at this level, this deep down—real fear.

Sakima had always prided herself on her fearlessness. She always climbed up trees higher than any of her friends. Skipped with glee through haunted houses and all the gruesome things there—the ghosts, the monsters, the "dead" people walking and talking with their guts spilling out. Sights that made her friends scream and cry and run out of the eerie longhouse.

Not that Sakima was brave because she thought it was pretend or a joke. No, she knew it was real, that these threats were legit, but she always, without exception, stood her ground. Ready to beat back the horrors one by one, if needed. Failure was not an option and never entered her mind.

But this, this was different, and she knew it. There was nothing to do battle with—no grotesque creatures to face down, no demons to stand up to. Just darkness. And she knew what she was actually thinking, the word she didn't want to say.

Death.

For the first time, she felt a terrible fear, and it was all based on knowledge she'd never allowed herself to recognize before.

She was going to die, and it was all her fault. Her fault for thinking this was a good idea to start with. And then to force herself down into this cave with no backup plan, no predetermined way out. And now there was a real chance she might die down here. Starve to death or freeze to death. And that her body might never be found. Or if one day it was, all they would find—her brother and sisters, her mother and father, as well as her relatives and friends—might be a small pile of her white bones.

Sakima sighed and stood up again. She opened only one eye—as if keeping the other closed might protect her somehow—and tried to see in the dark. She had never felt so scared in her life and was worried that maybe she'd wet herself accidentally. After a quick discreet check, she sighed, discovering she had not.

Determined not to be afraid, at least for a little while, young Sakima now wondered whether she'd picked the right direction to proceed in. She briefly thought about returning to where she'd first landed in the cave and trying to climb back out, but she knew that was pointless. Because she'd already determined that getting back out that way was impossible.

Then she reconsidered taking the path that would follow the sound of water. But after some rumination, she rejected that too.

The howl she heard might just be the wind, but the water was real, and she knew that it was potentially dangerous. Besides, her father, the tribe's leader and Sachem, had taught her that water always runs downstream. He was also a scientist and always told her things like that. So, if that water was more than just some dripping of dampness down from stalactites to the floor, then she would be following a path that would lead not out, but down and down and down.

Sakima couldn't take that chance. She had to continue on, if for no other reason than her mother expected her to be home in time for dinner. Sakima realized then that the time she had promised she would be returning had long since passed. She wondered if her father would be out looking for her now. Maybe he'd send warriors or police. Probably a drone or two, as well, because he preferred using technological solutions whenever possible.

The air in the cave was colder where she now found herself. And it felt damper, like a thick fog coming in off the coast. She took the tiniest, shortest steps she could, trying not to trip or fall into an unseen opening, taking her even deeper underground. Trying hard to stop weeping, she bit her lip. Tears still welled up in her eyes, but now they no longer ran down her cheeks.

She sniffed and moved forward, one hand on the rock face beside her, the other waving in the air in front of her as if she were blind because she was as good as blind in here. She couldn't even see her own hand in front of her face.

It was up to her other senses now: hearing, touching, smelling. If this were a game, she'd probably enjoy it a lot. But because it was real and dangerous—and because she knew she'd be in serious trouble, no matter how things turned out—she did not enjoy what was happening to her. Not that much at all.

The air grew colder still, like she was walking right into a monster's freezer. *What would be in a such a freezer? Yakwahe—the man-eater—ate people, so maybe frozen dead bodies?* Sakima shuddered.

Or bits and pieces of people: an eyeball, an ear? Maybe just a nose all by itself. Sakima felt herself wanting to cry again, so she shook her head and took three deep breaths. *One: air in and hold it. Now let it out. Two: do it again. Three: Okay, one more time.*

Sakima actually felt better after her deep breathing, something her grandmother had taught her to do when she felt scared or nervous. She smiled and then made herself concentrate. *Okay, getting colder,* she thought. *That means probably I am going lower into the ground, away from the warmth of the sun.*

Sakima noticed that it smelled a little like winter now. Not so much the stuffy smell of a freezer, but the fresh, bright scent the air gets right before the snow starts to fall, crisp and chilly and happy. Sakima pulled her shoulders back and bravely continued on, waving her hand in front of her again as her eyes were only good for crying now, not seeing. The way in front of her—in any direction now—showed only total, absolute black.

Except for a sudden light that popped into Sakima's field of vision, like a reflection of a lightning bug in a mirror in the dark. It was there, and then it was gone. At first, Sakima thought it was just her imagination, or maybe something in her eye. She'd "seen" things in her eyes before, little floating objects, tiny flecks of light that she'd follow around with her eyes but which really weren't there at all. But never did they emit their own light, light that reflected off of things, like this light had done off the shiny wet walls of the cave. Sakima had also experienced some headaches where light seemed to dance about in front of her eyes like sparkles, glitter that seemed to mock her pain.

But this wasn't a sparkling light. It was reflective. The way you can see an animal's eyes in the blackest of nights, even though there appeared to be no light source anywhere around whatsoever. As if the animal was generating a light internally and some of it gently escaped through its eyes.

Sakima inhaled hard. *An animal's eyes.* That's what she'd seen; she knew that now. But they were high, taller up than Daddy's eyes. Taller even than a cat in a tree. She wanted so much to shed tears, to collapse to the ground and sob. She also wanted so much for her mommy and her daddy to be there right now with her. To hold her, protect her, and take care of her. But she was all alone in the deep underground gloom.

Then the thing attacked.

CHAPTER 12

As Sakima launched out of the enemy vessel and entered the blackness of outer space, she was immediately struck by the silence and peacefulness, in contrast to her panicking. She shot out of the spacecraft at bullet speed, but after traveling only a few *shaèks* from the ship, she started to float.

Still breathing hard, Sakima forced herself to stop screaming and calm down. She knew that if there was any—however unlikely—chance of survival, she'd need a clear head. And as she tried to relax, she heard two things. One was the sound of the vacuum seals around every hinge and seam of the mechSuit snapping into place, completely sealing off her pilot area from the icy, death-bringing, extreme chill of space. The second was the whir of fans as the air system kicked on. A gauge on her dashboard showed a green light indicating that oxygen was being pumped into the enclosed space. Next to it, a readout showed how much O_2 versus CO_2 existed. It also gave information on which other gasses were currently in the air. The automatic system regulated all features to ensure that only safe, breathable air filled the cabin area of the *mechakgilik*.

So, Sakima thought, *those science guys, in their infinite Elder wisdom, put in a breathing unit. I guess they did it in anticipation of a gas attack, and they never expected me to be floating out here in deep space. I guess you never know…* She couldn't help but smile. *Reminder to self: give Daddy an extra-long hug when you get back, just for this. And Uncle Pahòke too, for that matter.*

Instantly after that thought, Sakima remembered: Uncle Pahòke was gone! Murdered by this malevolent race who so recently came to attack Mannahatta. She felt such sadness, she completely lost focus on the task at hand: to stay alive.

Sakima had the strangest feeling, one that was completely alien to her. She was experiencing what it felt like to give up.

It was as if a dead weight was pressing down on her, crushing her from the inside out. Sakima felt as if she were being buried alive, a terrible feeling. And the only reason she could stop it from shutting her down completely was simple. She absolutely hated the feeling.

This sucks. Do other people feel this way? Ugh, I hate it. I've been down, I've been afraid—I've even doubted myself. But giving up? No! No, I must not and will not go there. But how can I possibly pull myself—

Then space debris suddenly began hitting her—tiny bits off of some ancient meteorite that had long since crashed to Mannahatta. Sakima spun around, over and over again with such force she blacked out almost immediately. When she came to, she was much closer to the lower atmosphere of Mannahatta than she had been just before the debris struck. She estimated that before the small rocks pounded her, she would have been roughly three miles from Mannahatta's thermosphere. But now, she approached forty miles or so above the surface of Mannahatta, lost in the mesosphere somewhere near the so-called Kármán line.

If she kept the current velocity of her now downward trajectory, it would be mere minutes before she entered the stratosphere. This would happen after maybe, at worst, a twenty-mile plummet. After that, she'd be in the breathable atmosphere of the troposphere.

Then only another ten miles or so, or five minutes, through to the ground.

That is, if she and the *mechakgilik* suit didn't burst into flames and incinerate into nothing in the meantime.

Sakima tried to pull herself together. *Come on, girl, this ain't over yet,* she thought. *We just have to keep from being smashed to bits out here among the meteorites. Then escape being burned alive down there in initial reentry. Next, side step being crushed on impact into the ground below. And finally, skip running out of oxygen anywhere in between. Easy!*

She checked all sensors. Thankfully, no damage of any significance. Thank *Kishelë* for the mirror-matter substrate on this thing, she thought. Then she glanced to her right where the accelerometer was tapping the right side of the scale on her dashboard readout, showing that she was moving at incredible speed. *Gravity's got me. Much quicker than I expected!*

Sakima didn't know what to think as the *mechakgilik* began to glow red—and some sections of it even silver-white—from the intense heat of reentry. *Now what? This is happening way too fast.*

All sensors on her dash were in the red zone. The suit shook so fast everything quickly became a blur. Sakima wanted to scream but couldn't make any motion or sound. *This is it,* she thought. *Stupid Sakima dies accomplishing nothing... Hell of a monument.*

Sakima could feel herself passing out. Things were going from blurred to black. Her eyes rolled back in her head uncontrollably. And her blood pressure fell to distressingly low levels from the g-forces her body was experiencing.

Traveling at nearly four miles per second, the mechSuit rattled like old empty cans crashing down a set of stairs. Emergency sirens of many types and tones sounded all about her. Lights on the dash flashed dire warnings. But all this meant nothing to the unconscious warrior woman. Whether she burned up in the atmosphere or crashed into the earth below, it would make no difference to her now. Death was coming—that was certain—and it would be arriving within seconds.

Sakima woke up at that point, awake enough to witness her own impending death. She quickly scanned the readouts and could see there was no hope. She braced for the end and waited, her short life passing before her weary eyes.

CHAPTER 13

At first young Sakima, lost in the dark cave, didn't comprehend that she was now under attack. She just kept moving bravely forward, chin out, hands searching, eyes as big and wide as she could make them.

What tipped her off was that an unknown danger came from the sound of rapidly approaching distant footsteps. A galloping, scraping, pounding noise that grew louder and louder by the second. Approaching through the jet-black silence of the cave like a missile homing in on its target. It was near now—whatever it was—almost on her. The growling grew nearer and so loud she could hear it in the beast's throat, could hear its breathing, could smell the creature's damp, hot breath.

The eyes of the thing were what she saw next, briefly, and at the end. Eyes that glowed like fire, like beams of that light she was just learning about at school. *Emmy-pow-lon-liens*, or something like that. Its initials were easier for her to remember, though, because they matched the initials of one of her best friends, Mileen Pilsin. *Mp*.

Sakima trembled but held her ground. Nothing was going to kill her without a fight. She balled up her fists, ready to strike at whatever this might be that had chosen to attack her down in these dark depths. It showed up much closer now, so close the light of its eyes lit up the path and bounced off the slick walls, off the stalagmite and stalactite pyramids. So clear and bright Sakima could see her own fists now, out in front of her. Her brave, useless weapons.

And so bright that she could see the beast now, less than two *shaèk* away. It was the size of a large dog, cyan light emanating from shockingly blue eyes. The size of it: Sakima knew she had no chance, no chance at all. *Goodbye, Mommy*, she said to herself. *Goodbye, Daddy. I am so sorry…*

But the creature, whatever it was, halted its charge. It came to an abrupt end, skidding over to Sakima until it was only inches away. Then their eyes met.

Sakima didn't look away. She didn't blink. The thing wasn't a monster. Nor was it a wolf. Its coat of fur was pure white, as if it had never seen the sun, nor had any of its ancestors seen it. A white nose, pure white lashes, and bright white whiskers. The glowing blue light of the creature's eyes reflected off its bright fur and back into the cave. It lit the space around Sakima better than tungsten and LCD lighting could have done, the brightest of all torches.

Young Sakima stood frozen as the two beings studied each other. Neither of them blinked. Sakima held her breath. *Is this how my death begins?* she thought. *Is this how this thing kills? By studying its victim first? Looking for weakness? Assessing how much meat this kill might bring?*

Then, mysteriously, the beast whimpered. It lowered its head and knelt down until it was fully laying on the ground. It peered up at Sakima almost bashfully, it's fluffy tail wagging eagerly. And then it licked her hand.

In fright, Sakima snapped her hand away, thinking the thing was about to devour it. Then, realizing it had licked her, not bitten her, she cautiously returned her hand toward the creature's face. It licked her hand again.

A dog's kiss.

This wasn't a wolf; this was a dog: *mwekane*. Nearly albino. A cave-dweller. A cave dog: *mwekane hakink*.

Sakima bent over and lifted her hand from its mouth to its head. She gently petted the animal, and it seemed to calm down at her touch. She herself felt calmer, too.

"*Good dog…*" Sakima whispered. "*Good dog.*"

The animal panted, tongue out, and stared at Sakima. While it did so, it slowly tilted its head to one side.

"What's your name? Are you a boy? A girl? Who are you, fluffy one? How did you get here?" Tears of joy ran down Sakima's face, mixed with tears of relief.

The dog barked, as if in response to her questions.

"Okay, it's okay. We'll find out more about you in time, right?"

The animal jumped up suddenly with a cheerful bark, as if it had just remembered something important. It turned and happily trotted deeper into the cave. Sakima stayed motionless on her knees, her bottom resting on the heels of her feet under her, watching. In a few seconds, the *mwekane* returned, barked again, and ran off. Sakima got up and followed.

It was like being behind someone who was illuminating the way ahead with a bold flashlight. She couldn't see much right around her, and if she looked back from where she'd come, it was total blackness. But up ahead as the animal jogged along, Sakima could see everything clearly. The walls, the floor, and the ceiling of the cave. And all of it nearly perfectly because of the mechanical dog's lighting features in its eyes.

After about ten minutes, she slowed down so that she could follow the beast through a tight, narrow section of the path they were on. Which at that moment cut sharply to the right and then back to the left.

When she emerged from the maze, Sakima found herself in the company of a litter of pups.

"Oh, so you're a mommy!" Sakima said, almost squealing with delight. "That explains everything!"

The animal barked again and laid down next to her pups. Sakima took a few steps forward and then dropped softly to her knees. The air was different here. First, it was not as cold as it had been in the other parts of the cave. Sakima thought it felt warm by comparison. Second, the odor in the air was a good part dog. That smell of baked bread that dogs' paws have. The warmth from their breath. The smell of the outdoors on their fur.

Sakima leaned in to pet the puppies. Two of the little beasts skittered around to sit behind their mom. But one pup, who had eyes just like its mom, stayed put. The other two puppies who had sequestered themselves behind their mother appeared to have ordinary eyes, at least in the sense that their orbs didn't glow at all.

This pup moved cautiously toward Sakima. It was a girl pup, and when it reached Sakima's outstretched hand, it gleefully knocked it away and jumped up on Sakima, wildly licking her face. Sakima giggled at the unnecessary enthusiasm, as well as the sensation of the small but rough tongue on her face.

"Easy, girl, easy. I am not going anywhere. No need to lick my face off!" Sakima laughed as the young animal knocked her over and stood on top of her to continue licking Sakima's cheeks and lips.

The other pups made whimpering noises. Either because they were a bit scared or because they wanted to join in the fun but couldn't let themselves run over to where their sister and the stranger were now wrestling on the ground.

Sakima tickled the pup's tummy and pulled gently on its tail. The puppy squirmed with delight and then fell off her. Sakima immediately got the pup in a hug-hold and kissed the side of its muzzle.

"You are quite a playful little thing!" she said. "And quite a beautiful little *mwekanètët*. I will call you Wu' Lisa!"

The mother dog barked twice with authority, and the little

female ran back. The mother dog stood up again, and now so did her pups. Sakima noticed now that the other two puppies were boy dogs.

Oh! I see. It's the females who have this light in their eyes…

The mother dog barked again and trotted down the path at the other end of this vast open area. Sakima understood what the animal wanted and promptly followed her.

They wound around through this new part of the cave in a complicated maze of turns. Sakima could tell they were climbing up bit by bit as they traveled along. After just a few minutes, the cave path looked lighter, much brighter than the effect of the mother's eyes on things. In addition, Sakima could hear the sound of running water. To be more precise, the sound of rushing, crashing, and splashing water. She had no idea what that meant and for some reason she started to feel a little scared.

But before she could worry herself to tears again, they turned a tight and sharp corner, and she emerged on a short ledge alongside the animal. The dog barked and Sakima stared straight ahead at the water cascading down. It smelled so fresh and wonderful; the cleanest air Sakima had ever breathed.

"*Èchei*… wow!" she said.

Then she walked through the curtains of clear water and out into the shallow pool created by the waterfall.

She was safe. She had made it out and could go home now.

She turned to wave goodbye to the good mother, but the friendly, caring creature had already returned to the bowels of the cavern.

CHAPTER 14

Sakima rushed through the atmosphere down toward Mannahatta, knowing this was the end. But the end didn't arrive as expected. Instead, the suit handled the pressure and the heat. Survived the chaos of reentry. She only knew this because, as she emerged from having blacked out, she noticed that the vibrating had stopped. Not only that, but the steaming heat had dissipated, and Mannahatta was visible again. An island of pure green surrounded by a sea of crystal blue. She was not out of danger, however, because she was still falling—and fast.

Sakima tried the various functions built into the suit: *nulakìl* (jump) and *nkëshhatahkixi* (run), with red dots indicating the recommended option:

> Jump Long|Jump High|Leap|Hop

> Run|Sprint|Mega Dash|Supersonic

But no matter which she selected, nothing changed how fast she was falling. She needed a counterforce; jets in her boots would be perfect. Unfortunately, however, she had nothing.

How many times in a single day can one person be so near their death?

She continued to plummet toward the ground at a ferocious speed. There would be nothing left of her or her suit when she hit, just dust and splatter, with nothing to collect. Except the memories of her that would be held by her family, her friends, and people in her village forever.

Then there was a signal.

From the dashboard, a green light flashed, indicating, well— something. *What is this now?* Sakima wondered. *How many features have been built into my suit that nobody told me about?*

Before she could get too upset about being left out of the loop when the suit was being constructed, clearly adding to her original design, there was a loud *POP!* Like a giant cork escaping from the world's most humongous bottle of champagne. Her suit had opened at the top, which immediately shot away into the sky above her.

I did not know this suit could do that. The top comes off? Who knew?

And then, while she wondered about it all, the suit next ejected Sakima straight up and out of her half-chair into the sky. She watched as she zoomed up and away from the mechSuit, as if it had sacrificed itself to save her. She watched as the *mechakgilik* continued to plummet to Mannahatta while she, herself, did not. In fact, she was just hanging there, in midair, in the middle of the sky. Then, before she, too, could return to falling again, Sakima next heard a loud *whoosh* sound, then a loud flutter like a sail unraveling in the wind.

She peered up over her head to watch a huge parachute unfurl, painted in Mannahatta colors, the colors of the earth and water and trees and sky. She studied the thing as it filled with air and became taut, all the while enchanted by what was happening. And a bit confused. From the reentry blackout and the trauma of the fall, Sakima was having trouble making two plus two equal four.

But finally, she did. She knew she would survive this after all. She gazed back down at the ground about a mile below her and watched as her *mechakgilik* silently exploded on impact. A plume of gray smoke rose up into the air, like a signal telling her she was safe.

Sakima tugged at one of the parachute's ropes to move her direction of descent away from the fire which the suit was engulfed in. And which was now only several hundred *shaèk* away from her instead of a mile.

You are safe, little one.

Sakima, out of habit and not logic, said, "What? What did you say?"

But there was no one there. Just the sky and the clouds and the wind whistling past her.

"Grandmother—Grandmother of the South?"

But no other voices did she hear as she softly floated to the ground.

She landed and rolled and and attempted to pull the parachute to her as the giant sail tried to pull her along the ground. Sakima detached it and stood in the field as the parachute blew away. At first, it rippled and folded along the ground before cresting higher and finally catching itself in the low branches of a nearby elm tree.

"Or was that you, Mother?" Sakima asked, gazing about herself in the field. It was as if suffering from some kind of brain trouble or confusion because of her earthbound careening and the fear it had induced.

But it was all silent where she stood, far away from the battlefield, the sun shining in a blue sky as if it was a wonderful, perfect day. And not this day of horrifying massacre and extreme pain and death.

Sakima breathed hard and closed her eyes, steadying herself. She opened them to see that the parachute had freed itself and moved on into the woods. Almost as if she had dreamed of being attached to it, dreamed of falling from space from an alien spacecraft. She sighed and turned to face east, back toward where her village lay, back to the suffering people of her tribe.

She walked along at first, her aching muscles fighting her on every step. She wanted to simply collapse to the ground and rest there, eyes closed. Her body had been through so much and she was aching and tired and even a little hungry now. But Sakima ignored the pleading of her body and its list of wants and needs and picked up her pace. She ran faster and faster, desperate now to get home, to be with her people, to see what the true damage was. Her own pain was meaningless compared to what others were suffering. She bent her head down and sprinted as fast as she'd ever done. *I could use another mechSuit right about now. There is no time to waste. No time to wonder. No time for self-pity or self-reflection.*

People needed her, and they needed her now.

Sakima soon could make out the screaming, the crying, the moaning. She was getting closer, nearing the battlefield. But she couldn't lift her head to see. She wasn't ready to assess the damage, to count the dead. She wasn't ready to face the fact that paradise had been destroyed.

And she wasn't ready to face her failure to protect her people, either. Despite her overwhelming need to be with them, she wasn't ready for reality in any shape or form. But she had no choice: this responsibility was hers.

Sakima lifted her head higher to face straight ahead. Tears streamed from her eyes as she entered the world of the wounded, the dying, and the dead.

She gasped loudly and froze mid-stride, as if she were a malfunctioning robot. Her brain was overburdened with what she witnessed. With horrified disbelief, she stood as still as a statue, unable to take another step. Her mouth opened as if she were about to talk, and her eyes squinted tight. Then they opened slowly as she cried. An ocean of tears as sorrow and grief and hatred and anger filled her body and mind.

Just a few yards from where she stood, Sakima stared at the lifeless body being lifted into a stretcher. The medics zipped with care a black rubberized sheet up over the dead person's body and

face. The person who would no longer be a part of her life forever now that they had walked on.

It was the Sachem, Takachsin Tamanend, known affectionately as "TeeTee."

Her father.

CHAPTER 15

Silence. Deafening silence, like all sounds had somehow been sucked out of the world.

The flames and smoke whirling about Sakima meant nothing; they were something from a museum, a movie, a show that wasn't real, could not be real.

The screams and the crying she didn't hear either. It was as if the world and all its distractions had slid away from her. To instead reposition themselves off into the distance, where its chaos and cacophony might do less harm.

The warriors dotted about the field, calling her name for recognition or sympathy, made no impact. It was as if she'd become permanently and totally deaf. The eerie silence filled her mind. A mind that had shut itself off, closed down in rebellion against the truth, climbed into itself and shut off all communication with the outside world.

She barely processed what she was seeing. But somewhere deep inside her, a thought was forming—a message, a horrible realization.

I am an orphan now.

And in an instant, the world—hiding, fearful of the consequences of what it had done—returned in full force. First, the wind started up again with a vengeance, pushing the dark storm clouds faster and faster through the late afternoon sky to create a threatening look to the heavens. And it carried an odd smell. Of death, perhaps. Of defeat.

Then Sakima recognized the odor. At first, she didn't want to identify what it was or even admit to herself that she detected it. But she wasn't able to deny anything any longer. Denial wasn't her way, and she let her guard down, little by little. It wasn't her imagination, she finally had to recognize, but the wind where she stood downwind of the slaughter carried the scent of human blood through the air.

She closed her eyes in horror and pinched her nose.

No. Not this at all. Not this terrible day. And not, dear Kishelë, my father. Please, Kishelë, please Grandmother, oh Creator, oh God. Please, not my father.

A few drops of rain tapped her gently on her forehead and nose, forcing her to open her eyes. She glanced up at the sky to assess when the torrents of rain would begin. Any second now, she realized. She let go the grip she had on her nose and fell to her knees, bawling.

The crying grew worse as the rain began to fall hard, soaking Sakima. She slumped down, onto her hands and knees, barely holding herself up as grief wracked her body.

She was alone now, no mother to comfort and encourage her. No father to guide her, keep her on life's correct path.

No one at all.

But while she grieved, it hit her. The Sachem and his wife—the king and the queen of the Mannahatta—were both gone now. And that meant that she, Sakima, would become, of all things—what she never, ever wanted—the matriarch of her family. A family whose only remaining members included herself, her little sister, and her younger brother. Her older sister had married into a new family, which left her out of the line to the leadership throne.

Sakima took step after heavy step, increasing speed with each step or two. She at last sprinted to her father's side where she dropped to her knees beside him. The medics temporarily halted their work to allow her this instant of shocked realization, this moment to grieve.

All of the surrounding sounds returned to her ears with a resounding crash, as if surfacing from deep below the ocean. And the world filled with all the noises of anguish and pain and fear again. But none of it matched what she was suffering from.

"Dad—*Daddy!*" Sakima said, sniffing. "No, do not go. You cannot go!" She fell onto him, her head on his chest, and she wailed. *"Nooooo!"* She pulled at the zipper of the bag that held her father, her teeth gritting, her face red, and her eyes wide. But she was too distraught to get a good grip on it, to pull it open so she could see his face.

The indignity of her father, the Sachem of her community, being now in a black bag of death cut her deeply. It was wrong—impossible—that he had been taken from her, that he had chosen this day to walk on.

It made it worse somehow that he wasn't in a beautiful death bed surrounded by and covered in flowers. With candles and fires and mourners in long lines. A part of her, deep down and almost hidden, knew that scene would play out soon. But right now, to see him in a body bag hurt so severely, it compounded the pain that was already overwhelming her heart.

A medical worker softly approached Sakima and whispered to her. "It will be okay. Come with me, honey."

The woman tenderly helped the sobbing Sakima to her feet and held her for a long time. Sakima, still shaking, slowly pulled back, wiping at her nose and eyes.

"They will pay! I do not know how; I do not know when," she spoke, almost growling. "But if our paths cross again, I will destroy every single one of them! I will make them suffer!" She spat on the ground and hit her fist hard against her chest. She turned, taking in all the damage and all the injured that surrounded her across the enormous field of battle. Sakima then marched off with her jaw set and her eyes staring straight ahead, burning with anger, to console others as she had just been consoled.

Despite feeling weak in the knees and tired all over from her father's death, Sakima moved from victim to victim. She greeted them with kind words and held their hands or touched their shoulders.

Sakima realized that as much as she wanted the world to go away, it needed her. Her people needed her to be a strong, compassionate leader, now more than ever. She straightened her back with pride and purpose as she moved throughout the field, attempting to bring at least a little solace to the hurt and grieving. She realized that her presence alone would bring comfort—not what she said, not what she did—just being there where she could be seen would be, for some, enough.

It was slow going but necessary, and she knew she'd be at it for the rest of the day and throughout the night. Everyone had lost so much, not just her—and some much more than her: sons and daughters, husbands and wives. The pain Sakima was experiencing was an almost universal one across her entire city and all its villages and all who lived in there. She wanted to bring as much comfort as she could to her people. Although all she really wanted to do was just collapse to the ground and give in to her grief and sorrow and cry for days or months or years—or forever.

She glanced up at the trees on the other side of the field. They were cast in a yellow and red light. She looked to the west and noticed that the sun had almost finished retreating in the graying sky. She'd lost track of time, so intent was she on visiting everyone. But she hadn't even made it halfway across the field. Doctors, medics, and EMTs crisscrossed the battlefield, picking up the wounded and the dead and moving them away—to either the hospital or the morgue. From here, if she ever finished, Sakima understood that her next stop was the hospital. To visit with all the wounded whom she didn't get a chance to talk to out here.

But what Sakima saw a sight she couldn't process at all; it had been too much. All the deaths of people she knew, either quite well or quite limited, who had been murdered by invading beings she'd never seen before, invaders with whom she had no quarrel nor any knowledge of their existence. People from far away who arrived in big ships for no other purpose, it seemed, than to kill the people of Mannahatta.

But what she was seeing now, this might break her, might stop her from ever moving forward again. She had nothing left inside to give, nothing left to suffer through. She was broken, wasted, and exhausted—her mind empty and heart numb.

For in the field not more than fifty *shaèk* from her lay her brother, Nimàt, blood on his chest and face and no doctors or emergency personnel anywhere near him.

With legs as weak and useless as if they were made from thin rubber, she wobbled and weaved her way toward her brother.

This nightmare, it never will end. Now the only members with the Tamanend family name are Tangetta and me. Left all alone in this world.

Sakima had no tears left. She cried with dry gulps of air as she approached her brother's lifeless body. And then she fell to her knees yet again, with a heaviness in her heart so dark and hard she thought the emotion alone might kill her. Sakima took her brother's cold hand and held it to her breast. She closed her eyes and felt as if the world spun all around her, sending her to the darkest places in her mind and heart and universe that she previously hadn't even a notion existed.

CHAPTER 16

"Sakima, try to catch me!" young Nimàt hollered as he sprinted on ahead of her through the bright May morning.

Buds were finally everywhere after a long winter, Nimàt's tenth and Sakima's twelfth. Most of the bushes and some of the trees had baby leaves. Eager first bugs buzzed about, looking for nectar or trouble, depending upon their nature. A bluebird sailed through the air and passed Nimàt just barely above his head, playfully dive-bombing the boy, or so it appeared. He laughed joyously as he watched the bird fly off toward the woods. Then he returned to his original objective: taunting his sister.

"You will never be as fast as me!" he yelled. He chuckled to himself, enjoying his ability to run fast and his prowess at beating his sister at *something*. It was a rare moment. Nimàt understood (with extreme discomfort) that his sister could beat him—not just at this, but at everything. Shooting arrows, throwing tomahawks, hurling spears, jumping and climbing. All of it.

He turned around, running swiftly still but backwards now so that he could see her better and watch the pain his taunts caused her. But she was gone.

What? Nimàt thought, pedaling backward, slower now, and subsequently coming to an exhausted stop. He studied the bushes he'd run past earlier, thinking maybe she had crashed through them on some shortcut journey of her own. But the bushes looked untouched, dew still clinging to every leafy part and not a branch or a leaf shaking. So he turned back to face the direction in which he had been going, quickly returning to his best running speed.

Only to find Sakima standing in the middle of the path at the bottom of the hill, her hands on her hips.

"You are less than me, Nimàt! I'm Sakima the Great, Savior of all Mannahatta! The turtle and the wolf and the turkey all in one! I'm unbeatable!" She lifted her face to the sky, her long black hair nearly reaching her buttocks, and laughed.

Nimàt, confused and startled, lost his balance, stumbled, and fell. As he slid along the wet grass to land at Sakima's feet, she said, "Face it, brother. I'm the warrior, fleet of foot and tough as a rock. And you are the girl. Fumble of foot and tough as a peach!"

Nimàt laid there in the wet grass and the strip of mud his fall had created in the earth. He slowly stood up and went to slap his sister for mocking him. He stopped himself before she could even sense a threat. Hitting girls wasn't who he was. He turned, head down, and started to walk home.

"Nimàt? What are you doing? I was not serious. Come on, you are being silly. You are a great man. A talented athlete."

Nimàt kept walking. He mumbled angrily to himself, maybe at her, maybe at himself, maybe at nothing.

"Nimàt, I was just teasing you back! Sorry if I overdid it a little." Sakima jogged back to Nimàt and put her arm around his shoulder. He immediately batted it off like an annoying insect. She put it back regardless. This time he let it stay there.

An eagle called out in the distance and a mechBoar snorted its way through the bushes as the two siblings walked along.

"I can never do anything right," Nimàt finally said. "I just want Dad to be proud of me, but I'm not good at any of this, this physical stuff."

"It's fine, Nimàt. I think you are perfect just as you are."

"Dad hates my butterfly collection. He hates that I like to draw pictures of beautiful fairies. He hates that I like to dance. He hates *me*."

"Daddy can be a real jerk sometimes, Nimàt, but he does not *hate* you."

"Well, he's not proud of me, I can say for sure."

"Mommy is. And anyway, you're wrong. He loves you. And, yes, he is proud of you. I have heard him talking to Mommy about that. You're a Two Spirit, a free spirit, on a path of your own. You are unique and beautiful, and that is all. And we love you this way, the way you are." She raised her other arm in an attempt to give him a reassuring hug.

"Well, I don't love me," he said.

Nimàt hurried his pace, pulling free from her unwanted embrace and trying to increase the distance between himself and Sakima again as quickly as he could.

He was unsuccessful, however, because Sakima, with the speed and agility of a cougar, caught up to him again. Sakima placed her hand on his shoulder again, but this time not for comfort but to make him stop. "Wait a minute, please? Just wait for a second, Nimmy," she said. "Look at me."

He wouldn't, so she circled him until they were face to face. Then she lifted his chin with her hand.

"I love you," she said. "I always will. We are two halves of the same warrior soul. We are great *gachpees*—twins, you know? You will contribute mightily to this society; I know that to be true. But in order to do that, you have to love yourself. Nothing can be accomplished otherwise. You will never become *you*, and you won't ever do all the things you are destined to do in order to change how we all—our whole nation—view the world, the stars, and the universe."

A tear rolled down one of Nimàt's cheeks. "I don't know, sis. It's hard being me sometimes and—"

Sakima laughed gently. "Nimmy? Really? You are talking to the girl who wants to be a warrior. There has never, ever, been a girl warrior in Mannahatta history. You want to talk hard, and well, probably dumb—"

"We are both heading down tough paths, for different reasons, and for different outcomes, I guess," Nimàt said, sniffing his hurt away and straightening up to be just a little less slumped, a little bit taller.

"You just keep being you," Sakima said softly. "I will keep being me. And if we have to change every single mind in the entire solar system in order to be understood, then let's do it!"

Nimàt laughed at last and gave his sister a little squeeze. "Last one home is a big fat *kwëshkwëtët*! Oink, oink!" He sprinted away, laughing loudly as Sakima stood with her hands on her hips again, proudly watching him go. She smiled and nodded.

He'll be all right. He's going to be just fine. She shook her head lovingly. I mean, look at him: such a, a—Nimàt.

Her smile faded away, to be replaced by a steely-eyed look of determination.

But just because he is suffering doesn't mean I am going to let him win.

With a laugh and a loud whoop, she took off after him, increasing her speed bit by bit until she had him clearly in her sights once again. They roared down the hill toward home, both running at their top speeds, with Sakima gaining on Nimàt with every passing second.

They burst out of the *Tèkëne* forest and into the clearing that led to the path that would take them to their village and home. Sakima charged on, only seconds away from passing her brother. She watched the back of his head, almost studying it as he ran on. Until she realized something.

She didn't need to win this one. It went against everything she stood for and against her soul not to try her hardest to win. But she made herself slow down. Maybe slower by only a step or two.

They turned the corner, and she could see her house ahead, its metal and glass parts shining in the sun, the grasses on its roof rippling with the slight breeze. Sakima knew Nimàt never looked behind him to see if she was close or far. She knew that when he had ever done that in previous races, he either tripped and fell or freaked himself out. So much so that he couldn't concentrate on the race or even on moving his legs.

But today, he kept his eyes forward, his legs cranking, and just sprinted with all his energy and heart, running into their yard and through the front door, hollering with joy.

CHAPTER 17

"Sakima?"

Sakima opened her eyes and stared down at the face where the voice had come from. Her brother, Nimàt, looked up at her.

"Where am I?" Nimàt said slowly, as if learning to talk for the first time.

"You are with me," Sakima said. Her hand shot up to her face and she covered her mouth, as if that would keep her from crying. "You are…" She took a deep breath. "You are going to be just fine—we both are."

Despite her original assessment that she could no longer feel and was broken forever, tears filled Sakima's eyes as she smiled down on him.

"It's okay, it's okay," she said, breathing hard, knowing that she was telling lies but also knowing that lies were the right thing to say right now. Her hand dropped to her chest as she took another, even deeper breath. "Give me one minute, brother. I will be right back. Do not worry, okay?"

"Sakima, please, don't—"

But Sakima had already taken off, headed across the killing field to the nearest rescue squad with both medical supplies and a stretcher. She grabbed the first person she reached by her wrist and then quickly pointed back to where Nimàt was lying. The woman nodded and waved at two others, who brought the stretcher while she ran over carrying a large medical bag.

"Nimàt!" Sakima said when she returned. She dropped to her knees again by his side. "These people are here to help." With one hand, she gestured at the people behind her, and with the other, she grabbed his hand again and squeezed. It still felt too cold, frozen in fact. But she didn't want to think about why that might be. "This is my brother," she said, looking up at the EMTs. "His name is Nimàt Tamanend, and he of all victims here must live. He is destined for great things. He is in the Foretelling, the stories of the future."

"I am?" Nimàt said, raising an eyebrow.

"Sure, why not," Sakima whispered to him, giving him a wink. "You most *probably* are."

He shrugged. "Cool," he said and smiled.

"We'll take care of him," the woman with the medical bag said, pushing gently but with purpose past Sakima to crouch down beside Nimàt. Carefully taking his hand away from Sakima, she felt for his pulse. Then she felt around the bloody areas of his shirt, softly probing for wounds. Nimàt winced in pain a couple of distinct times as she did this. "He's been shot, twice," she said, glancing up at the two men. "And something's cut him, I'm afraid. Badly."

She extracted a wide roll of gauze out of her kit and then proceeded to remove Nimàt's shirt by cutting it open with a knife and pulling it back and off him in pieces. Next, she applied some ointment to the gauze pads and placed the glaze onto the wounds that she could now clearly see. She wrapped the pads with more gauze from the big roll, pulling it around his back carefully as she did so, lifting him gently off the ground each time. She taped it all in place and then stood up.

"You can take him now," she said, addressing her colleagues. "But easy, he's seriously hurt. Take him to the tent on the north side and wait for the next hoverbulance." Then she turned back to Sakima with a serious expression on her face, eyebrows knitted. "I can't make any promises. He has some serious wounds. One is deep and has caused internal bleeding across multiple organs. I don't want to give you false hope," she paused and took a deep breath. "But it does not look good."

Sakima closed her eyes, feeling the world spinning around her, almost like it felt when she was reentering the atmosphere from outer space a short while ago. "Do whatever is necessary. He is the son of the Sachem. No expense should be spared. Do everything. You understand?"

"We will, yes, of course," the woman said. "We do for every victim, royalty or not."

"I mean…" Sakima said, jolted back to reality from her self-absorption, "he is my brother and I, I already lost my father today…"

The woman didn't say another word. She placed her hand gently on Sakima's shoulder and then reached out for her hand. Sakima stood back up with the woman's help.

The two women embraced in silence. Then, after a minute or so, they pulled away from each other, but the woman held her hands on Sakima's strong shoulders.

"I must go… there are others…" she said, nearly in a whisper.

"Yes, I understand. Go, do your job."

The woman turned away and was about to hurry off when Sakima reached out to snatch her firmly by the wrist.

"And thank you," Sakima said. "For all you are doing. For everyone, not just my brother." Sakima gave the woman a weary smile. "Thank you," she repeated, barely audible.

The woman smiled back. "Thank *you*, ma'am," she said.

Sakima hesitated, not knowing what to say and wanting to not sound stupid. "Is there anything I can do to help? I have no training in this type of—"

"Yes."

Sakima's weary smile grew to a fully happy one. "Good, good!" she said. "What can I do?"

"Come with me," the woman said. "There's plenty to do, and I could use an extra pair of hands. A hundred pairs of extra hands, actually."

"You have got them," Sakima said as she took up a position behind the woman, who was already jogging to the next victim on the ground just a few yards away. "I mean, you have my hands, my two hands—"

"I know what you meant," the woman called back over her shoulders, smiling gently. "Just hurry up already!"

CHAPTER 18

"Tangetta, I should go."

"I know, Sakima. Don't worry about me; I'll be all right."

"So, I need to go see Nimàt." It had been almost two weeks since the attack and what appeared to be a Mannahatta victory, at least temporarily. Two long weeks with no good future in sight.

"Can I, um—"

"No, you cannot, Tangerine. He's badly hurt, and you should not see him like that. In a few days, maybe. *Maybe*. But not yet."

Tangetta glanced down at her feet. "I know. But I miss him."

"You will see him soon."

"I meant Daddy."

Sakima took a quick intake of breath. She grabbed her sister's hand. "Sit down," she said. The two sat on the couch close together. "Daddy is watching over us, still. Just like Mommy. Only our eyes cannot see them, but their eyes can see us perfectly." She gave her little sister a quick hug. "Okay, Mimi will be here soon. So will Aunt Ahoa—you know, Uncle Lippoe's wife."

"Lip-oh…" Tangetta said, tilting her head and scratching her cheek.

"Uncle Pahòke, I meant. Dad's bestie."

"Oh, okay!" Tangetta said, giggling in a nervous way. Sakima was glad her little sister was giggling again, nervously or not.

"You can play with your little cousin, Mimëntëta, too," Sakima continued. "Did you know it is her birthday next week? That will be fun! You can help bake the treats with us and help wrap her gifts."

"And fight! Fight the evil, like you do. Right Sakima?"

Sakima hesitated and then smiled. "Look," she said, deliberately ignoring the question. "I will be back in an hour, maybe less. Okay? And listen, the evil is being taken care of by grownups. You do not need to worry about such things."

Perhaps, but also perhaps not. This is a total mess, and I'm not sure we'll ever recover. Or even survive.

"Nimàt is asleep right now," Sakima continued. She softly ran her hand across Tangetta's head and stood up. "So I will just be there with him briefly, and then I'm going to head back here. I will make us all a nice dinner. Fry bread sound good? With stew, and well, I am not sure yet, but something tasty."

"And cake!"

"Cake?"

"Yes, Sakima. I told you about it. Cake that you make. You're good at it."

"Well, I'm not really that good at it," Sakima said, laughing a little. "But you know who makes amazing cake and cupcakes and all such sweet things?"

"Who?"

"Your big sister, that's who! Amimi."

"No! Is that true?"

"Yes!"

"Really?"

"Yes, Tangerine, really. Now you go play, and I will tell Mimi that she needs to make you cake."

"With frosting. Lots and lots of frosting."

"Of course. See you later, okay?" Sakima gave her sister a strong but gentle hug. The doorbell rang, and she slowly backed her way to the front door while still looking at her sister. "We can talk more when I get back. You are being very, very brave. You do not need to be, though. Trust me."

The best thing for her younger sister to do, thought Sakima, *is for her to have the cry of her life. With her Mommy gone and now her Daddy, too.*

Sakima was unable to utter another syllable, the words choking her with tears and grief. She turned and strode purposefully toward the door. As she opened it, she worked to try and hide her tears as best she could.

Her older sister, Mimi, stood there, instantly assessed the situation, and stepped forward to embrace her younger sister.

She and Sakima hugged each other tight, both girls now crying, but Mimi much harder—which truly surprised Sakima. The almost-two-year-old child by Mimi's side, Mimëntëta, simply looked around at the new surroundings as if unaware that anything might be wrong. But that didn't last long at all, and soon the child's little face turned red, and her tiny mouth turned into an upside down "U," and she began to bawl too.

"Now look what I've done," Mimi said, dabbing her eyes carefully so as to not ruin her makeup. She reached down and clutched her daughter's hand and instantly swung both her hand and her daughter's up toward Sakima. "Can you take her, please?"

"Of course, of course," Sakima said. "Come here, you. I have someone eager to play with you." Taking the child's hand, Sakima walked slowly—keeping pace with the child's small steps—back to the living room where Tangetta stood waiting.

Sakima crouched down so she was at eye level with Mimëntëta. "Look, Mimën, look!" Sakima said. "It's your cousin, Tangerine!"

The child burst into a frenzy of glee, stomping her feet and trying to clap, restricted as she was by Sakima's grip on her right hand.

Sakima let her go, and the little girl waddled happily over to Tangetta.

"Hi there, Mimën! Would you like to play with me?" Tangetta said. She'd also crouched down after watching her sister do so and spread her arms out to Mimëntëta. The child collapsed so hard in to Tangetta that she almost toppled her.

Mimëntëta and Tangetta both laughed with joy. Then the two girls, holding hands, went to sit on the rug right by the couch so that they could search through all the available toys and games in the trunk there, many of which were Tangetta's, but most of which had once been Sakima's, and before that Mimi's.

"Hey, sis, what are you still doing here?" Mimi said, entering the living room from the kitchen where she'd dropped off some groceries and homemade pie.

The smell of the apples and the cinnamon almost made Sakima forget her troubles for a moment. "That pie smells amazing," Sakima said, eyes wide. "Oh, that reminds me. Tangetta is expecting you to make her a cake. I mean a full layer cake, with lots of frosting, of which she will have most of the slices."

"A cake? I just baked a pie."

"Her heart will be broken."

"I doubt that."

"Well, no, but she is pretty upset, and a cake—"

"I'm not baking on demand, and I'm certainly not going to spoil Tangetta like that, now that Mom is gone."

Sakima peered at her sister with her biggest, saddest eyes.

"Cut that out, Sakima."

"Pretty please? I promised her."

"Then you bake it."

"Like that would ever be a good idea."

Mimi thought about that for a second. "Hmmm, yeah, you're right. Doorstop, yes. Edible dessert, not so much."

"Um, thanks?"

"I'll make it. Fine. No big deal. You know how much I love to bake and all that."

Sakima leaned in and gave Mimi a hug. "Thanks, sis. *Wanìshi*. Save me a slice!"

"You should get going," Mimi said, her smile vanishing. "Seriously. Or you will never make it back to eat with all of us."

"I guess you are right. I mean, of course you are, of course I should…"

Mimi held a finger up to her lips and shushed Sakima gently with the intention of calming her down.

"Easy, there." Mimi reached out and ran her hand over Sakima's hair and patted her gently on the cheek. "Off you go. Tell Nimàt I say hi. And tell him Mimëntëta, and I will be by to see him tomorrow. If he's even awake, I mean—"

"I will. Sure," Sakima said, wiping a finger under her nose as discretely as she could.

"Can I get anything started for dinner?" Mimi said, quickly ushering Sakima toward the door. "I have some recipes of my own that I am going to work on while the little ones play."

"Sure, that would be great, thanks. And, um… Mimi?"

"Yeah?"

"Um, just, uh—well, just don't let Tangetta hear you call her one of the 'little ones!' She's fierce now, or so she wants the world to think."

"Right, you're right," Mimi said, winking as she reached past Sakima to open the door. "I'll be careful. She's getting big now, isn't she? Be a teenager before we blink twice."

They both laughed, and Sakima was about to reply when someone interrupted the conversation.

"Hi, girls—you are a sight for sore eyes!"

They turned to see their Aunt Ahoaltuwi, "Ahoa," the wife of Pahòke, standing at the open doorway looking like a beat-up rag doll, destroyed by sadness. "Come." Ahoa held her arms out wide.

Sakima and Mimi fell into her, and the three sniffled together for a bit before Sakima pulled herself away.

"I really must be going, Aunt Ahoa," Sakima said. "Nimàt, he—"

"Of course, of course," her aunt said. "You go. We will carry on until you return." She wiped her nose with a tissue and jammed it back into a pocket of her sweater. She straightened her slumping shoulders and forced a smile on her face. "Where is my Tangetta?"

"In the living roo—"

"I'm in here, Aunt Ahoa!" Tangetta yelled from the other room.

"Go," Aunt Ahoaltuwi whispered loudly to Sakima, making a shooing motion with her arms. Then she turned to Mimi. "I brought food." She pointed at a few large boxes lined up along the front porch. "Bring them in while I go visit the little ones, would you?"

"Do not call them little—oh, never mind!" Mimi said as she watched her aunt trundle down the hall toward the laughter of the younger ones—a much needed sound, like the sound of rain falling after a long drought. She smiled and picked up one of the boxes as Sakima headed toward her ride.

Sakima climbed into the waiting hovercab, and without a backward glance, disappeared out of view.

PART TWO
MONSTERS & MORTALS

CHAPTER 19

Nimàt lay passed out in his hospital bed, a bright white sheet and pillowcase acting almost like a presentation background. He slept in the open area of the hospital, blissfully dreaming despite the noises emitting from his fellow patients. The moaning of those in pain and the grunting of those in extreme discomfort, as well as the announcements, bells sounding, carts rattling, and other hospital noises, could not wake him. Not even wipe away the seemingly inappropriate smile on his snoozing face.

Sakima stood and watched from across the room as her brother slept, oblivious to his new surroundings and to her. She saw his upper body was wrapped in gauze with various tubes and cables running to and from machines and other devices. These kept monitoring his heart and feeding him drugs, and who knows what else.

Despite the situation and her brother's wounds, Sakima smiled a bit, glad to see him breathing but not happy at all at what had brought him to this state of being. Only two years younger than her, barely seventeen, and she had just turned nineteen last month.

Her brother was alive, against all odds, and she was grateful beyond words for that. She loved him in such her own special way. It almost hurt more to see him dead than it did when she saw her father. She wasn't able to explain it, not even to herself. Their brother-and-sister relationship was important beyond worlds, beyond galaxies, beyond universes.

She sighed and noticed the smell of antiseptics of various types intermingled with something like chlorine or some other equally strong and equally obnoxious cleaning solution. She wrinkled her nose as she studied the scene surrounding her in the hospital. So many warriors down, so many innocent citizens hurt.

And so many dead in the morgue—or so she'd been informed about all who had walked on, all of the departed. She hadn't had the strength just yet to see for herself. She couldn't face that, at least not yet. And she was in no shape to deal with all those who were now no more, forever. And most especially, was still unable to face the sight of her own father laid out on a slab in that chilly place.

She sniffed and wiped at her nose before stepping into the enormous space. She quietly approached her brother's bed while side-stepping around one nurse in the middle of taking a blood sample from a downed warrior and another who was administering medication to a civilian.

There was no place to sit by Nimàt, and the bed was too small for her to even find a modest little place to rest herself. So she stood. Stood and watched over him, unsure what to do. The noises made her nervous, even a little jumpy. She wanted none of it to be here, including herself. She wanted all of it to go away, to merely be the worst nightmare she'd ever had. To have her father back, her friends. And the real world—the world before all this—back. To be safe and happy again. She closed her eyes, only to immediately open them at the next voice she heard.

"Hi, sis," Nimàt said, his voice scratchy and soft.

Sakima gazed down at her little brother and smiled. "Well, look who's awake." She reached out and ruffled his hair. "You do not look so good, Nimmy."

"That's funny, 'cause I've never felt better," he said, coughing. He smiled with a less-than-convincing smirk and then coughed a second time, even harder. "Ouch!" He closed his eyes. "Hurts to cough," he whispered to his sister by way of explanation, keeping his eyes closed.

"I imagine it hurts to do anything."

Nimàt opened his eyes again. "I'm glad you're here. How's everyone else? The family, I mean…" Sakima hesitated. Before she could speak, Nimàt added, "How's Tangetta?"

"Tangetta? She's fine. She was never in any danger. When this whole thing started, when those ships arrived, I sent all my little archers running—and screaming, of course—in the opposite direction. Back toward the village and safety."

"Good." Nimàt said. "That's good to hear."

"Yeah. She never really knew what happened. I mean, she was there when the ships first appeared, of course, but she never had a good look, and I—" The words caught in Sakima's throat, and she needed a minute to collect herself. "Those *këlulël* bastards…" she mumbled, almost to herself.

Nimàt said nothing. He waited for Sakima to be ready again to continue, a loving smile on his face despite the pain he was in.

"I have not told her much, yet. It is too, too… terrible." Sakima found it hard to talk, hard to think back on what had gone on only a few brief hours ago, a couple of miles from where they stood now. It was like a colossus had appeared from out of nowhere with the purpose of destroying their world and all the people in it. It was so unfathomable that Sakima still had trouble thinking it was even real.

"How's Dad?" Nimàt asked, the question startling his sister.

Sakima gasped and slumped against the wall by Nimàt's cot. She reflexively raised her hand to her heart and left it there. Then she cried. Cried in the way she had denied herself out on the field of battle. She'd wailed then, but not fully, not the way she needed to—wanted to. Because she still saw herself as a leader and couldn't let herself be seen by the other soldiers as a complete wreck in a puddle of tears, unable to control her emotions.

Nimàt, with the various tubes inserted in his arms and all the wraps and bandages, was unable to reach his sister to comfort her, unable to leave his bed to hold her. So he had to let her cry. Which turned out to be exactly what she needed.

After a few minutes of shuddering, body shaking with tears and sorrow, Sakima grew quiet. She sat there, unthinking, unfocused for several more minutes. She grabbed a fistful of tissues from the holder on the tiny table next to Nimàt and blew her nose.

"Dad—" the word caught in Sakima's throat, and again she lacked the emotional strength to go on. She cleared her throat a few times, swallowing back her tears. "Dad—" She swallowed hard. "Dad has joined Mom," she said. She went dead quiet again.

Nimàt shut his eyes and let his head sink back into his pillows, sighing loudly.

"I should get going," Sakima said, her voice still a bit broken. She forced herself to her feet. "I am not doing you any good being here."

"Wait, sis," Nimàt said, opening his eyes and reaching out to her. "I'd like to talk a little. About what happened."

Sakima kept her back to him. With her shoulders slowly slumping down, she turned to glance at her brother. "I guess we should, huh? No time like the present."

"Who were those people—those invaders?" Nimàt said.

"I have no idea. Honestly, I really don't, but I wish I did. They seemed to have arrived somehow through the multiverse to only want to destroy us. They had never seen us before, nor us them, but it was like hate at first sight. Of course, Dad and Pahòke wanted to do the right, diplomatic thing and welcome the invaders as friends. But that is not what the invaders wanted. Oh," she added as an afterthought. "Lippoe. Dad's best friend, Uncle Lippoe Pahòke. He, uh, he's walked on, too. They—damn it, I wanted to keep this from you for at least a few days longer. He's dead, Nimàt! They killed him. Right in front of us—in front of Dad!"

Nimàt sighed again, and this time it was his turn to clear his throat. "Anyone else?"

"Family, you mean? No, thank God, thank *Kishelë*." Sakima raised her arms and pointed her palms skyward, as if accepting a gift. After a brief moment, she let her arms drop back down.

"Did you get a chance to say goodbye? To Dad?"

Sakima took a quick breath, her lips curled in, covering her teeth. Leaving her mouth just a colorless straight line. "What do you mean?"

"You know, before he passed…"

Sakima shuddered and nearly tipped over. Then she straightened her shoulders and stuck her chin out. "I, well, I said goodbye to him, but he was already—he had already walked on to join the *awèninkahke*, the departed people, in the Land of the Dead."

They were both silent for a few seconds. Then Nimàt spoke.

"Why us?" he whispered harshly. "Why so much death in our small family? First Hìtami—Tommy—our older brother born before even you and I were conceived. Mom, who sacrificed herself to save you." Nimàt's eyes were glossing over, despite the drugs he was on interfering with his tear ducts. "And now Dad, killed in battle. They're gone, all gone." He paused. "Is that our destiny, too? Is every Tamanend destined to die young? And violently?"

Nimàt said nothing more, just studied his sister as she covered her mouth with her hand and shut her eyes tight, as if trying to keep the tears from escaping, as if trying to deny the pain. Sakima made a few whimpering sounds and then turned her back to her brother. She abruptly and purposefully strode toward the hospital's exit.

"Come back and visit me again, Sakima. Soon. Please? Tomorrow? We need each other, more than ever."

Sakima kept walking, faster now, not wanting to embarrass

herself a second time in this big hospital with another ocean of tears.

"Bring Tangetta!" Nimàt called after her.

Sakima ran from the hospital, and out into the cold air of early evening where the full yellow moon stared down at her with what she perceived to be pure, targeted contempt.

CHAPTER 20

Sakima took her place at the head of the big table, sitting down where her father, Sachem Takachsin, used to sit when he would call a meeting of the Elders in the Elder Council Longhouse, *Kìkay Achimulsikaon.*

It felt strange to Sakima to sit there, but she wasn't the only one who thought so. The murmuring and staring of the other eight members of the Elder Council told her as much. She could hear them discussing her personality and how to deal with it and who would be the one among them to make her sit in a more humble seat along the side of the table against the wall.

Sakima ignored them—she was used to negative feedback for pretty much her whole life and for virtually everything she ever tried to do. She gazed around the room, wondering about the various images there. Some were large paintings of the Mannahatta kings and queens through history, her father among them. They were all standing regally against a beautiful woodsy background with tall trees, splashing waterfalls, and various animals of the forest, including deer, wolf, bear, and boar.

They were wearing full headdresses, which Sakima had never

seen anyone wear in real life. They had various symbols painted on their arms and face, and their bodies were draped in fine woven cloth with intricate patterns made from colored beads and shell pieces. Each without exception had a stern look on their countenance.

Between each of the Sachem portraits were other objects, such as carved masks, painted shields, carved stone, and collections of jewelry, each of which was protected behind strong glass. *Pretty.* She glanced around the table to see if anyone might be observing her.

Everyone was. Of course they were.

Although they might talk to the person next to them or across from them, each stole glances at Sakima in intermittent moments. Others stared at her outright. And each time, Sakima stared back for a brief moment before looking away. She could see that they judged her. She knew she shouldn't acknowledge them or their inappropriate behavior at all. Why give them the satisfaction? She was the right person to lead the nation, as the daughter of the most recent leader and as the champion in the Land Below, a celebrated hero now ready to take on a bigger set of responsibilities.

Instead, she studied the wood of the table in front of her. It was embedded with nano-technology and had a living AI built in, which recorded every minute and every conversation of these meetings. Then the AI analyzed, categorized, and filed it and all bio-readings, including emotional states, into its database and information retrieval system.

But the wood itself wasn't technological at all. It wasn't even lab-made, which was rare these days. Instead, according to the stories her father told her, it came from an ancient tree, most likely maple. It was so old, one couldn't immediately determine that. In fact, in some of his stories, her father had said the table was walnut —other times, elm. Regardless, it was a thing of immense beauty.

Sakima studied the surface, lost in thought, and used the beauty and the history of the thing to calm herself down and focus. She thought about how all the hands and fingers and palms of thousands of people in these meetings over hundreds of years had added a kind of polish to the wood. The table was more worn in front of where each seat was and less worn in the center. It was scratched and pocked and dented here and there, and the years of clear finish being applied couldn't hide its age. But it was beautiful, warm and reassuring. A memory from the Mannahatta past and a promise of the future.

Sakima decided it was time for her to stop delaying the inevitable. It was time for her to talk, to perhaps even take over the meeting, as there didn't appear to be anyone else interested in doing so. She realized in an instant (and with a bit of embarrassment) that, of course, it was her father who ran these meetings. It was possible that even now, despite their scornful stares of disapproval, the Elders here were expecting her to take over his role, at least for the time being.

"May I speak?" she said. "I want to say something. Something about the incident… the attack…"

The chattering around the long table in the *Kikay Achimulsikaon*, the Elder Council Longhouse, continued unabated. Four people sat on each side of the eighteen-foot table with Sakima at the head, and no one was sitting at the foot of the table at the moment. Many were missing, casualties of the recent attack.

They all continued to jabber on and on, rehashing events, getting nowhere, and ignoring Sakima as if she were the impertinent child some still considered her to be.

"Please!" Sakima said, raising her voice a little, and then a little more. "Let me speak!"

Finally, the chatter around the table wound down enough that a woman sitting two seats down from Sakima, the Elder Rita Shim Olsen, said, "Sakima would like to speak. We should let her have her say. It's the least we can do."

Let her? Sakima bristled at the tone while appreciating that this woman at least tried to intervene to help her be heard.

"Go ahead, Sakima dear," Elder Rita said quietly, a smile painted on her face which, for now, Sakima could not fully decipher. Was it genuinely friendly or condescendingly false?

"Uh, um, okay? So, I wanted to point out a couple of things—"

"I believe it's my turn to speak," said another Elder, Ahi Manunsko. He cleared his throat with intentional theatricality, as if hoping to add a solemn and self-important tone to what he was about to say. "As the most senior member of this distinguished committee, I feel—no, I know—it's my duty to, um—"

"Ahi, let her speak!" Elder Rita said, turning to address him, her face flushed with anger. "If for no other reason than she is the daughter of our beloved Sachem, recently passed, but who will never be forgotten."

Ahi Manunsko's face turned dark, his lips a tight pale line across his face, his eyes staring, unblinking.

"Yes? Would that be okay?" Rita said, almost as if trying to egg him on to disagree.

"Fine. I'll permit it," he grumbled in a voice so somber it sounded like an oak tree talking. Or being cut down. "For now… but be quick about it, woman."

"Thank you both," Sakima went on, ignoring the man's petulant and disrespectful response. *One battle at a time.* "I wanted to discuss three large issues and their sub-issues accordingly. Firstly—"

The *Ntite Pikchëlhe* (the Think & Draw 2000™) burst into life, entering Sakima's intel onto its electronic white board as she reported it. The number "1" appeared, followed by a "." and then a space. "Why were we attacked? Second—"

The *Ntite Pikchëlhe* wrote those words and then "2."

"Second, who was it that attacked us? And third, and this is perhaps the most important, why were we not prepared—not even a little bit?"

She looked around at the Elders at the table. One or two were whispering to each other, but no one attempted to interrupt her.

"As to the why: from what I was able to gather when their

leader was speaking, they were here to take back all of the *Alànëmëskat* technologies that have been a part of our great culture for nearly half a millennium. Ironically, or really, thankfully, that same technology that they came to steal is what defeated them, sent them away. At least for now. Maybe only for the next day or so. Maybe, hopefully, forever."

The *Ntite* device wrote most of this down and displayed it to the group, but only after instantaneously editing what was discussed so that it was shorter and more to the point:

> THE ATTACK
>
> 1. Why attacked?
>
> A: For Alànëmëskat Tech: Mpoaolonium
>
> 2. Who attacked?
>
> 3. Why were we not prepared?

Sakima cleared her throat, a little embarrassed at how well the *Ntite Pìkchëlhe* 2000 had reinterpreted her words. *Perhaps I am a bit windy in my speeches. Need to work on that...*

"Going back to the question of who," she said, attempting to mimic the shorthand that the *Ntite* was employing, preventing her words from being edited in real time.

"This we don't know as of yet," Elder Nitis Tschutti interjected. "But our research personnel are all hard at work on this question. We know that, for example, they came from the *iiRàbe* galaxy."

"That's over fifteen lightyears away, isn't it?" Sakima said, reaching back deep into her schooling memory for that, mildly impressed with herself. "So, wouldn't you say they obviously have harnessed mirror matter and/or dark matter to travel at that speed?"

"Exactly, yes," Elder Tschutti continued. "In addition, they would have no doubt also found the requisite time-traveling wormhole. We are still not clear as to whether they came through from a parallel universe or whether they are in ours. The consensus—which the Quantum Team is still studying and searching for evidence to support this—is that they traveled through the Many Worlds to get here."

Elder Ahi Manunsko cut in now, unable to hold back any longer. "We don't know that for certain, as Elder Nitis Tschutti mentioned. But they said that they were in pursuit of the *Alànëmëskat*, the People Who Fell from the Sky. We know the *Alànëmëskat*, who are also known as the Star Walkers, crashed here from the Many Worlds. Our theorem so far—and I personally believe it has merit—is that they were most likely in the same universe as the Star Walkers and not directly from ours."

Manunsko intertwined his fingers together on top of the large table, looking quite satisfied that he had added excellent details to the discussion. He seemed to be looking around the table, searching for Sachem Takachsin, who'd always acknowledged him and would frequently turn to him during these meetings for his sage insight and advice.

"Thank you, Elder Manunsko. That was a very good point," Sakima said. "And thank you too, Elder Tschutti, for reporting on the Quantum Team's research and findings thus far."

While the two men made mumbling attempts at acknowledging her, Elder Rita Shim Olsen jumped in to say, "Shall we move on to point two?"

"Yes, thank you." Sakima nodded in her direction and then glanced back across the room at the machine's whiteboard UI. "So, secondly: who are they?"

The *Ntite* 2000's screen refreshed and now read:

THE ATTACK

1. Why: For Star People's Tech

A. Unsuccessful

B. Repelled by same

> C. Most likely used mirror/dark matter and wormhole to get to Mannahatta

> D. Most likely attackers live in an alternate universe, somewhere within the Many Worlds

> 2. Who:

Under "Who," there was nothing yet written.

"What do we know about them?" Sakima went on. "Other than where they most likely have originated—that is, the *iiRàbe* galaxy."

"May I?" Elder Olsen said. "Again, although we can't confirm the exact planet completely, we were able to capture from their ship's symbols, colors, and other information, including snippets of conversation in their native language. The *Wàni Quanti*, our designated team of quantum mechanics scientists, parsed this data through our AI quantum computer banks."

"And?" Sakima said politely.

"Initial analysis indicates the invaders are most likely Taturåkee, from the planet Taturåkis. We have set this determination at 85 percent certainty, pending any additional data we might be able to capture subsequently."

"Okay, that's good, that's very good," Sakima said, nodding. "What do we know about these *Taturåkees*? I've never even heard of them."

"We don't know much, I'm afraid," Elder Olsen said. "We have only recently discovered that their planet exists. Knowing anything at all about their culture at this point—beyond that, it is clearly highly advanced; Tier 3 most likely—will take time."

"Time that we don't have," Ahi Manunsko said. He grimaced sternly as he stared at her. "And, hopefully, Rita, we will know more, and sooner rather than later."

"Yes, I believe we will," she said. "We have a dedicated team on that task, *Wàni Quanti*, as I've made perfectly clear, our—"

"Good, good," Sakima said, jumping into the middle of their

growing antagonism in an attempt to diffuse it. "Then that leaves us with the third point: why weren't we ready for an attack like this?"

"If I may—" said Elder Nitis Tschutti, raising his hands palms forward as if to stop conversational traffic, "and this is by no means meant as an excuse—but we have not experienced an attack such as this since, well, since just before Mannahatta was first ejected into this parallel universe by the arrival of our benefactors and teachers, the *Alànëmëskat*, the Star Walkers. There has been no reason, during all this time, to be on alert. Even to be on mild alert other than normal common sense dictates. That said," he cleared his throat and took a sip of water from the cup in front of him on the table. "Excuse me. That said, our military acted immediately and with force—using all the technology and power we have available—in perfect formation and following all training."

"I agree," Sakima said. "But at the end of the day, and all truth be told, we were simply not ready."

Elder Rita Shim Olsen nodded as others around the table made quiet comments to themselves and to each other.

"We could not have seen this coming, this attack, and we should not let this happen ever again. What we must do is to be prepared for attacks, now and in the future." Sakima said. "Unpredictable is one thing. Unprepared, quite another."

"Preposterous!" Elder Manunsko banged his fist on the table, rattling a couple of cups as well as a few nerves around the table. "How can we possibly predict or be on the lookout for starships careening their way toward us at that almost unmeasurable speed across multiple universes and timelines!"

"It is not preposterous," Elder Olsen countered, "but absolutely necessary!" In response, and to emphasize her counterpoint, she spanked both of her hands loudly on the tabletop.

"Exactly," Sakima said. "You both make excellent points—you all do. But we must be ready for an inevitable 'next time,' which might come sooner than we think or would ever want. We need to build systems that give us a view not only into the surrounding galaxies in our universe, but to all galaxies across all the Many Worlds!"

Loud chatter whipped around the table as the rest of the Elder Council added their opinions, either loudly or to each other and not as loud. All this fervent discussion was interrupted by a sudden knock at the door.

A warrior of high rank stepped into the room. "I apologize for interrupting the meeting, and I understand it is forbidden, but we have grave news, and the inaction in informing you of it would have been an even greater transgression."

"What is this—" Sakima started to say, but she was interrupted and talked over by Ahi Manunsko.

"What is it?" he said, standing up, attempting to take control for himself and away from Sakima.

"They've been found."

"Well, who's been found, dammit, *këlulël*?" Manunsko barked. "What in the world are you yammering on about?"

"The invaders, sir. We have tracked them down."

Elder Manunsko looked as if he'd just been slapped in the face, but he recovered quickly enough. "I, uh, er—good! Good!" He cleared his throat as if buying time. "And, um, well, where are they then? Come, come, speak up. Speak up!"

The warrior's answer caused all the Elders at the *Kîkay Achimul-sikaon*—including their special guest, Sakima—to jump to their feet, almost as if the move was fully choreographed and carefully rehearsed.

"The enemies have made it to Mannahatta, my Elders," the man said gravely. No one said a word. No one moved at all. They just kept staring at the messenger. He stared back, his eyes slowly and partially squinting.

"To be clear," he said, speaking slower and a bit more loudly. "They are on The Land Below."

CHAPTER 21

"How can this be, Sergeant? We have the Land Below under constant surveillance!" Elder Manunsko pushed his way to the front of the group gathered at the warrior's workstation. Above his desk, the man had a small sign that read, SERGEANT GALANNEY. Above that desk sign were fifteen different screens showed various views of the Land Below, including readings for heat, moisture, seismic activity, infrared, and more.

"I can't say," the warrior stated. "It's as if they appeared out of nowhere. And they chose a hidden, disused location to hide in, one that our systems don't typically sweep. Especially for ships of this type and size." He paused for a moment before continuing. "Look —" He pressed a few keys on his keyboard. "This was 9:30 this morning."

On the screen was an empty set of tracks, the fences around it upright, with all the cement intact overhead on the opening to what was called the "Freedom Tunnel" near West 125th Street in Harlem. In the near distance stood a number of buildings of various heights and levels of construction. A blackbird flew past the camera, and in the far background, a striped cat scampered across the tracks, through an opening in the fence, and down a hill.

"Now," the warrior continued, "the same location, same angle—everything exactly the same. Only now it's 9:45 LBT (Land Below Time). Fifteen minutes later."

Sitting as clear as day deep inside the wide, airplane hangar-sized opening to the Freedom Tunnel sat three Taturåkee space-ships. They were lined in a row, with the big ship, *Ästra Ån Ima*, closest to the tunnel's opening. The top of the opening now smashed, the fences ripped down, and most of the surrounding areas looked burned and windswept. All of this being the result of a headlong, graceless entry into the tunnel by the three alien warships.

"Those are the ships, for sure," Manunsko said, grumbling.

"What's their game, though?" Elder Rita Shim Olsen asked, standing more upright as she rubbed her chin thoughtfully. "The Land Below is not an ally of ours—in fact, for the most part, they don't know we even exist. So, no need to attack the people of New York City in order to get at us. Perhaps, though, do the Taturåkee assume we are allies with New Yorkers? And by attacking them, they will somehow weaken us? Leave us with no one to help when they strike again?"

"That's the thing," Sergeant Galanney said. "They didn't attack. Not one bullet. And this was almost an hour ago. They've done nothing, actually. Nothing except sit and wait, I suppose."

"Why didn't you report this! An hour ago? That's an outrage," shouted Elder Manunsko. He was about to slam his fist in his well-known way onto the workstation's table, but Galanney caught Manunsko's hand before it hit.

"Sorry, sir, for the impertinence. But this is extremely sensitive equipment. Your beating at it with your fist would cause much more damage than you might imagine. And, sir," the warrior continued, clearing his throat first, "if you'll excuse me, but your interpretation of things is a misunderstanding…"

Manunsko made a *harrumph* sound as he pulled his wrist away from the other man's grip. His face compressed like a dying flower, turning two shades of red in the process. "How *dare* you think I misunderstood something. How dare you!"

"What I mean is," Galanney continued, unaffected by Manunsko's outburst, "we were able to figure out when the ships arrived by basic video analysis. But we only discovered the ships were there just now, which is when I went to alert all of you. The Taturåkee slipped in an hour ago, but we didn't notice. None of our systems picked it up. None, that is, except the passive video capture system. It didn't raise any alarms even though all images are fed to our AI analysis systems for potential threats."

"*Hmmm*, I see," Elder Nitis Tschutti said. "So some kind of cloaking mechanism that evades analysis and detection, even though we can see it with our bare eyes—"

"Our video systems are programmed to override that kind of cloaking system. Doesn't always work, but it did here," Sergeant Galanney said.

Sakima thought for a second and then said, "Do you think it's deliberate? I mean, do you think they wanted us to see them there? Such advanced cloaking, I find it hard to believe they couldn't stay 'invisible' if they wanted to—"

"We'll need to send a team," Elder Tschutti said. "The sooner, the better."

"I agree," Elder Manunsko said. "But how do we fight them? If it is, in fact, another fight they want."

Elder Olsen laughed. "Send Sakima! She kicked their asses with her mechSuit originally," she said. "Although I'm still not quite sure how she pulled that off—"

"I'm not sure, either, to tell the truth. But regardless, the *mechakgilik* no longer exists. It was a prototype, one of kind, Rita—I mean, Elder Olsen," Sakima said. "And it's destroyed now."

"Is it really the only one we have? I didn't know that—"

"Yes, unfortunately, the only one that worked. And we don't

have the time or resources to create another. All the same, to your point, I should go to the Land Below. I should lead a team."

"Agreed," Olsen said.

"Disagreed," Manunsko snarled. "Dammit, this is man's work! Always has been, always will be."

"Ahi, you are being ridiculous! Completely ridiculous. If it wasn't for Sakima, we'd all be dead or enslaved right now!"

"She got lucky, that was all. Lightning doesn't strike twice."

"It wasn't luck, Elder Manunsko," Sakima said quietly. "I designed that suit. My father and other scientists helped build it. By good fortune or by strategy, I was prepared for today, for something like this, for an attack by invaders using Mp. No one else was. And no one else is ready even now."

"Nonsense. Our warriors, they'll proceed as they've always—"

"What warriors, Ahi?" Rita said. "Most are dead. The rest are in the hospital, near death."

"That's one battalion. Well, it is the one and *only* Mannahatta battalion," Sakima said.

"Our Kanyen friends have three."

"Are you suggesting that—?"

"Yes, *of course* I am!" Manunsko roared. "They may be our enemies, but that's from long ago—centuries! And Mannahatta is their land, too. They should help us defend it. Now is the time for them to step up, use their legendary military expertise and go to the Land Below. A surprise attack by Kanyen warriors and any Mannahatta *ilaok*—no matter how few there are left—might just end this now!"

No one said anything for a long spell. Finally, Sergeant Mitch Galanney turned his chair away from his console and spoke.

"I will summon them. I will go with them to the Land Below, if needed. However, I am assigned to a different, but critical, task in the next few hours. So do I go to battle in *Mënatink Ohëlëmi* or stay here to help guard our city? To protect the women and children in case this is a trap and the enemy attempts another invasion."

"Good man," Elder Manunsko said. "Spoken like a true hero. I commend you!"

"But—"

"But? What do you mean, 'but?'"

"But Sakima must lead us," Sergeant Galanney said, looking Manunsko directly in the eyes.

"That's insane, I forbid it!"

"It's not for you to decide," Elder Olsen said. She glanced around at the other Elders clustered together around the workstation. "A show of hands, then."

There was some murmuring and sideways glances as Elder Rita Shim Olsen waited for silence to return.

"If you vote for Sakima, our bravest warrior, to lead this band of fighters into battle on the Land Below, raise your hand."

There was some more murmuring, and then quiet descended again. Elder Olsen raised her hand forcefully. Elder Tschutti followed suit, but just a bit tentatively. One by one, virtually all of the Elders present raised their hands, except for Elder Manunsko and one other Elder.

"Good," Elder Olsen said with finality. "It's settled."

"I go on record as opposed then," Manunsko said. "And history will show me as the wise one here."

"So noted and good for you," Elder Olsen said. Then, turning to face Sakima, she said. "Honey, how soon can you get started?"

"We'll need to communicate with the Kanyen leaders—"

"I can do that," Sergeant Galanney said. "I'll start right now."

"Then we'll need to wait for their arrival," Sakima said. "After that, we'll need to define a strategy, tactics—our approach."

"Ha! That much has already been decided," Manunsko said with a sneer. "Stealth and surprise!"

"With all due respect," Sakima said without looking at him, "we need more than that. We need to decide how to attack: straight on, flanking, from behind. And how many warriors per position. And the timing. For example, do we wait for dark or attack regardless of the time of day?"

Elder Manunsko rolled his eyes contemptuously. "You are not a soldier. You haven't been trained in these things. This is absurd, stupid, and dangerous. You are going to lead these men—these true *ilaok*, not this, this—" He made a disgusted face, his lip curling back to show a bit of his upper teeth. "This self-proclaimed 'warrior girl.' An abomination!"

Sakima stepped up right in Elder Ahi Manunsko's face at this remark, her hand raised to strike. She slowly lowered her arm.

"My father was a warrior, and he has left us now." She struggled to hold back her tears. "Perhaps the greatest warrior in our lifetimes. My brother was a warrior, and he's left us too. And you denied my mother the warrior status she craved all her life." Sakima paused, her lips tight, her eyes fiery. "You will *not* deny me," she said, her voice a harsh, resistant whisper.

There was silence now. Even Elder Manunsko dared not speak, for fear of making a further fool of himself. The air was heavy with tension as he looked away. The only sound was the clicking of computer keys.

"They're in," Sergeant Galanney said, staring at his computer screen and oblivious to the emotions in the room around him. "One battalion of the Kanyen army will be here first thing in the morning."

"Let's hope that's not too late," Elder Rita Shim Olsen muttered. "Get the portal ready, would you, Mitch?" she said to Galanney.

"I'll contact the *Skontay Chìpilësu* team, tell them to start prepping the portal."

"Good. Thank you. And Sakima?"

Sakima, whose gaze hadn't stopped burning into the side of Ahi Manunsko's face, blinked as if returning from a dream. "Yes?" she said slowly.

"You best start mapping out your plan of attack. Looks like we got help. And pray to *Kishelë* that it will be enough."

"Yes ma'am," Sakina said, bowing slightly. "I'll start now. And I believe the most effective initial response is to send our best stealthy explorers, the *Wematëgunis*. The People of the Woods."

"What is your plan, here?" Elder Olsen said. "How can you leverage those small, elf-like people?"

"They are experts at camouflage and making themselves nearly invisible and completely silent. We can send a squad of them down to assess the situation, as you know things aren't always how they appear. If the ships parked there in the shadows are a trap, the *Wematëgunis* will know. And they'll communicate that back to us before we begin our attack. It's a safety net that makes perfect sense, as they are always focused on helping Mannahatta in times of trouble. And we have never been in more trouble than we are now!"

Sakima turned and left the Elders, heading for the War Room in the building across the quad. She would assemble a *Wematëgunis* squad there as soon as possible, present to them the full situation, and ask for their advice and help. If they could get down to the Land Below and give them all of the intel on the situation, she and the other warriors would have a sudden advantage. Which they might never get again against these overly aggressive invaders.

In a minute, she was down to ground level, out the door, and crossing the grassy quad between buildings.

"Grandmother of the South," she whispered as she made her way to Building 2. "I really, *really* could use your help here. Where *are* you? Where have you been through all this?"

CHAPTER 22

Nimàt woke in his hospital bed and heard the sounds of nurses and doctors whispering in the hall and the click and dings of the equipment he was hooked up to, as well as the other medical machines scattered about the large room. He could also hear the moaning of his wounded compatriots at various pain levels as the effects of some medicines wore off, while some others kicked in.

He sighed and stared up at the vaulted ceiling where colorful Mannahatta mythical characters and symbols were painted. Not so much as a mural but more like graffiti with different styles and sizes and colors in disconnected locations.

He tried to raise himself up but immediately knew he was too drugged, tired, wired, and bandaged to get far at all. He lowered himself with care back down to the bed, resting his head against the somewhat stiff hospital pillow.

Nimàt pondered about how the day had transpired. He wondered whether anyone he knew had been hurt, too, and perhaps somewhere in this room in other beds with other wounds and diagnoses. He hoped his family might be saved the trauma of losing anyone else and wondered if his sister Mimi and her baby daughter were okay. The same with his little sister, Tangetta. Mimi's husband, Machto, was long gone and considered deceased, although there was no physical proof of this.

Then he reflected on his favorite sister and, in many ways, his best friend in life, Sakima. He sighed again. *She is a problem. No, I don't mean that. She is a worry. But only because she throws herself at danger and ignores risks and only worries about others, and never her own safety.*

This concerned him. If anyone would be in serious danger and end up here with him in this cavernous space, an overflow area from the regular hospital rooms, it would be Sakima. Then he had a horrible thought: *What if she gets killed one day soon?*

He closed his eyes and tried to steady his breathing. He knew he didn't make much of a threatening warrior—really not much of a warrior at all—but he wanted to be back out on the fields of battle, if only to help the wounded get to safety.

He wished he was already a qualified nurse, which was his dream. And also not here as a patient, hurt and in a hospital bed. He wanted to be tending to the wounded, not being one of them himself.

These amazingly handsome and strong *ilaok*—their bodies were so fit and toned he could hardly process it—could use his help at times like this, and he would love to be in that position. To nurture, to heal, to caress their sweaty foreheads gently and bring them drinks and food.

One day, perhaps. He sighed.

Then he reflected on the most handsome of all warriors, a man who made him feel funny inside. He'd had plenty of friends growing up and the occasional crush, but nothing that made him go through anything quite like this before. The man was only a Private at this time, but Nimàt understood he had great potential to rise in the ranks. His name was Lèke.

Nimàt experienced a warmth in his private parts and wasn't

sure if it was the medicine making him sense this. But either way, he liked the sensation.

He imagined spending time with Lèke. Heading off to places together, like museums and coffee shops and restaurants. Sitting close together, shoulders touching, in movie theaters and at plays. Sharing a bottle of wine. He couldn't let himself imagine the rest. The first hug. The first kiss. The first…

His cheeks flushed with embarrassment as he realized how thin and flimsy the hospital blanket was, so he forced himself to concentrate on something else, someone else. Anyone else.

And he focused on his sister again, Sakima. She was so beautiful that he was jealous of her, how the boys looked at her, how they wanted her. Although Nimàt himself was quite good looking, he was too skinny and still at an awkward stage in his growth to be a real head-turner. At least not yet. But he had his father and mother's genes, and with that, the potential to be as attractive, in his own way, as his sister.

He allowed himself a weak smile at that conclusion as he drifted back to sleep again to dream of the future and all its possibilities. The image of Lèke Gischileu floated like a spirit in front of him. Men's bodies made the most sense to Nimàt; he knew how they worked, how they felt, and what felt good.

After all, he himself had one of those bodies. He loved everything about the male form. The female form, on the other hand, often confused him. There seemed to be too much added on and somehow too much missing, all at the same time. Although he sometimes imagined himself as female, it wasn't necessary to be anything but who he truly was: a Two Spirit.

The image of two eagles, a male and a female flying off together straight up into the sky was the last image he had before blacking out, the image of the two birds at the top of their arc splitting off and heading in two different directions.

CHAPTER 23

Sakima poured over the maps of the Land Below, what the people there called Manhattan. She studied the close-up images Sergeant Galanney had provided for her from his recon database of the area. They seemed unthreatening, these alien ships filled with alien scoundrels—almost innocent, in fact. How they sat there in the early morning sunshine, looking like carnival booths waiting to open up and sell cotton candy and T-shirts.

She could ascertain two ways where Mannahatta warriors would have a distinct advantage. Behind the ships was a row of trees and bushes, gone wild almost completely because they were so unkempt. Behind that bank of growth was a small tributary of some kind, maybe feeding into the *Muhheakantuck*—which the people of the Land Below call the Hudson River—or perhaps connecting to a bigger waterway, which itself rolled down to the Hudson. A battalion of warriors could move almost silently up the river in Mp-powered hovercraft, barely above the water, and remain in position. Another battalion could utilize the streets and sidewalks up to ten blocks away. Then they could cross over into the cover of the trees and bushes.

All this assumes, thought Sakima, *that the ships weren't using any surveillance equipment of their own, nor any type of heat and noise sensors.* Based on the technology they revealed when they attacked, Sakima thought it unlikely to be the case.

"Hè, Sakima."

Sakima gazed up from her maps and images and notes and felt her knees give out a tiny bit. She exhaled, scratched the side of her neck, and finally responded to the friendly greeting.

"Uh, um… *hè,* Lèke," she said. Sakima coughed nervously and peered down at her papers.

"Thank you for picking me," he said. "For the advisor team, I mean."

Without looking up at him, she said, "Sure. No problem." But there was a problem. She experienced a high level of nervousness bordering on a fight-or-flight blast of adrenaline. She adjusted her shirt a bit and stared over his head at the wall.

"You okay, Sakima, I mean Miss Tamanend? I meant to say that it's not every day that a warrior with the rank of private gets to be invited to any kind of strategic meetings. Anyway, I've assembled a small squad of *Wematëgunis,* as you requested." He turned to the door and waved. "Come in, please. Meet Sakima."

Before Sakima could respond, a group of six *Wematëgunis* marched in, in full and regal outfits. Each of them were no more than two to two and a half feet high, with furry faces and arms. They resembled average Mannahatta people, but shrunk down to almost 30 percent of an adult Mannahatta's height, with long hair and hairy faces. Yet somehow they appeared attractive in their own way. They each wore long capes on their backs that draped behind them on the floor, necklaces of gems and seashells around their necks that descended to their knees.

"We are here to help!" the first one said, waving his hand high in the air above his head and right away dropping it down to where his knees were. "The name is Tuney. Pleased to meetcha."

"I am Amoe!" the next dwarf-like individual to enter the room said.

"I'm Topi!" another said.

"Elikus here!"

"Kikey!"

"Bambil!"

"Oleleu!"

"Well, hello," Sakima said, slightly surprised by the elf-like people's arrival. She'd heard many, many stories about the People of the Wood but had never actually seen one in person. "Thank you for helping us."

"Nope, happy to do it," Tuney said, the apparent leader of the group. "This is what we like to do. Spy on people (and make fun of them, mostly). Be invisible and play psychological games against our enemies. Now, who are we checking on?"

"Well, the Taturåkee."

"Um, the what now?"

"They're from another universe and have arrived here to enslave or exterminate the Mannahatta nation."

"Well, we can't let that happen, can we?" Tuney said. "Fellows! Let's get to work. Or technically, get to play!"

The squad jogged along, following their leader, and headed for the portal as Sakima and Lèke watched in confusion.

"Wait!" Sakima shouted. "How do you know where to go?"

"We know everything about Mannahatta," Kikey and Elikus yelled back.

"Skoden!" hollered Amoe.

The group began to sing what appeared to be their favorite tune.

"Down to the Land Below we go, we go.

To keep any eye on the bad guys, you know.

Hide ourselves and spy,

Make our enemies stomp and cry,

Down to the Land Below we go. We go!"

Sakima watched them leave, her mouth partially open and her eyebrows flattened. "What in the world… "

Two other warriors entered the room at that moment: a sergeant and a colonel.

"Good to finally meet you," the colonel said, extending his hand. Sakima returned to her normal, take-charge self and took it, giving it a single firm, no-nonsense shake. "I'm Colonel Jamie Skattek," the man continued.

"My pleasure, colonel."

"And this is Second Lieutenant Nuwingi."

"Pleasure."

"All mine."

"Sakima," said Colonel Skattek, "I have to say, you have done amazing work. I'm not yet ready to say that I'm okay with women joining our ranks, but you are a powerful argument in favor of it." He turned and shut the door gently behind him.

"Thank you," Sakima said, completely unsure how she should respond. Was it a compliment or was it condescension? She couldn't tell either way.

Colonel Skattek laughed. "I'm leaning in that direction, I have to tell you. After nearly twenty years in service, I can't believe I'm saying it, but I'm becoming very much pro-female in the warrior ranks more and more each day." He chuckled, mostly to himself. "Well, turns out you *can* teach old dogs after all, can't you?"

Sakima studied Skattek's face for a moment, still unsure how exactly to respond, but choosing to just go with the flow for now. "I am hoping so," she said. "Or it will be time for old dogs to set free on the farm." This was met with silence. "No offense, of course."

"None taken," Skattek said. "I agree. Change with the times, or move on to retirement." He motioned toward his colleague, Second Lieutenant Nuwingi, to take a seat as Skattek himself pulled out a chair and sat. "What are we looking at, Sakima *Tamned*?"

Sakima considered correcting him on her family name, but instead shrugged and signaled Lèke to take a seat as well. "We don't have much, to tell you the truth. The element of surprise, perhaps. Unless it is a trap, of course. And there is the possibility we might have of making a stealth attack. Which could work. Unless they have sensors, of course. Which, frankly, I would bet my life they do."

"I agree, again. I've seen the images. Something's not right. It has all of the elements of a well thought-out trap."

"Anything happening with their own forces? In the Land Below, I mean," Second Lieutenant Nuwingi jumped in to ask. "Are we picking up anything at all?"

"Nothing yet. They have only been on the ground for about two hours, in a remote part of the Land Below, if you can believe there's such a thing in a city that big. Seems to be a lot of overgrowth, abandoned buildings, that kind of thing, around the immediate area. And only now did our friendly volunteers, the *Wematë-gunis*..." She paused for a second to suppress her laughter. "...headed down there to check things out."

"Understood," Skattek said.

"But to be clear, it is populated right outside where they have landed, but not much in terms of people in the area closest to the tunnel the ships are hiding in. So, from an attack standpoint, it is fairly safe for the local populace. Minimal, if any, collateral damage."

"That's good then. Very good."

"On the other hand, the lack of people also means that there are not a whole lot of folks around to report the sighting of these alien ships in to New York City authorities. But someone will, I'm sure, and soon."

"I don't think, regardless of the support we may or may not have down there, that we should depend in any significant way on what those folks can do," Colonel Skattek said. "As proven when Sakima was down there a year ago—"

"A year and a half—almost two," Sakima said.

"Really? It's been that long? Two years, my goodness. Well, as I was saying, two years ago, they seemed to have only the most primitive defense system. Seem like good people, and well trained. But their weapons technologies left quite a bit to be desired."

"I agree," the sergeant said. "They'll be good for holding back crowds, creating diversions, that kind of thing. But that's all, I'm afraid. Also, I would hesitate to put the forces of the Land Below in danger when there's nothing they can do—as much as I appreciate the spirit of it."

"Agreed," Sakima and the colonel said at the same time. Lèke nodded respectfully in accord, but did not speak up to place any additional ideas into the conversation.

"I want to add one more thing—" the sergeant said. But before he could continue, the door swung open, and in strode a half dozen Kanyen warriors.

They stood like a threatening wall, not saying a word. A few crossed their arms over their chests. Others kept their hands down by their sides, where they had weapons on their belts. They stared from face to face in the room, as if assessing the enemy.

"Please, come in, come in" Sakima said, waving her hand over toward the nearly empty conference table. "There are plenty of seats."

The Kanyens continued to stare. Sakima expected one of them to growl. Eventually, the warrior in front who appeared to be their leader spoke up.

"We have been sent by our council to assist in a raid to the Land Below." He continued to look from face to face as if waiting for a tell, a sign that an attack on him and his men was coming from the men in the room, for which he was more than prepared.

"Yes, thank you. My name is Sakima Tamanend. I will lead this action. I am the acting Sachem here and—"

"Ha, ha! A female warrior *and* a female chief!" the Kanyen leader said. "Mannahatta is truly the land of the ladies! The female man."

The colonel stood up. "Say. That. Again," he growled, giving the other man an icy, unblinking stare.

"Ladies' club." The Kanyen leader narrowed his eyes, staring at the colonel while allowing his hand to slowly drift down to the large knife at his hip.

Colonel Skattek locked his gaze while at the same time, he too sent his hand quietly toward the weapon attached to his belt.

The two stood frozen, snarling expressions on their contorted faces.

"My *Kishelë*!" Sakima said, stepping in between them. "Back down, the both of you! This is why we need more women warriors, slightly less testosterone and a whole lot less d**k measuring." She met their stares, moving her head back and forth to stare them down. "And much clearer thinking."

Neither man broke their stare.

But Sakima did. "Seriously. Enough. Everyone, please sit." She grabbed the Kanyen leader's hand by the wrist. He reflexively moved to pull free, but Sakima was strong and held fast. "Please," she said in a quiet, non-threatening tone.

She guided him to the seat she had been seated in earlier, the place of honor where her father, Sachem Takachsin, always sat. "Here," she said, "is where you will sit. A place of honor. And power."

Sakima gathered up the papers and maps, the pens and markers and pulled them over to the center of the table, where she took her seat.

"Please, everyone," she said, again motioning toward the Kanyen warriors and then at the plethora of empty seats. "Sit, sit. We have important work to do."

Reluctantly and with an arrogant slowness, the warriors finally complied while checking silently with each other and with their leader that they would all actually sit down and not fight.

Lèke and Sakima caught each other's eyes, and Lèke gave her a subtle smile while Sakima rolled her eyes again ever so slightly.

"Now," Sakima said, focusing on the work ahead. "For the battle plan, I see two options." She tapped on the map spread out in front of her.

"Stop," Colonel Skattek said. He stretched out his hand across the table to his Kanyen counterpoint. "I believe we got off to a wrong start, and no surprise considering our histories together. Please accept my apologies. The name is Skattek. Colonel Skattek. I'm in command here."

The Kanyen leader glanced up and down the table at his compatriots. He appeared to be unsure what to do, perhaps even suspecting that he was being insulted and not wanting to lose face in front of his men. But at last, he let his guard down.

"No, allow me to apologize—with sincerity. It was I who stepped in with the wrong foot and overstepped with my insults. I retract them here and now. They were verbal needles meant to create tension, and I did not believe the words I spoke."

"Thank you. Apologies are unnecessary, but accepted."

"I am Major Ron:kwe Onanta. I am leading not only the squad you see here in this room with me but am in full command of two companies of three platoons each from the Kanyen Nation—all of whom will be taking part of this attack, as we have agreed it is a common threat and common goal to stop these invaders."

The two shook hands, and Sakima breathed a sigh of relief.

"Shall we get started, then?" she asked, smiling for the first time in quite a while.

CHAPTER 24

"The first thing we need to discuss, to solve, is how to attack ships carrying so much firepower and troops. Stealth appears to be a good option," Sakima said, "but the ships are sitting ducks where they are, with multiple avenues for a surprise attack. However, it's been brought up that the 'sitting duck' nature of their positions suggests a possible trap. I have sent a squad of the People of the Woods, *Wematëgunis*, down to investigate and get back to us."

"I have to agree with that assessment and with the sending of the invisible ones," the Kanyen leader, Major Onanta said. "I've been the engineer of many a trap such as this, and this one on the Land Below has all the earmarks of a snare for the gullible."

"Yes, to me it looks that way as well," Colonel Skattek, the leader of the Mannahatta divisions, said. "We should proceed as if it is a trap, with all the necessary precautions. Expect the worst and bring out the best."

"That being said," Sakima said, "what are our options? I've looked at approaching their hideout using the nearby river at the ship's rear, through the narrow swath of forest, as well as to the rear along the southern side of the target area. Problem is, we'll be seen approaching, no matter how 'stealthily' we proceed. We have to assume, based on their original attack, that they have all the latest tech for monitoring threats."

"Could we—" Lèke spoke up, causing all heads to swivel his way. He'd been quiet for so long that some attendees at this meeting had forgotten he was even in the room. "Could we, just a suggestion here, but I was thinking. Could we, um, set the portal to drop platoons directly *inside* each of the enemy ships?"

The military advisors looked at each other, then to Sakima and then back at each other. The idea was so simple, so smart, none of them wanted to admit that they hadn't been the first to come up with it.

"I think the soldier has made quite an interesting suggestion," Skattek said. "Your name, Private?"

"Uh, Private Second Class Lèke Gischileu. Sir!"

"Well, very good, Private, very good." He turned back to engage Sakima. "What do you think, ma'am?"

"I think it's brilliant. But I do not fully understand if the portal is capable of such pinpoint precision."

"It is." Standing at the door was Elder Rita Shim Olsen. "I was on the committee and engineering team that repaired it recently— well, a year or so gone by now, I suppose," she said as she strolled confidently into the room. "We were able to pinpoint the exact target where we wanted Wùnita—Sakima's mother, that is." Elder Olsen nodded in Sakima's direction. "Where we wanted Sakima's mother to appear. It was strategic, surgical, and worked like a charm." Elder Olsen smiled.

"That it did," Sakima said. "Saved my life with only minutes to spare. Being off by a few blocks, maybe even less, would have meant my mother would've arrived too late to help me."

"However," interrupted Elder Manunsko, who now stood with Elder Nitis Tschutti at the door where only seconds early Elder Rita Shim Olsen had been standing. "We have never tried to position someone—let alone an entire squad or platoon—inside of anything. The portal has always—and I don't really know the reason for it at all—been aimed at placing travelers somewhere in the open air. I don't know whether there is a risk of going inside of a building or craft, but I certainly don't see why there should be."

"Maybe fear of dropping someone into a wall or halfway in and halfway out, perhaps," Elder Nitis Tschutti said. "But I know for a fact that issue was overcome years ago. I just think no one has had a reason to transport someone inside of a building or anything else. It's just easier to select a clear location outdoors and *boom!*—over they go."

"Then we should try it," Sakima said, feeling good about things for the first time since this terrible crisis began. She nodded at Lèke. "Good job." Then she turned to the rest of the people in the room. "Now, let's get over to the portal and get these settings in place." She switched on the telecom, and in a second, a voice announced itself on the other end. "Sargent Galanney. Will you please join us in the War Room—*Puhùntèk Mahtakeyëwakàn*? We are heading over to the portal building soon and could use your expertise." Galanney responded in the affirmative and Sakima glanced around the table at her advisors. "Assuming we can place warriors within the enemy ships—and let's go with that—we still need a plan of action for the teams inside," she said. "And we need to determine how many and where. For example, how many troops are on the bridge, at the front entrance, in the equipment room, the armory, and so on —all the areas of each ship?"

"I have the plans for each, as best as we could determine," Colonel Skattek said. "I mean, the ships are just sitting there, and they're not blocking our penetration analysis beams. What we have is a set of schematics and blueprints for all three of the enemy craft."

"Unless, of course, it is a trap, as we've considered," Major Onanta said. "In which case they could well interfere with our probes and send back to us the wrong plans. We might send soldiers to their death inside walls or into fuel tanks or into an ambush."

"That would be one amazing technology, like none we've ever seen until now," said Second Lieutenant Nuwingi. "Not to say that this isn't what you're saying. But I'm suggesting that we lean into the scenario that we have real, accurate blueprints."

"I'm with the Lieutenant on this," Sakima said. "At some point we need to just say full steam ahead, damn the torpedoes, and all that. If this is nothing more than an elaborate trap, we will all die. We have to go in, all the same, as if we might just have the upper hand."

"And we might," Elder Olsen agreed. "So why not go into battle thinking we'll win? If it's a trap, then our hands are tied and we can do nothing. Nothing except waiting for our own doom."

"Both of you women here today have spoken the truth," Onanta said. "We attack, as planned, as soon as we hear back from the squad of *Wematëgunis*. Therefore, I officially retract my objections." For the first time since this nightmare began, Major Ron Onanta, leader of the Kanyen troops, allowed himself a small smile.

"Well, I totally disagree. It's a suicide mission!" Elder Ahi Manunsko appeared suddenly at the door, glowering, not quite in the room and not quite in the hallway. "Two women making this type of critical decision! Nonsense! Utter nonsense and stupidity and I won't stand by and watch as they sentence Mannahatta and our Kanyen friends and warriors to certain death."

"Ahi—you are so full of yourself!" Elder Olsen shouted, a grimace on her face. "This isn't about two women, or men versus women. It's about the best way to defeat a terrible enemy. The calculated risks. The timing."

Sakima stood up, her body weary from all it had been through in the past two weeks, all she had lost. Her soul and her heart were more battered still. She strode over and faced Elder Manusko with a firm jaw and strong eyes.

"My respected colleague," she said, in a somber tone. "My

father's true friend, and friend of all Mannahatta people. No one is intent on harming any warrior, Mannahatta or Kanyen or otherwise. No one is more reluctant than me to put anyone in harm's way. But they have brought the Armageddon to us, *Ekhokiike*. We have not sought this battle, but we will not walk away from the challenge, regardless of the costs." She sighed but did not take her eyes off the man's face.

"How dare you! How dare you speak to your superior—" Elder Manunsko raised his hand, the back of it to Sakima, and pulled it back to strike her across the face.

But before he could release it, Sakima caught him by the wrist, stopping it in mid-arc. Her other hand was on her knife, Chessi, without a thought. She had it out of its sheath and the tip pressed into the side of the Elder's wrist before she was even aware that she'd done so.

"Never," Sakima said between gritted teeth. "Never raise your hand to me or to any woman unless you are prepared to lose it." Her voice was a fierce whisper.

Elder Ahi Manunsko's eyes glared with hatred. "You forget yourself, madam. You forget my position."

"My good man," Colonel Skattek said. "Won't you please shut the hell up."

Sakima looked at the colonel, then back at the Elder.

"Do not stand in my way, Elder Manunsko," Sakima said, teeth gritted. "Though your intentions might be most honorable, the effect is most deleterious and dangerous. Please step down. These plans and this leadership that you mock are being defined by the best military minds available." She waited to be sure he was listening and then released his wrist and sheathed her knife again. "And they will be executed by the best warriors across both nations."

Manunsko's face turned a deep crimson as he slapped his hand back to his side and took an unbalanced step backward.

Elder Rita Olsen spoke up. "If you are offended by a so-called inferior speaking to you in the way you need to be spoken to"—she got to her feet—"I can fix that." She glanced across the table at all assembled there. "In light of the amazing and selfless bravery Sakima Tamanend has shown every time her people have called on her for help—and because her father, Sachem Takachsin, and her mother, Wùnita Tamanend, have both walked on to the Land of the Dead to be among their loved ones there—considering everything, I recommend that Sakima Tamanend, daughter of royalty, be named Sachem *pro tempore* until further notice and until this crisis has ended, one way or another."

Elder Olsen stared at Elder Manunsko and then from face to face around the table, her chin out, her neck tight, and her brow compressed. "And let me remind you, sir," she said, when her gaze returned to Manunsko and her face began to darken, "that in any other culture, a princess far outranks a mere Elder. Only here, in the Mannahatta world, would you have the effrontery to not only confront royalty, but to refrain from respecting, even bowing to her." Then she addressed the Mannahatta men present. "All in favor of Sakima being Sachem *pro temp* until another solution is determined down the road, raise your hand."

Second Lieutenant Nuwingi lifted his hand while looking about the table as Elder Olsen shot her own hand straight up into the air. Then the other advisors around the table followed suit. Finally, with a shrug and a smile, Colonel Skattek raised his too.

"Ahi?" Elder Olsen said. "Do you not vote in favor?"

A look of pure fury covered the man's face, a vein in both his forehead and his neck throbbing with anger. He turned and stormed out of the room.

"It is unanimous then," Elder Olsen said, "in a vote of all here and now present in this room. Sakima Tamanend is our new queen: our *kittakima!*"

The room filled with respectful, quiet applause.

"Well, for the time being, at any rate," Sakima said with a shrug. She reluctantly accepted what, to her, was an unnecessary honor, and frankly, a burden. But she knew better than to turn it down. Besides, she had no time nor inclination right then to worry about politics.

"Now, about how many warriors and in which ship and where within the ship—" She bent over the blueprints, maps, and other papers on the table in front of her as yet another person appeared at the door. Sakima glanced over at the door without actually seeing who was there. "We need a lock on that thing. We need the input and analysis from the *Wematëgunis*."

"Um, it's me, ma'am. You wanted to see me?"

Sakima looked up to see warrior and tech advisor, Sergeant Mitch Galanney, standing at attention in the doorway.

"What? Oh, yes, yes, thank you. We need you to help us program the portal to send a battalion to the Land Below. Please assemble as many people for your team as you require. I know the programming of the portal won't be easy or quick, but we need it done as close to immediately as you can do it. Get the *Wematëgunis* down there right away. And then, once we get a report back from them, send down the attack team."

"Understood, ma'am." Galanney didn't leave his spot.

"Was there something else, soldier?" Sakima said, returning to her full height. "And please, stop with the 'ma'am' and the 'princess' and the 'pro temp' and all that damn *maluwe* nonsense. It's Sakima, and that's all. Just Sakima." She smiled to soften the message.

"Yes, your highness. I mean Sakima, ma'am. I'm afraid I have some problematic news to share."

"Spit it out, warrior," Skattek said.

"Uh, would you all please accompany me back to my workstation? I've got something to show you that you need to know. But I'm finding it difficult to put it into words."

CHAPTER 25

The group in the War Room gathered up their papers and themselves and followed Sergeant Galanney down the hall.

As they walked along, he continued. "The thing is, well, it's a monster—I don't know any other way to describe it."

Sakima stopped. "Has Yakwahe returned?" She swallowed hard. "I mean, I had hoped that I had killed that hideous beast, but well, the truth is, it just kind of vanished into nothingness."

"Um, no," Galanney said. "It's new. Not as big, not as horrifying as Yakwahe, with its exposed bones and flesh. But big and horrifying enough in its own way."

"Well done finding this behemoth, soldier," Nuwingi said from the back of the crowd.

"Yes, well, I should clarify. It's not so much that we've found it, as it let itself be found."

"What are you saying?" Sakima said, raising an eyebrow and returning to walking along with the others.

"You'll see."

They entered the Logistics, Analysis, and Targeting (LAT) room and gathered around Galanney's workstation. He sat and began tapping at a keyboard.

"There," he said, pointing at the largest of the six screens laid out on the wall in front of him.

A stunned silence filled the room as the group stared at the video currently playing on the screen. On the monitor in front of them—as well as three of the other monitors showing different angles—was what could only be described as none other than the mythological monster, Mhuwe. A beast with horns and fur and a strangely human-like body of immense height and width.

"Oh, my *Kishelë*!" Elder Olsen exclaimed, clutching her hands to her chest.

Sakima felt a chill run down her spine. Mhuwe was a creature as evil on the outside as the evil that no doubt filled the beast entirely within. *This much evil, this much threat. How do we fight this thing from our Mannahatta nation's mythological past?* Sakima wondered. *In fact, will this horror even be impervious to the effects of weaponized Mp, their most powerful weapon?*

"What is going on here?" the Colonel said, almost shouting. "What is it doing?"

Sergeant Galanney coughed, covering his mouth with his fist, then spoke up. "He's conversing with the intruders. Now, watch what happens next."

The team gazed on in horror as Mhuwe bent his head, lowering his immense rack of horns, and entered the main spaceship, followed by what appeared to be a group of the largest dogs ever seen on the planet.

"They've invited him in. He's talked to them, and he got himself on board," Galanney said, almost shouting.

"This is all too much!" Sakima said, dropping abruptly into the nearest available seat. "What in the hell is going on? What is this creature? How did it find and tame all of those *manëtu* beasts from the underworld?" She leaned over and placed her face in her palms.

Elder Olsen placed her hand gently on Sakima's back. "Breathe, brave one," she said. "Just breathe."

Sakima thought about what had transpired in her life just under two years ago. How she'd lost so much, yet gained so much, too. New friends from the Land Below. New skills and strengths. And most important, new respect. For herself, from herself, and from the tribe.

But this new threat, although she had risen to the challenge, was so overwhelmingly different. She had thrown herself down to the Land Below to save her little sister. Just as she'd so recently thrown herself into the enemy ship to save her family—and all of the Mannahatta people.

But she was feeling now like she was an ordinary human and very much out of her element. The fall from space had nearly killed her. And the death of her father weighed so heavily on her, she didn't know how she'd be able to carry on with such grief. She felt almost powerless now.

Add to this the fact that this new monster, Mhuwe—looking horrific and gigantic and disproportionate—appeared to be befriending the Mannahatta's new, murderous enemies.

Sakima doubted her ability to change what was happening, to save the day. Against such foes, she just didn't know if she had what it took.

And the Grandmother, she thought, almost angrily but mostly feeling quite lonely. *Where was she? Why is she staying hidden and leaving me—and all Mannahatta people—on their own at their most dire time of need?*

Sakima felt sorry for herself, which caused her to chuckle quietly, to laugh at herself.

Look at me, the new temporary Queen of the Mannahatta, shaking in my boots. Too scared to go on. Crying for Mommy. Sakima stopped and bit her lip. Mom: that's another thing. Where is she? Why isn't she communicating with me, telling me what I need to do?

Sakima stared straight ahead, her eyes still and seeing nothing.

It's like everyone I have ever depended on has disappeared from the multiverse.

CHAPTER 26

The warm New York City air wafted across its face and matted fur in rapid gusts. The air smelled of faded roses and tarmac. Bugs landed and took off again on the thing as it lumbered through the small wooded area. Strange vines curled up, but not along the branches of trees, but instead, around the thing's almost-human arms and legs, which displayed exposed bits of bone here and there. Patches of mongrel fur teemed with fleas and ticks, but these pests were not able to draw blood from the desiccated skin. Birds flew near, toward the safe haven of a tree, but turned sharply at the last minute to fly away from the discovered danger.

The thing stunk like a field of manure where dead animals had collapsed and rotted and fallen apart. Its eyes worked independently of each other as they searched for something, searched everywhere. For food? For danger? For release from the burden of being trapped in the most hideous of bodies?

For the thing was part wolf, part deer buck, part tree, all horror. It stumbled through the morning's warm air like a giant from a fairytale gone mad. It strode on thin, bony legs, like deer's legs.

Legs that did not end in hooves, but in large, human-like feet. Feet covered in scale and moss. Toenails like large thorns. It lumbered through the morning toward the cave of spaceships, toward the visitors.

The creature of Mannahatta mythology known as *Mhuwe* was covered in dirt and moss and vines and bugs and lizards and snakes. Its long arms and outsized legs seemed stretched unnaturally, as if made from tree branches and not human bone. It hunched, its back looking more like the bulging back of a buck than a man, covered with blotchy fur. Its hands were grotesquely oversized, with fingers each close to a foot in length. At their tips were long nails, claws actually, curved like talons. These talons were darkened, almost black, the ends chipped and broken.

The face of the monstrosity appeared strangely extended, almost as if the creature had the muzzle of a wolf or part of the face of a male deer. The face of this beast, thought to be real only in Mannahatta mythology—and other nations too, especially the *Wendigo* of the Algonquin, Cree, and Ojibwa tribes—had blotchy patches of fur here and there about it. Its mouth was much larger than any large animal on Mannahatta. Inside the beast's strange grimace were hideous fangs of incredible length. They would be more fitting inside the mouth of a black bear, and they seemed to drip with some kind of dark, mucus-like liquid. Perhaps drool mixed with animal blood and some other strange things that the creature might have eaten over its lifetime, or at least its recent times.

Its eyes were red and glowing, like the werewolf legends of old. The eyes orbited about the eyeholes as if constantly hunting for prey. They moved sometimes in unison and sometimes independently, with each individual eyeball looking off in a direction of its own.

The visitors had appeared in the empty concrete space that had once been a large transit tunnel but which now was just a memory of one. The beast crunched along on the gravel and dirt that lined each side of the potholed route, getting closer to the visitors' crafts, spaceships that appeared first like a mirage and then like a threat. Through the multiverse maybe; through a wormhole most definitely.

The thing approached—angry, weary, deadly. It wanting revenge, but against what it couldn't say. But it also saw the sudden visitors as potential new allies; and if they choose not to align, then as corpses, as meals, as nothing.

It finally reached the biggest of the spacecrafts that sat in the middle like a giant frog on a giant lily pond, its metal skin twinkling from the sun's reflection along its rear like a fly's eye. Multiple iridescent layers of greenish material, almost transparent, gave the skin of the craft depth. The thing knew that this was not just for design; it was protection. Layers of nano-bots, nano-wire. Perhaps mpoaolonium—no, upon closer inspection, *definitely* mpoaolonium.

The creature stood there and waited. The craft was silent. No whirring, no buzzing. No sounds of footsteps within. No turrets turning toward it, creaking as they did. Instead, the ships—all three of them—sat and baked in the hot shadows like cows in a barn: content to do nothing but simply wait.

The thing pondered what it saw and stood still in its wooden, furry, not-quite-human giganticness. And it glared. Sometimes with red eyes in unison, sometimes with each eye on its own personal mission.

No rush, no urgency. The thing had all the time in the world. As it waited, a significant number of flies, gnats, yellow jackets, and beetles buzzed about the creature. They had become a constant presence, and nothing could be done about it. They were as much a part of Mhuwe as the creature's own body.

Once—*was it ever true?*—Mhuwe was only a man. An original man. A Mannahattan. Now, it had been transformed into this. When the thing used to be a man, it prided itself on its looks. But now it's prickly horrifying appearance was all anyone could see, its giant bigger-than-moose-like horns, its furry hair like the bristles on a porcupine. But its giant size was the thing that gave it the feeling of true power. Extreme, infinite power. *Like a god.*

Mhuwe, the giant and grotesque man-eater, was as content as a walking pile of broken branches, dung, and human and animal parts could ever be. The evil powers came from *Matanto*, the Mannahatta Devil, as had most of the deformity: the extended limbs, the long fingers, the gigantic tree-like height. And the horns. Those damned horns. Although recently, the thing had actually come to love those long, monstrous extensions on each side of its head—along with its molting skin, pockmarked fur, protruding bones, and branch-like deformities—simply for the fear they put into ordinary men, sometimes freezing them and leaving them whimpering in horror and disgust in their tracks.

The creature spat on the ground, the mucous-dense, pus-and-blood-filled saliva sizzling immediately on the hot pebbles below.

It called out in a screeching noise that sounded part tiger, part bear, and part hyena. The bushes behind it rustled and waved, and then creatures from the underworld burst out of the thick bushes and tall, spiky weeds, friends and cohorts of Mhuwe. And as focused on destruction, revenge, and malice as Mhuwe.

The demon creatures, the *manëtu*, crawled on all fours. Their eyeless, hideous faces bent strangely up and down and left and right as if they had four spines instead of just one. Creatures from the underworld, hell, hades. Wolf-like creatures with no morals and driven by pure hatred.

Much like Mhuwe.

Then the door in front of Mhuwe emitted a noise like an electrical connection gone bad—the snap of an electrical buzz right before the door slid open on its damaged track. The door was actually a replacement from the supply sector of the ship. The door itself looked good, better than new, in fact. But what operated it— all the wires and cables and pulleys and magnets—they were repaired or replaced as well as possible. Yet the door's operation was still buggy, still not quite right. This pleased Mhuwe, although it wasn't sure why. Perhaps the discovery of its ability to analyze broken things that are not human—inanimate objects made of metal and wires. It realized that it had more power and insight than it previously realized.

Mhuwe blinked as it peered into the cavernous entrance in front of itself from its position in the bright sun. After the creature's eyes adjusted, the thing could see that the interior of the craft was actually well lit, with giant lights along the high—twenty-feet, maybe?—ceiling. And when it blinked again to clear its red eyes and help them adjust, it saw soldiers. Men in dark red battle suits—the color of blood dried in the sun—wearing helmets with yellow visors. The battle suits were reinforced at the shoulders, chest, back, thighs, and knees. All the vulnerable area—except the neck, Mhuwe noticed.

The beast estimated there were about twenty soldiers in front of it, spanned out in an arc—all with weapons aimed at its face. The weapons were alien to Mhuwe, but the beast recognized power and technology. These were sophisticated machines. The creature had nothing to worry about in terms of dying. But the pain. The pain was a legitimate concern. Mhuwe had forgotten to negotiate that into its "I will live forever!" contract with *Matanto*. The beast grimaced out a smile so hideous that some of the soldiers stepped back quickly. This, of course, only caused the monster to grimace even wider, filthy scum dripping from its mouth and splashing on the ground.

"Take me to your leader," it said, quoting an old book it had found in a pile of garbage in the Land Below. And then it cackled out loud at how silly that sounded.

But this noise struck the soldiers' ears, not as laughter, but as a screeching zombie howl out from the depths of the underworlds.

CHAPTER 27

"Okay," Sakima said softly, composing herself. Then she said much louder, "Okay. *Okay*!" She wanted to believe she could handle this, that she could and would rise to the challenge, however much it made her feel scared and unqualified. "That devil, that Mhuwe—it can be defeated, I am sure," she said between gritted teeth. "Possibly not killed or destroyed, but sent away. Far away, forever. It is nothing like Yakwahe and should be easier to conquer than the thirty-foot tall and twenty-feet wide mythological monster, Yakwahe." She turned to look at Galanney and changed the subject. "What do we know about these alien ships? Anything? We need to understand what to expect, how to best plan our attack."

"Well, ma'am, we actually have learned quite a lot about these strange ships. Most of it gathered and processed in just the past half hour or so. There are three ships, as you know, in three different sizes and aspects." Galanney turned toward the whiteboard in the room, *Ntite Pìkchëlhe* (the Think & Draw 2000™). "Please display the Taturåkee ship diagrams."

The blueprints for each of the three ships displayed immediately on the *Ntite Pìkchëlhe's* whiteboard screen.

"We were able to do a complete scan of the ships right after we discovered them. They constitute a rather small armada. Our speculation is that they are a discovery unit and that bigger ships are out there somewhere in the Many Worlds, waiting for the signal to move forward." He cleared his throat. "But I hope not. *Kishelë* willing." He took a deep breath. "Let's look at what we have on them so far," he said, getting to his feet to stand by the whiteboard. "*Ntite* 2000, please zoom in on the *Ästra*, 200 percent."

The device zoomed in on the bigger ship and centered it on the display.

"Private Gischileu, why don't you take this one since you did much of the research yourself?"

Lèke Gischileu swiveled in his seat to face the others in the room. He turned his focus to the people there instead of the database he was studying and the code he was compiling to analyze the information even further. Across the room, he noticed Sakima. She blushed when their eyes met, and she immediately took her gaze down to the floor. Lèke hesitated for a moment, his heart having sped up and his mouth suddenly dry. He took a deep breath while focusing his vision on the *Ntite* 2000's whiteboard and the diagrams it displayed there.

"Yes, of course, Sergeant Galanney, happy to help." Lèke made a small scratching noise in his throat to give himself one last chance to forget, at least temporarily, that the beautiful Sakima shared the room with him. "Okay, well, um, what we're looking at here is the main ship, the first one to arrive on Mannahatta on that fateful day. The leader or king or whatever, the one who marched out after addressing us, the self-proclaimed 'god,' if you will—"

Two Elders chuckled with a mocking tone as one of the soldiers gritted his teeth and stared at the ground with laser intensity.

"We've been able to identify that person, if you will, as one 'Locus Mub,'" Private Gischileu continued. "He appears to be some kind of leader or actual king on his planet of Taturåkis. Anyway, the ship itself is called the *Ästra Ån Ima*, which approximately means 'Ghost of the Stars,' according to our linguistics algorithms." He paused, waiting for a response. When none came, he continued. "It's a destroyer-class ship, on the smaller end of the spectrum. Would you like to hear the details? Size, capacity, and so on?"

"Yes," Elder Nitis Tschutti said. "Please go on."

"Yes, sir." Gischileu cleared his throat, his eyes having caught a glance of Sakima again. "The, uh, the *Ästra Ån Ima* is a single-level ship; one story, in other words. Well, one for the crew; there's a second, lower level for the engine and fuel storage, HVAC, wiring, weapons bays, and so on." He pointed at the whiteboard to show a lower deck about half as long as the full deck above, like a shark swimming below a whale. "It's twenty-four feet tall, top to bottom. The main floor has twelve-foot high ceilings. The ship is sixty feet, or about twenty *shaèk* across, with eight-foot wide corridors and eleven feet across for the rooms—galley, sleeping quarters, medical area, and so on."

"What about the crew?" Elder Tschutti said.

"Thanks for asking; I didn't mean to leave that information out." He glanced at Sakima again, although he hadn't meant to, and their glances locked together for a moment. Lèke thought she had the prettiest eyes he'd ever seen, as well as the sweetest lashes, as she glanced down again. "Uh, well, where was I? Oh, yes, the crew. The crew is small but serviceable, correctly sized for the ship. Leadership, or royalty class, if you will—which also includes their advisors and servants—totals six. Flight control totals four: a captain, copilot, navigator, and communications officer."

"That's ten for leaders and pilots," Elder Rita Shim Olsen said. "What about soldiers? That's what we need to get a handle on. The forces we'll be facing."

"Yes, I'll get to that now. I just want to add, quickly, that the ship's support staff totals six: two maintenance workers, two engineers, one cook, and one medic. Okay, as for the military—the important bit, as you note—there are forty-five: ten officers and thirty-five soldiers. A ship total of sixty-one personnel, from what we could establish."

"Not a huge contingent."

"But effective. They rely on their advanced weaponry and technologies in battle, as opposed to headcount. A more advanced civilization than ours, in some ways. At least in terms of military technologies."

"So, we're dealing with a small battalion," Elder Ahi Manunsko said, ignoring Private Gischileu's note about the enemy's technological advantage. "We can take them with ease!" He clapped his hands together emphatically. "What about the other two ships?"

"Less to worry about there, fortunately," said Sergeant Galanney. "Private, if you don't mind, I'll jump in here."

"Not at all."

"Ntite 2000, display the schematic for the *Ästra Ån Pit*," Galanney said.

The Think & Draw 2000 complied, centering the diagram on its screen.

"The '*Ån*,' by the way, seems to be similar in function to HMS or USS in the Land Below. We haven't yet determined precisely what it stands for. And '*Ästra*' means starship, or something along those lines."

"Understood," Elder Tschutti said. "Please continue."

"Yes sir. The *Ästra Ån Pit* is the middle-size vessel in the group," Galanney continued. "It's a gunship-class light interceptor. It's eighteen feet high and thirty feet across and is also a single-level craft. The ship carries a full crew of twenty-three—five officers and twelve soldiers. The support and flight crews (maintenance, medical, pilots) accounts for the other six."

"And the last ship?" Elder Olsen asked.

"The last ship, the *Ästra Ån Ni*—"

The *Ntite* 2000 was smart enough to display this ship's blueprint without prompting.

"It's the smallest of the three ships, a destroyer escort class. Only twelve feet high, with nine feet of usable space from floor to ceiling. Private?"

"Thank you, sir. It is also a single-level craft, eighteen feet across from beam to beam," Lèke Gischileu said, taking over the description of the last ship. "It carries a twelve-man crew, five of which are fighters. But again, their AI-driven weaponry does virtually all the fighting for them."

"Thank you both, Sergeant Galanney and Private Gischileu," Sakima said, not looking at either man. "That was an excellent transfer of information. But just to be sure, I was counting along with you correctly as you spoke…" She took a deep breath. "They have seventy-one soldiers, including officers, across all three ships. That's assuming that they took no casualties during our initial encounter with them, which strikes me as unlikely. Do you agree with my math—is it correct?"

"Yes ma'am. Accurate."

"With the bulk of their officers and fighters, forty-five to be exact, on their flagship. Is that correct as well?"

"Yes ma'am, you are correct."

Sakima then turned to face the members of the Elder Council and the military representatives. "Strikes me that if we attack the main ship internally and don't worry about the others at the start, we'd have an excellent chance at victory. Take out the larger set of soldiers on the *Ästra Ån Ima*. Reduce or eliminate their forces there. The other ships will go down, and they might even surrender once we've taken the big ship. That wretched Mhuwe should be considered a serious problem and one not to be taken lightly. That said, that monster might be harder to take down, but not as difficult as a group of soldiers. We strike, we kill soldiers and the devil of a beast, we take no prisoners."

"This plan has legs," Colonel Skattek said, nodding.

"I have to agree," added the Kanyen leader, Major Onanta. "The element of surprise, along with hitting the biggest target first. It could all be over in an instant, with us seizing and securing victory."

"We will have surprise on our side, which will hopefully get in there and do our work before they can notify the mothership," Sakima continued. "Assuming as Sergeant Galanney implied that there might be such a thing out there in the Many Worlds somewhere."

"Maybe, maybe not," Galanney said. "We just don't know at this point. But we should assume it until proven otherwise."

"Yes, I second that," Private Gischileu said. "Expecting the worst is the best way to be physically and mentally prepared."

Sergeant Galanney gave his mentee a quick nod of approval.

"All right, good, good. Be that as it may. But they have, at best, forty or so healthy soldiers, probably less because I have to believe that we wounded or killed at least a few of them. Others will man their ship's bigger guns on the exterior, as well as handling communications, logistics, and so on." Sakima paused to be sure all present were following her train of thought. "So let's say, realistically, about thirty-five battle-ready fighters. We have over fifty still-healthy warriors. We keep twenty here to protect Mannahatta and send thirty to the Land Below. Coupled with the twenty-six Kanyen fighters, that gives us about fifty-six warriors; a two-to-one advantage here. At least, I hope so."

"I like those odds! I'll take them any day of the week," Colonel Skattek said. "Let's figure out the final details and get this ball rolling.The faster we act, the better our chances for victory over these bastards!"

Some people in the room cheered, while others remained silent. Sakima glanced about at the people in the room, trying to read their faces to see who was on board and who was not.

"Of course, there is still the unknown impact of this Mhuwe. But as I mentioned earlier, I knew Yakwahe. I battled Yakwahe. I destroyed Yakwahe. And this Mhuwe, sir, is no Yakwahe."

She let go a long sigh. Whether the brute might destroy the best laid plans or whether this group in this room supported her was not really the issue. It was *her* plan, and it must not fail.

This better work, Sakima thought. *Or my glorious Mannahatta, as well as the beloved Land Below, are finished. Forever. I must collect myself and find the strength I shall need.*

"I will be back soon," she said to the others. "Get the portal ready. Send our *Wematëgunis* friends to assess the situation and get ready to travel through the Many Worlds to attack these vicious enemies. I need a moment to prepare for battle, to get my thoughts straight, and to pray to our ancestors for help and guidance. I will see you at the portal soon."

"Understood," someone in the room said softly as others nodded their heads.

CHAPTER 28

The wispy clouds in the cerulean autumn sky hinted at the winter soon to come. But the day was still warm, with a cool breeze. Leaves seesawed through Sakima's view as she sat and studied the Land Below from the Edge of the World: *Nink Shawi*. This break in the time-space continuum had appeared shortly after her trip to the Land Below and back again. No Mannahatta scientist could explain this sudden window onto *Mënatink Ohëlëmi*. It was as if Mannahatta floated in the sky a hundred miles above the island of Manhattan. It was as if they were on a spaceship hovering somewhere between the Earth and outer space.

Sakima pulled her legs up to her chest and let the tears come. She couldn't believe this was all happening. The horrible attack with so many dead and wounded. The destroyed Mannahatta buildings—although, thank *Kishelë*, the attack was stopped at the fields outside of the village, and only a few structures nearby had burned down.

Mostly, the loss of spirit. Everyone in the village seemed to be in a state of shock. And many were acting irrationally—enough to make her the temporary "Queen of the Mannahatta." There was actually no such thing. They should have, in keeping with Manna-hatta traditions and history, chosen Nimàt. Yes, he was badly hurt and in and out of consciousness. But he was the male heir to the throne, and that's how these things worked and had always worked for millennia. But they chose her because she was their new favorite, everybody's hero.

Sakima sniffed twice and wiped her nose with the back of her hand as she watched one of the Manhattan's primitive jet planes arc across the sky far below her. The sun glistened off the metal of the jet, making it appear like a floating jewel. Sakima smiled at this. Despite the recent calamity, the peacefulness of the hill she sat on with the clean air and the trees casting shade and fluttering leaves on her—and especially the view of *Mënatink Ohëlëmi*—calmed Sakima, and actually made her a little happy.

Is there really hope? Is that what I am experiencing, or am I delusional? Suffering from shock, kidding myself.

She peered down at the glistening, bustling city below with all its life and positive energy and turned her gaze up high above her into the boundless blue sky of Mannahatta.

Where are you, Grandmother? And Mother, can't you talk to me from the Land of the Dead? Can't you try? And the Grandmother of the South, won't you say even a single word? Just a simple, 'hello?'

"Hello!"

Sakima startled and froze, like a squirrel afraid of the sound of a breaking branch. Timidly, she turned to face her greeter, expecting the Grandmother but seeing someone else entirely.

"Nimàt?"

"Hè, Sakima. What's up?"

"What are you—did they let you out of the hospital?"

Nimàt laughed and gestured to the gauze and other wraps around his body. "Yes, they did. But do you think they should have released me? I mean, I am a bit of a wreck."

"You look great, though," she said, laughing out loud in a more joyous way than she would have considered possible only twenty-four hours ago. "The color's back in your face, little brother. You don't appear to be a white man—a *Shëwanahkòk*—anymore!"

"Well, that's good, at least. But I feel like shit."

"That's the drugs talking."

"I wish that were true! They've given me almost nothing for the pain. Black Willow-bark tea. Can you believe it? Black Willow tea!"

"Yes, I can. The tea should have helped you, at least a bit."

"A tiny bit, yeah, sure—"

"So, how did you find me?"

"Come on, are you serious? Where else would you be? This is now your favorite place, night and day. Why do you love it so much? Why do you love gazing down at the people and the buildings in the Land Below?"

"Don't you?"

"Sometimes, maybe. Once in a while. But you practically live here."

"I guess…" Sakima's voice trailed off. She experienced a pain in her soul again. She'd enjoyed the minute of relief, but now it was back, as strong as ever.

"So," Nimàt said, trying to talk around the pain he could so clearly see in her eyes. "I heard they made you queen. You go, girl."

"Ha, it is you that should be Sachem, and you understand that. Besides, it is only temporary. What did they call it? '*Kittakima pro tempore*.' That's it. Queen for a day."

"Aw, knock it off, sis. You're queen now, and that's that. Pro or Tem or whatever. It doesn't mean a queen without power. It means a full-on *kittakima* until further notice—which could mean, you know, forever."

Sakima sighed. "I guess. I mean, I don't know what to think. All I ever wanted to be was a warrior, a leader of soldiers into battle. Not a queen. Certainly not a princess. You understand me. You know that's true."

"Yeah, I know. I've always known. But, hell, you're queen now. Queen Sakima. Deal with it."

"I can't. I mean, I don't want to."

Nimàt carefully lowered himself to the ground next to his sister. His hair blew gently in the breeze as the scent of nearby honeysuckle floated through the air past the two siblings. Smelled good to him. He picked up a stick and moved some of the dried maple leaves around with it.

"You need to hide."

"What?"

"Sakima, the last thing we need, the Mannahatta people need, is a dead or captured queen. You think we're all demoralized and beaten now? If you get killed or taken away, I think everyone in the entire nation will just lie down on the ground, give up, and die."

"Man, Nimmy, you paint a pretty picture. I am not dying. I am not getting kidnapped, and never will be. I promise you."

"So you say."

"Seriously. Such a thing will never happen. I will *never* be kidnapped, you understand? Never! Who in the world would even try such a thing? Wrap me in chains and toss me in a prison cell? No way! I would kill my kidnapper or myself, whichever was quickest."

"Okay, sure. But, well, I mean, could you have predicted what happened here a couple of weeks ago? Such a vicious attack by aliens? No. No, you couldn't. So you need to hear me out."

"What am I supposed to do, Nimàt, run and hide? I am the temporary queen, for *Kishelë's* sake! I was born to lead, and now I guess I must lead this new way, as a queen."

"No, Sakima. That won't work and it's too dangerous for Mannahatta. You must instead protect yourself—that has to be your first priority. You can't fight anymore, you understand? No more of that. You can't be all 'warrior girl' anymore; those days have now officially passed. You must protect yourself. You must protect the queen: you. For gosh sakes, you certainly can't be out here in the middle of nowhere all by yourself here at *Nink Shawi!*"

Sakima sighed. It was a harsh truth that she didn't want to face.

Elder Olsen had thought she'd done the right thing installing Sakima as the Queen of the Mannahatta. But all she'd really done was strip a warrior of her strength and her effectiveness. Made a powerful warrior impotent.

"But I cannot simply disappear. What queen would do that? I've got to lead my people, lead the troops. This is impossible, Nimmy. I am caught between a rock and a hard place. I might as well be dead already, for all the good I can do."

She stared off into the sky ahead, no longer looking up at the heavens or down at the city below.

"You can rally the troops first, I suppose," Nimàt said, sounding defeated. "I guess that's necessary. Rally the troops and then go into hiding? How's that sound?"

"I hate this idea of hiding, for the record. It goes against everything I believe in. I have a warrior's heart, and a warrior does not run and hide. A warrior fights!"

"Yes and no, sis. Sometimes a strategic retreat is a step toward winning the war. You aren't just a warrior anymore. You can't be killed because—well, you know why. Society will collapse. It's that simple. Without a strong leader, you, the Mannahatta, will defeat themselves—ourselves."

Sakima thought about this for a minute and said, reluctantly, "I guess you could be right." She closed her eyes and stretched her back, trying to relieve all the tension there that seemed to grow by the minute. "So, what next? Do I go into 'official' hiding with the help of the Elders? Or do I suddenly disappear, starting right now?"

"Option 'B,' Sakima, option 'B.' You need to hide. No Elders. No permissions. And nobody to know how to find you. You will be much safer that way. Because, you know, not every Elder can really be trusted."

"Okay, but where? Come on, Nimàt, where in this world can I go to be out of harm's way? Especially if the invaders return, which I know they will. What then? I just stay hidden? Do nothing?"

"Yes, Sakima, that's exactly what must happen. You, as the warrior Sakima, must do everything in your powers to protect Sakima, the queen, the *kittakima*. Talk to your troops; get them ready to fight. Send them to the Land Below. But—and I am dead serious about this, sis—you must *not* go with them."

Sakima rolled her eyes and fell back onto the ground. She slid her hands behind her head and watched the clouds skim past in the steel-blue sky for a few minutes. Nimàt awkwardly joined her; awkwardly because it required a lot of core muscle movements in the areas where he was wounded most severely to lay down.

"But where, Nimmy? Where am I supposed to go?" Sakima whispered. "I do not like this hiding idea, but I see your point. But there is nowhere to hide on Mannahatta where I will not be found by somebody, either deliberately or accidentally."

They lay there side by side in silence for a few minutes. The cool air rippled past them, exciting the yellow and orange leaves in the trees and scooting the dry ones on the ground in little soft bursts, like gentle mini-funnels. At last Nimàt spoke, quietly but determined.

"I've got it. The one place no one would ever even consider, on purpose or by luck." He forced himself, with much dramatic groaning and teeth-gritting, to sit up. "*Nagatamen Mùxul Allanque*," he said. "The original ship of the *Alànawènik*."

"I know what that is, dummy. Their spaceship that is currently dug into the side of *Òhchu* Peak." Sakima sat up. "That could work," she said, contemplating the idea. "But no one's ever gotten inside. We have no idea what it's like in there. Heck, it could be filled with poisonous air that might kill me instantly."

"Unlikely."

"Well, this all relies on the preposterous notion that I could get inside that ship, a feat no one in 500 years has been able to accomplish!"

"My money's on you, sis," Nimàt said, smiling. "Now help me get the heck up. I got no abs anymore, remember?"

"You got abs still, silly. You are just a baby, as always." Sakima laughed.

"Either way, I can't do it without you." Nimàt smiled, too.

Sakima, who in the meantime had stood up and extended her hand to Nimàt, froze in place. She retracted her hand.

"Well, that's it, isn't it?"

"What is?"

"If I'm going to successfully go into hiding, I can't do that without you, can I?"

"Just help me up already. We can talk once I'm vertical again."

"I can talk, you can listen." Sakima laughed.

"*There's* my sister. That's the girl I'm familiar with," Nimàt said. "The same tough girl, whether warrior, queen, or—even better, my sister." He extended his hand up to her.

Sakima grabbed his hand and, with her other hand, cupped him behind his upper arm and pulled him to his feet.

"*Ooww!*" he yelled.

"And there's the *brother* I've always known: drama queen."

"Two queens in one household. Has to be a new record!"

The siblings laughed well and for a stolen moment together, interrupted only by the occasional sounds of agony from Nimàt, suffering pains from the laughter.

"Let's get going. We still have a few hours of light," Nimàt said. "That's enough to time to get to the ship and poke around it a bit."

"I said I would do the talking."

"Right, right. Sorry, sis. And?"

"What *you* said." Sakima smiled. She picked up her things, and turned to march down the hill. "But first we have a ceremony to attend where I will give the speech of my life."

CHAPTER 29

The soldiers led Mhuwe through the labyrinth of corridors deep within the alien spacecraft. The beast observed everything, as if it wanted to know how the tech works, where the vulnerabilities might. be. This might be needed later, or it might be worthless information. The thing collected this data anyway, knowing it would know more after it met with the leaders of this group. With that intent, Mhuwe spoke up.

"Who," it growled. As if it had tripped on a stone and not its words, the beast stood rock still and started again. "Who… should… me talk, me talk to? *Who?*" The monster stared straight ahead, addressing no one and everyone at the same time.

After an awkward moment where no one responded or moved, the beast screamed, *"I. Said. Who?"* Dirt-encrusted drool cascaded out of the creature's mouth to the floor.

It still got no answers, just looks of abject fear in the eyes of the faces surrounding it. So the beast tried a different tack. Its brow curled into multiple waves as it concentrated, trying to remember how to talk. Speaking had never before been this difficult. The thing growled, but it sounded more like a broken engine trying to start. And then, as if reading the lines of a play that the beast had long since forgotten, it spoke almost clearly.

"What are you called… you people? Do you have, have a name? A culture? Location?" Then, as if it had consumed a magic elixir, it spoke like a college professor: "Are you Martians? Saturnites? Romulans? Gamorreans?"

Still no action. The soldiers kept their eyes straight ahead and their guns pointed at their new "guest."

A grimace grew on the monster's face that perhaps was meant to be a smile, a smile at the stupidity it was now encountering. It might have trouble talking, but it had no trouble thinking. No problem with assessing, evaluating, tracking, and predicting the behavior of both enemy and prey.

"I see," the beast said, its voice returning to a horrific snarl again. Mhuwe remained unaware of how its voice—a strained, growling noise—was received by others. All anyone heard was a monstrous guttural noise with words mixed in—a kind of horrible feedback noise from hell.

They approached a set of sliding doors, which glided apart after a scanning light shone slowly across the initial line of soldiers. The scan rejected the visitor, so one of the soldiers took a calculated risk and punched in a code indicating that Mhuwe was an authorized guest.

They marched through the doors into an even bigger hallway, maybe ten yards across. Vehicles of various kinds lined one wall. These were glistening, white-and-chrome military units with no visible wheels but many visible weapons. Only a single window opened the view of each to the outside, most likely the driver's view. Mhuwe assumed with its smart but hideous freak-brain that all other "views" of the outside world from these vehicles were done electronically with sensors and video screens and, most likely, AI.

The beast did not understand how it knew this, which made its monster head hurt. It remembered another era, when things were quite different yet normal, and full of possibilities. Memories rushed by its brain like leaves in the wind, each carrying the image of how the beast used to look, the things it used to do. And then these wisps of what felt like another life in another universe suddenly whisked away, and its brain grew dark and full of nothingness once again.

The thing studied the cables and chutes that covered and filled most of the walls: conduits for plumbing, electric, and communications. Various button-pads appeared here and there along the jet-black walls, as did other doors and the occasional perpendicular hallway leading off to who knows where.

The group passed through another set of doors into yet an even wider and taller hallway, this one twenty *shaèks* wide and twelve *shaèks* high. This new place teemed with other soldiers and individuals who appeared to be technicians, scientists, food workers, and other service people. There seemed to be no high-ranking leaders in this area, the same as in the two previous halls.

So, Mhuwe thought, *they are stupidly all in one place, a single cathedral for the leadership. Vulnerable to such a simple attack if their enemies knew of this and acted fast enough. Centralization of power will be their demise, if such an ending is in their future.*

Finally, they reached a large elevator, big enough to hold a good-sized Mannahatta hovertank. The entire squad of soldiers stepped in, forming a circle around Mhuwe as they ushered their uninvited visitor in. Right before the elevator doors closed the *manëtu* creatures dashed in. Mhuwe, who had to bend itself in half at the waist to fit in the freight elevator, despite its high ceiling—stared at his "pets" and said nothing.

Noises of creaking gears changing and shifting echoed in the elevator shaft. Mhuwe could feel the floor move in an odd way beneath its feet. Then it got a strange sensation, as if its stomach had dropped in its decrepit body. The beast felt almost dizzy for just a second. Then it realized what was happening.

We are not moving up in this car. We're moving sideways, horizontally. Mhuwe smiled. *Clever. Very clever.*

There was a digital *ping* noise, and the doors opened to reveal what could only be called a throne room. A high-tech throne room, but a throne room nonetheless.

The soldiers started moving, and the two nearest the monster's back poked Mhuwe with the barrels of their guns to get the beast moving. Mhuwe turned to stare at them with its oily red eyes. They were all anonymous in their matching suits and their yellow visors that hid their faces. But Mhuwe took in their personnel numbers emblazoned on each of their chest plates, and thought, *MI9222 and VS1434. You will be dealt with for your insolence soon enough.*

"Sit."

So, they can speak, Mhuwe thought. "Where, exactly? Exactly?" It said this in a voice that sounded distorted and broken, but they understood it all the same.

"The red seat. At the table."

"Please?" the beast uttered, a smirk on its bloated mouth.

"Yes, of course, sir. Please. Please sit." The man speaking gestured at the chair.

A red seat for visitors. Quaint, Mhuwe mused. *But I wonder what it means. I presume an honor of some kind. If that is not actually the case, I will go with that change and adjust. No sense starting off on too much of the wrong foot.*

Mhuwe tried to do as instructed and almost immediately gave up, the smirk growing. It held its hand against its throat to calm the roar and feedback noises.

"You see, see the problem, do you, you not? Too small, small, for a being of, a being of my stature." It glanced over at one enormous seat on the other side of the conference table—the throne. "That, on the other, the other hand, hand," it said, tightening its grip on its own filthy, scarred, partially hairy throat covered in insects and slime. "Seems to me, seems, seems it would be, be, a good, a good fit. Fit. Good."

Mhuwe, the hideous thing that it was, strode across the immense room toward the giant Mhuwe-sized chair. But before it could get to the throne and seat itself, it was interrupted by a newcomer in the room.

"That's *my* seat, friend," the person said, his voice booming across the room almost as if he had shouted into a microphone. He was a man, large of stature, with huge, bulky, artificially-enhanced muscles, draped in cloth and steel.

He stood at the entrance that had appeared out of the wall on the other side of the room, nearest to this throne. The man wore a crown of gold on his head, like some mythical king of ages past. Beneath the crown, a burgundy velvet cap laid crushed. Either the cap or the crown didn't belong on the man's head, but he was clearly not willing to give up either one.

The man has matching wide metal bracelets on his forearms and another, slightly narrower pair, on each bicep. A necklace of silver and gold, impregnated with a variety of exotic jewels, glistened around his neck and fell heavily on his broad chest.

A velvet cape the color of burgundy on his back hung attached to his bright metal chest protector, a thick sheet that has the look of the armor worn by Spanish Conquistadors long ago in another galaxy and timeline. There were intricate designs carved into the armor, which seemed to represent ships and islands and planets and stars. At least that was how Mhuwe interpreted them, and it wasn't concerned with learning more about the symbols or whether it was correct in its thinking. The hideous beast just wanted to get the conversation going and finish this irritating but necessary negotiation.

The ermine cloak was closed in the front, up by the man's neck by a gold clasp, which has at its center the portrait of a beautiful woman holding a scepter and looking quite stern.

On the man's giant, sausage-like fingers sat enormous rings of gold. Most were bedecked with at least one jewel; some with as many as a dozen or more. There was at least one ring per finger, including the thumb. Some fingers had two rings, others three.

On his feet were leather and metal boots, festooned with feathers and ribbon, which intertwine the boots like laces. The heels were tall and added at least three inches to the man's height.

The man's face was like granite, chiseled features carved into it at sharp angles. His eyes glowed in deep-set sockets. His large mouth seemed to be in a perpetual sneer. He wore a hoop earring in his right ear, nearly covered by his long, wavy, black hair cropped just at his chin.

"Lord Locus Mub…" the man said. "…is pleased to meet you. I'm the leader 'round here. In fact, I'm typically referred to as Supreme Leader Mub, but I can take it or leave it." He withdrew his hand, unshaken and untouched by Mhuwe. "And you are?"

"You know who, who I am," the thing growled. "I am, I am Mhuwe. Mhuwe. I am a god, a god."

"I'm sure you are," Mub said, filtering enough of the noises from the beast to get the gist of its meaning. He began climbing a short staircase before settling himself into the throne-like chair. "Like to consider myself about the same. God, I mean. Some have called me El Diablo Blanco: the White Devil. Which, personally, I love. Either way, though, it amounts to about the same thing. Obey me or worship me, I'm fine with both. But refuse to do either and you're dead. And just between you and me, no fast death, you understand?"

"I quite, I quite understand," Mhuwe said, scanning the room for anything else that might be throne-like and thus suitable for its frame and shape. Failing to discover any such object, it cleared the chairs away from the side of the table facing the throne with one swipe of his elongated arm. Then it backed up and leaned against the thick, sturdy table half sitting, half propped up. It liked it, it turned out. Not especially comfortable, but not uncomfortable either.

The best part is, due to Mhuwe's incredible height, the creature was now situated so that it was above this Mub person. *That's how it was meant to be. If I had to, I'd have climbed right up on the table itself to give me that physical and psychological advantage.*

But that move wasn't necessary. The creature was higher up now, looking down at Locus Mub, despite the other, this Mub, being in a large seat at the top of a set of stairs that wrapped around the throne on all four sides like a pyramid.

"In fact," Mhuwe growled and barked, "I live by the same, the same decree. Surrender or die. Sometimes die, anyway, even after, after surrender." It smiled a wretched, twisted grin. "So, which of the two of us, of us, will do the bowing? Or which, alternatively, which of us, which will do the dying?"

Mub chuckled. "This is good," he said. "Two men of like mind. Two leaders with the same objective. But of course, only one can survive; nature demands it. But you're in my house now, sir. Surrounded by my guards, my soldiers, my weapons. You have no army. No gun or knife. And from what I can tell, no friends other than those odd dogs-wolf-monster things that followed you in." He pointed at the demon creatures, the *manëtu*, who now sat on the marble floor below Mhuwe.

"All true, all true. But you know, you know, what they say about underestimating your, your enemies, eh?" Mhuwe remarked in a gutter-like mumble. With that, the beast swept ten soldiers into each of its arm and pulled them in against his trunk of a body, crushing all of them to death in an instant. Their blood ran down from their mouths and noses and eyes to the ornate Spanish tiles on the floor, staining the grout.

At first, Locus Mub didn't blink, as he was trying hard not to reveal his rage. Tried not to command all his men to destroy this vile intruder. But Mub was too interested in what this walking tree-buck wanted, this towering horror of a being. He wanted to know what he could learn from this beast—or take from him—which might be useful in his search. Something that might help him in his future subjugation of all who crossed his path.

But when Mhuwe then chewed at the neck of one of the dead soldiers and ripped the man's head from his body, Mub had not only second thoughts, but feelings of intense revulsion. He thought he'd seen all the horrors the universe could offer, but he had never seen anything like Mhuwe.

That feeling grew ten times stronger when Mhuwe bit open the man's head like biscuit and chewed on the brain therein as if it was a fine, soft cheese.

After the devilish creature swallowed a sizeable chunk of brain, Locus Mub thought for a moment that he—the most powerful man in any of the universes he had ever encountered—might just pass out like a young maiden.

PART THREE
IN THE LAND BELOW

CHAPTER 30

Mannahatta warriors of all ranks assembled in the large yard, called *Elgixin Field*, in the center of *Lëpweichik Èlikhatink Mannahatta*—the Mannahatta Technology and Research Campus.

Sakima emerged from *Wîkëwam Shawken Obroa*—the Manna-hatta Technology building—wearing a full headdress, a *psikali*. This had been her father's. She would ordinarily have worn the women's version of this piece, an *ansiptakàn*, but this occasion required a genuine leader's headdress. Sakina also wore a tradi-tional, but custom made, gown.

The gown was constructed from leather and suede which had been worked until it became as smooth as baby skin and as pale as cornmeal. Fine thread and bead work covered the front and back in many intricate designs repeating patterns of corn-silk blue, forest green, crimson red, purple, and white. The patterns were boxes within boxes, triangles like arrowheads, and strips and rows of color like river currents. Tassels of leather were held together with the finest, silkiest fiber that gave the illusion of turkey feathers of red, tan, and black. Across her middle, Sakima wore a *kèkwi këlamapisun,* a beautiful belt with colorful seashell bits integrated in patterns across the entire belt.

On her feet, Sakima wore her favorite shoes—the dressy ones she only wore once before, at the celebration in her honor years ago now. They seemed appropriate for today, this solemn yet celebratory occasion. Sakima tried her best, with the help of her sister Mimi, to look as elegant and royal as she could. She was the temporary queen, after all. But she felt most at home when she was ready to battle, to target her eyes and her arrows at foes and pretenders. Being dressed up was nice, and she enjoyed it, but she wasn't completely in her comfort zone like this.

Sakima wore dark eyeshadow, the color of earth, and dramatic eyeliner: a thick black line on each eyelid ending with a swoop. Her eyelashes were dark and thick, and a band of red paint ran across her eyes from ear to ear. A mark of class, but also the sign of the warrior—something she had insisted on for today. A dot of red was dabbed on her forehead and her neck. Jewelry of stones, gems, gold, silver, and seashell decorated her wrists, neck, and ankles. Sakima's full hair was tied in multiple braids. Some twirled onto the crown of her head, others falling free. The braids were intertwined with ribbons that matched the colorful pattern of her outfit.

The crowd of local onlookers and their warrior family members —over a thousand in total—milled about in the grand open space. At Sakima's entrance, soldiers fell into parallel lines of uniform length, their backs stiff, their chins out, and their eyes straight ahead. They were neither looking away nor looking at their new— albeit temporary—queen, but respectfully somewhere in the space between.

Onlookers who were not military personnel, cheered and clapped. The news of Sakima's role as the *kittakima pro tempore* had spread throughout the community as quickly as an emergency. The excitement in the air—which was crisp and the coldest it had been so far this early fall—was electric with people talking, clapping, dancing, and shouting. A red-tailed hawk circled above the crowd in the crystal blue sky.

Sakima raised her right hand, her fingers together in a tight fist formation. The crowd hushed, and the warriors stood a bit taller and a bit straighter.

"My friends, my people, my Mannahatta," Sakima started. "My warriors." She turned to face the warriors in the field more directly —all fifty-one of them. "We start today on a noble mission. Bless us *Kishelë*, hear our prayers and have pity on us! To the Land Below, to *Mënatink Ohëlëmi*, on this grand quest for revenge and right-eousness. We go there first and foremost to avenge our fallen soldiers, our loved ones who were our family, and second, to set the world right. Today, more of our loved ones leave on a mission to destroy our enemy, save the people of Manhattan, and return Mannahatta to glory! We thank you, oh great *Kishelë*, and we humbly ask for your protection!"

Some people in the crowd of onlookers at the outskirts of the field cheered, and someone hollered, "Go, Sakima!"

Sakima paid them no attention, but continued to address the troops. She allowed her eyes to skim across the faces in from of her. Most were unfamiliar, but many were from the same troop she had joined upon returning from her victory on The Land Below. The ones she trained with, improving her skills, getting stronger, better. Then she caught a pair of startling gray eyes in the crowd, three rows back and a bit to her right.

Lèke Gischileu.

He seemed to be at least a foot taller than the warriors nearest him. His black hair appeared darker, thicker, and longer than the warriors around him. And his smile was in a class of its own. Sweet and sexy and charming and seductive.

Could a smile be all that, Sakima wondered, *or am I making it so?*

She smiled back; how could she not? But she made it a subtle, repressed smile on her lips and left the biggest part of the smile in her eyes. Because she had a job to do and was determined to give the best speech of her life—as if her life depended on it. And in many, many ways, she knew it did.

"You are the best of all warriors—*ilaok-wulit!* As you go to this war—this mission with which you are all solemnly charged—do not let your fears or your nightmares affect your souls. Let your strong arms be your conscience—and your spears, your guns, your bows, and arrows your law. Be brave; march on through *Skontay Chìpilësu*, the portal, and on down to the Land Below. Hand and hand to victory or to walk on to the Land of the Dead! May *Kishelë* be with you, always!"

The crowd cheered, and some people started wildly dancing.

"And so," Sakima continued, raising her voice to be heard above the excitement. "What else can I possibly say that I haven't already hinted at or said outright here today?"

Sakima paused and scanned the warriors' faces again, searching for cowardice and bravery, boldness and caution. Again, she caught the steel-colored eyes of Lèke and found it hard to break away his stare.

When did he become so passionate, she wondered, *and why now? When there is no hope for either of us, let alone a new romance?*

Regardless, Sakima continued, as was her duty, but also as was above and beyond. "Might I remind you who you go off to do battle with: the scum of the universe, of *all* universes. Morally corrupt vagabonds and rascals whom the galaxies have vomited upon us and upon *Mënatink Ohëlëmi*. You were all asleep, safe in your beds when they brought unrest, poison, destruction, and death to Mannahatta. You with your lives ahead, your beautiful wives and your handsome husbands in your bed. Pulled out like rotting weeds and thrown onto the fire. But today and tomorrow and as long as it takes, we shall whip these devils, these evil entities from across the Many Worlds. For if it is to be our sad destiny to be conquered, then I say let *people* conquer us, not these bastardly cowards!" Her voice rose dramatically, although she didn't intend it to or plan for it, but nevertheless was swept away by her emotions of sadness and anger.

The crowd in the back cheered wildly, and a few of the warriors broke rank to fist pump or call out, or both while some leaped up in a midair tumble.

"Shall we let these heirs of shame sow and cultivate and harvest on our lands?" Sakima shouted, her voice hoarse now. "To lie with our women, ravish the daughters of Mannahatta? Fight, you men of Mannahatta, fight bold! Draw your arrows, run forth, amaze, and shock these *aèsës* with your spears, your knives, your guns! Draw blood as rivers and leave no enemy standing! Now go! And may *Kishelë* grant you the most glorious of victories!"

Sakima stepped dramatically aside to gesture at the great doors of the *Wîkëwam Shawken Obroa*.

"Go, fight, bring to these wretches the death they brought here to our Mannahatta. I ache as a warrior to go with you, to fight alongside you. But I grieve that as your queen, I must not put the throne in danger until the last possible moment, which has not yet come, and which I hope will never arrive, thanks to your bravery and your skills. Go forth now, and come back alive, healthy, and proud! We send you to battle now as warriors but will welcome you back soon as victors, heroes, and legends!"

A sergeant just to the left of Sakima gave the signal. The warriors jogged slowly in place. Then the first man in the first row closest to the great door moved toward it and through. He was then followed by all the men in his row, and then all the men in each of the rows behind.

When Lèke passed by, Sakima noticed her heart jump in her chest. *Who was this man to her? They had flirted more than once, but nothing beyond that. Not even time alone together, let alone what might have happened during such an encounter. But something about this seemed different somehow—real, maybe.* More real than anything she'd ever experienced before. Even, she had to admit, the feelings she'd once held for her first love at fourteen years old, Apatschin: her Pat.

How can this be? Such feelings for someone who is practically a stranger to me?

At that moment, the *Wematëgunis* squad appeared from out of the *Wîkëwam Shawken Obroa*. They marched across the field to give the queen their assessment of the dangers currently lurking in the Land Below.

"No trap," Tuney said, the top of his head covered in dust for no apparent reason.

"Could find nothing suspicious," Amoe said, his hands and arms muddy.

"The same," Topi said, weeds and dirt on his cape.

"Agreed!" Elikus shouted.

"Yep," Kikey said.

"Yep, yep," Bambil said.

"Yep, yep, yep!" Oleleu cried out, jumping in place.

Then they all stopped, stood still, and all gave Sakima a firm, serious salute. Sakima responded by pressing her hand against her heart. "Thank you, all," she said. "You are dismissed with honor."

With that, the *Wematëgunis* bolted to the edge of the forest, disappearing in seconds. Almost as if they'd never been on the field at all, never been involved in this military assessment process.

As Sakima studied the forest where they'd ran into, she turned and realized how surprisingly fast all of the troops had made it inside the building. As they disappeared within the dark halls of the great structure, Sakima's eyes welled with tears. She longed to go into battle with her compatriots, the warriors she'd trained with and come to know—and love.

She fought back tears while gazing around at the large and boisterous crowd, searching for her brother as the people moved closer and closer with each warrior's departure.

Another soldier, one of the military police, stepped in front of Sakima. "No civilians allowed inside." That was it. No explanation, no apologies. The man glanced over at Sakima and nodded in respect. She noticed right before he turned quickly away to face the crowd again that there had been tears in his eyes too.

Okay, let's get this over with.

At last she spied Nimàt in the crowd, trying to fight his weakened way toward her through the throngs. He occasionally pushed people gently but deliberately in an attempt to move them out of his way.

He approached her finally. "We should get going." He sighed, a bit tired from the effort to get to her.

"Let me change, and then we are off to the safe place."

Nimàt nodded to show that he'd heard and understood because she'd said what she said without opening her mouth, instead whispering through clenched teeth and nearly closed lips.

She indicated "five minutes" by holding her hand up at her waist, fingers spread. She closed her hand without looking at her brother. Then she turned and headed across to *Kèkayëmhès Wikwahëmink*—the government building—that was used for planning, strategy, and government meetings. But which also held the so-called "royal quarters" where she'd left her warrior's clothes and weapons.

Sakima couldn't wait to be on her way as quickly as possible because she now found herself suddenly crying hard. She kept her face turned from the crowd and tried not to suffer shame. She sprinted across *Elgixin Field* in perhaps the last of the Mannahatta sunshine she'd see in a long while, if not forever.

As she ran, a battalion of Kanyen warriors arrived at the opposite end of the field, having received a similar, but perhaps less eloquent, speech from their Sachem earlier that morning.

———

Meanwhile, Major Ron:kwe Onanta stood glancing up at the sky. He said a silent prayer as he took in a deep breath of the fresh, crisp air. *A good day to die, but not for Kanyens, not today.*

CHAPTER 31

Brother and sister, Nimàt and Sakima, dashed through the woods behind the Mannahatta technology campus with a single purpose: to get Sakima to a safe place where she could be hidden and protected. They were heading for the *Òhchu* Peak, hoping to find a way into the spaceship, *Nagatamen Mùxul Allanque*—or simply *NaMùxAll*. No one, over the centuries since it crashed on Mannahatta, had figured out how to get inside this craft. Despite all the knowledge gained from the *Alànëmëskat*, the Star Walkers, that information was not transferred or discovered. Despite this and the odds of making their way into the spaceship, the two were determined to give it their best shot. Because in that ship was their only chance for Sakima to survive all that was happening now to Mannahatta and the Land Below.

"I want you to know that I still don't feel great about this, Nimàt. I feel like a coward." Sakima moved swiftly through the forest, leaping easily over undergrowth and around obstacles, including stumps and large rocks. She was a wild deer moving in her natural element, with nearly unsurpassed energy and agility.

"But you're not, though. Trust me, trust your own instincts,"

Nimàt said, panting and trying his best to keep up with his warrior sister. "You, of all people, need to stay alive. I don't care if we are down to two dozen survivors; they'll need their queen to shepherd them into the next phase of our civilization. Whatever that turns out to be."

"I know what you say is the right thing to do; it is just hard. It is difficult for me to face this necessity. I mean, it goes against my natural inclinations."

"Look," Nimàt said, gasping for breath. His sister was a toned warrior with amazing strength and endurance and was running at a considerable clip. He was none of those things. If fact, he'd been barely able to keep up for the first mile, and now he was fading fast, his tank nearly empty. "Look, we can discuss... all your feelings..." Nimàt took another desperate breath like a man trapped in a cage without oxygen. "When we get... to the... ship."

"This plan of yours is only partially brilliant, my brother. If I am to stay hidden and undiscovered, no one should come close to where I am hiding, correct? Yet—" Sakima continued, as if she were relaxing on her couch at home instead of running through the forest at a near sprint. "—we both get that the ship is a teen hangout and always has been, with each new generation. Practically everyone hangs out there after high school anymore. Like, you know, doing drugs, hooking up—"

"Not today. The attack... the deaths... the warriors being sent... through the portal has... refocused everyone." Nimàt sucked in all the air he could. He grabbed at a side stitch that he had tried to ignore but which now insisted on being noticed. "Maybe they'll start... again tomorrow or the next day, but..." Nimàt took in yet another deep breath. "But for today, I'm 99.89 percent certain that no one will be there—"

"Well, I hope you are 100 percent right."

"Sakima?"

"What?"

"Can we slow down?"

"What?"

"Can we, you know... reduce the pace a bit?"

"I already have reduced for you considerably. About six times now. Any slower and we will be strolling."

"Yeah, but you have an advantage over the person with the bullet holes."

Sakima smiled and then downshifted to a brisk walk for her brother's sake. "Sorry, Nimàt! I totally forgot for a minute. In my mind, I was racing along with my healthy, unhurt brother. Is this better?" she said, slowing down even more.

"Almost perfect."

"What would be perfect, then?"

"Sitting down—no, lying down—and just not moving at all, for like an hour. Except to eat. Like pan bread with maple sugar on top."

Sakima laughed and shook her head. "You are ridiculous."

"Right, I get it. Hey!" Nimàt said, catching up to his sister and walking alongside her as she slowed down even more.

"What is it?" Sakima said.

"Just noticed something."

"What now, Nimmy?"

"You never took off your makeup after the ceremony."

"No time."

"Looks good, though, sis."

"Thanks."

"Looks like you're ready for battle. Lots of red. I like it."

"That was the intent. Tough but glamorous." She laughed. "Or something like that."

"Yeah. I mean, I get you. It's like perhaps you're gonna be in a dance battle!"

Sakima snorted at her brother's nonsense; she couldn't help herself. "You idiot. What are you, jealous?"

"A little, yeah. Of your makeup. And also of your shoes. Which I see you wisely left behind."

"Couldn't imagine running in them. I mean, I *can* run in them. But we needed to move fast and far. Thus, my moccasin boots." She gestured down at them gracefully. "Made for speed."

Nimàt nodded as he glanced at her boots. Then he looked back at her, nodding for a different reason. "You left your necklaces in place, too. Cool."

"I did?" Sakima reached up and felt the metal and stone around her neck. "*Këlulël!* Didn't mean to do that."

"Well, you're all dressed up, that's for sure. And nowhere to go. Seriously, we're getting you safely hidden, and then you're not going anywhere."

"Whatever, Nimàt. Again, I am still not completely on board with this idea."

"Not your decision to make. For once."

"What's that supposed to mean?"

"You're a bit of a control freak; I mean, you gotta admit that."

"Not really."

"Totally."

"Maybe."

"And you hate anyone making decisions for you. No one can tell you what to do, as you often point out."

"Well, they cannot. Never will."

"I made this decision for you."

"No, you did not, not really."

"Did too."

"No, you raised it as a possibility and—after some queenly contemplation—I approved your decision."

"Same thing."

"Not, Nimmy! *I* decided to do this. And if you keep yammering, I might just change my mind."

Nimàt went silent.

"I suppose you could," he said. "Your prerogative."

"Darn right it is."

She stopped in her tracks then, staring up ahead. "My, we made great time."

Nimàt stopped next to her, looking ahead as well.

They were at the top of *Òhchu* Peak in record time. The sun shone brightly on them as they emerged from the forest's canopy. But there was new shade ahead, cast by a large, circular, metal object the size of a gigantic building, which was embedded there in the rocks and dirt. The half-buried ship was surrounded by vines, and parts were covered in dense moss.

The *Nagatamen Mùxul Allanque* spacecraft. Inscrutable, impenetrable. As it had always been.

Until today. Or so the two siblings hoped.

"Let's get to work figuring this thing out," Sakima said in a hushed tone. "Before it gets dark and people start showing up. Even though you say they will not, Nimmy."

But neither of them moved. Instead, they both stood there, held in wonder at the humongous spacecraft and in considerable awe of the quixotic task in front of them: to do what had never been done before.

Yellow and orange and brown elm, maple, and oak leaves fluttered slowly and almost silently to the ground around them. The air was clear, filled with the late afternoon songs of bluebirds and cardinals, and it smelled of cold earth and the approaching fall and winter seasons.

"You first," Nimàt said, with a sly grin on his face. "My queen."

CHAPTER 32

"You seem, seem confused, my new, my friend. New friend." Mhuwe wiped his filthy, tree-like arm across his mouth in a weak attempt to remove some of the blood that coated them. "Did you think you, you were in charge, charge? That you have the power, the power here? What do you think, do you think, what is the right answer, answer to that? I'll wait."

Mhuwe broke an arm off another dead Taturåkee soldier's body and removed the armor surrounding it like cracking a crab claw. The monster extracted the meat of the man's arm in a similar way, sucking it out of the remaining metal enclosure.

"Yum," it said. "Very young. Delicate flavor. Almost no, almost no gristle. Tell me, can you get me a bowl—a large tureen would be, be ideal—of melted butter?" The creature's growling voice hid most the words it was speaking, making it hard but not impossible to understand. "I'd like to keep snack, keep snacking, while we chat."

Locus Mub froze, unable to speak. The calm exterior he'd intended to maintain had quickly crumbled. His face was crimson and his eyes bulged in their sockets. He managed to holler a directive through gritted teeth while waving at the remaining soldiers in the room to attack.

"Kill. This. *Abomination!*"

Which they tried to do, and which had absolutely no effect on the monster. Bullets bounced off the creature like they were made of soft foam. Laser shots got absorbed by the beast like a flashlight's beam through a window. Even Mp weapons, the strongest in the known multiverse, only cut the beast like pinpricks, producing ineffective wounds on the thing's body. The wounds healed themselves almost as fast as the soldiers inflicted them. But their attack somehow killed all the beasts from hell, the *manëtu*, all of which laid on the ground with various levels of destruction to their bodies.

When the onslaught by the guards and military supporting Mub finally abated, the creature hurled itself through the air like a crazed, twelve-foot tall monkey. It leaped from soldier to soldier, pulling heads from torsos, arms from shoulders, one after another, over and over again, a weird grimace rippling across the monster's face as if it were enjoying every moment.

"Enough!" Locus Mub screamed. "I command you to stop this. *At once!*"

Mhuwe, the monstrous and despicable thing, stopped tearing people apart and stood with its back to Mub, its shoulders slumped —almost as if it were embarrassed at being caught being so naughty.

"So," Mhuwe said in low, guttural tones and without turning around. "You are ready, ready to, to talk, yes?"

"Yes! Just quit your—whatever you call that. Quit it and sit, please."

This time, Mub pointed to a throne-like chair at his right. It was nearly as big as Mub's, but not quite. Anyone's first guess upon seeing it there would assume it belonged to Mub's queen, but no such queen seemed to exist.

"I'd be happy to. But first, let me clean, let me clean up real quick. Quick." With that, Mhuwe somehow set itself on fire, burning away the blood and excrement and skin and gore from his tree-like body. The fire flashed on for a few seconds and suddenly shut off. Mhuwe was now clean of the detritus of war, but its body was left unscathed, unburned—the fire had not affected the creature. It strode purposefully and slowly toward the other throne-like seat where it positioned itself after some awkward and aborted attempts.

Locus Mub stared in terrified disbelief at all he had just witnessed. He wasn't a man who was familiar with the feelings of terror and fright, and they hit him like a punch to the soul. He swallowed hard as he watched the beast seat itself near him, way too near.

"*Aaaah...* that's more, more like it," Mhuwe snorted. "Fits a big man better, better. Not as good, not as good as yours would, but, but good enough."

"I'd be happy to switch. Temporarily, of course."

"Not necessary, my new, my new friend. Not necessary. Now, where, where were we?"

"Negotiating, I think. If you can call it that," Mub mumbled.

"Yes, right. Negotiating. So, here's what I'm, what I'm thinking." Mhuwe cleared its throat while it used its pinky talon to pick at a chunk of Taturåkee flesh caught between a couple of his back teeth. "We attack, attack together, Mannahatta." It made slurping noises as the thing continued to fish out the stuck pieces of Taturåkee meat. "I finish my business, my business there, and take its queen—Sakima, isn't it? I take Sakima, to be my personal, my personal plaything. For, for eternity." The monster burped, a sound more like a small explosion than anything natural. "Once we've fully, fully decimated—how do like, like, my word choice by the way? 'Decimated.' I like it so much, so much better, better than 'destroyed.' Yes, so," Mhuwe continued, stroking the mossy growth on its chin with newfound enjoyment. "I am smart. Did you know, did you know that? Smartest being in the world, the world, quite possibly. Yes, I'd say so. Say so. Anyway, where was, where was I?"

"Your plan of attack?" Locus Mub said, looking straight ahead, afraid to turn and gaze upon the beast from hell.

"Right, right. When Mannahatta is a smoking, fiery hellhole, hellhole, and all Mannahatta, all of any age, age or sex lies rotting, rotting on the ground—or burning, burning, burning." The nightmare almost sounded like a bear chuckling while munching on a dead body. "They can certainly, certainly be lying there burning. I'm fine with that; either way, either way. Both scenarios work for me. Once this is done, we can head back to the Land Below again. By which I mean, I mean, of course, back here. Since I, since I assume you are gleefully ignorant of many things, many things. Including all things Mannahatta. And then we take this shit city and all the cities, one by one. All cities and all countries of this pathetic, this pathetic backwater planet. Now, how's that, King, KingMub, how's that sound?" Mhuwe picked at a different bit of something between its teeth at the front of his mouth, making an offensive sucking noise as it did so.

"You know, my hideous friend, I could easily blow you up. I could do that," Locus Mub stated in a near monotone. "I'd be willing to sacrifice this ship and all the people in it just to teach you a lesson. But I won't. And you know why?"

"I don't care, don't care. No."

"Because you disgust me, and I'd rather be doing a deal with Satan himself, rather than his freaking proxy."

"Be that as it may, I'm here now. Here right now, and you, you old windbag, aren't blowing this ship up, ship up. Me in it or not in it, or not."

"No? Well I…"

"Shut up! Stop wasting my time, my time. I'll rip your throat out before you even tried. And about the evil one—we call him *Matanto*, for your, your information—if you'd like to meet him, to meet, I can arrange that, arrange it. Arrange all."

Locus Mub stared at this creature and shook his head. He didn't know how to deal with such a horror. Couldn't deal that there was one such as this, so vile and hideous. And more arrogant and vain than even Mub himself. No, that he couldn't take. Not at all. Not in the slightest. Mub himself was the big man, the one and only Emperor Locus Mub. And having this strange competition was an alien concept to him. Mub was used to crushing and destroying entire nations and civilizations the way most people are used to getting up in the morning and brushing their teeth.

But having a nemesis like this *thing*, when Mub himself was the quintessential enemy of all in his path, was, well... odd. A nemesis with a nemesis. Although, the way he liked to think of himself was as Locus Mub, the authentic hero. Doing what he did for the greater good of his people and to honor his beloved queen.

"What's going on here?" said a commanding yet feminine voice from the back of the room.

"Speak of the devil," Mub said, mostly to himself.

"Where?" Mhuwe said in a mocking tone. The beast peered about the big room with exaggerated surprise. It snorted out what must have been the monster's equivalent of a laugh. "Her? You have obviously never met, met the devil, never, my pathetic friend, pathetic... You would not mistake, mistake, anyone or anything else in the multiverse for *Matanto, Matanto*!" Mhuwe victoriously spat the bit of flesh it had been picking at onto the floor, where it landed with a loud and sickening splat.

A woman with sharp features, tight lips, and large green eyes stood at the doorway where Mub had previously entered. She tightly shouted her next sentence. "My Lord Mub, who—or rather *what*—is this frightful wretch doing on *my* throne in *my* throne room *on my ship*?"

Both Mub and the beast stared at the woman with her straw-colored hair piled high on her head where, at the apex of the hairdo, there squatted a gold and bejeweled crown. About half the size and weight of the one currently atop Locus Mub's enormous head. Huge pearls in the shape of raindrops hung on gold threads from the woman's crown. They cascaded down the side of her face where they neatly met the pearl earrings in her ears.

She squinted her eyes and sneered at the two of them before pronouncing, "Get this wretched beast off *of my most holy ship!*"

"My dearest," Mub said, addressing the woman with surprising deference. "This is..." Mub paused. "You know, I don't believe I know your name."

A wretched smirk slithered across Mhuwe's face.

"I am Mhuwe, servant for eternity of the great, the great and all-knowing ultimate, ultimate devil himself, *Matanto!*" The creature raised its head high and beat his fists against its chest like a gorilla.

"Do we call you that? 'The Devil's Servant'?" the woman said, unimpressed. "*Mah Hoo Way?* Is that it? Or is it pronounced 'Whoo-hoo?'"

"Where are, are my manners?" Mhuwe uttered gravely as it extracted itself with much effort from the velvet, steel, and leather throne that was half the right size for the beast. It loped over to the woman, its hand extended. When she accepted its grizzly, boney hand, Mhuwe curtsied in an awkward and contemptuous way. "M'lady, lady. My..." it grunted.

"This is my wife, Mister Mhuwe, or mister or whatever you want to be called," Mub stated with his jaw clenched, ignoring the monster's attempt at disrespectful posturing. "She is queen here—Queen Leia Blas. And, until our recent bonding by matrimony, also my benefactor and financial supporter. She is from a royal family and quite a wealthy woman when I met her. Now we *both* are. Forever!"

"I am, I am charmed," Mhuwe said, staying frozen in its mocking curtsy pose, its head bowed.

"Get up, you disgusting beast! And quit your mocking. You are not so clever as you'd like to believe." Queen Leia Blas turned to her husband. "Get this mess scrubbed. Get these bodies to the incinerator. This is my home away from home, and you and this shitty creature have made it a disgrace!"

"Yes, mum," Mub muttered, properly chastised and a little hurt by his wife's reprimand. He pressed a push switch on the arm of his throne, and in less than a minute the room swarmed with medics, morticians, and workers with large buckets and mops. In less than twenty minutes, the throne room sparkled once again, wiped clean of cadavers, blood and guts, human heads, and other parts—chewed or not.

"That's better," Queen Leia Blas pronounced when it was all over. She clapped her hands sharply for one beat and proceeded to her now spotless throne beside Locus Mub.

"Let's start again, shall we, Mr. Woo Way? What is your business here with us today?" She leaned on her gold staff, which had pearls along the top just like her crown. She held it between her open legs, the long skirt of her outfit stretching tightly around it, and waited for a plausible explanation with one eyebrow cocked.

"Funny enough, mum, business has, it has concluded. We have an agreement where I, Mr. Hoo Hay, as you call me, assist you. And where, and where and you and Mub assist me. Quid pro fuckin' quo."

She sat silently for a long moment. Then her one eyebrow dropped back down, and she said, slowly and with much suspicion, "What kind of agreement?"

"War, my love. Military stuff. Your favorite," Mub said.

"The best kind of agreement! And an extermination? I assume there will be extermination of an entire race somewhere in this plan, yes?"

"We have yet to finalize that discussion, but yes, likely—"

"That's the only way it could, it could possibly be, Queen," Mhuwe said, interrupting Mub. "No survivors—and that applies to the flora, to all the flora and fauna of native lands, both here and in Mannahatta. Everything, everything wiped, wiped out."

"Mannahatta—is that the dreadful place we attacked recently, dear?" Queen Blas asked stared at husband, flattering him with flutter eyes and kissy lips. "Or was it before that, perhaps? I find it hard to keep all of our invasions and timelines straight in my head."

"Yes it was, dearest; it most certainly was. Our friend here has suggested that if we give it the old college try one more time, we shall, with his help, achieve complete victory."

"Good," the queen said, smiling in a way that made her look less cunning and a bit hungry as she licked her lips. "In that case, I approve."

"Good, my love. I'm glad you're with us on this."

"Yes, good," Mhuwe snorted. "Good for all of us, all of us. Except those not in any of your three, three little ships. For them, the people of Mannahatta, the world—the world is about to end."

"Good, I say again," Queen Leia Blas squealed. "Very good indeed!" And with that, she tapped the tip of her scepter against the marble floor repeatedly, and with considerable glee.

CHAPTER 33

The two siblings stood in the shadow of the legendary space craft as it blocked the sun. The scent of pine wafted through the cooling air.

"Now what?" Sakima said, gently flicking away a small beetle off her brother's neck.

"What?" Nimàt said, watching the beetle flutter away and wondering where it was headed and if it had a family.

"Now that we're here, how do we get in? Hello?"

Nimàt blinked and turned back to face his sister. "First of all, sis," he said, taking one final curious look at the bug as it disappeared into the woods. "You should appreciate that we are the only ones here. Remember how convinced you were that this place would be crawling with teenagers?"

"So?"

"Well, it ain't."

"Not yet; school has not let out."

"We can worry about that if and when it happens. For now, let's snack!"

With that, Nimàt pulled out some food that he'd stolen away

into his rucksack from the ceremony. Fry bread, roasted corn, venison chunks in gravy, succotash, fried potato strips, and sweet cake.

"Where did you get—"

"The buffet tables at your big-deal speech to straighten the spines of your fellow 'warriohs,' that's where."

"Stop saying 'warriohs' in that creepy way of yours, you free food thief."

"I prefer 'opportunist.'"

Nimàt munched on a piece of fry bread, extended it as an offering to Sakima, shrugged when she turned him down, and took another bite.

Sakima glanced up at the towering—though half-buried—monolith. It was steely black, and despite having originally been crawling with nano-life, the surface of the ship appeared about as ordinary—and as old—as it could be. In fact, it looked more like an ancient monument than anything that once was metal, openable, or flyable.

"Even if we could get in, what am I supposed to do? Hang out in total darkness and eat bugs?"

"Maybe. Maybe not. But you'll be alive, that I can guarantee. Well, almost guarantee. 90 percent."

Sakima rolled her eyes and continued scrutinizing the exterior of the craft. She bent on to one knee and took the rucksack off her back. She ruffled about for a minute until she emerged with a mysterious black box in her hand.

"What's that?" Nimàt said. "An all-black Rubik's Cube?"

"Ha, ha," she said in a mocking tone with her face like stone. Giving no indication whatsoever that she found him funny. "Funny."

She twisted a small lever and the interesting, black box that she'd taken from the parlor of *Alànëmëskat* materials in the *Wîkëwam Shawken Obroa* made a slight hum. Then she pressed a button. There was a loud click. The hum increased, and a blue light fanned across the ship and circled it slowly as Sakima held the device up in her open hand.

After less than a minute, the light shut off. The cube made some noises like an old-time computer crunching numbers: a lot of beeps and squeaks and clunks. A small piece of paper, like a cash register tape, chugged its way out of the top of the cube. With a shudder and a clank, the cube returned to silence.

"Quite the modern contraption you have there, sis."

"Shut up, Nimmy. It is old, but that does not mean the thing ain't any good."

"Okay, so what does it say?"

"Nothing."

Nimàt stared at his sister as she studied the boxy thing on her palm.

"What do you mean, nothing? What's the little paper say?"

"It is empty. Blank. Thus my reporting to you, 'nothing.'"

"Yep. Old but good, I agree."

"Back off, will you? Look, no one has found a way into this thing, and probably thousands of minds better than ours have tried, generation after generation."

"Maybe."

"Not maybe, they have. Same result. Because it's nothing filled with nothing, like a melted structure burned closed forever."

With little care, she shoved the device back into her rucksack and let herself fall back against the ship's exterior wall, landing sadly on a patch of moss. Nimàt joined her, sliding down as dramatically as he could onto a napkin he'd placed down before beginning his slide.

"We're doomed," he said, dropping his chin into his upturned hands while turning down his mouth into a frown.

"Not doomed, Nimmy. Thwarted is all, and temporarily at that. Where should we try next?"

"Remember that hideout that we used to play in when we were kids, Sakima?"

"Not a good hideout. Mom found us every single time."

"I mean, wouldn't it be great if we had a place like that? I mean bigger and more hidden, obviously."

"We did. The cave I found. But Dad filled the openings in with big rocks. He said he transplanted the *mwekane* and the pups to a safe place—although he never said where." Her shoulders slumped, and she lowered her head, suddenly feeling overwhelmed. She picked up a few pebbles and threw them half-heartedly down the hill. "This is ridiculous. What am I doing? I should go back, I—" She stopped. "_um… did you hear that?"

"Hear what?"

"That, uh, scratching sound?"

"I don't hear no scratching—"

"*Sssh!*" Sakima turned around and got on her knees. She pressed her ear against the side of the alien ship. "It's coming from inside the craft!" she yelled.

She jumped up excitedly.

"No way!" Nimàt said, getting slowly to his feet.

"Yes way! *You* listen. Go ahead; come on!"

Nimàt did as he was told. He listened for a bit, then looked back at his sister with an apologetic expression, his eyebrows raised high. He shrugged and was about to say something when he practically leaped from the wall and took a few fast steps backward. "Hot *maluwe*, hot damn!" He stopped in his tracks and stood frozen, staring at the side of the spaceship, his eyes growing huge.

Sakima leaned against the exterior wall and listened again. "Yep, scratching. Someone—or something—is inside." She extracted her knife and continued listening. "Sounds like…" She paused. "Wait a minute. I think I heard something. I, I—well, whatever is inside, I think they are crying?"

Now it was her turn to step away from the craft. When she was standing side by side with Nimàt, she looked at him, and her brother looked back at her. They locked eyes for a bit as if two stares would reveal the mystery. Finally, Sakima turned back to the ship.

"Who's there?" she said in her best commanding voice. "I demand that you state your name! I am the queen *pro tem* of the Mannahatta people, and I tell you that you must come out now, or risk the consequences!"

The scratching and the whining or crying or whatever it was stopped abruptly, leaving nothing but the whispering winds. The two siblings waited, wondering what might happen next.

"Enough of this," Sakima said, a look of disgust on her face. "There has to be a way in. I mean, whoever that is has gotten in, right? So, let's go." She waved for Nimàt to follow her and the two walked around the perimeter of the ship again, but with guarded steps.

As they came around the front of the ship and back down the other side, Nimàt pointed.

"What's that?"

"What's what?"

"*That!*" he said, shoving his finger through the air at a small pile of brush. "That is not natural, that pile of branches and stuff. It's definitely manmade. Didn't fall like that; it's been stacked."

Sakima held her finger to her lips and made a motion for him to stop talking. "Homeless vagrant. Or perhaps a drug addict," she whispered, nodding. She kept her knife firmly in her hand, her arm pressed against her side so the weapon could not be dislodged from her.

She reached down and whipped the top branches away, revealing just more and more branches.

She looked over at Nimàt, who held his palms up, a puzzled expression on his face, eyebrows high, mouth twisted. Sakima grabbed another stack of branches and bushes and threw them aside. Still more branches remained.

"Come, give me a hand," she whispered. "Or I will be here all night whittling away at this pile of *mwichti*, shit."

Nimàt ambled over as Sakima sheathed her blade for the time being. Together they pulled layer after layer of branch until at last they revealed a boulder wedged into what looked like a small opening in the ground.

"It's a burrow!" Nimàt said. "An animal's shelter."

"I know what a burrow is, you *tèpahtu* dumb ass. Wait, there it is again!" This time, they both could clearly hear the sound of whimpering. "It was not someone crying," she said. "It is an animal! Maybe it has been hurt!"

"So the animal we first heard wasn't actually *in* the ship," Nimàt said. "But *under* it."

"I think I see what happened," Sakima said. "This boulder got dislodged somehow, crashed through the branches and landed here, trapping the poor creature in its little home. The branches must have dislodged when the boulder arrived and fell on top of it, hiding the rock and this place completely."

"Well, we found it. So what do we do now?"

"Help me get this boulder out of the way. I want to see if the creature is hurting. If there are babies."

"What if it's a *kwèn'shùkwënay* or a *mechquikan*? We'll be dead in seconds!"

"Unlikely. None of those creatures are known to burrow. Mountain lions live in the trees, and bears live in caves—even mechBears. And this is neither, I am sure of it."

"Better safe than mauled to death, I always say."

Sakima smiled at him with both love and weariness. "Just help me, you idiot. Would you, please?" she said.

CHAPTER 34

nside the invaders' ships on the island of Manhattan, hidden in an abandoned train tunnel, soldiers of all ranks and backgrounds were busy preparing for their next attack on Mannahatta. There was a smell inside the ships where they worked of motor oil and cleaning fluid and had that antiseptic smell of overly-cleaned air.

The attack on Mannahatta, along with the concurrent planned massacre of all Mannahatta people, would be followed by the total destruction of this island city of Manhattan as well. But these were only steps 1 and 2 of their violent plans. The remaining steps covered the devastation and subjugation of the entire planet known as Earth, within this universe and the current given timeline.

"Listen up, soldiers of Taturåkis! This is our finest moment," Locus Mub stood and gestured dramatically as he addressed his men. "Although we won't be capturing and killing any of our actual sworn enemies of *Eldëror*, we will destroy their pet civilization on Mannahatta."

The soldiers surrounding him let out a loud and aggressive cheer. Locus Mub went on, energized by the crowd.

"The elimination of every last person on Mannahatta will be complete, thorough, bloody—and glorious!"

More whoops and shouts, even louder now, filled the large space on *Ästra Ån Ima.*

"Our great, noble armies were only stopped by some unexpected technology worn, apparently, by this—this *thing*! This 'warrior woman'—if you can believe that there is even such a horror in existence! She got lucky with her little robo-suit and her pathetic attempt at bravery and selflessness." Mub stopped to spit on the floor in contempt as more hoots and hollers rang out.

"But my fellow Taturåkee, we are prepared now for her second attempt at defeating *our* second attempt. She will fail! Amass your weapons, load all our bays with them until they are fit to burst! Get ready to kill anything and everything you see! This will be our most glorious hour—the slaughter of one civilization and the subjugation of another!"

A roar went up from the crowd of Taturåkee soldiers and mercenaries. Most wore the full white protective uniform with the red cross on the chest plate. Others wore bits and pieces which, where their skin was exposed, nearly matched the strange alabaster hue of their own skin.

The Taturåkee were a pale people and wore their translucence proudly. It was a sign that no Taturåkee had ever commingled with the people of the conquered planets. Their skin tone was the palest white, and all of the Taturåkee people believed that it was as intended by their true and only God.

They were convinced that no pollution of any other color or genetics could be—or would ever be—found in Taturåkis history, or in their future, as if that was somehow a good thing. In fact, a Taturåkee would rather die than procreate with an alien from another planet and race. Although many took alien women whenever they wanted, to satisfy themselves as much as to humiliate their victims.

The Taturåkee fighters chanted and danced like demons, spinning in circles, mock-attacking each other, and yet some purposely making contact and injuring their compatriots, all with much loud laughter.

"We are Taturåkee! We destroy all that we find!"

"For our God, Ziåd, makes it so, leading us to find the weak and has made us understand how to destroy all our inferior enemies!" Locus Mub shouted at the top of his lungs.

The crowd responded enthusiastically. "Destroy! *Destroy!*"

Mub raised his hands to hush the mob. After a minute, the crowd calmed down just enough to listen, although quite a few continued to talk and push at each other with eagerness.

"We are not alone in this pursuit. Our most Holy Ziåd has sent us a helper—a savior, if you will—who will make sure that we are victorious! I give you, my new friend and fellow destroyer, Mhuwe!"

The crowd immediately went completely quiet. All dancing and celebration stopped cold. The silence was deafening as the men looked back and forth at each other in puzzlement.

Then the grotesque Mhuwe creature stepped out from the shadows where it had been waiting.

And that's when the boos began.

"Murderer of the Taturåkee!"

"Monster from Mannahatta!"

"Devil!"

Locus Mub smiled, having expected a bit of "push back" from his people. Again, he lifted both hands high to quiet the unrest so that he could address them all. But before Mub could get a word out, Mhuwe raised its voice above the booing and the shouting.

"I know, I know I'm not the partner you desire, desire for war," it growled loudly out to the crowd as they all jostled for a better view of the monster. Or perhaps for a better vantage point from which to kill it. Mhuwe was okay with it either way. "I know you'd rather, rather another albino, albino martyr like your secondary god, god of yours, King Mub, Mub. He who gave you gave you permission to freely take others' lives, lives," it went on. The beast waited for the new wave of fury to subside. "But there can be only, only one of him, just as there is, there is only one of me. The one, true *Mhuwe*. Executioner, executioner of men. Annihilator of all, all worlds."

The crowd began enjoying Mhuwe's rhetoric, and the booing and angry chants morphed through confused grunting into cheers and hurrahs of acclamation and encouragement. The soldiers shook their weapons high, and then many started dancing again.

"Good," Mhuwe said, a greasy smile creeping across its hideous face. "You're with me, with me then. You serve two gods, *two* gods now."

But the crowd was in too much an uproar to hear Mhuwe's closing remark. Instead, they were content to push and shove each other in a primitive imitation of dancing. Flailing their arms around, pounding into each other's stomachs, punching randomly at different parts of others' bodies, and spitting into the air.

Then things got weird.

There was a shaking sensation, like they were all standing atop a giant gelatin mold.

"What is this?" Locus Mub said to Mhuwe, shouting above the noise of the crowd. He assumed it was Mhuwe's doing—and for once, and for most likely the last time in this bizarre relationship, it wasn't.

"I do not know, not know," Mhuwe screeched angrily, stretching its arms out in front of it to watch the hair and moss repeatedly stand up and sit down. It felt a chill go up its spine, and for just a second, it felt almost dizzy.

"What is this feeling I'm feeling?" Locus Mub continued. "It feels the same as when I am about to vomit, but I don't need to vomit, I don't think. But it's that same queasy, dizzying sensation."

"Me, too!" a woman's voice called out loudly behind him.

Locus Mub turned to see his queen entering the great room. "Came to see what all the hubbub was about, but now I'm feeling goosebumps in all the wrong places, mostly. But some in the right places, too." She looked at Mub in a way that could be interpreted as either flirty or completely nuts, and winked.

Then Locus Mub turned to watch his men, who had stopped their odd shoving dance and were now acting skittish, like nervous mice in a trap. Most of them had flipped their guns into the firing position, wedged between their arms and their shoulders. They aimed their blasters at the ceiling high above the room, changing where they were aiming, over and over again. Like they thought something was about to happen, but they didn't know from which direction it would come. So they covered all directions.

Then the ceiling—painted dusty black to hide the pipes and conduits that ran across it, overlapping many times, being ten layers deep of the various electronic and air conditioning and heating pipes and vents—began to ripple and weave. As if the entire mass of it all was about to explode apart.

The soldiers were unprepared for such an event and began running around unhinged and acting like crazy monkeys. They deliberately ignored direct orders from their superiors to fall into ranks and prepare for battle. Although, if they were to be completely honest, these men of superior rank seemed to have no idea what was happening or what was about to happen, either.

The men continued to run amok, aiming their weapons at the weird undulating ceiling, when they all noticed round blobs on the surface or beneath it—they couldn't tell. All they knew was that these blobs appeared to be getting bigger and bigger—and closer and closer—by the second.

Finally, the blobby things started to come into focus. Mub's men —and Mub himself, along with Mhuwe—were then staring at the bottom of military boots, as clear as day, just hovering there in the wriggling ceiling above them.

Then, in a flash, the boots crashed through the wavering blackness, and along with the Mannahatta soldiers who wore them, arrived on the ground. As they landed, the warriors toppled or crushed those Taturåkee soldiers unfortunate enough to be in the line of their trajectory.

Immediately, the Mannahatta military squads opened fire, spraying the room with Mp-based rays. Doing this obliterated anyone and everyone the Mp made contact with and sliced through walls and weapon cases and anything else made of nonliving material the rays happened to encounter.

The only other sound—other than the electronic buzz of the weapons and the shrieking of the wounded and the dying—were the screams of fear and outrage from the royal highness of Taturåkees, Queen Leia Blas.

CHAPTER 35

With the boulder removed and the rest of the branches taken away, Sakima got down on her belly to survey the scene.

"Definitely an animal burrow," she announced, taking a flashlight from out of her rucksack and aiming the beam at the opening, which was about three feet in diameter. "Looks like it goes in there pretty deep. Hey, this is interesting—"

"What's that?"

"It looks like it gets a lot bigger, right after the opening here, kind of cavernous, actually."

"Why can't you just say 'cave?'"

"Because it's not a cave. A cave is a natural formation. This has been dug by an animal. It's huge, unexpectedly so. Cavernous, I would call it. Which is why I did so."

"Fine, fine. Whatever." Nimàt shook his head and briefly shut his eyes. "Well, then, what's your assessment? Can we fit in there, or should we try to cajole the animal out?"

"If it is hurt or if it's protecting babies, it will not come out, no matter how much 'cajoling' we do. Talk about odd word choices, bro—"

"Coax, inveigle, sweet talk. Take your pick."

"We're going in," Sakima said. "That's all there is to it. You go first."

"Wait, what? Me? Why?"

"Dude, you're smaller than me, and that's a small opening. You need to go through that opening and kick-scrape to make the hole bigger as you go. That way we can be pretty sure I'll fit too. It doesn't work the other way around."

Nimàt smirked his disapproval of the plan, but then, in classic Nimàt style, he shrugged his shoulders, got down on his stomach next to Sakima, and began slithering down the slope toward the opening.

"Take this." Sakima held out her flashlight to him. "So you can see whatever it is that's about to rip you to shreds."

"Ha, ha. But that's not funny. I already told you there could easily be a killer critter down here."

"I was only kidding, jeez. Get going."

"I'm going, I'm going. Just let me look around first a bit."

Nimàt jammed his flashlight-holding hand into the rough entryway and then inserted his head with great care. His eyes darted everywhere while he shone the light in all possible directions, at each and every shadow and crevice.

"Coast seems clear," he said. "But I swear, sis, if I get attacked, I am coming back to haunt you!"

"Just get through. Once you are in, I will get in and I will take the lead," Sakima said. "Like always," she added in a whisper.

"What was that?"

"Nothing. Just please go on through before I die of old age." She rolled her eyes briefly.

Nimàt began making his way in a bit, then bumped his head on the top of the hole and knocked a clump of earth onto his head.

"Maluwe!" He spit dirt from his mouth and wiped at his eyes with his free hand. "Should've known. I should have known."

"Well, at least you made the opening bigger for me. Thanks, little brother."

"Drop dead, girl," Nimàt said, scrambling through the now partially collapsed opening, pulling his legs through as gingerly and carefully as he could. He crawled on his hands and knees further into the underground place, and then he was in the middle of it.

The center was indeed cavernous. About twelve feet across and nearly seven feet tall at the tallest point. Nimàt had no trouble standing at his full height.

Using the flashlight beam, he examined the "room." The beam fell on Sakima, who was now squeezing her way in too, but she was doing it feet first—making Nimàt wonder why he hadn't thought of that. Most of the walls had that scratched up, dug by hand—or more likely, by paw—look. The walls appeared to be sturdy, with stones and rocks of various sizes embedded here and there by nature. Roots from bushes also had managed to find their way into the space, mostly through the "ceiling" part of the cave. And this Nimàt thought was odd, considering the only thing above them was the spaceship.

"Hey, bro," Sakima said, in a deliberately loud timbre. As expected, Nimàt jumped, nearly hitting his head on the surface he had studied intently until that moment.

"Cut that out! What's wrong with you?"

"Um, Nimmy?"

Nimàt rubbed his neck worriedly before mumbling, "What?"

Sakima said nothing, so he kept wiping the flashlight beam over the interior of the big hole they'd gotten themselves into.

"Nimàt?"

"What, already!" he said, nearly shouting as he cut around to stare at her.

Sakima raised her eyebrows in a conspiratorial way and looked at Nimàt, then at something to her left, then deliberately back at Nimàt. She needed to repeat this a couple of times before he caught on.

"*Ohhh…*" he whispered, nodding to let her know that he'd picked up her signals.

Then, nerves taut, he turned slowly around to look in the direction his sister had indicated with her eyes.

In the pitch black darkness at the back of the cave-like hole, two blue eyes glowed. Shone so bright Nimàt was worried he'd done some kind of damage to his eyes and wasn't actually seeing what he was seeing. Like the effect after staring at a welder's arc or at the sun in summer. Both of which he'd done many times while growing up because he liked the strange way his eyes felt afterward. They felt heavy, more globular. And the dark spots chased around his field of vision for nearly an hour after, like an ember from a fire being carried by a frivolous breeze.

But then the growling started. A low, guttural, menacing growl.

Nimàt took a few quick steps backward. "Crap! I *toooold you*, Sakima!"

But his sister wasn't moving—a human statue. Not from fear, but from familiarity. She'd been here before. Something in the deep recesses of her mind told her that everything would be all right.

"*Easy, easy…*" she whispered.

"I'm trying."

"Not you—it, or her, or him," she said, pointing toward the bright blue shining eyes. "Easy, now."

She took a cautious step forward and cautiously lifted her hand out in front of her, palm facing the animal. She then took another step as the growling increased in both volume and ferocity. Ignoring the obvious threat and trusting her gut, Sakima took yet another step forward.

The growling stopped like brakes had been applied.

"*That can't be good,*" Nimàt muttered. He kept the light shining into the corner like a spotlight. It did no good, though, as the creature, whatever it was, was far back in another tunnel where the light couldn't reach. And yet, the light of its eyes reached them easily.

"*No, it is not good, not at all,*" Sakima said softly, nodding her head.

And then the creature barked.

"Crap, again!" Nimàt yelled.

"Do not yell," Sakima yelled. "Please."

"Don't yell at me not to yell!"

The creature barked again.

"That is a *mwekane*," Sakima said. "It is not the sound of a wolf or coyote or anything else. That is a dog's bark, plain as day."

The eyes came closer, like tiny torches through the night. Then closer still, until finally a snout peaked out of the blackness. Then the entire face of a dog appeared, a dog that was more wolf-like than dog.

"It's a mech-*mwekane*!" Nimàt said. "Look at the metal around its neck. That's not a collar, that *is* its actual neck. A mech-dog!"

But Sakima didn't respond; she was too busy smiling. She'd seen that face before, the white fur with the black diamond in the middle at the top of the snout, and a second diamond on its forehead.

"*Lisa?*" she said in a quiet but clear voice. She was both unsure and astonished.

"What did you say?" asked Nimàt.

"This one, we met years ago, she and I, when I was, um, a little lost. I named her Wu' Lisa. Lisa for short..."

The dog suddenly leaped into the air as if attacking Sakima. It knocked her over roughly to the ground—being that it weighed close to one hundred pounds—then licked her face with joy.

"Wu' Lisa!" Sakima called out, laughing. "Okay, girl, cut it out. That is a bit too much, really." Sakima sniffed the strong *mwekane* smell of warm earth and love that Wu'Lisa was giving off as Sakima wiped her face with her shirt sleeve.

But after a brief break, Wu' Lisa jumped up, having pinned Sakima beneath itself as her prisoner. It scampered back near where they'd first spotted it and crouched down on her front legs only, her tail slapping against the ground with excitement.

Nimàt took a run at Sakima to help her get back up. As he did so, a small and thin gun barrel emerged from the animal's metallic neck. It cocked into a loaded state with a loud click. Nimàt froze.

"Lisa, no! Friend, *friend!*"

Nimàt held his hands up.

"Yeah, man. Friend. Friend of Sakima. Brother, actually. Family."

The gun ticked a few notches left and then a few notches to the right, tracking Nimàt. The firing mechanism of the nozzle glowed, and a deep humming sound came emitted from the full metal collar.

"Wu' Lisa!" Sakima said, shouting this time as she jumped to stand between the dog and her brother.

The *mwekane* looked up at Sakima and into her eyes. Then it started to whine, a bit pathetically.

"I think she's just trying to protect you," Nimàt said, being careful not to move any muscles except the ones controlling his mouth.

"I think you are right. Yes, I am sure of it."

The weapon made the sound of powering down, and then it retracted back into the dog's metal neck.

"Good girl, Lisa. Now let us all calm down."

Wu' Lisa stepped back a foot or two, but not before giving Sakima one additional lick. Then it barked and ran back eagerly into the dark passage from which it had emerged.

"What in the world?" Nimàt said.

"I do not know, I—"

Wu' Lisa burst out of the passage, barked again happily, then ran back into the dark.

"I think she wants us to follow her," Nimàt said.

"I think you are right. Yet again. Super annoying, by the way."

Sakima grabbed the flashlight from her brother's limp hand and charged into the dark without waiting for him to follow.

The tunnel was only five *shaèks*—or roughly about fifteen feet in length. At the end of it, Wu' Lisa stood proudly, her head high, her back straight, her tail upright and curled. Then she barked at a metal box that was on the wall there about four feet from the ground.

When Sakima caught up with her, she noticed that the box was some kind of binary mechanism: on or off. In this case, she presumed, open or closed. She noticed that the metal box was part of a metal wall, a wall mostly covered with dirt and clay. And to the right of it, also covered in earth, was clearly a door.

The escape hatch.

"This is the bottom of the ship. This is an emergency way in or out."

"Why has no one in almost 500 years thought to dig around the spaceship?" Nimàt said.

Sakima shrugged. "Well, the ship has always been left 'as is' as a monument to the Sky Walkers, you know. And we have all always concentrated on the part above ground. It's most of the ship, after all. Hard to imagine that there'd be a door here at the—what part of the ship is this? The back?"

"Yeah, aft," Nimàt said.

"Aft?"

"Fore and aft; starboard and leeward."

"Huh?"

"Spaceships are still ships, right? That's standard navigational terminology."

"Okay, thanks, Captain Nemo."

"Whatever. Basic knowledge."

"I don't care. Anyway, let's try to get it open, right?"

"Sure, sis. But, um..." Nimàt glanced at the box, which gave no indication of its proper use or function, then back at Sakima. He spread his hands at his sides and shrugged. "How?"

"That box is a panel. That panel has buttons. Let's push them. One at a time, I mean."

Nimàt did so. Nothing happened. "Maybe it's for eye-scanning or fingerprints," he said.

"Maybe, maybe not. Maybe just broken. Been buried down here in moist conditions for half a millennium. I mean, look at it; it is a rusty old thing."

"That it is. And moisture and dirt would certainly screw up any electronics or tech, for sure," Nimàt said.

"Thanks, Captain Leela."

"Stop calling me those weird names. I don't even know what you're talking about."

"Okay, whatever. Now, about this door—"

"What about your thingy?"

"What are you talking about, my 'thingy?'"

"Your cuff thing. Doesn't it have special Star Walker abilities?"

Sakima nearly hit herself on the forehead with the palm of her hand.

"I am an idiot. I could have used the cuff outside when we first got here. This whole invasion has gotten my thinking muscles all messed up."

"Who cares? Just use it now."

"It is in my quiver, which I have left topside. With my bow."

"Let's go get that stuff, then."

"I will get it. You stay here and make small talk with Lisa."

"Um, *okay*…"

"You're a good girl, aren't you, Wu' Lisa?" Sakima said in a kind of baby talk. "Who's a good girl? Wu' Lisa's a good girl!"

Wu' Lisa jumped and licked Sakima and barked happily. Sakima rubbed the top of the dog's head and scratched the scruff of its neck.

"You stay with Nimàt, okay girl? He's good, too, just like Lisa!"

Sakima laughed, gave Wu' Lisa one last pet, turned, and screamed.

She had come face to face with another being in this closed, dark, damp, lonely, secret place. Someone or something as quiet as a mouse and as sneaky as a rat.

"*Hè* guys! It's me!" Tangetta called out cheerily. "Whatcha' doing?"

CHAPTER 36

Private First Class Lèke Gischileu flexed his leg muscles as he squatted with his back pressed hard against a metal wall near the back of the ship. He propped a massive gun that looked almost like a miniature tank in both arms while he scanned the area, hunting down the horrifying beast. It was his job, which he had volunteered to do, to find and take out that monstrous beast. They instructed him that this mission would be his only one once they boarded the alien ship. Find the monster and smash it to pieces. A critical part of their victory plan.

He scanned the room as the two teams of warriors fought side by side against Taturåkee soldiers. At first, the warriors had the element of surprise on their side. But as the fighting wore on, the Taturåkee soldiers recovered and attacked with more venom and energy. After a while, heavy casualties were being taken on both sides; for every one of the enemy felled, an ally fell, too. The tide turned against the Mannahatta warriors, and they were pushed back bit by bit.

Mhuwe glared at the battle scene with growing rage and disgust. It could no longer stand by and watch the scene play out. If the Mannahatta fighters were to emerge victorious, the beast's plans to destroy this "Sakima" person, as well as the entirety of Mannahatta, would become far less likely to succeed.

Private Gischileu at last spotted the nightmarish creature, when at last it stepped out from behind the large protective wall where it no doubt had waited for the right time to engage. With a giant step forward into the fray, Mhuwe began systematically ripping warrior after warrior apart, with a vengeance and hatred never before seen on any fields of battle on any worlds. Blood splattered on the floors and walls as if sprayed from broken pipes. And not just blood: intestines, organs, muscles—all torn from the bodies of the Mannahatta warriors. Gischileu felt extremely nauseous and could not get himself back into the mindset of destroying Mhuwe.

Even the Taturåkee soldiers stalled in their own attacks, no doubt frozen for a second by the shock of what they saw. Lèke figured, as he watched, that these aggressors had seen much of the horror of war, and even thought most of it resulted from their own actions. But he could tell by the looks on their faces that they'd never witnessed this level of insanity and destruction. Many Taturåkee soldiers seemed unable to refocus and get back to the fight, and they thus lost their lives at the hands of warriors not so terribly affected by the sight. Others wretched up their day's food. Some even passed out. This was occurring across the lines, with many Kanyen and Mannahatta fighters also losing their concentration—and their stomachs for fighting.

Lèke stared at Mhuwe as it continued sweeping through the crowd of battlers like a thresher taking down wheat in human form. Then he heard Major Onanta across the room, shouting with obvious panic into his communicator.

"This is Onanta," Major Ron:kwe Onanta shouted into his shoulder-mounted comm device. "We're outnumbered. Taking heavy casualties down here. Many, many deaths. Request return to Mannahatta of all Kanyen and Mannahatta troops immediately." He clicked off the comm and awaited a response, but one never came. He tried again. "Major Onanta here. Request permission to evacuate now! Under heavy fire, heavy losses. Do you copy?"

Again, only static. The Mannahatta squadron was being pressured step-by-step toward the far wall and no doubt to their execution.

"Go for the door!" Onanta shouted, waving over his head to signal his troops. "Retreat. Retreat!"

The warriors did not need to be told twice, especially those closest to the horrible thing ripping bodies in half. They jogged backward, still fighting with knives and guns, with Lèke slowly catching up to them, leaping over dead bodies and circling around enemy fighters. He couldn't try to kill the monster at this moment because too many of his Mannahatta brethren were too close to the beast they surrounded. But before any of the Mannahatta or Kanyen soldiers could reach the giant open area leading to the next room, a massive metal wall slid across, shutting them in with a loud clunk.

"Oh, *hell*," Onanta spat. Without missing a beat, he turned and signaled Lèke and waved toward his squat, fat gun. "Shoot the door!" he said.

Private Gischelieu nodded, turned, and pressed with determination on the largest trigger on the gigantic gun. The weapon instantly released a loud whine like an emergency alarm, and a large pale red beam about ten inches in diameter poured out of it. He aimed it at the metal barrier as the weapon hit the thick closed door in pulses. The light continued to jackhammer the door, at first making no apparent change in the metal. Then, slowly, dents could be seen in the structure. The dents, looking like the result of cannonballs, got both bigger and deeper second by second until at last the beam of energy and heat blasted through the thick metal. Once it did, Lèke used the beam to cut an opening in the door big enough for a single warrior to get through.

"Go, go, go!" Major Onanta shouted above the mayhem,

guiding his men through the opening and to safety, however temporary it might be.

"Turn the weapon on that brute!" Onanta shouted to Lèke. "It's designed to kill things like that, so let's at least destroy that demon before we leave here or die, whichever comes first."

Lèke nodded and did as instructed, arcing the weapon over those battling in the current theater of war. He directed the beam of death at the gigantic freak, Mhuwe, who towered over all as it continued its wave of hideous, horrific destruction.

Once the deadly beam reached its target, the monster turned its massive, hideous stag-devil-man head to glare over at the warrior. Mhuwe was chewing a Kanyen soldier alive, but quickly spat the poor soul out and began a lumbering charge toward the soldier with the irritating, big-beam weapon.

Now that the beast was no longer eating and tearing its way through the vast throng of fighters, its forward progress was slowed to a considerable degree. This gave the weapon's beam the chance to crash into the monster's chest repeatedly.

At first, this method of attack had no effect. But then, Mhuwe slowed, as if it were trying to power its way through a sludge swamp, knee deep in mud and roots.

But the diabolical creature wasn't being hurt; Lèke could see that. At least it was being slowed down, thank *Kishelë*. The cannonball shapes appeared on the monster's chest, but they disappeared as if the wounds were spontaneously healing. Or worse, as if they'd never even happened.

"Get in!" Onanta continued his shouting encouragement to the Mannahatta forces, waving them through the rough opening into the next chamber as the creature staggered toward them. He tried again to communicate through the multiverse to the people at home, but to no avail.

Across the crowded space, Colonel Skattek, the Mannahatta team leader, waved and guided the men on that side to rush toward the door. At the door itself, there was a logjam of warriors trying to get through the opening, yet they were able to somehow maintain a certain level of forward motion.

Lèke kept the beam blaster focused on Mhuwe, hitting the thing again and again. But the beam was getting paler by the minute and was closer to an eight-inch diameter now. Lèke kept his back to the door all the same and kept firing at the grotesque monster. The effect on the towering beast was more like an strong firehose: it held the creature back but was not doing any permanent damage at all.

"That thing is going to be upon us any minute now," he shouted to Onanta. "I'm losing power."

"We're almost all in," Onanta said, firing at an approaching group of Taturåkee soldiers in a spraying pattern. "Once they're in, you get in too. And fast!"

Lèke nodded and pressed harder on the firing switch, as if doing so would make the beam more powerful.

As the last of the Mannahatta warriors approached and squeezed into the opening to the other side, Colonel Skattek motioned Major Onanta to head on through.

"No sir, you outrank me. You first."

"I'd prefer you to go in," Skattek said.

"Is that an order, sir?"

"Well, no, but—"

"In that case, I suggest you get a move on and get through. The Taturåkee outnumber us and are about to overtake the last of us. So, please sir, get in. We can't afford to lose you."

Skattek placed his hand on Onanta's shoulder in a sign of respect and edged through into the next chamber.

"Warrior, you next!" Onanta yelled.

"But, sir, I—" Lèke said.

"No backtalk. Get through. I'll hold them off until you do. Go! I'll be right behind you."

Lèke did as he was told, shutting down the beam that was keeping Mhuwe at bay. He ducked through the severed opening as Onanta took a shot to his leg and fell on one knee, groaning.

"I'm hit!"

Skattek reached through the opening and grabbed Onanta under his arms, and pulled him in. "You'll be fine, Onanta. We'll get you fixed up in no time."

Skattek pulled with all his might and had the Kanyen leader halfway through when the man screamed in agony.

"*Aaaaahh!*"

Skattek used every ounce of his strength to pull Onanta to safety, but Mhuwe reached the door and ripped the Kanyen in half. Skattek went flying backward, crashing to the ground, still holding the upper half of the major.

"*Kishelë!*" he said. "Oh my dear *Kishelë*, what is happening? Why have you permitted this horror?"

Skattek remained on the ground, stunned and hurt, unable to get the dead half-body off. Meanwhile, the warriors were savvy enough to keep firing at anyone else attempting to enter through the opening torn into the metal door.

After a moment, Skattek came to his senses. He pushed the half-corpse off himself and stumbled away from the opening carved into the thick metal door.

"Close it up," he shouted. "Seal it!"

Another warrior with a similar but much smaller red beam device fired it up and pointed it at the opening. From their new position, the opening looked like a flower petal turned in. Firing the beam at the bent metal pushed the folded pieces back together. The soldier redirected the beam at the door seal, where the metal met the wall. He welded it shut on one side and halfway down the other before the gun's energy gave out.

Lèke stepped forward, and with the last of his gun's power, welded the remaining open slit completely. Then he unstrapped the weapon from his body and let it drop to the floor.

Skattek closed his eyes and took a deep and slow breathe while saying a silent prayer.

"Good work," he then said to the man who had sealed the opening. Skattek got to his feet, exhausted. He nodded at Private Lèke Gischileu, who suddenly remembered to salute his military superior.

"Everyone, fall in," Colonel Skattek said, turning to face the bloody and exhausted warriors scattered throughout the area. "Prepare for the inevitable attack, from one direction or the other, or both. They aren't going to give up. Let's get into formation, in two rows, back to back, your weapons ready to fire. Cannibalize from broken guns as necessary. We're setting up a full area defense, and we're going to blast these bastards straight to hell!"

The weary soldiers got up from their squatting or sitting positions and did as directed, checking their weapons and reloading or refilling as needed.

"This is Colonel Skattek," he hollered into his comm device. "Requesting return to base! Repeat, we have been overrun and need to evac immediately!"

And as it was for the late Major Onanta, all Colonel Skattek heard in response was crackling static from across the multiverse.

CHAPTER 37

"You've got to be kidding me," Sakima sighed, drooping her head down. "Why is this happening again? Why are you always where you are not supposed to be, Tangerine?"

"I don't know, Sakima! Nobody knows!"

Sakima bit her lip. "Well, Nimàt is taking you home as soon as we get inside this thing. I just need to get my cuff. You both stay here until I—"

"You mean these?" Tangetta lifted her arms up. She had been clutching Sakima's cuff, rucksack, quiver, and bow in one untidy clump between her arms. The bow fell to the ground and bounced off a rock. An arrow dropped from the quiver. And then another, and another. And after all of them fell, Tangetta let go of the quiver helplessly and shrugged at Sakima.

Sakima rolled her eyes and snatched her cuff from her little sister as Nimàt bent over to recover her quiver and arrows. Sakima picked up her bow and swung it around onto her back. Then she slid the cuff onto her wrist and pressed all three jewel-toggles at once.

With a high-pitched hum, the cuff immediately began a scanning process on the dirt and metal in the small burrow they were in. It stopped on the control box, and the beam quickly constricted until only the box was highlighted. The beam changed from light blue to white, and then the control box emitted a quiet beep just before the door slid up and open.

By a single inch.

Trapped by years of dirt and moisture, the door had stopped before it even got started.

"Oh great," Nimàt said. "So close and yet so far."

"No one else has ever gotten inside this spaceship," Sakima said, her mouth in a twist. "But *we* will. I don't know how, but I know we will and—"

"What's that?" Tangetta interrupted.

"What's *what*, Tangetta?" She removed her cuff to avoid getting any more mud on it or inside its mechanisms.

"That big rock!" Tangetta pointed straight ahead at the door.

Sakima turned to see what Tangetta was talking about. A rock about the size of a human skull was wedged up near the top of the door, at the only corner that they could see because most of the door was still buried behind mud and dirt.

Sakima took out her knife, Chessi, then got up and went over to where Tangetta had indicated. Once there, she began hacking at the dirt around the rock.

After a few hits, the rock moved slightly, and the door moved open an additional inch. She tapped at the dirt around it, again trying to dig it free. But one of her blows hit the rock instead. Which wasn't a rock at all, it turned out. The rock that resembled a skull was actually a skull.

The skull popped out of where it was wedged after Sakima pulled out her knife. Then it fell to the floor by her feet with a thud, rolling about a yard, one *shaèk*, before stopping. The door moved up another inch and then another, in a constipated attempt to open all the way.

Sakima bent and picked up the skull. It was deformed, with an elongated back portion of the skull. But Sakima couldn't tell if, after 500 years, the skull was representing its original shape or the shape imposed on by half a millennium of underground pressure.

So, not everyone made it out alive that day. I wonder how many did? Or why some were trying to come out this way, through the ground? Why didn't they, instead, use a different exit more likely to lead successfully to freedom? And are there more like this, more who were trapped here and died like this?

Sakima placed the skull gently back on the ground. Then she moved to position herself under the half-open door to help Nimàt push it the rest of the way up.

They managed to get the opening about three-quarters revealed when Sakima said, "Good enough. Let's get inside. We need to see if we can shut it from the inside." She kicked a couple of small rocks out of the way at the bottom of the door's track as she said this. She guided Nimàt through and then Tangetta, and finally Wu' Lisa.

"Go ahead, girl," she said to the mechDog. "It's okay. In you go."

Wu' Lisa barked one quick, quiet message that Sakima interpreted to mean that she should go first.

"Okay, okay. Got it." She ducked under the partially open door and ducked in. "You come on then," she said, waving the dog in.

Wu' Lisa hesitated and then, with her tail wagging, leaped right past Sakima and into the ship.

Sakima peered into the craft.

"Let's close this door first to be safe and—*what the...*"

She stood alone, Nimàt and Tangetta having sped on into the ship proper, followed by an excited and eager Wu' Lisa. She shook her head with mild disappointment. *No discipline, the lot of them.*

She quickly found the internal device and used the cuff to shut the door. It closed efficiently and quietly, which surprised her, as she was ready for another struggle.

"Nimàt! Tangetta! Where are you?" she shouted into the dusky darkness of the *Alànëmëskat* ship.

No one replied, which irritated Sakima to no end.

Then she heard Wu' Lisa barking in response somewhere deep in the ship.

Good dog, Lisa, Sakima thought as she proceeded in the direction the barks had come from.

After a brief run, which included a couple of stairways heading up to the top level, she arrived at a main deck, which included the captain's area. This room she ended up in had massive panels and controls lining the walls of the circular room.

Nimàt lounged in one of the chairs, experimenting with the various switches and knobs in front of him. Tangetta was sitting next to him but upon the console itself, her legs crossed daintily as if she were at a fancy tea party. Lisa sat on the ground panting, looking at the two of them expectantly.

There were two chairs side by side—one where Nimàt was sitting and swiveling about and another near it, currently empty. A large console wrapped the entire wall in front of him, including a set of large monitors—creating an effect more akin to a huge windshield than interlocked data monitors. The rest of the walls in this small room were all lined with gadgets that must certainly do important things. But Sakima had no idea what.

"Nice to see you, guys. Thanks for waiting," she said, hoping her greeting dripped with obvious irony. Even if it was perceived that way, her sarcasm was also ignored by all parties.

"Check out these cool buttons!" Nimàt shouted with glee. "So many colors and shapes and sizes—"

"And functions, but whatever."

"I feel like I'm in the biggest, best recording studio in the universe!"

"It's not a music studio, moron."

"I know that, dummy. I said, 'like.' If you ever paid attention in school, that's a metaphor. Means it is akin to a thing, but not the thing itself."

"Simile."

"Sim-*what?*"

"Nothing," Sakima sighed, plopping into the nearest chair she could find. "So, this is to be my new home, then?" She made a twisted expression with her face to show her distaste with that reality.

"New home? What are you talking about, Sakima?" Tangetta said. She turned to stare at her brother. "What is Sakima talking about, Nimmy?"

"Uh... well, you see—"

"I am staying here awhile, Tangerine," Sakima said. "Safety reasons."

"What do you mean?"

"Sakima is the queen now—" Nimàt interjected.

"*Temporary* queen," Sakima interjected.

"Whatever. Temporary, not temporary. You're still the queen, right? And our *kittakima*," Nimàt said, turning his attention back to Tangetta, "must be protected at all costs."

"Why?"

"Why?" Nimàt repeated, pulling his head in and making a confused face.

"Why is she staying here?" Tangetta looked back at Sakima and pointed. "Why are you staying here? Why aren't you doing battles? *Sakima!*" Tangetta said, switching to a good, loud holler now and holding both of her fists up by her face. "You *love* battles!"

Sakima had to glance away. First, to laugh at her little sister. Then, as the truth hit her, she stayed looking away because the truth hurt. *Good question, my Tangerine.*

"It's only for a little while. While I assess the actual danger. And more importantly," Sakima said, getting up out of her chair, "while I develop the most effective strategy, the best plan of attack."

"Yes! I *knew* you was goin' to do a battle!" Tangetta said. She hopped down from the console and ran to Sakima and hugged her. "I knew you was not afraid, Sakima." Her voice grew quiet. "I just *knew* it," she whispered.

Sakima hugged Tangetta and then softly pushed her back by her shoulders. She then squatted down so that she could look her in the eyes. Tangetta had grown so much taller in the last year, so just leaning down a bit would have been sufficient to make eye contact. But the habit of bringing herself to Tangetta's height, even though now it wasn't much of an adjustment, was a hard one to break.

"Being afraid is fine, Tangetta. Fighting, despite your own fears, is practically the definition of being a hero. You remember that the next time you feel really scared." She gently patted the top of Tangetta's head.

"I will, Sakima. I promise."

"Good. Now help me see if there is anything to eat in this big tin can."

"There is."

"You mean you *think* there is."

"No, really. We already looked." Tangetta pointed down to the end of their room, to the door at the far end. Her pointing at things appeared to be her new communication technique. "That staircase leads down to the kitchen. We passed it on the way up here. There's a whole room with beds too! No, wait," she said, rubbing her chin dramatically with her little fingers. "That's not what you call the kitchen on a ship, is it. The gallery?"

"Close enough," Sakima said, smiling. "The galley."

"Yeah, Sakima, the galley. I peeked in, and it has everything you want, I think. It has a machine or a robot or something. It makes stuff, I think—"

"Okay, we need to get you something to eat. But first..." Sakima strode over to a narrow half-door to the left, and below the console, as she and her sister talked. She tapped it lightly, and the door sprung open. "Perfect," she said. "Storage!"

She slipped the bow off her back and slid it into the cubby

there. Sakima put the quiver and arrows in as well. She glanced down at her cuff and studied it for a second. With a shrug, she pulled it off and put it in the cubby, too, and shut the door.

That should keep my weapons and tech safe and at hand.

Tangetta came over and grabbed her sister's hand and practically dragged her to the door and down to the galley.

On the floor below, the room was also circular, like above, but smaller than the one they were just in. It was nearly all stainless steel. Stoves and refrigerators, or at least the *Alànëmëskat* equivalent, filled a semicircle of the wall. The other side was almost entirely blank except for a computer-like device that had been installed in the exact center of the wall.

"That's the thing I was telling you about," Tangetta said, continuing to nearly drag her sister to it.

"Interesting," Sakima said when she stood in front of it. "But how can you tell that it makes food?"

"The markings. Look!" She gestured to the machine.

Sakima followed her sister's prompt—she was right. There was an alien-looking hieroglyphic that clearly represented various food categories. Sakima assumed that these included meat, veggies, and fruit. But there were also other odd symbols that Sakima didn't recognize.

"Well, we need to get this thing going," she said. "So we can get these machines and robots and all of that fully activated."

"Well, how, Sakima? How do we do that?"

"First, I have to get back upstairs, to the navigation room, or captain's deck, or whatever you call it." Sakima tussled her sister's hair. "I'm guessing the power switch for this entire ship is up there somewhere. Let's get back upstairs, okay?"

"Okay!" Tangerine said, giggling.

"And after you eat, we get you home. Is that okay?"

"No," Tangetta said in a barely audible whisper. "*Not* okay."

They headed back upstairs where Nimàt was still fiddling with buttons and beating his hand against the console table as if he were listening to music and recording it too in his "studio."

"Um, wait a minute," Sakima said.

"What is it?"

"You know what? I just realized something. I didn't notice at first because it seemed so normal, but—"

"What did you figure out?" Nimàt said, climbing up the last step to join them in the galley.

"What's wrong with this picture?" Sakima said.

"What are you getting at?" he said, tilting his head slightly. Wu' Lisa, on the floor by his feet, mirrored his head tilt and gazed from one Mannahatta to the other.

"We are all standing upright, at the appropriate angle to the walls, floors, and ceilings. Agreed?"

"Duh. That's normal, you know."

"It shouldn't be, though. The ship crashed into the ground vertically. Or so we thought."

"You lost me," Nimàt said, scratching his head while still playing with the dials and switches.

"We should be walking or crawling or lying on the ground, which is the wall. Like, against all this equipment. But we're not."

Nimàt finally caught on. "My *Kishelë*!" He said. "This craft doesn't fly like we thought."

"It flies vertically. The way it is embedded here in the ground."

"So, it didn't crash!"

Wu' Lisa barked with enthusiasm to join in the excitement.

"It did not crash at all. This was a skillful landing in difficult terrain—mushy soil, but filled with rocks and covered with boulders and pine trees. This is the position that this craft was designed to fly in and land in."

"Well, I'll be," Nimàt said, laughing. "We're geniuses!"

CHAPTER 38

Lèke had lowered himself to the floor, exhausted and horrified, when a sudden loud pounding at the burnished metal door filled the room like bombs exploding. It sounded as if the Taturåkee soldiers were handling a huge, robotic battering ram that would make short work of breaking into the room. The space where the exhausted Mannahatta and Kanyen warriors tried to steady their nerves and their resolve, readying for one final battle on this alien ship from some alternate version of hell.

The piledriver's constant *boom, boom, boom* over and over again was like a personal judgement day for every single warrior in the cramped space. A place in which they were reloading, checking weapons for damage—and themselves for wounds. Lèke among them.

A number of warriors stood at a distance from the far door, firing into the controller and the sections of metal track where the large metal sheet normally slid open and closed. They destroyed the mechanism and stepped back, ready to fire at whoever might get the door open anyway and come through guns-blazing. Lèke and his compatriots were as ready as they ever could be for what might be the last fight of their lives.

This metal protected an opening that was large enough to drive a tank through. And that's what it sounded like when the second door started to receive the same battering as the first door on the other side of the room. The opening through which they had all climbed and sealed back up only minutes before.

Then came the sound no one there wanted to hear: the creaking, screaming noise of metal buckling. It was only a matter of time now, and not much at that, before the waves of Taturåkee soldiers—and that horrific, tree-monster cannibal—would burst through and finish them all off.

They won't get into here without a fight, thought Lèke. *For the men I am here with are brave warriors. But a futile fight it will be, nonetheless. We are outnumbered now more than ten-to-one, and the power supplies for our weapons are near exhausted. Futile, indeed.*

The booming on one side was echoed by the booming on the other, frazzling nerves, destroying confidence and willpower. But the warriors kept their weapons held high and strong, aimed at the door in front of them. Half the battalion—what remained of it, at any rate—faced the front door, the other half the back door.

"This is Colonel Skattek. Do you read me? Repeat. Do. You. Read?" Skattek wiped the sweat off his brow. He peered up from his squatting position at all the warriors around him, all preparing to die. Lèke watched his leader and thought that if Skattek were a different kind of man, he might appear to be crying, but Lèke knew that couldn't be. *It could be the man's allergies starting up,* he thought. *Like me, he's probably allergic to something on this damn ship.* Lèke's eyes reacted with unexpected wateriness.

This wasn't how it was supposed to go down, he thought, his brain filling with anger. *We had surprise on our side. And the latest weaponry. And the ability to move through the Many Worlds to get here, strike, and get out—key, that getting out part.*

It wasn't foolproof, but it was solid. But right away they started to lose ground to Taturåkee soldiers, all of whom seemed possessed or fueled by something unearthly. Taking hits, even losing a hand or an arm, and fighting on, blood flowing. With smiles on their faces. That was the part that caused Lèke to shudder. They fought —and he knew even as he thought this that it was a ridiculous notion—like the undead, like zombies. Unlike zombies, however, once killed they stayed killed.

Meanwhile, Skattek tried again. "Base, this is the Green Team. Please acknowledge. Extraction required right now. Over." Skattek swayed his head, the look in his eyes no longer showing fear, but defeat.

Lèke, however, wasn't surprised by the lack of response. In fact, he expected it. He wiped his sleeve across his forehead and stood up. Communication attempts were now pointless, and he faced this fact with stoic resolve. *No time left, even if they could get us out of here. Time to fight, to kill or be killed.* Either way, there was no future now where they would be leaving the Land Below.

He picked up a discarded weapon and cocked it. He checked his reserves: only a quarter of the Mp remained. *Good enough for now.*

The booming crash of the battering rams on both of the doors continued. The squealing of the metal being bent and torn grew louder. They had minutes left, or perhaps only seconds.

Then, out of nowhere, Private Lèke had a plan. It was farfetched and pretty close to hopeless. But it might give them a sliver of a chance, and that was quite a bit more than they had right now.

"Men! Gather 'round. Quick." He stared over at Skattek, who was now leaning with one hand against the wall, staring at the ground and mumbling to himself.

Lèke took a deep breath and looked away. He waited until most of the warriors had turned to face him, closing in to form a loose circle around him. "Look, our only hope is to pick a side and attack. They have us trapped, yes. But only if they enter here at the same time. We are sitting ducks here, waiting."

There was some subdued discussion among the men. He waited for it to subside a bit.

"See, my idea is that we attack the side where we know the monster *isn't*." Lèke pointed at the large door at the rear of the room. "We take our chances there. We know behind the first door is the beast and at least a hundred Taturåkee soldiers."

More mumbling and nervous glances at both doors.

"For all we know, there's only a robotic battering ram on the far side and a handful of men." Lèke waited for that to sink in. "It's our best bet. We blast that door and come out shooting. We all won't survive, but some of us will. After, we head for the main door of this godforsaken ship and get the hell out of here!"

The warriors let out a cheer, some less enthusiastic than others, others coughing in pain.

Second Lieutenant Nuwingi, who stood closest of the group to the rear door, nodded in agreement, one eyebrow raised. He appeared to be impressed with this new soldier's vision. So he raised his hand high and waved it at the three warriors who still carried serious artillery in the form of Mp cannon blasters. The men swiveled, loaded, and aimed at the door.

They began firing, so much Mp and so fast that almost immediately the heavy door blew apart after a final, single blast from all three of the large guns in tandem, the door having been crippled by the battering ram to near collapse.

The door shot into the next room like a tornado threw it, knocking over the ten or so Taturåkee soldiers near it who were manning the battering ram on the other side. Soldiers behind it further back were also slapped to the ground.

Nuwingi gave a two-fingered wave toward the new blasted opening, and the warriors all gave their best frightening whoops and cries at the top of their lungs, then rushed forward into the darkness.

"This is it, boys! Kill or be killed! Blast or be blasted!"

The warriors roared into the crowd of less than thirty enemy soldiers and blasted anything and everyone that got in their way.

Lèke could see the ship's main exit door straight ahead, and as if a miracle, it stood wide open.

"Move it, men! *Go, go!*" Nuwingi yelled, encouraging his weary fighters to give it their all, even if this was for the last time. He stepped aside to wave them all through, and when the bullet hit him in the back of his skull, he fell first to his knees as if praying to the Creator, then flat on his face as if falling asleep.

The warriors were less than twenty-five yards from the main door when Mhuwe appeared with the other, larger band of enemy soldiers, having heard the Mannahatta fighters bash through the rear metal barrier. The creature and the Mub men had abandoned their attack on the other wall and had sped down the hallway in time to cut off the Mannahatta and Kanyen warriors from their escape route. A Taturåkee soldier slammed his hand against a black switch on the wall that stuck out like a large mushroom. The door to the outside—to freedom—slid shut with a resounding boom that echoed throughout the ship.

Mhuwe roared with delight up at the ceiling, pounding its bony chest with its fists. Before anyone could move, the monster lifted Skattek by the neck and twisted the colonel in half like the beast was breaking bread for a ceremony.

"Looks who's going to die!" Queen Leia Blas squealed, coming behind Mhuwe and visible between its two, impossibly tall legs. "You, that's who! *You* are all going to die!" She jumped and danced about, laughing like a maniac, spinning her scepter through her fingers like a cheerleader with a baton.

CHAPTER 39

"Well, we have food, I think. At least there's a good chance of it," Sakima said.

"And I saw weapons in the chamber on the other side of where we came in—a whole artillery of strange guns and things, but definitely weapons," Nimàt said.

"So, we only need to get the power on in here."

"Is that wise, sis? I mean, we might draw ever-so-much attention if we're in here with lights on inside and maybe strobing outside and who knows how many odd noises this baby makes once she's fired up."

"Babies always make a fuss!" Tangetta said, laughing.

Her siblings stared at her with blank expressions.

"Um… okay," Sakima said after a few long seconds, turning back to the ship's dashboard. "So… anyway, let's see exactly what these buttons and dials and levers are built to do. And hope one of them powers us up. As opposed to activating the self-destruct system."

"Sakima!" Nimàt said, eyes wide. "Don't even freakin' joke!"

She chuckled as she cracked her knuckles by pushing her intertwined hands together and pushing out and away from herself. Sakima next shook her hands by her sides like she was trying to shed water off of them. But in reality, she was doing it to psych herself up.

"Okay, for power, I am thinking we start with the biggest ones and work our way down."

She reached up above her head where a lever—well, two levers connected by a long metal bar—stood out as being the biggest in the bunch.

She grabbed one lever from right above her head and back and pushed it forward.

"This thing either weighs a ton or it is rusted in place. Either way," she said, grunting, "it's a beast to move!"

But it did move at last and settled into the slot in front with a loud clicking sound.

Then: nothing. Absolutely, positively no change.

"Do you hear anything?" she asked her siblings. "'Cause I did not see anything happen."

"I don't think it did anything at all. Try another," Nimàt said.

"Okay, here goes."

She grabbed the next biggest lever, which once again was really two levers connected by a solid metal bar. This one was about half the size of the first, about eight inches from end to end.

Nothing, again.

"Seriously?" Sakima said.

"What about that one?" Tangetta used her well-refined pointing technique to highlight a lever of similar construction, but only about four inches across, right in front of Sakima on the console.

"Good as any," Sakima said.

"Let me try!" Tangetta exclaimed.

"Sure, why not? Knock yourself out."

Tangetta put both her small hands on the lever, side by side. She pushed with all her might and using most of her body weight and strength. This one snapped into place and made a kind of *bing* noise, like a microwave when it's done cooking. Other than that, however, nothing else happened.

"This is getting ridiculous," Sakima said.

She slapped every switch on the console table in front of her to the opposite position. In the end, when she jumped from the chair and yelled, "*Aaaargh!*" it was 124 switches.

And 124 nothings.

"I give up. Maybe this thing has been too long in the ground, powered down, and just has no juice left. "

"Could be," Nimàt said. "Or perhaps the power-on sequence is in some other part of the ship, like where the power cells are located. Like maybe the engine room."

"Could be. Not sure I care."

"You giving up already? Are you really? This sure is a different —and not at all good—side of Sakima, the so-called 'warrior.'" Nimàt teased.

"Drop dead."

"You first."

"What's this little pink button do?" Tangetta said, again leveraging her pointing skills. "It's pretty."

"Probably turns on the night light or something dumb like—"

Tangetta pressed the tiny, all-pink button. It clicked.

Something whirred.

Something else whooshed.

Then every light on the console, and on every panel, and every light in the ceiling and along the floor slammed on with a visceral thud that they all felt in their feet and stomachs.

"*Èchei!*" Tangetta whispered. "Wow."

"Well, I'll be *maluwied, damned!*" Sakima said, also under her breath.

She peered over at her little sister with admiration and smiled. "High five, kid. Well done."

Sakima and Tangetta tapped palms while they continued, with Nimàt, to look around the bright space with wonder.

"Let's eat!" Tangetta said, running off to the galley. "I'm making mac 'n' cheese for everyone!"

Sakima laughed for a bit and shook her head. "That little idiot," she said, "can sure be good luck sometimes to have around."

"I just missed it, is all. I would have chosen that pink button eventually," Nimàt said with a down-turned mouth.

"I am sure you would have, kiddo. 'Eventually' and in some parallel universe."

She got up, followed by Nimàt, to join her little sister in the mess hall where Tangetta had already placed two servings of mac 'n' cheese on one of the stainless steel tables.

"Looks yummy," she said. "How in the world did you figure that machine out, though?"

"You just talk to it is all, Sakima."

"Well, so, how in the world did you figure out that you just talk to it?"

"It said, 'Hi! I'm your Chef Quanta, version 12.47.1, at your service!'" Tangetta saluted crisply, hand to her forehead. "'What is your pleasure?' So I said my pleasure was three macs and cheeses."

"But how did it know what mac and cheese was?"

"I told the Chef thing the ingredients and I said make it yummy!"

:Well, now I understand. You go ahead and sit down with Nimàt, and I'll join you soon. I have one more thing I wanted to do real quick in the cockpit."

"Okay, Sakima."

Sakima strolled back up to the cockpit/captain's deck, still marveling that they'd gotten all the lights on and all systems working. She flopped down in one of the big, comfortable seats at the main console again and stared from screen to screen in front of her and slightly to both sides. A voice out of nowhere announced in a deep, but still metallic, voice:

Attention, this is the Threat Evaluation and
Detection system, version 20.3.171. But
you can call me TED.

There is a threat in a nearby universe
containing sentient and sympathetic
beings. Would you like to know more?

"Um, I guess—"

I cannot interpret. Please repeat.

"I said: I guess!"

Please answer in the affirmative or the
negative.

"Affirmative. All right? You satisfied now, you stupid AI?"
The deep voice boomed on:

To clarify, please respond with either yes
or no.

Sakima squinted her eyes, her eyebrows descending in anger.
"'Yes, 'idiot.'"

Please clarify 'idiot.'

"Just 'yes,' okay?" Sakima scrunched up her face with frustration. "*Y-e-s*. Yes!"

Understood.

There was a momentary set of beeps, and the monitors across
Sakima's field of vision flashed black, then white, then black again.
Video images appeared on all the screens.

At first, Sakima didn't understand what she was seeing. The

images were blurry and shaky, as if they were being beamed from an earthquake region. After a minute, the images sharpened. She could see that each screen displayed what looked like crowds of people at what—a sporting event?

Sakima realized it wasn't sports at all, but an actual battle. At first, she couldn't tell where it was taking place or who was involved. But suddenly, she recognized that monster, Mhuwe.

Once she had realized it was there, she then began to clearly see the Taturåkee soldiers. She couldn't make out any Mannahatta or Kanyen warriors and breathed a sigh of relief.

But she didn't relax for long. On the next monitor, she discovered her compatriots. They looked beaten and exhausted, and, well, scared shitless. She also understood that they were trapped in one room while Mhuwe and the Taturåkee soldiers attempted to pound and shoot their way through the door that separated them.

On the third giant monitor, she noticed at last that the same thing was happening outside the other door. Her warriors were in a deadly trap, and they were about to face certain death.

Sakima jumped to her feet, scanning the screens, trying to make sense of it all. All of a sudden, one face in particular caught her eye. A face she knew well, looking up at her somehow.

Lèke Gischileu. The man of her dreams. Maybe... hopefully.

"TED, what is going on? How are we seeing this other reality so easily?"

> Technology on this ship is far advanced than what most galaxies and planets have at the present time. It is complicated to explain. Basically the search system on this ship can see into any dimension or universe requested.

"How did you know to pick the Land Below, though?"

> I am AI-driven, after all. It was a logical
> assumption that residents of Mannahatta
> would initially want to view other
> Mannahatta people in the nearest
> alternative reality, which would be, naturally,
> Manhattan.

Sakima said nothing, scratching her forehead absentmindedly and not knowing what, if anything, to do or say.

After an extended pause, the sonorous metallic voice of the TED AI asked:

> Would you like to send help?

"Yes! Yes," Sakima said, panicking but remembering the protocol for speaking with the Threat Evaluation and Defense system.

> Please prepare yourself.

"Prepare myself? What in the world are you talking about?"

> Please return to your seat and buckle up.

"I see no reason to buckle up or—"

The ship started to shake, gently at first, and then more violently, as if it were trying to dig itself out of a tight space. Which, Sakima realized with a start, was precisely what it was doing.

"Nimmy!" Sakima shouted as loud as she could.

"What's going on?" Nimàt called from the mess hall. "What have you done, Sakima?"

"I have no idea, but you better grab Tangetta and get back in here right now—I think the *NaMùxAll* is taking off!"

Nimàt and Tangetta, holding hands, seemed to appear at the door instantaneously.

"Sit!" Sakima yelled. "Buckle!"

She collapsed back into her chair and strapped on her seat and shoulder belts. Nimàt, still holding his little sister's hand, staggered to the first available seat and shoved her in it, snugging her in place with the seatbelt. He proceeded like a very drunk person to the next chair in from to the console and did likewise. The shuddering and vibrating got worse, and they could all tell that the ship was pulling up out of the ground, and soon enough, leaving the surface of Mannahatta.

"*Maluwe! Èchei!*" Nimàt screamed.

"*Hold on to Wu' Lisa!*" Sakima shouted.

The main monitor in front of them went black and, in a flash, reappeared as a windshield, showing them the trees they were rising above and the skies ahead. In no time, the skies ahead turned into the stars of their galaxy.

"*What's happening!*" Nimàt yelled.

"*I'm still hungry!*" Tangetta hollered.

"*I think… I think we're headed for the Land Below!*" Sakima shouted.

The universe in front of them began to wiggle and wave like an old television losing the signal. What they next witnessed stood out like a rainbow connected to an electrical storm. Colors so vibrant they hurt their eyes. A throbbing-like effect pulled half the galaxy straight at them at insane speed while the rest was pushed to the ends of the universe and beyond. Over and over and over.

"*Hang on!*" Sakima screamed, barely able to control her vocal chords.

The universe rippled past them in technicolor, all a blur now, as they traveled on a kaleidoscope rollercoaster of space-time. A million of Schrödinger's cats of every type—from Bengal to Bombay, Manx to Munchkin, Savannah to Serengeti—zoomed by, both asleep and awake as the Tamanends sped through the Many Worlds to the Earth Below.

CHAPTER 40

The *Alànëmëskat* spaceship, the *NaMùxAll*, burst through the multiverse and appeared shimmering in the skies above Manhattan like an angel from the heavens.

Below, most New Yorkers went about their day as if there was nothing new under the sun to see. Those who spotted Sakima's ship would've missed it had they blinked and peered up again because it was already gone.

The ship swept from its entry space-time coordinates to where the Taturåkee spaceships sat inside the Freedom Tunnel near 125th Street and Riverside Drive in upper Manhattan. Even those standing at or driving by that exact location would most likely have missed her as the ship continued to shine in and out of focus brightly, like the sun reflecting on a twisting mirror, miles above the ground.

Inside the ship, the three passengers were still getting used to travel through the Many Worlds, and one young girl in particular was having issues with a serious case of motion sickness.

"You all right, Tangerine?" Sakima shouted.

"No, I feel, I feel—" Tangetta threw up on the floor in front of her. Thanks to the fact that it was projectile vomit, it shot past her before splatting onto the tile, missing her completely but painting the tile floor as well as the back of Nimàt's seat with a thin coating of vomitus.

"Poor baby!" Sakima said, snapping herself out of her seat and shoulder harnesses in a second and dashing back to be by her sister's side. "Let's get you some soda. Nimmy, you okay?"

Nimàt shook his head as if waking from a dream. He felt his head, shoulders, and chest. "Good enough, considering."

"Can you take care of Tangetta? I need to figure out how to help our warriors and—" Before she could finish, the ship was hurled to one side, as if it had hit an obstacle.

"*Kishelë!*" Sakima said. She jumped up and peered at the view monitors. "*Maluwe!* Are we under attack already?"

Nimàt took Tangetta's hand from Sakima and gently escorted the shaky child into the mess hall. "I'll be back to help in two minutes, Sakima."

But Sakima wasn't listening. She was trying to figure out in the few seconds they had left before the next blast how to counterattack, evade, or escape.

A deep voice in the air said:

> My bad.

"What is that, now?" Sakima said, one eyebrow raised high. "Is that you, TED?"

The Threat Evaluation and Defense system intoned:

> Yes, and greetings. I was running post-multiverse checks through all onboard systems. Pulled exterior sensors sequencers offline for 3.275 seconds for repair. That is when we came under attack.

"I don't follow you, but I don't need to. I only want to know one thing: can you do something about this?"

Defensive shields are operational. We are under no further threat. Would you like me to eliminate the attacking vessel?

"If that's not asking too much—"

Roger that.

"What?"

Roger is an affirmative response.

"What?"

Like the word, 'yes.' It means I have understood your orders and are acting in accordance.

"You mean I could've said 'roger' earlier and we could have avoided all that back and forth?"

Roger. But I did not want to complicate our initial interaction too much.

"Not complicate it? If only you had... it was all knotted up for no reason, you, you—TED."

"Uh, Sakima?"

Sakima turned around to see Nimàt motioning toward the left monitor with his head.

"Shouldn't we do something?" he said.

Sakima glanced over at the monitor to see that the *Ästra Ån Pit*, the medium-sized gunship, had done a barrel roll and swept past them. It was now headed straight at their ship from an extreme altitude, with guns no doubt about to be blazing.

"Roger? I mean, TED? You got this?"

The Threat Evaluation and Defense system didn't need to answer. Sakima could see it with her own eyes, and so could Nimàt.

The *Ästra Ån Pit* ship had exploded into millions of pieces.

Wanting to applaud or cheer or jump up and down—or really, to fall to the ground exhausted—Sakima knew she still had other business to attend to.

The main monitor screen now showed the warriors battling the horrendous Mhuwe. And they were being defeated in the most quick and thorough way possible.

Sakima could not watch another second of this. She leaped into the captain's chair and yelled to TED for help.

"TED, get me down there and make it quick, and when you get down there, blast that *maluwe,* damn, door off its hinges!"

> Excuse me, ma'am, I'm good. As a defensive, tactical, multiverse-transversing AI, I am not too shy to admit that I am the best. But alas, I have not been programmed to navigate through simple space.

"What?"

> Well, ma'am, I am always paired with a capable, well-trained captain. Now, if you want to go through a black hole, through hyperspace, and at warp speed through the multiverse, well, I am your AI—ready, able, and willing. But if you need to get from point A to point B on an ordinary plane of existence, I'm sorry, but you'll have to do that yourself.

"You dolt!" Sakima yelled. "There are human lives at stake. You must understand and obey the first directive!"

Of course I do.

There was a mechanical scratching sound, almost as if the system were clearing its thought.

The First Directive: an AI must not harm a human, or through its own inaction, allow a human to come to harm.

"That's right, you bag of chips! There are many, many humans about to come to harm because of you. Now get me down there, keeping in mind the second directive."

That being so, an AI entity must obey instructions given to it by human beings, except where doing so would violate the first directive.

"So, therefore, do it."

I cannot. It's not in my programming.

"What the fry bread! Well, you better figure it out and damn fast."

Sakima waited, petting Wu' Lisa, who had walked over and sat next to her as the AI system ran some calculations. TED announced:

Done!

"That was the longest nanosecond of my life. Now get us down there!"

Nimàt was thrown to the ground, Sakima thrown back into her seat, while Wu' Lisa scraped her claws along the floor as she fought to stop sliding backward. And in the background, Tangetta sat against the wall and tossed her *ahpòn'tëta* (cookies) again.

And in 1.16.43 seconds, the ship hovered outside the opening of the Freedom Tunnel on the Land Below. TED then announced:

On your signal, ma'am.

"Fire away," Sakima said, rubbing her neck and head where it had slammed against the back of the head rest. "TED, a reminder: you are blowing the door off. You are not harming anyone inside."

Understood. Recalculating.

In an instant, with a fiery explosion, the door to the *Ästra Ån Ima* smashed into many large pieces, a few of them flying into the ship.

Inside the *Ästra Ån Ima*, pieces of the giant door, some as big as compact cars, flew by like escapees from a tornado's funnel. They pierced the walls and ceilings of the ship, shattering electric systems, sending sparks flying everywhere.

The giant pieces took out a few of the Taturåkee soldiers, mostly by decapitation, although some were simply crushed.

As luck would have it, none of the pieces hit any Mannahatta or Kanyen warriors. Luck being a cruel mistress, however, neither did any of the debris kill or hit or harm Mhuwe.

Sakima noticed this immediately on her view monitors. But the blast had done the trick nonetheless. The majority of the Taturåkee soldiers had been hurled backward, most right back down the hall from which they had charged through minutes earlier. Even better, the mighty Mhuwe was now on its back, legs up in the air like a flipped turtle. Because of its structure and size, the monster was having a difficult time righting itself.

"Missed him!" Sakima said, upset that Mhuwe still lived. She made a sneering face with some anger thrown in. She slammed her fist on the console, inadvertently hitting the button that opened and with no pause closed a keyboard drawer of some kind. The drawer opened with a slight whooshing sound before meekly sliding back into hiding again.

Sakima ignored the unnecessary activity happening on the console in front of her because something in the view screen distracted her. She was studying a certain somebody in the invaders' ship to determine if he'd been hit by debris from the door and whether he was wounded. And if so, how hurt he might be.

It was the intriguing Lèke Gischileu, and he had also been spared by both the battle and the flying bits of door, but barely. She could see small parts of the door embedded in the wall next to his neck on both sides, as well as above his head.

"*Këlulël!* Missed him again!" she said, her sneer turning into a smile, with some sense of relief thrown in. She took a deep breath and got right back to work.

"Circle back around!" she called out to TED. TED responded with:

> Roger.

They ship followed a mobius-strip path through the air and returned to the damaged, blown-apart entrance to the *Ästra Ån Ima*.

"Lower," Sakima said, and TED lowered the ship.

It now hovered a few feet below the overpass that acted as the roof of the Freedom Tunnel, a few feet above the train tracks.

And that's when the warriors came streaming out of the Taturåkee ship like bees from an upset hive. Sakima hit the "lower the door" button on the dashboard labeled in hieroglyphs.

The intended purpose of the symbols was to make their functions understandable to anyone, regardless of language or universe. This was because the button label was an animation on a continuous loop, showing a simple diagram of a door sliding open and a ramp sliding out and down.

Within seconds, she could hear the warriors thundering into her ship, the *NaMùxAll*, on the bottom floor.

"Nimmy!" she shouted. "Go help them in. Get them to sick bay, wherever that is. Hold on... " She typed in the words "sick bay" into the AI system, which was designed with a universal-language interpreter built in.

"Uh, *èchei*. This is a *small* vessel," Sakima said, more to herself than to anyone who might be listening. "A crazy small vessel." She turned to gaze back at Nimàt, who stood by the exit stairs waiting for direction. "There are only two other rooms here that we haven't yet seen: the sick bay and the sleeping quarters."

She raised her voice to Nimàt, who was now slip sliding his way down the corridor as the *NaMùxAll*—short for *Nagatamen Mùxul Allanque*—bobbed in the air like a hummingbird. "Sick bay is below the galley, which is right below this floor. Oh wait... " she said, peering at the ship's schematic, which the helpful AI had displayed on one of the monitors. "It is a sick bay-slash-sleeping quarters. Or the other way around. Anyway, that is it. That is this whole darn ship, more or less. I mean not counting the various bathrooms and stuff." She turned back around, but Nimàt had already left, no doubt a while ago.

"I'm hungry," a small voice said.

Sakima glanced over at Tangetta, who was still collapsed against the back wall.

"Tangerine, I'm not surprised, considering everything you ate earlier made its way up and out and onto the floor, like *everywhere*." She smiled at her little sister, with warm eyes full of love.

"Can you wait just a few minutes? We are kind of in a lot of danger right now—"

"Why don't you go out there an' kill everybody, Sakima? Especially that ugly monster! That's what you do. *You* are the monster killer!"

Sakima made a face that was halfway between a laugh and a look of horror.

"Rather not be considered the killer of anything, sweetie, if I am honest. But I see what you are saying. And under ordinary circumstances, I would be down there right now. Unfortunately, and to be honest not what I personally wanted—ever—I am also now the 'queen'—*kittakima*—and not merely a warrior. Seems the queen part overrides the warrior part." Sakima sighed and shrugged.

Tangetta pursed her lips and squinted her eyes with deep dissatisfaction.

"That's so dumb," she said, folding her arms across her chest.

"You're *pëmëtunhe* to the choir."

"What does that mean?"

"It means that you and me feel the same way about it."

"What's a choir?"

"*Ehasuwichik*? Well, it's a group of people that sing together, I think. It is just an expression—"

"What's preaching?"

"I never should have said that. I picked it up in the Land Below —well, down here where we are right now. I just liked the way it sounded. Does not matter, though; I will not ever use it again."

"Good, because it's so dumb."

Sakima let out a short laugh and tilted her head to look at her opinionated sister. *Was I ever like this?*

"All in! Leave now!" Nimàt said, crashing into the captain's deck.

"Everyone?"

"Everyone that survived, which isn't many."

"Okay, we're out. TED?"

I heard, ma'am.

The ship began to shake, almost too calm to notice at first. Next, it swung backward, away from the tunnel opening, and shot up into the sky.

Forgive me for not realizing you were royalty.

"Don't worry about it. I barely realize it myself," Sakima said, clutching her sister's shoulder with one arm, the other around Wu' Lisa's neck. She pushed her feet against the metal floor as hard as she could to stabilize all three of them. The ship sped up into the sky, entered Earth's highest atmosphere, and in the blink of an eye, left for space in the current universe.

"Thanks for getting us out of that tight spot, TED."

You're welcome, your highness.

"None of that; no royal name-calling."

Very good, ma'am.

"TED?"

Yes, ma'am?

"You know I wanted to destroy those ships down there, right? But I didn't want to endanger everyone on board. That's why I wanted you to get us out of there right away. You get that, right?"

A commendable and wise decision, Queen Ma'am. I would have suggested the same. Besides, it would have been a fool's errand ultimately.

"Huh? What do you mean?"

The remaining two Taturåkee ships had already left.

"Left the tunnel?"

Yes.

"Left the planet?"

That, too.

"Are they in pursuit?"

No ma'am. They have left the galaxy.

"Which galaxy are they in?"

The question now, to be clear, is which universe.

"Okay. Which universe?"

Yours, ma'am.

"What do you mean, mine?"

They've returned to Mannahatta.

"Oh, *këlulël*—damn!"

Sakima pounded her fist on the control panel. Again, and by accident, the keyboard revealed itself, paused for a second, and rolled back into place and out of view.

"Can I get something to eat now?" Tangetta said, taking a breath and closing her eyes. She sat on the floor, petting Wu' Lisa, who lay on the floor beside her.

"And I think the nice *mwekane* is hungry, too." She gave Wu' Lisa a quick, tight hug.

"Hope that food machine can make dog-machine dog food, Sakima said. Then she thought: *How can dog food be the topmost item in my brain right now, at this terrible moment in Mannahatta history?*

Wu' Lisa barked, stood up, and followed Tangetta as the girl ran back down the stairs to the mess hall.

"Sakima! Come *on!*" Tangetta called back without looking.

"*Woof!*" Wu' Lisa said, her tail wagging and her eyes following Tangetta as they both scurried down to the deck below.

PART FOUR
THE BEGINNING
OF THE END

CHAPTER 41

With Tangetta and Wu' Lisa fed and happy, Sakima left the captain's deck and made her way to sick bay. What she found there shocked her and caused her to doubt every decision she'd made since the Taturåkees had first appeared.

About forty cots filled the space, a room which was more or less the size of the average high school gymnasium, but with a much lower ceiling. Like the rest of the ship, about seven and a half feet at the highest points of the ceiling but seven feet in the majority of spots.

The black metal cots had blue canvas covers stretched across them. On less than half of the cots, warriors lay, many clearly in pain. A handful of warriors, who appeared to be mostly of higher-rank, stood in small clusters here and there around the room.

Sakima required every ounce of her emotional strength not to cry. *I must not show any weakness, not today. Empathy, yes.* She would soon do so by visiting each and every warrior in the sick bay, enlisted or officer, Mannahatta or Kanyen.

Sakima reflected back on the military that Mannahatta had at its disposal only days before. So many of the best and the brightest. So many of whom died in battle that day, and more so badly wounded or crippled that they would fight no more forever.

That left about fifty good men, matched by about the same number of Kanyen warriors, give or take. Some left on Manna-hatta to guard the villages. Which meant approximately seventy-five warriors were sent through the portal to the Land Below to fight the Taturåkee. She gazed about the big room of the wounded and the exhausted, and the horrible truth became instantly clear to her: another fifty warriors had been lost in the latest battle. A battle which turned into a massacre because of Mhuwe. A battle that should have been an easy win as the Mannahatta warriors were infiltrating with a surprise attack through the multiverse. Get in. Destroy. Return victorious.

But so many never made it out. *Why weren't they extracted as soon as the tide turned? How come the Elders did not pull them back to Mannahatta? What had gone wrong?* Sakima thought about it for just a few seconds before realizing: *Everything had gone wrong, terribly wrong.*

She entered the room and stopped next to the first warrior laying on the first cot she came to.

"How are you?" she whispered.

The man looked up, blood covering his face and hiding his eyes. "May the Creator bless you, Sakima." He closed his eyes and turned his head away from her.

She looked at the man, who was no doubt near death and wished there was something she could have done to stop the inva-sion sooner, to act quicker. To kill the enemy army before they even wounded a single Mannahatta person. But fate denied her that, made her suffer now, surrounded by the wounded and the dying, and still mourning her father's death. The raid had been a mistake; that was clear now. But on paper, it didn't look like a suicide mission, it looked like an easy win.

"Get well," she whispered to him as she patted his arm. Then she moved on to the next wounded warrior.

Being a part of the authority, the aristocracy, *sucked*. She yearned to join the fight, not just console the hurt and the dying.

She saw Nimàt up ahead and walked over to him, tenderly touching the arms or shoulders of the warriors sitting or laying down in the cots she passed.

"What's your assessment, Nimmy?"

"A lot of wounds, Sakima, I'm—I'm kind of shocked. In my nursing training, it was all pretend really, and even with the robotic patients, they never simulated anything like this—"

"And why should they?" Sakima said. "The Mannahatta people haven't been at war with anyone in centuries. Training for military personnel wounded on the battlefield would have been, well, kind of a dumb waste of time."

"Except for now."

"Right," Sakima said, her voice dropping to a whisper. "Except for now."

There was a short, quiet pause.

"We should've known better, sis. Should've known that Mannahatta wouldn't stay a paradise forever. That someone would invade, try to conquer us. Someone with values opposed to ours of peace and live and let live. The values of the Taturåkee are horrifying, based on death and war and destruction." He paused to wipe his eyes. "How can such people exist, Sakima? How?"

Sakima put her arm around her brother and gave him a gentle squeeze. "I do not know. I wish they did not exist. I wish nothing had happened. But now we must deal with it."

"I know."

"Did you find supplies?"

"Yes, there's an entire locker of everything we'd ever need here. Most of it is familiar, some different from what we usually use. Anyway, I'll try to figure it out once everyone here has been tended to in the traditional way."

"Need help?"

"Yes, but not from you. I already talked to the officers in charge, and they've assigned about half a dozen warriors who weren't hurt at all—other than mentally, perhaps—to help me out. I should be fine until we get back to Mannahatta. By the way, the soldiers found a huge arsenal right in the hall. Sliding doors opened to show an enormous number of weapons, *Alànëmëskat* machine guns, no doubt Mp-based. Lots of other weapons. It's kind of relief to hear about it all, to tell the truth."

"Yes, definitely helps knowing we can still defend ourselves. And, um, Nimmy?"

"Yeah?"

"Think about getting Tangetta to help. She might be a pretty good thing for the spirits of these men. I mean, she can visit them and perhaps cheer them up a little with the ridiculous things she says and does sometimes. Might be just what they need to think about: something other than the horrors they saw."

"Yeah, sure, I agree, could be good. I'll get her for sure, but later. After everyone has been bandaged and has been given pain meds. Then, I'm guessing, they'll sleep. In a couple of hours, could you and Tangetta distribute some food around?"

"Sure, that works."

They smiled at each other, but their eyes showed the pain they were both feeling.

"You take it easy, okay, Nim?"

"You too, sis."

She started to walk away but then returned to her brother.

"Do not let this get to you. You have such a great spirit, and I know this could destroy you, if you let it. All this negative energy. All the death and—" Sakima regretted her pep talk the second the words left her mouth.

"I'll be fine," he said quietly. "Simply too much to do here to have any time to wallow in self-pity, although I am the best at that, as you know." He smiled again, and this time his eyes did too.

Sakima smiled back. "I am going to visit a few more of these warriors, and then I need to get back to the captain's deck and—"

"I understand, Sakima."

"I'll check in on you as soon as I can, though. And Nimàt?"

"Yeah?"

"Thank you."

She took a deep breath and Nimàt stared at the ground.

"Gotta get back to work," he said.

"Right," she said. "Me too."

Sakima left him and spent a few minutes consoling and encouraging the handful of warriors on the cots between her and the exit.

At the fifth one, she stopped in her tracks. Her heart fluttered. Under any other circumstances, she'd have berated herself for her feminine ways. *Fluttering? Is that even a real word? Ridiculous.*

But in the cot, with his shirt off and an icepack on his head where a small piece of the exploding door had skipped off him, sat Lèke.

"Hey," she whispered.

Lèke sat up straight, removing the icepack from his head for the moment. He was covered in dried blood, obviously not his own, and had a couple of bad bruises on his chest and upper arms. Other than that, he appeared to be doing all right.

"How are you feeling?"

He smile wryly. "I've been better."

"So have I, frankly. May I sit for a second?"

Lèke scooted over to give Sakima room. She sat on his cot, their shoulders touching because of a lack of space. Her leg just barely resting against his, however, had nothing to do with the amount of room available on the cot.

She reached up and felt the bump on his head. The skin had broken there, and he'd need a stitch or two, but it wasn't too bad, all things considered.

Their faces were close as she leaned in to examine his wound.

She glanced at him just then and met his eyes. They locked gazes, and neither of them blinked.

Then Lèke moved his head a few inches closer, almost touching face to face.

"Sakima!" The voice echoed in the room. It was Nimàt. "I need your help. Quickly!"

Sakima stood up and turned toward her brother, who was already out the door. She rushed out of the room, practically tumbling over Wu' Lisa, who had instinctively come over to the sick bay to nuzzle and lick the wounded.

"Good girl," Sakima said as they crossed paths, giving Lisa a quick pet.

Back at the furthest wall in the room, a stunned Nimàt stood, mouth agape, hands holding gauze and scissors at his side, tears misting his eyes. *Had his sister been just about to kiss his crush, Lèke? No. How could that be?*

"You needed me for something, Nimmy?" Sakima said, walking up to him.

He turned his back and pretended to be gathering medical equipment.

"No, no, um, it's over now. Never mind. It's fine."

CHAPTER 42

Elder Rita Shim Olsen studied the scene from the large window at the top of the *Kèkayëmhès Wikwahëmink* government building. They'd assembled there quickly after being alerted of the Taturåkee threat by those Mannahatta warriors responsible for tactical and defense monitoring, led by Sergeant Mitch Galanney.

Elder Olsen peered out the window at the change in the weather when she noticed something strange. They appeared in the skies above Mannahatta just as they did the first time they had arrived weeks ago. Starting with the strangely hued overcast skies and the thunderclouds. Then the same waving and warping of the air in the sky and the strong winds and lashing rain.

She watched as two spaceships shimmered into being from out of nothing, hovering a few thousand feet above the ground, waiting. They were suspended there in the sky like bombs dropped but caught in space-time, unable to finish falling. The menace of imminent doom was the same as the last time, too.

She watched as Mannahatta citizens gazed up at the sky, weary and afraid. Some pointed up at the ships; others pulled their children inside and away from harm. Dogs yelped, some whined. Creatures of the forest—both bio and mech—ran for cover, above and below ground as suited their species or their programmed settings. Or a bit of both.

Orange lightning snapped across the sky horizontally, followed by a tremendous *boom*. Still, the two ships—only two this time—waited. Hanging there as if they had all the time in the world to do whatever murderous, destructive acts they were planning.

People began running away, looking for shelter, in fear for their lives. They wanted no part of what was to happen next, regardless of what it might turn out to be. Because they knew it would not be good. In fact, it would be horrible.

Elder Ahi Manunsko, Elder Nitis Tschutti, and all the others joined Elder Olsen at the windows. They watched the lowering sky as the bigger ship, the *Ästra Ån Ima*, began to steadily drop itself down toward the ground—almost imperceptibly at first, and then with greater and greater velocity. As it did so, the fact that it no longer had the massive front door in place became obvious. The great door that had so dramatically opened and revealed the pompous man—the so-called "Supreme Leader" Locus Mub—who was so clearly filled with such irrational hate and ignorance and vanity. A bit later, as the craft moved even closer to the observers, other brokenness revealed itself: torn sheets of metal with gaps and cracks in those pieces that hadn't been destroyed or gone missing. The large crimson cross that once adorned the gigantic loading door was the thing most glaringly gone.

Elder Olsen and the others stood and stared in controlled horror. They had no idea what to do, although it was their sole job to think, work together, and develop solutions. She thought about the terrible cost to her beloved Mannahatta that might be taking place once again. They had some protection from the Mannahatta military, the *ilaok*, and other groups. But it had been the minimum, and now, clearly not enough at all.

This was because only the smallest of armies had remained

behind on Mannahatta while the rest were sent through the *Skontay Chìpilësu* portal to the Land Below—*Mënatink Ohëlëmi*. These warriors were currently dispatched for the civil duty of protecting the remaining Mannahatta citizens, the last tens thousands of us. But people were scattered among miles and trails, in different villages and groups, with great distances between. The alert had gone out almost immediately, and any Mannahatta individual with a bio-communicator or brain processor would have known to get to the safety of the *yakaon hakink*—the various underground shelters throughout the villages—immediately.

Elder Olsen shut her eyes and lowered her head. So many Mannahatta people were at the hospitals, either victims or helping care for the wounded. Others were in the areas that had been destroyed, clearing rubble and hunting for any survivors who were missed in the initial searches, however unlikely that might be. Still others tilled the burned land, removing debris from the battle, attempting to return the good soil back to at least some semblance of what it used to be. To try to get it ready for winter, with the hope of planting on the decimated fields in the spring, *Kishelë* willing. While they had access to these emergency bulletins, for their own reasons, they did not or could not respond.

Despite the Mannahatta warriors' best efforts at corralling the people to shelter quickly and quietly, panic had broken out, as was to be expected. After all, Elder Olsen thought, people had their own eyes and could see clearly that the invaders had returned. They had their own hearts, in which they could feel quite solidly the heaviness of *Ekhokiike*, the End of the World and *Wikhakamik*, the soul being a part of the End of the World.

Olsen heard screaming, even louder than before. Her eyes opened wide as she witnessed with great trepidation her people running through the streets, shoving, and screaming. The warriors assigned to protect the people tried to control the mobs, but they were severely outnumbered. Many Mannahatta citizens managed to get to the shelters, with or without warriors' help. Many more of the people remained above ground, panicking and sprinting through the woods and forests, or into their own homes—neither of which could provide any protection at all once the shooting started.

But the attack and the bombing expected of the Taturåkee hadn't started, and that was disconcerting.

"What are they waiting for?" She asked Elder Manunsko. "Why are they toying with us? Could it be that they've come to surrender to us?"

Elder Manunsko glared at her intensely, as if he were staring at a crazy person. "Why would they surrender?" he drawled, his teeth clenched. "They are the victors!"

"We don't know that, Ahi. We don't know what happened in *Mënatink Ohëlëmi*. Our warriors might have won!"

"Really, Elder Olsen? Okay, if that's the case, then where are they? We lost communication with them almost the second we sent them through the portal and have not heard a peep since. Deadly silence. In my opinion, we simply dropped our best fighters through the multiverse into an ambush. Just as I'd feared. We were set up to send our lambs to the slaughter. All at the design of a foolish, self-proclaimed leader and warrior, Sakima Tamanend!" He sneered with contempt as he said her name, and looked back out the window at the sickening mayhem.

"Elder Olsen has a point, though, regardless," Elder Tschutti said. "We don't actually know for a fact what went down in the Land Below."

"I think we do, Nitis, and I disagree with both of you totally. We *perceive* the enemy in our skies above. But our warriors are not to be found here or in any other universe. Further, where is our great new so-called 'queen?' The great female warrior. Well? Did she run away and hide when the real battle began?"

Elder Olsen felt her face turning red. "Elder Manunsko, you are, excuse my language, a fucking idiot. I say that with all due respect. But it was Sakima who chased them away the first time. Who gave us a fighting chance. She did that all by herself, at great personal risk." Elder Olsen took a deep breath. "And further, it is *protocol* to protect the queen. She didn't run away; she is in a secret place, awaiting the day she can return in triumph! It's always been that way and always—"

"Yes, Rita, true," Elder Manunsko said, shouting her down and not using her official, required title. "But only with the *female members* of the royal family: queen, princesses, ladies. The Sachem always fought with the warriors—leading them into battle!"

"What battle, Ahi?" she said, returning the disrespect he had shown when he used her first name, by referring to him with his. "There hasn't been a battle worth talking about for half a millennium. What you espouse as the glory of the Sachem line hasn't been reality for generations. It's all glorified myth, as far as I'm concerned."

"Doesn't matter," Elder Nitis Tschutti broke in. "Look!"

The darkened sky was becoming blacker still, with a purple essence of some kind. It looked sickly, unearthly, spreading through the air like a sticky, thick inkblot.

"What in *Kishelë's* name is that?" one of the other Elders said in a hushed tone, walking slowly forward while staring out the window.

The other Elders sighed, or turned away, or closed their eyes, wary and worried about what they might soon see—and how this could possibly get any worse.

CHAPTER 43

The purple-black cloud came out of the spaceships in a heavy plume. It descended to the ground and spread like a black fog, a fog tinged with palatinate purple, covering everything and everyone in its path.

The effects of the strange gas became immediately apparent as the Elders continued to peer out the window. Whomever the substance enveloped instantly fell to their knees, or if weaker, onto their stomachs or back. People were staring at their hands and their arms, rubbing at something that none of the Elders could see from where they stood. Suddenly, these victims scratched furiously at their faces, wailing in pain.

The Elders in the *Kèkayëmhès Wikwahëmink* building stared, eyes wide, at the spectacle playing out below them.

"We should—" one of them said, but they all stood there frozen, unable to move, incapable of a coherent thought. Tears choked them all now, and no one uttered another word as they watched the horrific carnage taking place on the streets below.

Here and there, Mannahatta military men—the handful who were tasked with staying behind to protect Mannahatta should the invaders return—were rushing toward the people still standing. They were trying to guide people—the old and infirm, children, pregnant women—to shelter. They did this in some cases pulling them by the hand to speed them up, to get out of the path of the encroaching purple-black cloud.

Others elsewhere—parents and teachers and neighbors—were running through the streets and taking children into their homes or buildings in an attempt to flee the cloud of poison.

At this point, however, it was unclear if the windows and walls would be able to stop the evil fog of sickness and misery. Warriors were directing as many people as possible to the underground shelters, which were gas-proof, bulletproof, fireproof, and had many other safety capabilities. But the shelters were a considerable distance apart, sometimes a few miles, and the warriors herding the populace were sparse. They did what they had to, but soon they too began to succumb to the invasive gas and what it did to a person.

Elder Olsen tapped Sergeant Galanney on the shoulder and gestured with her head toward the door. They both quickly turned and dashed down the hall to the Warrior Technology & Early Warning Center. Once there, Galanney switched on the external monitoring system in the room. While virtually all the visuals across each of the video monitors were currently focused on the Land Below, he was able to hit a few switches. Doing so rerouted the multiverse security camera system to the monitors as they watched.

What they saw made Elder Olsen involuntarily gasp, slapping her palms to her mouth, her eyes growing wide and filling fast with tears.

The monitor showed the effects the horrible cloud was having on her Mannahatta brethren close up. An older man was closest to the security camera by the front gate that sat at the furthest end of the *Elgixin Field* of the Mannahatta Technology and Research Campus, the *Lëpweichik Èlikhatink Mannahatta*.

The rest of the Elder Council soon joined Elder Olsen and

Sergeant Galanney. They gathered around the large monitor, and together they watched in alarm as the man fell in a bumpy way to the ground, first letting go of his walking stick and clutching his chest. He dropped to one knee but looked as if he were still trying to move forward, to run away. His other knee fell, and he collapsed to the ground, hitting his face and one palm hard. He lay there still for a moment, but they heard him scream—even at this distance and behind windows, they heard it. Low at first, growing louder and more high pitched.

Red dots out of nowhere started to form on the man's face and arms. He tried to lift himself up but stopped after achieving only a foot or so of space between him and the ground. He projected a powerful stream of vomitus onto the ground in front of him. The man next twisted himself around, still trying to stand, but unable to. He fell over again, this time onto his back.

The Elders zoomed in on the poor fellow as he lay on the ground. He wore shorts, and they observed that his legs, too, were now covered in pox, sores, and rashes. The man scratched desperately at it all and as he did so, the rash transformed itself into larger bumps. These filled with a fluid with an indent at the top. Some were scabbing over already, like an accelerated case of disease. Whatever was happening to these people was something no one had ever seen before on Mannahatta.

"What *is* that?" Elder Ahi Manunsko said.

"I have no idea," Elder Rita Shim Olsen answered. "It's something new—but yet—and I don't know why I'm saying this, familiar?"

"Well, we can be sure, therefore," Elder Nitis Tschutti said, "that because it's new and alien, we as a people will have no defenses against it. This will be catastrophic. This will truly be the end of the Mannahatta people!"

"We might all be wiped out, and quickly, if that happens to each of us..." Elder Olsen whispered.

They continued to witness in horror what was happening to the man on the screen. His skin, everywhere it was visible, was covered in either the red dots—the way the infection starts—or medium to big lesions, which seemed to enlarge even as they watched.

The man desperately tried to stand again, clearly wanting to get away, to hide, to save himself. But now his joints were visibly swollen. None of the Elders were aware of when this new symptom had begun, but the condition became noticeable now. It was as if, in the space of a few minutes, the man had developed the most advanced stage of arthritis. His joints were so swollen that they were causing deformations. The man's left arm bent at the elbow almost entirely behind his back. His right shoulder pulled his arm up near his head, while the newly deformed elbow sent his forearm off at nearly a ninety-degree angle, in a direction nature was not prepared to support. And the subsequent pain forced the victim to scream even louder.

With a shock, they all noticed that his lips, tongue, and the mucous membranes of his nose were also covered with the strange pink dots. The man desperately swept his hands to his mouth, trying to figure out what was happening. And that's when they saw that the disease had affected his fingers as well. They were bent in all directions, some so bent over they appeared to be only stubs.

He was dying in front of their eyes, the most hideous of deaths.

Elder Olsen tore herself away from the group. She couldn't watch any longer; she'd seen enough of this atrocity, this tragedy that the Taturåkee had inflicted—deliberately and knowing exactly what would happen—to the peace-loving people of Mannahatta. And soon, no doubt, everywhere across Mannahatta, to infect the Kanyen people as well.

And the children.

Elder Olsen would not allow herself to imagine that happening out there across her country to the littlest individuals of Manna-hatta. The tears came fast and free, and she crashed down hard in the nearest chair. She bent over and held her face in her hands and let the tears flow.

"Elder Olsen!" Elder Ahi Manunsko said.

She ignored whoever dared to summon her from her mortuary of grief.

Manunsko tried again. "Elder Rita Shim Olsen. Come here to the window. Look at the sky above!"

She raised her head only an inch or two up from her now-damp hands.

"It's—something is happening there. Far above the black clouds. Above even the two Taturåkee ships, which still hover there like angels of death—"

"What?" Elder Olsen said, barely able to let the word leave her lips and fall into the air below her. She was emotionally and psychologically defeated by all that had happened in the past days, and this disease was the last straw. She had nothing left and almost didn't care what she was being summoned to view or why.

"The sky. It's warping again... wavering—"

"It's the other Taturåkee ship. The missing one, I'm sure," Elder Ahi Manunsko said. "To add to our grief and humiliation."

"Um, I don't think so, sir," Sergeant Galanney said. "That ship, emerging from the multicolored warp, it's—it's an *Alànëmëskat* ship!"

There was a general mumbling and chattering as the people in the room tried to figure out what was happening.

"It's not *any Alànëmëskat* ship, sergeant. It's *the Alànëmëskat* ship!" Elder Tschutti said. "The one from *Òhchu Peak!*"

Elder Olsen sat bolt upright as if she'd been slapped in the face and doused with ice. She stood up and rushed to the window.

There, arcing down in attack mode on the Taturåkee spacecrafts was indeed the *Alànëmëskat* ship from the mountain.

And look at that. It flies the way in the same aspect as it was embedded in the mountaintop: it flies vertically, up and down, not flat like a saucer.

Without any warning, the sound of loud whirring, like something being whipped to a frenzy, filled the air. Next, a mpoaolonium blast from the *Alànëmëskat* ship's front-mounted blaster shot out and hit the smaller of the two ships squarely at its rear. This attack caused the ship to begin slowly circling in the sky, plumes of smoke pouring into the air from where it was hit.

"Who is flying that machine!" Elder Manunsko hollered, actually pumping his fist in the air. "They deserve a medal. No, not just any medal but the highest that can be conferred on any Mannahatta citizen!"

"If I had to guess, and I don't think I'm guessing at all, you awarded that honor to Sakima," Elder Olsen said, a wry smile on her face. A smile based on her new hope that arrived, and her pride in Sakima Tamanend.

That's my girl. That's my girl. You go, Sakima!

CHAPTER 44

They felt like they were riding a ship constructed from gelatin, and not the firm kind. The walls and ceilings wobbled. The ship itself seemed to pass in and out of focus. An aurora borealis of weaving watercolors passed through the ship and around it.

Abruptly, the *Alànëmëskat* spacecraft shook violently. Sakima held on as hard as possible. This time she put Wu' Lisa into a small cubbyhole in the floor, which seemed specifically designed to hold a mech animal. She also managed to get Tangetta strapped into her seat before they jumped through the Many Worlds toward home again. Nimàt squeezed his eyes shut as if it would help him survive the journey. Meanwhile, Tangetta gazed about the starship in wonder with a look that seemed to ask, *Is this a dream?* Wu' Lisa whimpered nervously from her hidden and protected space, and Sakima herself white-knuckled the armrest of her captain's chair.

Sakima heard shouts wafting up to her ears from two levels below. The hollering came from wounded warriors who tried to all of their focus their courage and bravery in trying to not fly off their cots onto the floor.

The monitors all around Sakima appeared to be showing what dreams and nightmares inside the mind look like. It was actually a pretty good representation of what Sakima and everyone else on the small *Alànëmëskat* craft felt.

But, in an instant, all that stopped: the shaking and shuddering. The crazy light show. The wobbling and waving.

And then they were there. In the Mannahatta skies. In the same universe that they'd left to go to the Land Below a short while ago. But something wasn't right. Sakima pulled herself upright and leaned forward to study what the monitors were showing her.

Two Taturåkee ships hovered in midair below them, a few thousand feet above Mannahatta soil. But that was pretty much what Sakima had expected. She knew they'd moved on, had returned to Mannahatta in this universe. What she didn't understand, however, was the crawling, churning, sickening, and worm-like black and purple cloud that was slowly covering the land she knew and loved.

What is that? What is going on?

Her instincts kicked in. She didn't need to understand, didn't require an explanation. It had to be bad because the Taturåkee were evil. Terrible. It would not be a joyous black cloud of goodness. No. So she had only one clear, overarching thought in her mind now: *stop the Taturåkee.*

"What's happening?" a voice behind her said. Sakima swiveled around.

Lèke.

They locked eyes again, something that seemed to happen whenever they were in the same room. Finally, after a moment, Sakima blinked a couple of times, and Lèke peered down at his feet.

"See those two ships there?" Sakima said, pointing over her shoulder with her thumb back at the display monitors. "See? The Taturåkee are up to no good, that's clear."

"Yes, definitely."

"And I know they are not landing for a reason. Literally hanging out up there. Now, see that black fog on the ground?"

"What in the—?"

"Exactly. That's the 'not good' part," she said. "I bet it is poison and they do not want to be anywhere near that cloud until it has done its work and completely dissipated."

"I get you, I see... " Lèke said, struggling to sit down in the chair next to her on the captain's deck. "Ow," he said, lowering himself to the seat with extra care.

"Is something wrong?"

"Nah, only a flesh wound."

"Oh—"

"In the wrong place," he said.

"Aren't they all in the wrong place?"

Lèke laughed. "Yes, good point. This particular flesh wound doesn't allow me to sit all that easily, though."

"But everything else works?"

"What?"

"I mean, that entire area is kind of vulnerable—"

"Oh!" Lèke said, blushing a bit. Instantly, he blushed harder when he realized he had blushed at all. "You mean—"

"The family jewels. I believe that is how some refer to them."

"The meat and potatoes, yes," Lèke said. "The gentleman's sausage—"

"Wait, what?" Sakima said, her eyebrows shooting up her forehead.

"Oh, I meant jewels, gentleman's jewels. Pretty jewels."

"That's better, I guess..."

"Yes, good. It's all fine down there—"

"Now that we have thoroughly covered that topic," Sakima said, suppressing both her laughter at him and her desire for him. "How 'bout you help me figure out what to do here?"

Lèke studied the display screens for a moment and scratched his head.

"Well," he said, "I don't know what to do about those deadly clouds, or whatever you want to call them. We'll need to figure that out right away, of course. But my instinct would be to take out those two ships. My guess is that they're too busy in their gloating over their purple-black monstrosity to notice that we've arrived."

"I bet you are right."

"Strike while the iron's hot, eh?"

"Could not have said it better myself. TED?"

"Who's that? Ted?" Lèke said, gazing at Sakima quizzically.

Yes, sir?

"Ted?" Lèke said again, looking all around as if expecting another man to walk into the room.

"T-E-D," Sakima continued. "We have a problem ahead. Need to attack those two ships."

Very good, ma'am.

"Give me control," she added.

Allow me to handle the problem. If you don't mind my saying so, time would appear to be of the essence, and there's insufficient time to teach you the basics of flying this machine, let alone the finer points of—

"TED, I'm waiting!"

... the finer points of complicated movements involved in loading, aiming, shooting, and so on. Especially while in motion, perhaps even in evasive patterns while attacking.

"TED, *now!*" Sakima said, getting angrier by the second.

Ma'am, I highly advise against—

"Do it, dammit! Do I need to remind you of the prime directives again?"

No, that won't be necessary.

"Oh," Lèke said, nodding to himself with satisfaction. "TED is the AI on board this ship. Got it."

There was a whirring sound like of something powering down before TED spoke again.

You have full control. I will be your copilot. Might I offer one tactical suggestion, however?

"*Hmmm*, I am not sure. You are being pretty stubborn—"

Regardless. I recommend taking out the smaller ship first. It can be more easily dispatched. If you target the big ship first, the smaller one is more agile. You could circle around, come up on the ship's rear and do what you want—that is to say, blow it out of the sky.

Sakima considered that advice for a few milliseconds.

"You know what, TED? I concur. Only because that is exactly what I would have decided on anyway, with or without your advice. So, we attack—" Sakima leaned in closer to the giant monitors and squinted. "The *Ästra Ån Pit*. I think that is what it says. So, come on, let's do this!"

"Very good, then. You have complete control, so please go on."

"I sure do. And I know *what* to do, too. I can see the buttons and switches necessary, and I get how this center stick thing works—especially for flying up and down and left and right; roll, pitch, and yaw; and velocity, acceleration, and all the things like that. It is your basic joystick, really. And this—" Sakima pointed to the red button at the top of the stick. "This is your basic 'bomb them to kingdom come' button. Therefore, don't interfere, TED."

I wouldn't dare," the AI said. "However, should you require my assistance, I am right here.

"Thank you, TED."

"Yeah, good man, TED," Lèke said. He looked away from the monitors and control panel and glanced back at Sakima.

"What can I do, 'ma'am?'"

"Hang on, that's what. With all your strength," Sakima said. She switched on her comm system. "Attention. 'Dog fight' mode enabled. If you can, strap yourselves in. If you can't do that, well then, hang on to something strong, and hold on real tight."

Sakima flicked the engine switch up, turned the propulsion dial to 11, and squeezed the other button—the propulsion-forward one —on the joystick.

They shot through the sky like fireworks. Lèke's head snapped backward and Wu' Lisa, who had been earlier freed from her floor cage, jumped up on him right away for comfort and protection, yelping her displeasure with their sudden speed.

Sakima next hit the 'blow the mofos up' button on the joystick, sending an Mp-torpedo straight at the smaller of the two ships.

Mpoaolonium, even in the tiniest amounts, is still powerful. A teaspoon's worth can power an entire home, including all appliances, as well as the heat and air, for three years. A five tablespoon-sized portion might power a whole city for three months.

A missile loaded with Mp—a missile in this case about the length and thickness of a golf club shaft—would easily take out a giant skyscraper as if it had never been there. And the *Ästra Ån Pit* was significantly smaller than any gigantic building.

The missile collided with the Taturåkee craft in silence. There was a flash of blue-green light, but it seemed that no sound came from the explosion. At least that anyone aboard the ship could hear. Suddenly, the alien spacecraft and everyone on it vanished from the viewport.

Now only a single, final Taturåkee ship stood between Sakima and victory.

This is almost too easy, Sakima realized, a gleeful smile dancing on her lips. *I'm kicking ass and taking names, and we'll soon have this one in the bag.*

CHAPTER 45

"Nice shot, Sakima!" Lèke shouted.

"One more target to destroy and we will land this thing," she said.

"Thank you, um... both," Sakima said with a broad smile on her face. "Beginner's luck, really. Now let's end this!"

Sakima grabbed the throttle of the joystick and did a barrel-house roll as everyone screamed—some with joy, some in fear, others in anger—as they rolled and fell about the ship. Hurt warriors who were not yet strapped to their beds, fell out and hit the ground, hit the ceiling, and hit the ground again. Once there, as the ship zoomed forward, they slid across the room, banging into cots and bedpans and dinnerware.

In the mess hall, where she had returned hungry once more, Tangetta squealed with delight. It reminded her of the roller-coasters she'd ridden all her young life. Although she wouldn't appreciate what the term meant, she was the original adrenaline junkie, loving every minute of the heightened excitement and physical changes that this kind of extreme motion elicited from her. She wasn't frightened for even one second.

"More!" she called out to no one at all, as the ship banked out of the roll and started its attack. "Again, again!"

On the captain's deck, Sakima was securely strapped in, as were Lèke with Wu' Lisa. Nimàt hung on for dear life in the copilot's chair. He had both hands clamped onto the dashboard in front of him, eyes squeezed shut, teeth clenched in anticipation of certain death.

Once the ship was upright again, Sakima prepared the next Mp-missile. In fact, she prepared two. If one took out that medium-sized ship, better to be sure to use two mpoaolonium missiles this time. Sakima figured the two together should do the trick on the big one.

Sakima glanced up to ensure that she had the ship pointing in the direction she had intended, and it was. There was no reason to get a visual on the target, as the Mp missiles were self-guiding: they sped after whatever was directly in their coordinate system at the time of launch. It wouldn't matter what evasive maneuvers the target made; the missiles would be on it like glue until impact.

The problem here, however, as Sakima now realized, was that there was no target to impact. No enemy ship.

The *Ästra Ån Ima* had disappeared.

To be sure she wasn't mistaken, Sakima glided the ship through the Mannahatta skies, looking for anything that might show a large spaceship in hiding. She saw nothing above, or below, or to the left or the right of her. On the ground, no ship hovering or hidden away under trees and branches. She checked for any signs of the shimmering you could sometimes see when a ship, having such capabilities, moved into stealth mode. And they did this by reflecting the surrounding sky so as to blend in nearly 99 percent with its surroundings.

Sakima witnessed no such conditions in the skies around her, but she wanted to be sure.

"TED, please scan the immediate area, up to two miles, for any spacecraft or strange phenomena."

DONE!

"'Done' as in you're going to do it right now? Or 'done' as in you already did it?"

The later.

"'Done and done,' in other words?"

Yes ma'am. Done and done. No alien ship within an extended range, just to be sure, of twenty miles.

"That was fast," Sakima said, casually impressed by the AI's abilities in this area. Well, in all areas.

If I may, ma'am, I'd like to inform you of certain physical evidence, which I detected while in search mode.

"Uh, sure, why not?"

I came upon evidence of a recent jump through space-time. I believe the ship has reentered the Many Worlds.

Sakima's shoulders slumped. She had been ready for a fight. More than prepared to blow the sons of bitches who killed her father—along with so many other Mannahatta people, including her uncle—back to the hell from which they'd come.

"All right," she said. "Are you sure, though?"

> There is no margin for error. They have left
> Mannahatta's universe and space-time,
> without a doubt.

"All right," Sakima said again, twisting up one side of her mouth. She breathed slowly in an attempt to calm herself down from the battle mode she'd put herself in at the start of her attack. "Do you know where they've gone, by any chance?"

> Unable to determine. They've not appeared
> yet in any of the known universes.

Sakima hit a switch on the console, and the weapons systems loudly powered down. She grabbed the joystick, and applying gentle pressure to the accelerator, guided the ship down to the ground.

Nimàt stood up. "We're done? Battle over?"

"Yep, looks like it. For now, anyway."

"You plan on going after them?"

"Yep. As soon as TED gets a reading on their new universe location, I will take the fight straight to these cowards."

"Good, great. Uh, but can you drop me and Tangetta off first?"

"That is the idea."

"That was so much fun, Sakima!" Tangetta yelled as she appeared on the captain's deck from below, her clothes covered in the dust and crumbs of various snacks, and her fingers sticky with chocolate. "Can we do it again?"

"That is enough for now, Tangerine. I am taking you and Nimàt and Wu' Lisa home now."

"Aw! But I don't want to go home!" Tangetta made an obviously fake sour face, her mouth an upside down U. "Please, please, Sakima, can't I stay with you?"

"No, little one. I am taking you to safety. And being on this ship is not safe, not at all. And being on the ground is not either, unfortunately. I am taking you both to the *Wîkëwam Shawken Obroa*.

Among its many spaces and floors, the entire two-level basement is impermeable to any gas. And it has got beds, games—including VR in six dimensions and translocations and all that. But you know what is best about it, Tangerine?"

"What, Sakima? Tell me! Tell me!" Tangetta clapped her hands together twice and then left them under her chin as if she were praying.

"They have *snacks*!" Sakima emphasized that last word strongly.

"Yay! Let's go!" Tangetta said, spinning over and over again until she lost her balance and collapsed to the metal and rubber floor.

"I thought you would like that, girl. And I bet most of your friends from school and the neighborhood are already down there. So, fun times ahead."

"Yay! Skoden!" Tangetta said, this time shouting with excitement as she struggled to get upright again.

"Indoor voice, Tangerine, indoor voice," Sakima said. She turned to Nimàt. "And you will take care of her, right?"

"Of course."

"I am sure Mimi and everyone else are already there," she added. *Oh, Kishële, I hope so.* "So you won't have to babysit her for too long."

"I'm not a baby!" Tangetta said in a harsh whisper, trying to adhere to the "indoor voice" policy. She shot her elbows akimbo and planted her fists on her hips.

"I know that, baby," Sakima said, laughing.

"I'm not a baby, I said! I already told you about it!"

"I know, I know," Sakima said, still chuckling. "I was just teasing you. When you call somebody 'baby,' it can also mean that you love them a lot."

"Is that true, Sakima? I didn't know about that."

"Well, now you do," Sakima said, patting her sister on the head.

"Better watch where you're going," Lèke said, having been

quiet on purpose this whole time. "We're getting a bit too close to the treetops, I think."

Lèke petted Wu' Lisa and then undid the dog's seatbelt and shoulder straps, but that wasn't as easy as it might sound. Wu' Lisa squirmed around so much that the straps connected across in various, random positions around her partially cyborg body. As soon as she was free, Wu' Lisa ran around the room twice before heading over to Sakima where she gave her a cheerful bark.

"I get you, and I am sorry, but safety first," Sakima said, ruffling the animal's fur. She addressed Lèke. "Sit back down, would you? I could use a copilot with good eyes for this last part. It is a little tricky going through the hills and the trees like this, everything having their own heights and deceiving locations."

"Sure," Lèke said. "Speaking of which, you might want to take it up a few more feet, right? Not that you don't have knowledge of what you're doing and not that I don't trust you. You do, and I do. You're great at this, by the way..."

Sakima pulled back on the joystick in time to avoid crashing the *Alànëmëskat's* ship, the *NaMùxAll*, into *Òhchu* Peak for the second time in Mannahatta history.

"That would have been too ironic," Sakima said, giggling. She glance over at Lèke, and she blushed, upset by his good looks and his compliments and not knowing quite how to handle her emotions.

"You ain't kidding," Lèke said.

"Get a room," Nimàt said, rolling his eyes playfully while an expression of sadness covered the rest of his face.

Sakima was amazed by how Lèke, whom she barely knew, made her feel. How he made her sense a tingle in so many places. She'd experienced something similar when she and Pat were together years ago. She had barely reached puberty at that time, and the sensations were so new and strange and, seemingly, forbidden and yet made her feel so—how did she describe it to herself back then? Delicious. That was it. Her whole body seemed as if it was enjoying the most luscious chocolate all the time when Pat was around. Even when he wasn't and she was alone in her bed at night, the delicious, chocolaty feeling overwhelming her.

In the interceding years since Apatschin was killed, she learned to finally let him go. To let him be in the Land of the Dead and allow herself to enjoy being in this world. There had been other crushes—how could there have not been? Twice had been crushes on other girls who she wanted to be like because they were fabulous. But those crushes hadn't lasted like the ones she had on the boys, although those crushes faded, too.

But none of those crushes—not even the love she had had for Pat—could compete with how Lèke affected her. And why, oh why, did he smell so *good*?

Sakima noticed a hand brush her neck, snapping her out of her wonderful reverie.

"Let's get down there, okay?" Lèke said, gently touching her back. "Without crashing and killing us all. Deal?"

"*Tèpahtu lënu*! Stupid man," Sakima said, a small smile on her face. "Just watch me." She gave him a look of total satisfaction and winked at him. Sakima then made a precision landing on the *Elgixin Field*, the enormous expanse of manicured grass in the center of the *Lëpweichik Èlikhatink Mannahatta* campus.

CHAPTER 46

"I need to assess the situation outside. *No one* goes out until after I have cleared it."

"Well, your babeness—I mean, Sakima! So sorry!" Lèke said. "I meant highness. Highness. *Your* most highness!" An over-ripe tomato would have nothing on the color of Lèke's face right now.

Both Sakima and her brother gave Lèke the side eye.

"Whatever," Sakima said, irritated and yet simultaneously amused at Lèke's slip up or attempt at humor or whatever the heck it was.

"I meant to say—" Lèke cleared his throat. "How can you go outside, as the Queen of the Mannahatta—"

"Tem-por-ary," Sakima said in a slow, deliberate way.

"Okay, fine, temporary. But still, you should be the last person to go outside into that poison, and especially not the only person."

"You don't tell me what I can and cannot do. And besides, I am not going out there unprotected."

"What are you talking about?"

"Yeah?" Nimàt said, chiming in. "What are you talking about?"

Sakima hit a shiny metal button on the wall next to the console. A narrow cubby door popped open silently, and a blue metallic suit meant to protect against the effects of hazardous materials rolled out into view. She slapped another chrome button, and the door on a second cubby rose up to reveal the hood and gloves.

"With that," she said.

"How did you know that was there?" Nimàt said.

"On the console. There is a bright, blinking arrow indicator, which showed there was a hazmat suit available. I imagine TED detected the gasses as we were landing and highlighted the buttons for me."

"That's quite an assist from TED," Lèke said, rubbing the back of his neck for a second.

"I will take any advantage I can get," Sakima said. She reached toward the hazmat cubby with both hands. "Hey, help me get into this, will you?" She pulled the suit on its hanger off the extended rack and unzipped the long chest-to-ankle zipper. The rack automatically receded, and the cubby door closed without a sound.

The boys helped zip her up and get the helmet-like hood into place and secured that as well with a zipper. Next, they pressed the zipper's cover tap into place. Finally, gloves were slid over each hand.

Sakima activated the self-contained breathing apparatus and gave the thumbs up signal to show that it was working well. She activated the comm device using the buttons on her sleeve.

In a modified and slightly deeper voice, she said, "Wait here until I get back. Lèke and Nimàt, would you mind watching Tangetta? And would you please go make sure everyone is okay down in sick bay below?"

"Sure, sis, but how long will you be gone?"

"A few minutes at most. I need to go down to the gas-proof shelter at the Technology & Research Center's campus and check on whoever is down there. Hopefully, most everyone is. And, *Kishelë* willing, they are all fine."

"What after that?" Lèke said, still looking a bit pink from his previous social gaffe.

"Well, when I am done and satisfied with what I learn there, I will return and get you all back to the shelter—one by one, I suppose. After that, I am not sure what I will do."

"Be careful," Nimàt said.

Tangetta ran her hand over the rubberized suit.

"You look scary, Sakima," she said, her eyes wide. "I can't even see your face."

"That is just the protection and a bit of my breath steaming up the visor. I am still in here, Tangerine. And I will be back to get you before you know it."

Sakima awkwardly patted Tangetta's head with the inaccuracy of her very oversizes gloves. She made her way to the stairwell and headed down.

"Take care of yourself," Lèke said.

"Bring me back some cake!" Tangetta shouted.

"What the heck, little one?" Nimàt said, giving her a tiny, affectionate push. "We will get you some cake next, but only after we check on the warriors." With that, the three headed down to the bunk area with Wu' Lisa trotting happily after them.

Alone on the ground floor of the ship, Sakima unlocked and passed through the first barrier door. She waited until she could hear the vacuum seal activate again. She pressed the exit code as TED dictated it to her through her earpiece.

The number pad beeped angrily.

"TED, read that number again."

He did, and she pressed it digit-by-digit into the pad.

The angry buzz sounded again.

"Jeez, man. Are you giving me the correct sequence or what?"

> Beg your pardon, ma'am, but I have been monitoring your key input. You are not pressing the correct buttons.

"Of course I am. I am not *tèpahtu*, you know."

> Not at all, ma'am. It's your gloves, I'm afraid. Their oversized clumsiness is not conducive to accuracy when attempting to push small buttons.

Sakima shrugged. "No, I guess not," she shrugged. "Let's try again. I'll take the gloves off for just a second."

> Ill-advised. Any gasses outside will seep in immediately and infiltrate your suit with the end result of poisoning you thoroughly.

"Well, what do you suggest?"

> Let me enter the sequence.

"You can do that?"

> Of course.

"Well, why in the world did you not at least—"

> Not protocol. Human interaction with doors on this ship always takes priority. Unless assistance is requested.

"Well, it is, *TED*," she said in a mocking tone. "Please open the door."

The door slid up with almost no sound, except for where it was broken and bent, which therefore elicited a minor scraping noise at the final moment.

"Thank you," Sakima said, still continuing her mocking tone.

> My pleasure.

TED said this as it closed the door behind her. It wasn't entirely clear if TED was mocking her or not.

Sakima stood motionless outside in what struck her as an alien landscape. Whatever this blackish gas was, it wasn't restricted to debilitating the Mannahatta people—it was also destroying the vegetation. The lawn here was scorched, the flowers in the circular gardens wilted and black. Some of the smaller trees were leafless and bent. The bigger trees looked sick along their lowest branches. Birds had fallen from the sky, their eyes opaque circles. The nearby bio- and mech-animals in the forest, at least the few she could see from where she was standing, had died or malfunctioned and appeared dead.

Tears filled Sakima's eyes as she peered around her at the destruction. Her SCBA unit (self-contained breathing apparatus) made her sound like a mechanical being herself as she breathed in and out.

And then she saw the bodies.

Mannahatta men, women—and *children*. Laying still and stiff where they'd fallen while hovering ambulances continuously passed by in all directions.

A group of warriors and first responders, who also wore more conventional hazmat suits, assisted those still alive get to their feet and climb into the ambulances. The rescuers lifted the children into their arms and carried them to medical vehicles. Sakima was relieved to see that the children, at least these children here in front of her, were still alive. For now.

All the people who had been exposed were covered in strange pink and red spots, some of which were oozing and some of which had already scabbed. And they weren't a little covered: the affliction was everywhere, more disease than skin. The pustules and red bumps were tight next to each other, one after another. It was as if a new, horrible skin had grown in to replace what was originally there.

Sakima had never seen anything like it. A disease this terrible—

like leprosy—but one which acted so fast, manifesting its symptoms almost immediately.

Who would do such a thing? What kind of hideous, hateful monsters would deliberately perpetrate this upon an entire people? Sakima's tears flowed freely down her cheeks and blurred her vision. She gritted her teeth as her hands balled up into fists—as much as they could in the poorly fitting rubber gloves.

She took a deep breath and then forced herself to take one step forward, and then another, to get inside the building. In order to see how many of her people, if any at all, had made it to safety and had avoided becoming impaired to the monstrous disease.

They were her people, always had been. But now, she was their leader. Temporary or not, she was their new queen. *Everything is temporary. What does it matter? Today I am their queen, Kittakima Sakima. And today they need me like they have never needed anyone before. I will not fail them. I cannot fail them!*

She reached the front door of the Mannahatta Science, Research, & Technology building and raised her floppy hand to the keypad. *Oh, if only TED could work here, too.* She was about to try to enter the passcode when the door slid open with a beep and someone pulled her roughly inside.

CHAPTER 47

"Sakima! You made it home!"

The other person was also in a hazmat suit, with their face unclear behind the protective mask, but Sakima recognized the voice instantly, regardless of the distortion.

"Mimi!"

The two sisters squeezed together in an awkward hug. Their two bulky suits of many layers prohibited them from getting close enough for a heartfelt hug, but it worked. This attempt was more than good enough.

"Let me look at you!" Mimi said. "I say that, but I can't see you," she added, laughing.

"My visor has fogged up. The stupid air cleaner couldn't keep up with my moisture-emitting tears."

"Neither could mine. Who designed these stupid things? Not a wise woman or a wise man—*Mannahatta sapien*. But a complete idiot. Because if you're wearing these, you're going to see terrible things. And there will be, consequently and naturally, tears."

Sakima smiled. It was so good to see her big sister. Even among this nightmarish devastation it brought Sakima some comfort, some hope.

"Come," Mimi said. "I want to show you the survivors, the untouched. You'll be happy to see that most of us got down here in time. The sensors in this particular building, the rooftop ones, detected the danger minutes before the cloud had descended."

The two sisters walked along, arm and arm, through many hallways until they entered into the large room dedicated to the technologies of the Star Walkers. Sakima gazed out through the clear parts of her visor at all the weapons and displays. She smiled at her memory of when she first found this place, the first time she put on that mysterious cuff that now felt like an organic part of herself. The cuff designed specifically for her by the Grandmother of the South and the *Alànëmëskat* people. They knew Sakima would find it, wear it, and use it perfectly. Even though that moment wouldn't occur for a few hundred years.

I do not know everything about it, but I will one day. With the Grandmother's help. She thought again about how she hadn't seen or heard from anyone from the Land of the Dead. *Why not? What could they be waiting for?* She needed their help and advice far more now than she did a few years ago in the Land Below.

Instead of heading toward the gigantic doors and into the mythical monster prison/museum and beyond into the labs and the portal, *Skontay Chìpilësu,* Mimi continued to guide Sakima to the other side of the building. A part of the building that Sakima had never before visited.

They entered an airlock system—three airlocks, one after another—and ended up approaching an enormous staircase, the kind you'd see at a ballroom in a fairytale. Mimi helped Sakima take off her headgear, and Sakima did the same for Mimi.

"We're safe in here now. You could take off the entire suit now, if you wanted to."

"Can't. Buck naked under this."

Mimi burst out laughing. "No, you are not!"

"Not really. But I'll keep it on for now, if it is all the same to you. Pain in the backside to put it all back on again," Sakima said, snapping off her rubber gloves from each hand as her sister did the same.

"Watch your step, Sakima," Mimi said, nodding at the stairs in front of them. "It's not too easy going up and down marble stairs in these suits."

"But why, sister? I ask you: why a marble entrance to a safe room?"

"Not only a 'safe room'—a 'safe entire floor,' actually. Anyway, from what I've heard, that's because the original purpose was to be a ballroom, believe it or not. With thirty-foot ceilings, a row of magnificent skylights high above, and beautiful chandeliers hanging from long, golden chains. But for some reason, they were never able to finish it after the Many Worlds were discovered and the Star Walkers arrived."

The basement "ballroom," which was now a gas-impervious bomb shelter, was filled with cots. This looked a little too familiar to Sakima. What was different here in this safe room, however, were the many crates of food and drink, the boxes of toys and books, and the way everyone here seemed to be for the most part healthy and unhurt.

"Very nice, Mimi," Sakima said, gazing about at the people sitting and standing, mostly in small groups, around the gigantic space. "How many are here, do you think? What percent, I mean? Is this everybody? It does not look like everybody—"

"Not even close, I'm afraid," Mimi said, leading Sakima deeper into the room. "We have some scientists down here, and some are statisticians. Perhaps they can tell us. Here, let me introduce you—"

"No, seriously, that's all right. I don't need to meet any stat—"

"This is Dr. Shèshkulha. He's been working on this campus since his twenties, and now he's, well, older." Mimi giggled at her self-created embarrassing moment. "Dr. Shèshkulha, this is *Kittakima* Sakima, *Pro Tempore*."

"Jeez, sis—"

"Call me Lëwis, please," Dr. Shèshkulha said, extending his hand.

Sakima moved both of her rubber gloves to her left fist so that she could shake his hand. "Nice to meet you," she said.

Dr. Shèshkulha nodded.

"So, um, 'Lëwis,'" Sakima said, clearing her throat. "What are we looking at here? How much of the Mannahatta population is down here and safe?"

"Well, let me see here," Dr. Shèshkulha said, flipping through some hand-drawn charts on a stack of graph paper. "I've got the numbers right here. Oh, I should mention, Mimi did the counting, by the way. She's helpful indeed!" He pointed at Mimi as if Sakima might not know to which Mimi he was referring. He smiled and waited for Mimi to acknowledge his praise.

Mimi watched him for a second, glanced over at Sakima, and chuckled. "Oh, yes, excuse my manners. Thank you for the compliment, Dr. Shèshkulha!" She curtsied dramatically, and Sakima couldn't resist giving her sister a quick, and probably a too vigorous, shove. Mimi laughed as she was forced to take a few balancing steps backward after Sakima's playful but strong push. The tension had gotten to both of them and it was nice to relieve it a bit by being playful—even if they looked silly and somewhat inappropriate for the seriousness of the occasion.

"It's Lëwis, please," the man corrected, sliding his thick glasses back up on his nose. He lifted a stack of the papers and sat down in a folding chair, pressing his knees together tightly. He rested the ends of the papers against his belly so they wouldn't fall. Then, with an occasional lick of his fingers, he flipped through the stack.

"Statistics by gender, *hmmm*," he mumbled. "By age. By village. By tribal association. *Hmmm*, let's see. *Hmmm*."

Sakima peered back at her sister and shrugged, hoping Mimi could detect her bemused-but-irritated expression despite her attempt to keep it hidden from the statistician. Sakima was then gently shoved by Mimi and knew her expression had been received.

"Right, here we go!" the man said triumphantly. "The 'Total Count of Secure Mannahatta Citizens within the Mannahatta Technology & Research Campus Shelter' report. By Lëwis Shèshkulha." He cleared his throat and added, "PhD."

"And?" Sakima said, ignoring his over-introduction. She slid her hands precariously onto the slippery surface covering her hips. Her hands almost immediately slid right off. She put them back instantly, trying harder to keep them in place this time. Ignoring her wishes, her hands slowly slid down her hips as the statistician answered her.

"And?" he said.

"And what does it say?" Sakima rolled her eyes reflexively but then returned them to stare with mock fascination at the professor.

"Oh, you wouldn't be interested," the man said shyly, his cheeks turning pink. "Just a lot of mathematical formulae and postulates. Nothing *too* impressive."

Sakima opened her mouth wide in frustration and stared at her sister, her hands now off her hips and her palms facing out.

"What she means," Mimi said, turning away from Sakima while suppressing a laugh. "What my sister wants to know is, first, how many people are down here?" She looked back at Sakima and whispered loudly, *"That was my contribution, as you know..."* Mimi paused and then talked to the doctor of science again. "And based on that count and the most recent census, what percentage of the population does that represent?"

"Ah, yes, yes! Excellent questions, both. Now, here's what's interesting—"

Sakima exhaled loudly.

"The last census, which was merely a few months ago, conveniently, gave us these values: 240,137 residents. About a third are Kanyen, but those numbers are somewhat questionable. This is because they were given to us, and we didn't take part in the

Kanyen census taking." He made a grimace that the two assumed was meant to be a "what can you do, right?" kind of smile.

He returned to listing the population statistics. "So, for Mannahatta only, that's a head count of 163,293. Of those, 66,950 are male, and 96,343 female. 53,886 were under the age of twenty-one, and thus 109,407 were over. Of those, 14,222 were over the age of sixty-five. Of those under twenty-one years old, 21,015 were between the ages of zero and twelve."

"*And?*" Sakima said, almost shouting.

"Um, sorry?" he said.

"Of that total—and seriously, man, that is all I am concerned with at the moment—how many are here, in this building, with us?"

"All right, no need for rudeness," he said.

"She's not being rude," Mimi said, "she's just being the queen."

"Oh, really," the man said, licking his lip nervously. "I suppose that's acceptable."

"Good," Mimi said.

"Times like right now, I wish I had beheading authority, like a real queen," Sakima whispered to her sister.

"So, if you could tell us, Dr. Shès—I mean, Lëwis—who exactly is missing? Not who, but how many of the Mannahatta population did not make it down here in time?"

"Well, of course, I was getting to that."

"You were?"

"Excuse me, my Queen?"

"Nothing. Please continue."

"Very good. So, as I've previously made clear, we have a total population of 240,137. Mimi's manual headcount gave us this number: 3,202. Thus, we are looking at—"

"Virtually everyone else is in another shelter, in the hospital, or dead. Thank you, sir." Sakima turned to her sister and gently slapped her on her shoulder. "Let's go."

"What do you mean? Don't you want to 'meet and greet' your

people?" Mimi gave her sister a quizzical look as they walked away from the statistician and back toward the main entrance and its ballroom steps.

"Not now. These people are safe and unharmed. I want to meet those who are not as fortunate."

"In the hospital, you mean."

"Yes. Everywhere else, too. And sooner rather than later. I also have warriors on the *Alànëmëskat* ship that I need to get inside here right away. Before we leave for anywhere else, actually."

"Okay, that makes sense. Perhaps you could come back here to give everyone a kind of pep talk? Everyone's pretty frazzled—worse than that, actually. Everyone is completely freaked out. By the gas attack and the earlier 'conventional attack.'" Mimi sneered bitterly by reflex.

"I understand. I will address them all, after I see the suffering ones in the hospital and after the warriors have been safely transferred into this shelter."

"Understood."

"So where do I get about thirty hazmat suits?"

"Sakima, seriously? We don't have anywhere near that many, and the ones we do have are currently in use by the early responders, EMTs, and a few of the warriors still looking for victims outside."

"What?" Sakima said, more frustrated than angry. "How am I supposed to get the wounded warriors from the ship through the remaining gas outside and into here?"

"Relax, sis, will you? We have a small transport vehicle."

"What do mean, 'we have a small transport vehicle?' Is it a golf cart or something?"

"I mean, we have a bomb-shelter vehicle. Holds twenty people plus the driver, so you'll need to make two trips."

"Is it gas proof, though? That's what I meant to ask."

"It's gas proof, bulletproof, and, depending on the size of the attack, somewhat bombproof."

"Sounds like it should be the royal limousine."

"If we keep suffering these attacks, that's exactly what it will be used for. To take you someplace secret and safe to wait out the war."

"Does that sound like me?"

"Not even close. But you are the queen—"

"Don't you start." Sakima gave Mimi a shove, a much gentler and softer one than the time before. "Okay, can you take me to the transport?"

"What do you think I'm doing? Just keep walking. I'll tell you when to turn." Mimi pushed her sister once again, but this time quite gently to move her forward. Her shove was a gentle one. "Put your headgear and gloves back on. We're leaving this safe place in just a few minutes."

CHAPTER 48

"Well, what do you think?" Mimi said, waving her hand majestically in front of her.

"You know, sister," Sakima said. "This will do just fine." She smiled at what her sister had called a "small transport vehicle." In reality, it looked like a bulky bus. And a good-sized one at that, with heavy armor all around and satellite and other navigation-related equipment on top. Except for the driver's main half of the front of the truck, all the reinforced windows were more rectangular peepholes than actual windows.

"How can this transport possibly be gasproof? The other stuff—the bulletproofness and the bombproofness—that is common these days. But gasproof?"

"Seals upon seals upon seals—the place is practically a freakin' vacuum on the inside. No air, other than the filtered air the system provides, gets in or out. The first chamber is for entering from the street to the interior, but you can't just walk all the way in. You're blocked by a second door. Once inside, that little chamber is flushed. Then they step into the next chamber. This is where the driver sits. The driver, for safety's sake, has an option to wear a gas mask for worst-case scenarios where the system is compromised. Should that ever happen, that is. This initial foyer area, if you want to call it that, is also flushed of all air by blasting the old air out as new, uncontaminated air enters. The entire process takes about three minutes. After which they enter the main body of the transport and take a seat."

"One person every three minutes? It will take hours to get everyone on the ship to safety."

"No, Sakima, it won't. The door and the chambers aren't normal sized. They're way oversized. The first chamber can hold either ten people at once, or four people in wheelchairs, or two stretchers. Or any combination thereof."

"How many people can it hold—the bus, I mean?"

"Well, it only has twenty-four seats, plus room for the driver. The oversized driver area up front is where the wheelchairs are parked. Folded, of course. And any stretchers that the wounded can be helped out of can go there too. Occupied stretchers are simply parked in a line along the floor, as needed. Last on, first off."

"So, more like ten or fifteen minutes to load up and disembark. Then one more round trip."

"The whole thing could take less than an hour. Likely a lot less, depending only on how many warriors on your ship need help or must stay in stretchers."

"What about the gap between the ship and the bus entrance, though?"

"Check this out."

Mimi entered a code on a keypad and pressed a green button. A canopy of plastic and rubber extracted itself from the side of the bus over the large door. Wheels hit the ground, and it continued to roll forward, fully covered in advanced protective materials. When it ceased moving, a rubber-encased metal horizontal system covered any gaps between the ground and the walls of the canopy by conforming to the terrain perfectly.

"Um, wow. I am impressed. The engineers and architects of this vehicle have thought of everything," Sakima said.

"They sure have. Someone in a hazmat suit seals the tunnel from the outside using flexi-tape if needed. If there are any visible gaps, that is. Which can happen."

"Then there is no reason to wait. Let's go get them before the Taturåkee return."

"Yes, let's."

In mere minutes, the canopy tunnel retracted, the sisters were in, and the bus was shooting up the ramp at speed. Mimi drove it around the corner nearly on two wheels, and then she guided the bus to the ship as Sakima directed her. They arrived at the ship in record time.

"You drive like a racing driver gone mad!" Sakima said. "Where did you learn all those moves?"

"I've been training for the last six months, believe it or not, as an EMT vehicle driver. It's something I've always wanted to do."

"Amazing."

"And I'll take your 'mad racer' comment as a compliment," Mimi said.

"It is how I meant it. Okay, I will be right back with the first of them," Sakima said. She slapped the button for the door and waited for it to open.

When it did, Mimi got up and joined her sister in the next sealed chamber. "I'll hop out and set the canopy up and make sure it's all sealed. Anything dangerous will be expelled into the air, and the pathway to the bus will be safe as it can be, Sakima."

Sakima then flipped the switch. The door to the driving chamber shut. Then the door to the outside immediately opened.

"Here we go," Sakima said. "Wish me luck."

"You got it!"

Sakima hopped out and marched up to the outside of the spacecraft. She entered the code to open the ship's door as Mimi began assembling the sealed path the warriors would use to get to the bus. Inside, Sakima waited for the air in the first chamber to be cleared out and her suit to be decontaminated. As soon as that was completed, she entered the ship proper and dashed up to the next floor, where the warriors were recuperating. She peeled off her mask and gloves as she made her way up to them.

"Sakima!" Tangetta shouted, running over to hug her the instant her big sister had stepped into the sick bay.

Many of the warriors who weren't strapped to stretchers or on their beds waiting to be so strapped were already standing up. Others, chatting in small groups, turned to watch their queen *pro tem* as she entered and made a commotion, thanks mostly to her little sister.

"We have safe transport to a shelter, poisonous gas-free the entire way."

A joyous whooping rippled through the crowd of the wounded and the weary.

"We can only take half of you at a time, though. But that's no real problem because we are only going about a few city blocks, drive-wise."

General nodding and chatting ensued as this information was absorbed.

"I am going to suggest the weak go first. If you cannot get out of your stretcher or need help walking or are otherwise incapacitated to any degree, you go with the first group. Anyone who helps you goes too, of course. Then we will backfill with the first group that can travel on their own with little to no assistance."

More nodding and agreeable noises. Nimàt broke from the small group of men he was with to talk to his sister.

"In the spirit of women and children first, sis, Tangetta should go back with the first wave."

"I agree. Children, yes."

"And obviously, to avoid the appearance of favoritism, I should go with the second wave."

"No, Nimàt, that is not necessary!"

"Yes, it is."

They looked into each other's eyes briefly, and Sakima knew it was an argument that, sadly, she wouldn't be able to win.

"And don't worry, I'll make sure Lèke gets out with the initial group." Nimàt winked, looking like a go-to, stand-up guy, and not the lovesick boy he really felt at that moment.

"He is hardly hurt, you know," Sakima said, hoping that what Nimàt was saying wasn't what she was afraid it might be. That her new relationship with Lèke was obvious, if not to everyone on board, at least to her brother.

"But he is hurt. And you didn't say incapacitated, just hurt. He's wounded, right? Besides," Nimàt added, "he means something to you."

Sakima paused, unsure what to say, but feeling her cheeks turn warm. "Well, Nimmy," she said. "So do you."

"Not the same thing."

Sakima thought this over for a few seconds. "Okay, fine. We will do that. But I am coming back for the second group—and you—without delay, and everything will work out just fine. You will hardly know I was gone, and you will all be safe inside the shelter in the blink of an eye. I promise."

"I know, Sakima. Gee, this isn't the end. No way Mhuwe and his new friends are coming back in the next ten minutes to specifically bomb our ship."

"No, of course not. But Nimàt? Stay alert."

"Will do, sis." They fell into each other's arms briefly. "Okay. Get going. Get Tangetta to safety."

"Will do, back at ya," Sakima said. "And see if you can put on a bit of muscle by the time I get back, so you can actually fight with the rest of us."

"And you try to get a face transplant in the meantime. Then we'll be invincible together."

They both laughed, and Sakima gave her brother a gentle push. "Okay, you idiot, I'm out. See you soon," she said.

Most of the wounded had already moved to the staircase. Those who couldn't walk on their own were in stretchers, being lowered carefully down to the stairs on their way to the exit below. Others were being helped as needed. Eventually a full contingent of soldiers and others were ready and waiting by the exit where Mimi had connected the ship to the transport in a gasproof link.

"We gotta go, Tangetta." She bent down and took the girl's small hand in hers. "Stay right with me, okay? The whole time. No matter what happens."

"Yes, Sakima!"

"You take care of yourself," Sakima said to Nimàt, looking up at him. "And the rest of these men."

"You got it."

Sakima returned to her full height and headed for the stairs with her sister, not daring to look back because she couldn't trust herself not to cry.

She slapped her thigh and made a quick "tick tick" noise with her tongue as she passed by Wu' Lisa. The dog jumped to its feet, tail wagging. Wu' Lisa followed Sakima and Tangetta down the stairs and finally—and safely—out into the LS&T transport.

"Everyone ready? I'll take it nice and slow, so don't worry," Mimi said, addressing her passengers once the first group were safe inside. "Try to get comfortable, but it's a quick trip. Bumpy, but brief."

The trip back to the ship was uneventful, for which Sakima was extremely grateful. With so many bad things seeming to fall from the skies recently, she was psychologically ready for a major disaster. Even on such a quick trip over a short and almost straight line to drive. Point A to point B.

They arrived at the safe place with great speed, and Sakima and Mimi assisted the hurt ones out of the transport and over to beds and chairs set up for the wounded. Many of the people already in the space ran over in tears and greeted their sons and brothers, fathers and uncles. Hugs and tears were as common now as the safe air they breathed.

Sakima was thankful that the first run had gone so well. She glowed on the inside to see the faces of the families of the warriors looking so joyous at the return of their loved ones. But she couldn't bear to look at the expectant faces of those whose sons and boyfriends and husbands and fathers were not among this initial group from the spaceship. She didn't want to face them when she returned with the second and final group, should those they love not be among those warriors either.

Sakima left her two sisters in each other's care and returned to the transport, following all protocols for safety as had been outlined to her thoroughly by Mimi. Once inside the transport, she said a quick prayer to herself.

Mother and Grandmother and the Grandmother of the South—and Tommy too, if you can hear me. Please come and help us. I am lost and afraid, and all I am doing is reacting. Reacting without planning, reacting without thinking of the future consequences. I am just trying my best. But all this tragedy is above my current abilities, and I don't want to fail. I need your help. I need your guidance. And maybe even your intervention —please. Help me save your people, the Mannahatta folks that you love, before it's too late and there are none of us left. Oh, Keshële. Oh, Spirits of the animals and the sky and the trees and the water. Please help me—help us all—now. Don't let this be our ultimate fate.

She wiped at her tears with her thick rubber glove but only succeeded in smearing them around and creating a small abrasion on her face. Giving up trying to wipe tears away, Sakima blinked hard a few of times and then started the engine up. She rolled up the ramp and waited for the door to slide open. As soon as it did, she pressed the accelerator and got on her way. Back to work, back to saving the Mannahatta heroes of war, of which she did not at all feel she was one, nor that she belonged. Despite her best efforts, they were losing to the invaders and doing so horribly. No, Sakima by no means considered herself a hero right now. She was using most of her emotional energy just to convince herself that she wasn't a completely full-of-crap loser girl.

She bumped up the ramp to the outdoors again, startled that on such a horrific day in Mannahatta history the sun was shining—that it dared to shine.

The black fog had, for the most part, dissipated. But that was no matter. It had done its damage. Sakima guided the transport around the corner of the Science & Research building and zoomed back to the ship to rescue those she'd left behind.

Only there was a problem. A rather significant problem.

The ship was no longer there.

Sakima slammed on the brakes and skidded onto the patch of grass where the *Alànëmëskat* craft she had piloted back to Mannahatta had so recently been sitting.

The transport spun sideways like the slow hands of a clock swinging to the quarter hour. It came to a stop precisely on top of the pressed-down grass where the ship had been, only a handful of minutes ago.

Sakima's eyes opened as wide as saucers.

No. This can't be, she thought, slamming her fist into the steering wheel. *They are gone. The ships gone. Are they all dead?* She let her rubber-and-vinyl encased head fall onto the steering wheel. *How deep can my failure go? Is there no end?*

She wanted desperately to weep, to give up, but she wouldn't allow herself to fall apart. Not yet, anyway. Not until she found out what happened to her brother and all the others.

CHAPTER 49

Sakima raised her head off the steering wheel and exhaled a slow, deep sigh. She climbed out of her seat and waited for the first door to unseal, tapping her rubberized boots with steel toes with anxious anticipation. The warrior she truly was filled her heart, returning her to her natural states of animal-like aggression and eagerness. As more seconds clicked by, she folded her arms across her chest and stared at the big, stupid doors. She was ready for action, and it was killing her to be standing doing nothing.

The door smacked open with a loud *pop*. Sakima pushed her way into the antechamber when it was only barely open. In the degassing chamber, she stopped with fierce restlessness to wait for the door to the outside to unseal. Fortunately, since she was exiting the transport, there was no need for a full wash down or an oxygen cleansing of the space. Yet, it still seemed to her like time stood still. She kept transferring her weight from one leg to another, amazed at how long it was taking just to get out of the transport vehicle.

At last, the door opened with an intense and odd deflation

noise, almost like a wet fart from an overgrown giant of a mech-Beast. Sakima propelled herself out onto the grass.

"Thank *Kishelë*, already!" she said. And then she peered about still in disbelief. It had been less than fifteen minutes since she'd left with the first group of wounded warriors and returned here. The ship would almost have had no time to power up and take off. But it was clearly gone. Vanished. Disappeared.

So where are you? Sakima glanced up at the dark and cloudy sky but saw nothing. If TED jumped them somewhere to be out of danger, where exactly was that danger? *Are you hiding somewhere? 'Cause you are not in the sky. Did you go to another universe? Just explode? Disintegrate? Shrink to the size of an atom?*

Sakima quit puzzling about it, as such thoughts were getting her nowhere. She jogged around in incomplete circles, looking and trying to figure this all out. Although it had seemed like an eternity since she'd arrived and slammed on the brakes of the transport, skidding across the field. In reality, it was less than two minutes.

She stopped dashing about in circles, picked a direction, and darted that way. Sakima ran as best she could in her clumsy hazmat suit, farther and farther away from where she'd abandoned her transport. Only a few more *shaèks* from the entering the edge of the *Tèkëne* forest, she stopped to look around. *Where have you gone? And more importantly, why?*

She got her answer the next second.

Sakima was thrown backward, and she lay there for a moment, trying to figure out what had just happened. She watched in disbelief at the wreckage of the transport, which had exploded with a shocking sound of metal shattering.

Giant pieces of the bus—doors, windows, the hood, chunks of the roof—had blown haphazardly everywhere through the air and crashed around the fields and lawns. A few had crashed into the sides of the buildings on the campus. The transport had been reduced to an enormous ball of fire, a black plume of smoke spewing higher and higher into the sky.

Sakima struggled to prop herself up on her elbows, her head spinning and her ears ringing. Looking up at the dark clouds above her, she saw the one thing she'd hoped she'd never have to see again as it emerged from the looming sky.

The Taturåkee main ship, the *Ästra Ån Ima*, was back, hovering in a menacing way in the skies above her beloved Mannahatta once again. The blast it sent at the transport had been programmed for her spaceship, not the bus, because it was at least ten times the power needed to destroy a small truck, but enough to blast a good-sized spaceship into dust.

Sakima stood up in slow movements, feeling shaky, and felt around her head and her torso to see if anything was broken—or missing. As she tried to piece it all together, she heard a strange whirring noise to her left. With trepidation and eyes squinting, she glanced over in that direction.

The missing *Alànëmëskat* spacecraft, the ship of the Star Walkers, was rippling into view, like a mirage becoming solid, just thirty feet from where she stood.

What in the actual këlulël?

She stared at the ship, as it hovered just a few inches off the grass. She tilted her head to the side a bit to take it all in, to try to make sense of it. Then she moved toward the spaceship, slowly at first, and then with ever-increasing speed. At last, she was all out-out running, despite the awkwardness of the hazmat suit and the way it restricted her athletic movements.

Sakima ran at close to her natural top speed right toward the ship. The main door of the craft was already raising up to let her in. Not waiting for it to open entirely this time, she ducked her head under and dashed through the door and into the ship. The door slid back into place and locked. She waited—again!—for the various airlocks to let her through. Once she was all the way inside, she tore off her hazmat helmet and ran up the stairs. She sprinted by the sick bay floor, past the mess hall floor, and all the way to the captain's deck.

"What happened?" she shouted the second she arrived.

"What happened?" Nimàt said, turning to look at her. "That's what we were going to ask you."

"The Taturåkee are back! I just saw their ship emerge from the clouds."

"We know," said Nimàt and a couple of warriors who'd run up to the deck earlier.

"They blew up the transport."

"Yes, we saw."

"I think the blast, though, was intended for *this* ship, not the transport," Sakima said, stripping off her purple gloves and boots.

"I think so, too," Nimàt said.

"So, we need to get off the freakin' ground, like yesterday." She turned back to face the console while continuing her fast progress toward it.

"Get us out of here, TED!" she hollered at the console while she untapped and unzipped her hazmat suit. She slipped out of it and slid into the captain's seat—her seat—and buckled up.

'Out of here' meaning to another universe, another geography, or simply 'up?'

"Out of here meaning, *out of here!*" Sakima yelled. She glanced across the room and noticed for the first time a large purple switch. Above it read:

Emergency Atmospheric Temporal Evasion
and Maneuverability System
Warning! Do not engage in atmosphere!

"Just never mind, TED." Without hesitation, Sakima grabbed the lever and yanked it down, like pulling a fire alarm.

The ship shook somewhat as it rose from the grass. Nimàt jumped into the other seat close to his sister and attempted to buckle himself in. The other warriors who were on the deck waiting for Sakima to return for them grabbed at anything they could hold on to. The ship shot into the air at the speed of sound, creating an enormous *boo-oo-oom!* that echoed through the air for miles around.

While the TED AI was busy guiding the ship into the stratosphere and then back around to Mannahatta, the Taturåkee ship blasted another smoking crater into the ground, where, a hundredth of a second ago, the ship had been sitting.

The emergency system banked the craft around and headed it back to the center of the main Mannahatta village.

This ship has some amazing capabilities, Sakima thought, her hands now on the joystick while she maneuvered the spacecraft of the People Who Fell from the Sky into position.

"Wow," Sakima said, unsure of what else to say. "Who knew this ship could do any of that?"

"Yeah, well, looks like it can. And I'm guessing just as we bounded out of the way, you showed up. At the worst possible time and the worst possible location," Nimàt concluded. "Classic Sakima."

"Pretty much," Sakima said, allowing herself to laugh for just a second.

In the meantime, the *Ästra Ån Ima* had come now in her sights as they returned from the upper atmosphere. The Taturåkee ship looked like a bug so far below them, and Sakima was more than ready to squash it.

"There it is," Nimàt said.

"Right, I see it! I am going to blow it up before its defense systems pick up our—"

"Um, too late, sis." Nimàt pointed at the giant viewscreens where a minor explosion appeared in the middle of the top of the Taturåkee ship. "Look! I think they're shooting at us!"

Threat detected. Threat detected. Repeat, threat—

"No kidding, TED," Sakima said.

Requesting control.

"No way," she said, white-knuckling the joystick.

Evasive action needed then. In three, two—

"No, TED, not yet! I'm not ready!"
And then, all went silent and black.

CHAPTER 50

The beep, beep, beep of some alarm system on the ship pulled Sakima out of the darkness and into the world of the living. Her eyelids fluttered open bit by bit until her blurry surroundings registered. She fought to pull herself from unconsciousness to consciousness with every passing second, with every loud warning *beep*.

BEEP.

BEEP.

BEEEEEP!

Sakima glanced about, her eyes now perfectly focused. All around her were broken, bent walls. Electrical wires hung from the ceiling, and whips of smoke curled from the console in front of her. As her senses returned to her, she noticed she felt sick to her stomach. As she struggled to sit up and peer at the monitors, she understood why.

The ship was in a tailspin, plunging straight for Mannahatta below at maximum velocity.

This woke Sakima up, fast. She took a quick glance over at Nimàt. He was passed out, but he seemed to be unhurt. No blood.

No machinery piled on top of him. Checking on him would have to wait. She'd make sure he was all right after she either got them out of this downward spiral or safely crash-landed this ship. Either option would be fine, but right now neither seemed likely.

"TED," Sakima yelled, but with more of a sickly croak than a note of command in her voice. She cleared her throat and tried again. "Err... TED!" She tried to make herself heard above the roar of the noises both inside and outside the craft.

Despite her best attempt and giving her best and loudest shout, the AI didn't respond. Sakima made some adjustments on the console. Some took, some didn't. Some failed with a loud *pop* to indicate that, no, that didn't work that way, or at all. Others failed with a whimper or a whine; still others made no signal at all. This meant the autopilot system was out. Not that Sakima thought it would do much in this circumstance. In fact, it occurred to her, it made sense for the auto-piloting system to turn itself off and return control to the pilot. Sakima was not as grateful as she perhaps should've been for this safety, and allegedly fail-safe, automatic response.

She decided to try one more time to rouse the AI.

"TED, for crying out loud. *Answer me!*" Sakima was nauseous and dizzy and worried she might lose consciousness again. But finally, a response.

"What? Stop shouting already!"

There was still no response from the TED system, but her yelling had awoken Nimàt.

"We are crashing. I am yelling to get TED's attention."

"Holy crap!" Nimàt hollered, seeing the blur of the spiral through the main group of monitors. "TED!"

"Now we are *both* yelling," Sakima said, "for all the good it's doing."

"Why won't TED answer?" Nimàt snapped.

"I do not know. I mean, maybe the blast shorted out his CPU.

Or perhaps just the comm speakers here. Either way, we're on our own and running out of time."

Sakima grabbed the joystick and pulled it back as hard as she could. She understood she might just break the stick right off its stand. But stick or no stick, she would try to do everything she could to avoid what seemed to be the inevitable: a fiery explosion of the ship in their last, fatal, and permanent collision into the ground of Mannahatta.

She noticed the spinning had begun to miraculously slow down. The horizon line on the captain's console was swaying back and forth like a baby's cradle instead of spinning like a top. It was almost straight horizontal across now, for the most part. Better still, some of the system's emergency alarms had been shut off by whichever one of the ship's computers handle that sort of thing. The screaming sirens, which warned of imminent death and destruction, remained blaring, their honking and beeping continuing throughout the ship.

Sakima continued to pull back on the joystick with all her might. She identified the reverse thrusters because the symbol used there was self-evident. She smashed that button with her fist and fell backward in her seat as the reverse tachyon engines kicked in. The full force of their power blasted the ship to the opposite direction of its plummeting course.

Sakima then sensed the nose of the ship pull up a bit. As this *Alànëmëskat* spacecraft was disc-shaped and almost perfectly round, there was technically no "nose." But what made up the front of the ship—with the captain's deck and chairs, the console, the view monitors, and the command layout—constituted the "front" by default. It was in this part of the disc that Sakima sensed the rolling up so that she was no longer looking straight at the ground. Instead, she now ever so slightly observed a mere slice of the horizon in the distance.

And the horizon grew. The ship was rolling up and raising Sakima's view—as well as the room she was in—higher and higher up the disc, rotating her up and away from the ground.

And Sakima felt "right." She was situated in a vertical position in relation to the ground and peering straight ahead at the far distant horizon. And, in somewhat of a surprise to her, the craft was slowing down.

We have a chance now, Sakima thought. *Not much of a chance. But if I can just ride this out a little longer here before touching down—more like hitting hard—we might just be lucky enough, Kishelë willing, to have the ship slow down. Enough for me to have a chance of landing it.*

Before she'd even fully formed these thoughts, the spacecraft crashed into the ground with incredible impact and the sound of crunching metal. Sakima worked as hard as possible to control the craft, which had wobbled almost out of control even as it plowed through the dirt of the expansive Mannahatta fields of grain.

The ship plowed deeper into the dirt, uprooting corn stalks and the small rocks and boulders that had laid deep below the fields for centuries. It uprooted all medium and large bushes and small trees in its path, setting some of them on fire.

It continued its line of destruction all the way across the football and lacrosse fields. Slowing at last, it cut through the practice archery fields where Sakima used to teach young girls the art and science of the bow and arrow. An activity that seemed to have taken place in another lifetime now, and not just a few days ago.

Back when friends and family were alive. When her father ruled Mannahatta, before her temporary rule. Before the sickness was brought in to kill off the remaining warriors and the rest of the civilian population. When skies shone bright blue, and the clouds floated by in white wisps and puffs, and the air so fresh and full of promise. Back when life was still good. And not this horrible nightmare that seemed never to end.

The ship smashed through the long line of targets and crashed into the oak and elm and chestnut trees just behind the targets. The targets were crumpled and on fire, and the old trees—some hundreds of years old—cracked and split apart. Many fell to the ground in wretched defeat.

But the ship came to a stop, the bottom part of the craft embedded in the ground, the power completely off both to the various engines and the electrical components. It was an echo of the original crash landing of the *Alànëmëskat* starship on *Òhchu* almost half a millennium ago. Silence filled the air where the sirens and alarms and engine sounds and crashing noises had so furiously been. The ship stood there upright like a monolithic homage to some gods long forgotten.

And inside the ship, all was still, not a soul moving, all appearing to be dead as they sat strapped in chairs or cots, or lay on the floor where they'd tumbled.

CHAPTER 51

Barely conscious, for the second time this day, Sakima slouched in her chair with her head lolling about slowly from side to side before dropping toward her chest.

Steam, smoke, sparking wires everywhere. Debris on the floor and more still fluttering and drifting down from the ceiling. Damage at virtually every inch. The sparking stopped as the ship completely powered down. Everything broken, failed, and ruined. Exactly like Sakima.

Sakima reached up painfully to unbuckle her shoulder strap. Once she'd managed that, she reached down and around her waist —again with considerable aching—to click open her seatbelt. With great care, she stood up, hands pushing into the armrests of her chair. A dizzying sense overcame her and she fell to the floor. She lay there, once again looking up at the broken ship's interior all around her. She forced herself to sit up and struggled to get back on her feet. Using the console edge to guide her, Sakima made her way over to her brother. This time, he was wide awake, staring straight ahead at nothingness.

"You okay?" She watched him closely to see if he was wincing, but Nimàt's face stayed calm, and his eyes looked up at her.

"Yeah, I think so. You?"

"I am still breathing, I can say that much at least. So, I am going down to sick bay to check on the others. Can you make sure these guys,"—she motioned at the warriors who now sat with their backs to the wall, their heads in their hands, having crawled there after the crash. "Can you make sure they are okay? I will be back as soon as I can."

"Yeah, sure." Nimàt rubbed the back of his neck but made no attempt to get out of his seat to check on anybody. He closed his eyes and allowed himself to simply rest. In a minute, he was out cold.

Sakima cautiously made her way to the staircase. She was careful to avoid tripping over the bits and pieces of what formerly were the walls, ceilings, and gear of the captain's deck. Sakima was not quite herself either, as she still felt a little dizzy, and her legs seemed to be made of rubber.

She concentrated on simply moving away from where Nimàt was sleeping and over to the stairs. She would take the stairs one careful, slow step at a time once she got there.

Sakima was able to go down a couple of steps upright but realized she wouldn't be able to make it all the way down in her current condition. So she simply sat on the next step. She cautiously made her way down the rest of the way by lowering her rear from one step to the next to the next.

When she got to the deck below, Sakima was surprised to discover that she was actually feeling better. She stood up, brushed the dust off her bottom and her hands, and strode with some renewed confidence and even some energy—as little as it was—into the sick bay.

Most of the warriors were standing now. These were the warriors who'd somehow survived the attack on the Land Below without getting wounded. A little banged up, but nothing serious.

Only at the next moment to crash into the ground of their home-land. *If it wasn't one thing, it was another.* She studied the men briefly before continuing. They were talking in groups, checking on each other, and supporting their brothers. However, they instantly stopped what they were doing and turned to face Sakima when she walked in.

A few of the warriors snapped to attention to greet their military leader and compatriot. A few others bowed to acknowledge their new queen. The rest had no idea what to do when the battered and bruised woman they'd slowly grown to respect over the past many months stepped into their area.

"At ease, warriors, please," Sakima said, waving her hands down like fanning a fire. "So, how are you all? Did anyone get hurt when we crash-landed?"

"No," a few voices rang out.

"Not so much," a few others said.

One of the warriors replied, "We were investigating that, ma'am, when you came in. It doesn't look like anyone was signifi-cantly hurt when we crashed. We were all thrown around the room a few times. But we can handle that!"

He turned to receive a high five from a friend as some others chuckled loudly at his bravado.

"Okay, that is good. That is fantastic news, for sure." Sakima wanted to cry, despite the great news. The reason these men were here, whether or not hurt, was because of her many failures in lead-ership. She sucked in her breath sharply and pulled herself more upright, fighting off the tears and the dark desire to hate herself, to let herself be filled with self-loathing and self-pity. To become the loser that deep down inside she'd always perceived might be the "real" her.

"Okay, glad it is all right. I am going outside, check on the air situation," she forced herself to say. "I've got the only hazmat suit, and I am somewhat certain it has not been compromised. Let me go out and run a few quick tests on the air quality and the amount of poison, if any, still out there. If it is safe, I will come and get you all and we can get out of here. If not, perhaps we stay right here. Wait for rescue."

Honestly, I do not know if that is really an option. There's no doubt that Locus Mub is going to target this ship and with considerable speed. We are all basically sitting ducks.

"I will go get ready. Be back inside from outside with a report in ten minutes or less. In the meantime, hang tight, but be on alert. The Taturåkee aren't done with us, not yet."

"Yes, ma'am," a few of the men said. A couple of warriors saluted awkwardly and then gave up with a shrug, still unsure how to react to orders from a female-in-charge, even if she was their interim queen.

"Keep checking on each other," Sakima said as she turned to leave. "I want a full rundown of this group's condition. We might have to leave here in a hurry and move real fast through the forest. I need to know who can and cannot keep up."

"Will do," someone shouted from the back of the room, perhaps a bit too eagerly.

Sakima ran upstairs, this time with more strength and less dizziness, collecting the various pieces of her hazmat suit. When she had it all in place, she lined it up along the floor. Next, she walked over to the cabinet beneath the captain's console and pulled out her cuff, her bow, and her quiver of arrows. She'd slipped them all into a small drawer in the console, and fortunately, the location turned out to be an excellent one. All her belongings had survived the blast and the crash with no visible damage.

The cuff she needed for testing the air quality. Her bow and arrows she took for good luck and because it seemed like the right thing to do so.

And because, well, you just never know.

She pulled the cuff onto her forearm. It felt good. Real good. She'd missed the feeling of having it there.

I might never take this off ever again.

She propped her bow and quiver against the wall and slipped on the hazmat suit. Nimàt, awake again, walked over and helped her make sure it was tightly air-proof again. He pulled here and there on the suit, checking for holes or gaps, and pressing the tape in places where it had loosened up.

Sakima slipped the helmet on and checked the breathing apparatus and the comm system. She gave Nimàt the thumbs up and then slid a purple rubber glove on each hand. She turned and headed down the stairs two levels. Sakima jogged past the sick bay, past the mess hall, and down one last short set of stairs to the airlock system where she began the exit procedure.

Once she had made it through the two airlocks, Sakima warily stepped out into the open, peering in all directions and up above in the sky. There was no sign of any Taturåkee on the ground. No sign of the last of their attack ships, the *Ästra Ån Ima*. At least not at this moment.

So we have time, maybe. No doubt only minutes, though. Need to check the air and get the warriors out of the ship as fast as possible.

When she was finally outside all the way, Sakima noticed that the air seemed cleaner, clearer. More like the ordinary, crisp fall day it was before the invasion and the dreadful chemical attack.

Sakima had strapped her cuff on inside the hazmat suit to be safe. She could manipulate it, although somewhat clumsily, from outside the suit, pressing through the vinyl material with her big rubber gloves. She was able to activate—after a few initial fumble-fingered tries—three turtle keys and the wolf key: *tulpe-tulpe-xinkwtëme-tulpe*. This gave her a reading of her surroundings.

After her solo trip to the Land Below to chase Machto and save her sister—in Mannahatta *and* the Land Below—she'd spent the last year or so analyzing and testing the cuff. She was confident that she knew most of what the cuff was capable of and how to activate each function. She had more than memorized the key sequences; they were as much a part of her now as her own DNA—in fact, the cuff itself was, too.

The cuff scanned the immediate area and next expanded automatically two more times to take readings as far as half a mile away. The readings for all the dangerous chemicals, gasses, and viruses all came back zero. All other information on the surrounding air showed readings well within the normal, livable range.

Thank Kishële. At least we have a minor change in our luck today.

Sakima pulled the hazmat helmet off and dropped it on the ground with a relaxed sigh. She yanked off the thick purple boots. Finally, she removed the bulky suit and concentrated on tugging her sweaty gloves off. She turned to walk back into the ship and report to her fellow soldiers and Nimàt with the good news. But when she swept around, her smile froze on her face like a stain.

"Hello, Sakima, you *tèpahtu* bitch, bitch."

Mhuwe towered over her, impossibly big and completely horrifying. Despite being nearly fifty feet away, the creature's rank smell accosted her senses. The stench of dried blood, dead things, decay.

The monster grimaced a mocking sneer at her. It continued in a strange, garbled voice. "It's going to be so enjoyable, to rip you, to rip you apart. Hear your screams of agony, agony. Watch you die. But not before I violate, violate you. As I'd always intended to."

Sakima stared at the beast with unblinking eyes. *What is this horrible thing talking about? Why so personal?*

The monster continued, slime oozing out its sickening mouth and onto its chin. "I wish I had done so, left you, left you a completely worthless nothing. Left you to hide, to hide, in the bushes with your shame, shame. Remember that?"

Remember what? Sakima was unable to move, unable to do anything at all but stare at this mythological creature that she always thought was just a made-up story. Nothing real and nothing to worry about. How wrong she was.

"Seems like only yesterday, yesterday, near the forest. So close. So close to where we now stand once again. Together."

Why does this horror think I would have any memory of it at all?

"Fate, wouldn't you agree, agree? And now, finally, as I deserve, I will take, take you. Have you seen what I have now between, between my legs? Its mangled thorniness will tear you, tear you apart as I enjoy having you, having you, taking everything away from you, forever. Forever!"

And that's when all the pieces came together in the most terrible way.

This sickening creature was someone she knew.

This disgusting beast was actually once human.

This hideous monster was once a person long presumed dead. A manifestation of her brother-in-law.

It was Machto!

CHAPTER 52

Sakima found herself unable to identify exactly what she was feeling right at that moment, but it was not fear, which surprised her. It wasn't even that dullness of shock.

No, instead she was dealing with a mixture of disgust and shock.

And rage. Pure, unadulterated rage.

"Bring it, *kèpchat*," she said, her face bending into a snarl as she crouched a bit lower, ready for battle. "Let's finish this, asshole."

In the time since they'd last crossed paths, much work had been done on Sakima's—and all Mannahatta warriors'—arrows. Sakima had reported back on the ineffectiveness of her weapons against Yakwahe, the giant, hairless, bear monster of Mannahatta myth she attacked in the Land Below. That is, until the double-split shot by both her and her mother using the magic arrows given to them by the Grandmother of the South. The fact that the Mp and other tech-arrows had failed them had greatly bothered her father, Takachsin, and the Elders. They had immediately assigned a task force to research, design, and build stronger, Mp-based arrows with better targeting and killing capabilities.

The result was arrows of three, four, even ten times the power of the previous generation of mpoaolonium arrows. Arrows that, with artificial intelligence built in, could virtually "think." The arrows now approached their victims doing instantaneous evaluations and calculations to find the most vulnerable points of attack. Then, depending on the opponent's defenses, activate one or more Mp bombs and delivery mechanisms, such as the subatomic Mp bombs delivered directly into the victim's bloodstream.

Sakima pulled just such an arrow out of her quiver now and shot it at Mhuwe. Its roar sounded like some kind of sickening combination of an insane man's death rattle and the scream of an army of lost souls.

But Sakima was not frightened. Yet.

She knew Machto before he'd made a pact with the devil, *Matanto*, deep in hell to transform himself into the true Mhuwe—the man-eater—of Mannahatta legend. And she knew that some-where inside that gargantuan freak was that little runt of a human monster: Machto.

Sakima hated him fiercely. Disrespected him; mocked him. And she wanted to kill him even more than she wanted to save herself.

Her arrow sailed so fast through the air that it vanished in a blink of any eye, as if the arrow never existed, as if she never shot it at all. Mhuwe reared back, roaring in pain and anger. Then it stood fully upright and grabbed at the piercing pain in its forehead. Luckily for Mhuwe, it had swatted the arrow and ducked at the last second. Sakima had been aiming for his eye.

Mhuwe pulled at the thing, seething as it drilled into its head, all motors on the forward drill working to full capacity. Of course, the shaft had barbs facing in such a way that the harder Mhuwe pulled at the tech-arrow, the more the shaft dug into its brain and the more it screamed.

And then it snapped in half, and he pulled out part of it. The rest was pushed out—after a battle between evil energy and Mp energy—by a bony branch that grew almost by magic to dislodge the arrow from its brain within to push it out of its head. The creature snatched the other half of the arrow with one hand as it fell. With its other hand, it crushed the loaded end, extinguishing the 10X Mp before the arrow had a chance to explode and make Mhuwe/Machto disappear forever.

Sakima froze again. This time not because of the shock of seeing Mhuwe so close up. But because of what it just did: dismiss her best weapon as derisively as if the arrow had been a foam-rubber, suction-cup-tipped dart.

I would kill to have a mechSuit suit right now, she thought as she backpedaled. *Or an army to help me.*

A mechSuit wasn't available at the moment, but help was. As she watched, warrior after warrior—having witnessed Sakima remove her hazmat head cover on the viewer with Nimàt—poured out of their spacecraft, firing at Mhuwe over and over.

The monster bellowed in agony.

And then it grew again. From twelve feet to fifteen feet high, both bigger and stronger. And as it grew, the arrows simply popped out of its molted skin like shedding raindrops.

The warriors, both Mannahatta and Kanyen, attacked with new ferocity, firing the *Alànëmëskat* Mp machine guns they discovered within the ship's armory. With each blast, a part of the monster Mhuwe disappeared and then instantly healed. If 'healed' was the right word. Because its body regrew the rotting, moldy flesh and dry branch-bones that had been shot away. It staggered with each blast, but it ignored the warriors, its sole focus being on Sakima herself.

Mhuwe swept its arms back and forth in front of it like a wheat thresher, throwing warriors left and right the length of football fields. Most who landed, if they even lived, broke many of the bones in their bodies.

Sakima, backing up this whole time, now turned and bolted for the forest's edge. She ran not out of cowardice or fear. But with the somber knowledge that she couldn't do anything to help her people if she was dead or maimed. And with her arrows being no match at all for the *Alànëmëskat* weapons they all were using. It was imperative that she stay alive, queen or no queen.

She crashed through the brush into the *Tèkëne* forest, not wasting time searching for any of the actual entrance paths in. The brambles scratched at her skin, and the branches slapped her arms and legs and face, slowing her down but not stopping her. At last, with the sounds of the battle fading behind her, she found a good path and picked up her speed on it.

Sakima sprinted as fast as she was able to with the last of her strength. Trying to put as much distance between herself and Mhuwe as possible. She peered around as she ran, desperate to find a place to hide, but none revealed itself.

She continued up a hill and down the other side. And that's when she saw it: her hiding place in the woods that she used to go to when she was young. She and Nimàt would sneak out of the house, rush to the forest, and ferret themselves into this secret space in the thicket. So covered in vines and thorns you couldn't see the hiding place, nor could you see out of it once you were in it. The only way to get into it was through a sizable gap in the roots of an ancient, giant oak that grew tall in the thickets. It wasn't an obvious opening, and no one else, as far as she knew, had ever found her secret place.

Sakima wondered if she'd grown too big to fit through that gap; the last time she'd been there and crawled through that hole was almost ten years ago. She veered off the path into the thicket. It was painful going, this part. She was jabbed and scraped and poked.

She suddenly found herself stuck in thorny branches and vines, which stopped her forward progress as effectively as quicksand. With nowhere to go and while struggling to free herself, she spied back through the brush and branches toward where the battle was still taking place. Sakima instantly felt sick to her stomach.

Nearly as high as some of the taller trees, and higher even than some younger pines and cedars, towered the creepy horns of Mhuwe. Sakima gasped loudly and her heart beat fiercely.

How can this be happening? How can the mighty, conquering hero, the vanquisher of Yakwahe in the Land Below, now be running like a frightened, desperate rabbit would from a mechWolf? Sakima felt tears welling in her eyes and was ashamed. Ashamed to have ever been called a hero, to have ever wanted to be a warrior.

What hubris. What ego. I was nothing but a foolish little girl, Sakima thought, furious with herself. *And now I am personally responsible for this death and destruction raining down on my people in their beautiful, peaceful garden of a place called Mannahatta. I have failed, more miserably than any other Mannahatta person in history. I have brought the ruin, the end of our civilization, to my beloved people.*

And so Sakima simply stopped.

Stopped running. Stopped trying to hide. Stopped trying to save herself.

And stopped trying to fool herself. Fool herself anymore into thinking she was anyone of any importance whatsoever. That she would be the hero to save anyone at all, when she couldn't even save herself.

The earth shook as Mhuwe pounded its way closer to her through the dark and damp forest, crushing bushes and bugs and snakes and even small animals. Snapping large branches in two like they were celery stalks when they appeared in his way. Breaking the trunks of small trees rather than go around them, sending birds panicking into the darkening skies above.

Sakima fell to her knees, her head bowed in shame as she felt the monster approach, heard its heavy breathing, smelled its putrid odor.

She stayed put, not moving a muscle, not making a sound. This is what Sakima once did best.

But she had done it hunting. And winning. And it was such a long time ago. Not the result of losing everything and everyone and every single battle, as had so recently been her history as the first female Mannahatta warrior and Queen of the Mannahatta. It was over for her people, for her land. And soon, quite soon, it would be over for Sakima Tamanend, "Legendary Female Warrior and Queen of Mannahatta."

Sakima sensed the monster's presence, sensed its large hand hovering over her, the shadow covering her and the thicket all around her. Heard its sickening gurgle of a laugh. With a shudder, she felt a drop of its drool slap onto the top of her head and part of her shoulder.

Get it over with, already. Destroy me, you hideous piece of mwichti, you piece of shit.

Sakima squeezed her eyes closed and began to shudder uncontrollably with terror and revulsion.

Just do what you want, Machto. End me now.

CHAPTER 53

"You are mine now!" the monster roared, its feedback voice gurgling like the sounds of an electric sewer. "First, I will take everything, everything from you! Your womanhood, your flower, your virgin, virginity. Call it what you will, will. And I will make you hate. Hate it all every minute and wish you were dead, dead. Then I will with glee, glee. I will grant you that wish. Death, slow death!"

The thumb and fingers on the monster's now-giant hand pinched Sakima's skull and lifted her up off the ground in the most painful way possible. Sakima reached up to grab at its fingers, but its fingers moved separately like each was the paw of a gorilla as they held her head tight. She couldn't move them at all, and kicking and struggling only seemed to make it much, much worse.

With the flick of a fingernail on his other hand, Mhuwe tore off her pants, exposing her underwear as her pants plummeted down to the ground. Sakima was nearly in shock. *He has not changed at all. Still the same sex-obsessed monster he always was, just bigger now, and even more ugly.*

Horrified, Sakima suddenly remembered that she'd worn new

underwear beneath her ceremonial dress. The prettiest, sexiest bra and panties she had ever worn in her life—she deserved it. That's exactly what she was thinking at the time. On the eve of battle, and her a warrior of renown and acting queen of the occasion, known for her fighting skills and bravery. She deserved something for that momentous occasion. And she loved it. This all filled her with dread now. Dread, and shame, and fear.

In the next instance, Mhuwe flicked at her quiver and bow, snapping them free from her back and dropping her weapons to the ground. He did the same with her extra belt, and thus she lost both her knives, including her favorite, Chessi. Finally, he cut her shirt free, leaving her virtually naked with her new underwear exposed.

He drooled lasciviously and made a strange groaning sound. As he did this, Sakima had another thought that made her feel sicker still, and more afraid. She suddenly remembered that she was wearing the dramatic makeup of the ceremony. The swath of red paint across her eyes. Eyes made up with false lashes and lots of color, thick eyeliner. Made up for broadcasting on the large screens that had been set up around the lawns, as well as for those watching at home. Her shiny, bright red lipstick, her long hoop earrings. All of it was still there. She hadn't time to wash it off. She should've stopped at a stream and cleaned it off after Nimàt made his comment about her makeup, as nice as he meant it to be. But who had the time? It never crossed her mind until this exact second. That her elegant dressy look at the ceremony would someday put her in gross, disgusting danger.

Sakima wanted to cry. But her sudden self-loathing, coupled with the fear of being violated, would not let her. And it wouldn't matter if it was some small, pathetic creep or this gigantic, repulsive monster; the fear and disgust were the same. It was in her DNA, in her shared history with all women since the beginning of time. It was as if she had frozen up inside, unable to fight for herself at last. Unable to even feel sorry for herself. Just wishing it was over and she was dead. Wishing she had a way, right here and now, to kill herself quickly, to exit before it began.

"And now you will suffer, will suffer down to your soul, soul of your womanhood," Mhuwe growled, interrupting Sakima's thoughts, which had almost succeeded in shielding her from the reality of the moment. "Then you will, you will suffer more. As I tear you, tear you apart limb by limb. But I won't, won't let you die, or even pass out. No, no! I will make sure you are awake, are awake for every ounce of the pain, the pain, until I send your wretched, wretched soul to hell. To hell!" The monster snorted, a laugh that sounded like it was choking.

His long, pustule-covered tongue slithered out of his foul mouth full of rotten fangs and fungus. It licked Sakima's face like a dog with a bone. Mhuwe pulled his tongue back and thrust it forward again, sloshing its sogginess across her bra.

"Good, nice, tasty," the monster said. The sentiment was clearly Machto's own and not the derangement of the monster he'd become; Sakima recognized his debased thoughts. "Wish only, only that I could be man-sized again, man again, to enjoy taking you as I was destined to, destiny! But this will work. I shall make it work, make it work."

With one fur-and-vine covered hand he reached down between his own legs, his eyes rolling back in his head for a second. Sakima thought she was going to throw up and was surprised that she hadn't been vomiting this whole time. But the vomit, like her tears, seemed to have turned to dust within her.

Mhuwe's rotting tongue wriggled around Sakima's ankles and started to slowly work its way up her legs, over each calf, and then creeping further and further up her thighs. The monster again emitted a horrifying moan.

"You excited?" it said in a hoarse, almost mechanical sounding voice. "Because I am, oh I certainly am. You are mine now, mine now, and for eternity our lives will forever be intertwined. Forever!"

He cackled with a strange animal-robot sound as he began to pull Sakima toward himself with a rocking motion, perhaps something the monster considered seductive, his tongue throbbing with arousal each time it touched a part of Sakima.

"Mine, mine, mi—"

"What in the actual name of His High Holy Master, *Dorado Bej Rigor*, King of All Worlds, Maker of All Things is going on here?" a voice barked from behind Mhuwe, interrupting the hideous monster's big moment.

"Who dares speak, dares!" Mhuwe snarled, whipping around to cast a gaze on whoever had the temerity to interrupt him so he could see their face and squash them out of existence.

Locus Mub stood before and below him, his arrogant metal-clad chest puffed out, his soldiers in formation behind him, all with weapons drawn.

"How dare you interrupt, interrupt my pleasures!" the man-eating Mhuwe roared.

"This, we did not agree to."

"What?"

"We—you and I, as gentlemen—we had an agreement."

"Yes, that she is mine, mine. To do with as I will, will."

"Close, but not exactly. To kill: that was the agreement. Even to kill as slowly and as painfully as you wished, yes. That has honor in it, vengeance does. But not this thing, this assault of yours, it has no honor."

"And?" Mhuwe sneered, growling impatiently, eager to get on with his delights. After first killing Mub and his men, of course, for their impertinence.

"We had no agreement as to her womanhood. As to taking her this way."

"No?"

"The violation of a maiden? No sir." Mub snapped.

"Killing her in any way I desired, desired anyway, covers this moment," the monster raged. "My taking of her, taking her. It is all along the same gilded path, pathway." Mhuwe's words were that of a well-educated bully, but the sound of his voice was like a thousand tortured screams ringing out from the underworld.

Mub's eyebrows shot upward as his eyes popped like white mushrooms in darkness. "No, sir," he said, clearing his throat before continuing. "It does not. And as a gentleman, and in the name of fair play, I cannot allow it. Women are by far our inferiors, barely at all significant. But they *are* our mothers and sisters—and wives and courtesans and concubines as well. Not to be taken without permission."

"I have all the permission I need, need to have, from the authority invested in me as a freakin' giant monster, monster from freakin' hell, you insolent son of, son of a bitch!"

"Put her down, sir. I shall not ask again." Locus Mub withdrew his Mp-encrusted sword from its sheath and held it out in front of him.

"You must be kidding, kidding!" Mhuwe barked, rolling its eyes around for a bit. Then, it tossed Sakima to the ground with disdain. But not to kill her. Not yet. Hurting her was fine, but the beast looked forward to its extended period of fun with an odd sense of glee.

"Say your prayers, foul one," Locus Mub said.

"I put her down, down, see? Like you asked, you asked. I'm playing all nice-nice. Nice. What's your problem, shit, shithead?"

And with that, Mhuwe kicked at the man with his gigantic foot. However, Mhuwe hadn't yet grown into his new humongous body in terms of balance, and so the monster tilted a bit in the opposite direction. Thus its foot unexpectedly passed without harm over the head of Locus Mub.

"Fire!" Locus Mub hollered, his mouth shutting down to a straight and serious line, a flicker of delight in his eyes, as if he'd wanted, expected—even planned for—this moment all along. And his men complied immediately and joyfully, blasting Mhuwe repeatedly with their Mp weapons. Wounds appeared all over

Mhuwe's body. But just as it did during the battle between the Taturåkee soldiers and the Mannahatta and Kanyen fighters on the *Ästra Ån Ima* ship, Mhuwe's wounds healed almost as fast as they appeared.

But unlike the previous battle wherein Mhuwe's body took damage from just a hundred or so shots, here there were thousands and thousands. Despite the monster now having grown to more than double in size and strength of even the tallest human, the amount of hits took a toll. While one wound healed, three other gaping, bloody wounds opened up. Soon, there were more holes than substance, more wounds than flesh and bone.

Then Mhuwe's form, granted him by the devil himself, *Matanto*, began to fail. But more than fail, it simply began to disappear, like it was being sucked into a black hole. Which is exactly what was happening. The Mp was creating rips in the multiverse one after another after another. Where a single blast was effective against any human and most things—to rip it down to the atomic elements before blasting the pieces throughout the multiverse—many more were needed against Mhuwe.

His body opened up, torn to the atomic and subatomic levels, yanked toward some part of the multiverse. But then, almost instantly, it was pulled back and surprisingly reformed, again and again. And Mhuwe the monster might possibly have been able to do that trick over and over forever. But soon, holes in his body couldn't be retrieved in time. There were just too many, too fast. And bit by bit, chunks of Mhuwe disappeared. They could not be retrieved, no matter how much evil magic and power it leveraged against the damage in order to save itself.

In front of their eyes, Mhuwe flailed, trying to strike out at his torturers. But he could hardly take a step without a thigh or a knee or a foot vanishing, with great pain. And then returning and reconstructing itself—even more painfully.

The monster grimaced in agony, and his face contorted with anger. It wanted to kill them all, make them all suffer and beg for death. It wanted destruction, victory, satisfaction. But instead, all it could do was stumble, teeter, and suffer the explosions on every inch of its body, including its head and face.

Sakima stood up, nerves rattled and muscles exhausted, unnoticed by anyone. She shakily picked up her clothing and held them tight against herself, like a shield of cloth, but with the saddest face she'd ever displayed.

The monster's basic shape somehow remained as neutrons, protons, and positrons—matter and antimatter—pulled back and forth and back again from this plane of existence to many, many others. It was as if he had been cut apart by giant, malformed cookie cutters, taking bites out of his body. Bit by horrifying bit, the bites, the hollow places, were overtaking the remaining parts of Machto.

Mhuwe spun left and right, trying to deflect the blasts, making futile attempts to attack his new nemeses. All the monster's entire twelve feet high and four feet across body disintegrated when its heart exploded. The flimsy remaining outline of the horrific monster began to be transported elsewhere in the multiverse.

"You are nothing but a savage, you poor brute," Locus Mub called out to the vanishing Mhuwe. "Nothing but a myth and a joke. A massive and imposing one, to be sure. But you are nothing but your origins. You are one of them, a native of Mannahatta." Mub spat this last word out with contempt. "And I used you to help me destroy your own people. The people you betrayed with your selfish ignorance." Locus Mub laughed a terrible laugh. "And I enjoyed doing it. Using a fool, a betrayer, to take down his own people. You may hate them. You may have disowned them, laid curses upon them, murdered them and even devoured many of them. But they are you, and you are they. And you are…" Mub roared his next word at the top of his lungs. "…*Nothing!*"

The Mhuwe creature spit back, "I can be leaving, yes. Yes. But don't you think for a minute, minute, that it will be forever, ever." The monster became nothing for real, disappearing like a ghost into fog, the solid pieces of it the last to go. One hand dissolved, then one hip, and the opposite shoulder. The last thing sucked into the multiverse and off Mannahatta forever was his eye. The gigantic eye that, just for a second, as it searched the world in front of it for the last time, showed its terror.

Then all was quiet. The Taturåkee powering down their weapons as a dusting of something—a patch of Mhuwe's fur, perhaps?—flittered softly to the ground.

Sakima had watched it all in disbelief as she sat in tremendous pain. She closed her eyes, not sure she'd really seen what had played out in front of her. Not wanting to think about how close she had been to being sexually assaulted.

When she opened them again, Locus Mub's hand was outstretched to her, just a few inches from her face.

"Take my hand, won't you?" he stated.

CHAPTER 54

Locus Mub had an odor about him that was, while not strictly offensive, strong. Strong like the scent of an animal, if that animal also used a significant amount of cheap cologne and body spray.

"Let me help you to your feet, your majesty," he said. While he waited, Locus Mub turned to face his troops. "Bring me something to cover this lovely lady with. Now!"

Am I in hell? Or have I completely lost my mind? Or both? Sakima wondered.

"I can get up by myself," she said. Sakima struggled to get to her feet again, but fell back down, her back and arms and legs burning in pain. "*Mwichti!* Ow, *ow!*"

"Please, Queen of Mannahatta. Allow me to be of service."

Sakima squinted her eyes at the man. *How much of that last statement was in mocking? 50 percent? 90 percent? I'm guessing 100 percent.*

"Please allow me. It was my honor to rescue you from that aggressor."

Sakima forced herself to speak. In a raspy voice full of heat and dirt, she said, "You did not rescue me. You came to kill Mhuwe.

Which was always your plan. My being saved from a monster's abuse was coincidental fallout. You got lucky."

"No, madam, begging your pardon. But it was truly *you* who got lucky."

Around a dozen Taturåkee soldiers approached Locus Mub, their king, and handed him an olive T-shirt and a pair of pants with a camouflage pattern on them.

Mub turned to Sakima and gave them to her. "Put these on."

He motioned to the soldiers to form a circle around Sakima, their backs to her. She peered around, surprised by the graciousness of that move and grateful for the clothing they'd brought to her. But she remained deeply suspicious as well. She stood, unable or unwilling to move for a full minute. Without taking her eyes off the backs of the men, or off Mub, she slipped the shirt over her head.

It was too big, of course, but did the job of covering her, almost like a small dress. Sakima slipped on the pants, which were cut for a man and not a woman. They fit awkwardly around her hips, and there was a ridiculous gap at her waist. With some effort, she was able to tear the bottom of the too-long T-shirt in a strip. Next, she weaved the strip through the belt loops of the pants and tied it in a rough bow, creating a makeshift belt. *It might not look at all fashionable, but it will certainly keep these pants where they belong.*

"Ready?"

"Yes," she sighed. "I guess I am."

Locus Mub and his soldiers turned around, and a few of them laughed.

"Not haute couture, to be sure, but not too bad." Locus Mub lowered his voice and said, "Get the queen."

Sakima assumed he was talking about her. She didn't understand the context of "getting" her. Her muscles tensed automatically, and with the last of her strained strength and courage she had left, she adopted a weak, defensive stance of a slight crouch, arms and fists out in front of her, shaking. From sheer exhaustion, she weaved almost unnoticeably as she tried to hold her stance.

Locus Mub raised an eyebrow.

"What?" he said. He thought for a minute. "Oh! No, madam, not you. My apologies. Her—" He turned dramatically to his left to point at a woman walking forward wearing regal clothing and a crown.

The Taturåkee queen walked over to the Mannahatta queen, using her scepter as a walking stick, and put her hand on Sakima's shoulder. "Pleased to meet you. I am Queen Leia Blas. And I know all about you, my poor dear." The queen propped her scepter against the ship and put her other hand on Sakima's other shoulder. "You've been through so much, through no fault of your own. Only from being in the wrong place at the wrong time. You poor thing. And almost defiled, too. Horrible, horrible..."

With that, Sakima had nothing left. She burst into tears, her legs trembling, sobbing as her shoulders shook. The royal-looking woman, by intent and also from a genetic mother's instinct, gathered the crying girl in her arms and held her close. She gently stroked the top of Sakima's head and let her cry it out for as long as she might need to.

"There, there," the woman said in a hushed, quiet tone. "*Sssh*. It will all be all right. You'll see... *Now shush. Shhhhh...*"

Sakima let herself collapse into the woman's arms, needing the comfort, needing the release. Although she didn't trust what was happening at all. Or at the least, didn't understand it.

These are the killers of my people, the destroyers of my land, Sakima thought. *They killed my soldiers on the battlefield, as well as women and children in their innocence in their homes and sidewalks and stores and school. They are the very essence of evil. But now, they seem to take pity on me. Seem to care. Maybe I have left my senses, gone out of my mind. Perhaps none of this is happening and Machto—or Mhuwe or whatever— is destroying me on the outside as I hide within a nice, safe fantasy on the inside.*

It was the clang of the heavy chains that brought Sakima back to the here and now with an icy cold feeling as thick, heavy metal cuffs clicked onto both of her wrists.

"What are you doing?" Sakima whispered, eyes huge, peering about her like a deer in a trap, her voice barely audible.

Queen Leia Blas stepped away from Sakima. "I'm so sorry, my dear, but you are our prisoner now. Our trophy, if you will," she said. "You'll join us on our ship now, and we will head home to Taturåkis. Our mission is done. We'll need to return at a different point in the space-time continuum to get what we came to get. Back when our sworn enemies, the people of Eldëror—the *Alànëmëskat*—first arrived in your quaint land. We'll succeed in our next attempt to capture our adversaries. A few tweaks and adjustments in the navigation and time systems, and we shall destroy them before they even arrive, crashing into the 'Land Below,' as you like to call planet Earth, sending your people, your ancestors off to a parallel world of Mannahatta. Before they have a chance to alter the direction of your people's destiny. It will be as if it never happened." She paused and stared at Sakima. "My! Hold on. What is this...?"

Queen Leia Blas pulled the leather and steel *Alànëmëskat* arm cuff off Sakima's forearm. The cuff her ancestors had created only for Sakima. The cuff that gave her the advantage and the connection to the Grandmother of the South.

Sakima was too sad, and tired, and surprised to resist in time, and before she knew it, her precious, magical cuff was in the hands of the enemy.

"Tighten that!" Blas said, gesturing toward the metal handcuffs on Sakima's wrists. By removing Sakima's Alànëmëskat cuff, the queen had created enough of a gap that Sakima might have been able to pull her hand out of the handcuff on that arm. But that possibility ended as soon as it revealed itself.

Two other soldiers stepped up to Sakima and ran a large chain through the cuffs on her hands, connecting them. They dropped the heavy chain to the ground. It momentarily pulled Sakima with it.

Two additional cuffs were slapped onto each of Sakima's ankles. They ran the chain through these as well, making it impossible for Sakima to run away—or even walk away without considerable effort and discomfort. Making it impossible, really, for Sakima to do anything at all.

"Why don't you just kill me?" Sakima said in frustration. "Why take me from my people? After all this, this—"

"It's called 'war,' dear. Something you lost—and quite spectacularly, I might add. You are the spoils. And besides—" Queen Blas grabbed the chain that hung between Sakima's wrists, where she was now forced to hold her arms out in front of her and up at chest height. The Queen of the Taturåkee tugged Sakima forward as she was shoved from behind by some of the soldiers. "Besides, you'll keep these sad specimens in line. You're being dead would cause more trouble that it—or you—are worth."

With that, the soldiers shoved and yanked Sakima out of the woods and into the field again, where she had crash-landed her spaceship a only minutes earlier. There, sitting along the side of the craft in chains were the last of the grand Mannahatta and Kanyen co-armies, looking beaten and exhausted—and even, in a few cases, clearly frightened.

Sakima looked at the brave *ilaok*, both Mannahatta and Kanyen. She was proud of them still; in fact, even more proud that they had never given up, even during these darkest of moments. Her eyes stopped, and she stared at one warrior in particular. It couldn't be. But it was—him.

Lèke.

And as she realized she loved him and that he too was now in mortal danger and a prisoner like her, a group of Taturåkee soldiers appeared and hollered at the men to get up. Suddenly, and without provocation, they began beating the warriors with the butts of their weapons. Some of the Mannahatta warriors' noses bled profusely. Other fighters dropped to the ground, knocked unconscious. Many of them cursed, cried out for the unnecessary beating to stop.

"My *Kishelë!*" Sakima shouted at the top of her lungs. "What is *wrong* with you people?"

Queen Leia Blas slapped Sakima hard across the face, leaving Sakima shocked and her cheek stinging.

"Oh no, my dear," Leia Blas said. "Disrespect will not be permitted. You will speak when spoken to. And do as you are told. You will, my sweet Queen of Mannahatta, behave yourself. Like a good little queen."

Sakima's jaw hung open for a minute as she tried to take in all that had happened in a few brief seconds. As she did so, Locus Mub swept by her with a dozen men. He struck at the warriors sitting on the ground with a large stick he'd picked up in the *Tèkëne* forest—in fact, it was one of the branches snapped in two by Mhuwe. He roused them viciously up onto their feet.

"Let's get a move on," he shouted. "We got a long way to go, and you are as expendable—or as valuable—as you make yourself. Get going, get *going.*" He slapped contemptuously at a few of the warriors at random with the stick before tossing it onto the grass. "Get them into the ship and locked in," he said, directing himself to his soldiers. "We leave immediately."

Locus Mub turned to Queen Leia Blas and took her hand. "Please, allow me." He guided her arm around his in a practiced move while pointing the way ahead with the palm of his hand. Queen Blas smiled and made a curtsey-like movement as they walked on.

Sakima was shoved from behind. "Move it, bitch," a gravelly voice said.

Why? It's always "bitch." That was always what they say. She almost laughed for a second, but her body, heart, and soul were in far too much pain to allow that to happen.

The defeated soldiers and their temporary queen were all herded roughly and without ceremony aboard the *Ästra Ån Ima*—Sakima along with the Mannahatta *ilaok* and the Kanyen warriors. She tried to imagine a way out of this disastrous turn of events, but could think of nothing. Once she got on that ship, she'd be gone forever—they all would—never to return. She had no way of knowing in which of the Many Worlds they might end up. Nor any way of possibly getting back to her own universe in her own time period.

It was as over, as over as it could possibly get. Her reign as queen, if you could even call it that, could be measured in days—or really just in hours and minutes.

And what of my people? Sakima thought, feeling the tears start again. *Who will take care of them? Who will fight for them? Who will cure them of this horrid disease, if a cure is even possible? There are no warriors with them now. Half the population is deathly sick; another good size group has been killed in battle or murdered outright as collateral damage.*

She took one long, exhausted breath.

Mannahatta is doomed, she thought, trembling now with anger and deep, profound sorrow. *And there is nothing I can do about it. Or will be able to do, ever again.* Sakima closed her eyes and sighed. *Mannahatta is over, done, finished.*

And so am I.

CHAPTER 55

nside the *Alànëmëskat* spacecraft—which Sakima had miraculously saved with her daring crash landing—her brother Nimàt began to open his tired eyes.

"Hello? Anyone?" He reached up and grabbed the back of his neck, where he'd experienced some not insignificant whiplash. "Ow! Jeez, that hurts." He cleared his throat and focused his eyes. The place was a wrecked mess. Abruptly, he remembered that they'd crashed. He peered over to where he expected to find his sister sitting in the captain's chair. But it was empty, she was gone.

"Sakima?" he called out in a shaky voice. He unsnapped himself from his seat and stood up with care, his muscles everywhere aching. "Where is everybody? Hello? Wu' Lisa? Come, girl!"

But he received no response. And then, as if remembering a dream, he pictured the soldiers escaping, along with his sisters and their new dog friend. Nimàt grunted and sighed as he made his way down the first set of stairs. He checked the mess hall to find out if there was anyone else there, but came up empty-handed. He walked down to the bunk area where the last group of warriors had waited to get to safety via the now-destroyed transport. Again, there was no one else on board but him and him alone.

Odd, he thought. *Sakima wouldn't have gone and gotten another transport and returned for the remaining warriors. Wouldn't have driven back to the shelter with everyone else on it except for me. He swallowed hard. Would she...?*

He screwed up his bravery and strength and dismissed a growing demand from his psyche to hit him with the double-whammy of panic and self-pity.

Maybe they're waiting until everyone is on the transit ready to go. Sakima was going to come back for her kid brother. He smiled and nodded his head. *That's it, of course. Makes sense. She was letting me rest. She's sweet like that.*

He glanced down the short flight of steps to the exit door and noticed that, strangely, the door to the airlock was open.

Well, that shouldn't be. I know that much for sure. Hmmm. He scratched his head, then suddenly snapped his fingers. *It's open because the air is clean again! That's it, the coast is clear.*

He ran down the stairs, taking two at a time.

The door to the outside was also open. No one would have left both doors like that if the air was still poisonous.

How are they staying open? It was then that he noticed the swords jammed into the track for each door, preventing them from auto-matically shutting.

Why in the world would anyone do that?

He shrugged his shoulders and jauntily stepped outside, expecting to find his compatriots milling about, enjoying the fresh air and the euphoric feeling of victory.

But there was no one milling about. Only lots and lots of kicked-up clumps of grass and mud. Some broken weapons were strewn about, too.

A battle? Again?

Nimàt was having a hard time piecing together what had tran-spired while he was asleep. But it hit him soon enough: the

Taturåkis ship must have landed shortly after they crashed. A fight ensued: Mannahatta and Kanyen versus Taturåkees.

But who won? Nimàt shook his head and smiled. *'Who won?' What an idiotic question. The side with Sakima on it, of course! Sakima could not lose! She is not a loser, no way.*

He heard an odd sound: the whirring of tachyon engines. It was a low, almost quiet noise at first. But it grew louder and louder as the engines torqued up to speed.

The sound of revving engines was coming from the other side of the ship, Nimàt realized. He ran around the ship as fast as he could.

But when he got there, he froze.

The great door of the *Ästra Ån Ima* banged shut. But he had been able to catch a glimpse of the Mannahatta warriors inside the ship and was quite certain he had spied his sister among them, all of them bound in chains.

And as he stood there, unable to move, the ship lifted off the ground, and in seconds it was gone. Gone from this universe and this time to *Kishelë* knows where.

In the ensuing eerie silence, Nimàt collapsed to his knees in shock. He wavered there, tilting back and forth as the enormity of the situation hit him.

Mannahatta was defeated. There were no warriors left. Most of the population was sick or dying or dead. And their temporary queen—his beloved sister—had been taken away in chains, a prisoner of the invaders, the monstrous Taturåkees.

For a few long minutes, Nimàt felt like dropping onto the grass and giving into his emotions, his feelings of despair and sorrow. But he forced himself to stand up again. He turned and gazed back at his world—a world torn apart, buildings smashed, some trees and bushes still smoldering.

He dragged himself back down the low hill toward the shelter inside the *Wîkëwam Shawken Obroa*—the Mannahatta Science, Research, & Technology building. As he approached, his sister Mimi ran out toward him. Seeing him with no hazmat suit nor oxygen mask of any kind, she threw off her helmet and her gloves and embraced him when they met.

"What has happened?" she said. "Where are the other men? The other *ilaok*? Where—where is Sakima?"

"They're... they're gone."

"What do you mean, 'gone?' Gone where? To battle?"

"They've been taken."

"Nimàt, are you all right? Are you hurt? Are you sure you've understood my questions? Who has taken them?"

"The Taturåkees. Locus Mub. I saw them, Mimi! All of them in chains!"

"No!" Mimi screamed. Tears of anger filled her eyes. "No, this absolutely can't be. And Sakima?"

Nimàt was unable to speak.

"Alive?"

He slowly tipped his head, but Mimi had her answer.

"They have her too, but where are they?" she said in an almost inaudible whisper.

"Back to Taturåkis, I suppose, wherever that is." He sniffed and drew a breath. "We'll never see her again. They've gone who knows where, deep through the Many Worlds, I'm sure."

They fell into each other again and hugged for a long time. When they separated at last, the sky was already darkening, and some stars had appeared. They both stared up at the cosmos, lost in their own thoughts.

"It's what they foretold," Mimi said, her voice quiet and shaky and deep. "It's the end now. The end days. *Ekhokiike*..."

Nimàt lowered his gaze from the sky and seemed to stare at something in the distance. "It is not the end," he said, his eyes boring into the deepening darkness, his mouth a thin, grim line. "Not if I have anything to say about it."

CHAPTER 56

Two days later, the Council of Elders managed to rise above their emotional pain and hold an emergency meeting. They gathered with solemnity around the same table as always. Some gravely took their seats, while others remained standing, heads down.

Present were the most senior Elders: Elder Ahi Manunsko, Elder Rita Shim Olsen, and Elder Nitis Tschutti. Also present were all the Elders who'd survived the attack, which were too few. Two died during the initial attack, two more after the poisonous gassing, and three were currently hospitalized. No one represented the military because there were scant few officers who'd lived to see this day— or warriors of any class. All others were in the hospital receiving as much treatment as they could from the overworked and under-staffed doctors, nurses, and technicians there.

Elder Ahi Manunsko motioned for quiet. He seemed weaker than before the attacks, and much older, clutching the back of his chair for support as he spoke. "First, let me say we are grateful that this building and even this room still stand today," he said. "Now, a moment if you would, to honor those we lost. Elder Olsen?" He addressed her without looking up at her, hiding his tear-filled, red eyes.

"Yes, of course," Elder Rita Shim Olsen said, clearing her throat. She got up as Elder Manunsko sat down. "We remember with fondness the ones we've lost, and the ones wounded. Many in mortal danger. We remember especially our leader, the wise and brave Sachem, Takachsin Tamanend. May he enjoy the fullness of the Land of the Dead. May he be blessed again with the presence of his wife, the wise and loving Wùnita, and of his firstborn, Hìtami, a brave warrior and the pride of Mannahatta."

There were many sounds of agreement and whispered words of prayer good wishes as heads nodded.

"And we remember our lost friends, Dr. Lippoe Pahòke, a scientist with true vision and a genuine friend to all. Colonel Skattek, a brave leader who always fought alongside his men and sacrificed himself so they might have a chance to live. Second Lieutenant Nuwingi, a mighty warrior. Our Kanyen friend, Major Ron:kwe Onanta, who stood beside us to battle our enemies at this, our darkest hour. And all the warriors who fell fighting for Mannahatta. And last but not least, to all the ones we loved, who have left us for the Land of the Dead during this terrible time."

"*Ànkùntëwakàn*. Many blessings to them all."

There followed some more sad mumbling and then complete silence.

"And to our queen," Nimàt said, taking over the eulogy. "Sakima Tamanend, a brave, wise, and loving sister, daughter, and warrior to the very end. May they all find joy and fulfillment in the Land of the Dead forever." Nimàt bent his head and closed his eyes. He didn't know if his sister was, in fact, among the deceased now. But he knew he'd never see her again and wanted to send blessings her way regardless.

"*Na në lekèch*," the Elders all said in unison. "Let it be so."

There were a few scattered amens and *ànkùntëwakàns* and then silence again. Elder Rita Shim Olsen sat back down.

"Your attention please, on another matter," Elder Ahi Manunsko said, looking at his hands as he talked. "As Nimàt Tamanend—the youngest and last remaining son of our lost sachem, Takachsin Tamanend, and sister of our Queen *Pro Tempore*, Sakima Tamanend —has rightfully pointed out: we are without a leader now. I call that now as our first and only other order of business for this meeting."

"Agreed," some of the Elders called out. Others simply nodded or took notes on the electronic pads in front of them.

"So now, I'd like to nominate Nimàt Tamanend as our new Sachem *Pro Tempore*. Can I get a second?"

"I second that, Elder Manunsko," Elder Olsen said, raising her hand.

"Let us vote on it," Elder Nitis Tschutti said. "All in favor?"

There were many yays around the table—some shouted, others uttered softly, respectively.

"Any against?"

Nimàt considered for a second speaking up, raising his hand against the idea. He wasn't ready, didn't want this. At least not yet, not this soon. He was young and inexperienced. Too apprehensive about what might come next to Mannahatta. But he stayed silent. For he understood that's what Sakima would want: for her brother to take over the helm. Now that the Tamanend family was, in the most tragic way, reduced to only himself, his sisters, Tangetta and Mimi, and Mimi's little daughter.

Mimi had turned down the position, he knew, when she had been earlier offered the position in private consultation. She did not want this either. Or perhaps not yet. Or maybe she wanted Nimàt to have a chance—however short and without glory that might be —to stand in his father's shoes. To sit in the throne of power where his father had once sat. At least once in his life. Or perhaps, for the rest of his life, should the Elders decide or fate intervene.

"It's unanimous," Elder Tschutti said in a solemn tone.

"Good. Praise *Kishelë*," Elder Manunsko said, and around the table everyone joined in the praising.

Nimàt peered out the window up into the blue autumn sky, as high as he could see, imagining that on the other side of that blue existed the blackness of space. And somewhere within that infinite space in some other timeline in another one of the Many Worlds, he imagined his sister still alive, fighting to be free.

But he felt no joy in that thought, as it felt like a lie—a fairytale, a myth he was telling himself. He absently returned his gaze to the group seated around the table.

"It's your job to dismiss this meeting, Nimàt. Or should I now say, *Sachem* Nimàt," Elder Rita Shim Olsen said. "In fact, from here on and until further notice, you will run these meetings as the leader of the Mannahatta people and the head of the Council of Elders."

"Oh, um, okay," Nimàt restlessly tapped the pad in front of him, searching for a clue about what to say. "Well, then, um," he cleared his throat. "Uh, so, I say—dismissed?"

"We typically say, if I may be so bold," Elder Tschutti said, "something like, 'If there are no further agenda items, I move to adjourn.' And next, and also normally, we all agree."

"Oh, right, I see." In a voice he hoped came across serious and weighty, Nimàt said, "If there's nothing else, I call to adjourn."

"I second that," Elder Manunsko said.

There were words of agreement, and with that, the first meeting of the Council of Elders under the direction of their new leader, Sachem Nimàt Tamanend, came to its natural conclusion. All the members of the council rose up and left the room.

Except Nimàt, who remained in the room, sitting in silence with his eyes closed. Taking slow, sad, and deep breaths.

Sakima, I pray you are safe. But more than that, I pray you can somehow return to us. Nimàt gazed back up at the sky. *I get that that's foolish of me. "Look at Nimàt," everyone says. "Always dreaming." But I,*

I can't accept that you're gone forever. This is your land, your throne, Sakima. I don't want it. I only want to dance and laugh. And be myself.

Nimàt let his head fall to his chest and allowed the tears to drip down. Even he, the frivolous one of the family, understood that the time of dancing and laughter and any joy at all was over and gone forever.

CHAPTER 57

Sakima crouched in the small prison room where she and all the other warriors were locked with heavy chains against shiny metal walls that contrasted gravely with the worn and rusty shackles. Cameras mounted along the top of the walls, positioned every five feet, whirring slowly as they monitored the new prisoners up and down the line. She peered about at her friends, both Mannahattas and a few Kanyens, and wondered how —why—this was happening.

She closed her eyes and tried to think as the ship sped through the Many Worlds. What she didn't understand was how she'd lost her connection to the Grandmother of the South. While she didn't really have expectations that she'd be visited by her own mother, she secretly hoped she'd receive some help, some advice, from her all the same.

She wished that somehow Janie Jones from the Land Below was here. Not in this same predicament. Just have her here to talk to her. To ask her to take a peek into the Land of the Dead with that gift she had. To perhaps find out what was going on with the lack of communication. It would be good to just understand what was happening, anywhere at all. Because nothing that had happened in the last few days and weeks made any sense to her whatsoever.

Sakima thought about the statue that her ancestors made with the help of the Star Walkers that her father had revealed to her at the wonderful celebration almost two years ago. Why should such a statue exist in her honor and likeness? Could her ancestors and the *Alànëmëskat* only see into the future up to a year ago, and all that has happened since then was actually completely unknown to them?

Stupid statue. It should never have existed. It was a lie, showing me as some kind of hero, some type of savior of the Mannahatta people. A complete lie—a stupid, terrible, mocking joke of a lie.

Her recent failures were of such a magnitude as to almost be unfathomable. No one in history could have failed as hard as Sakima had.

A statue for me? That is just embarrassing.

Sakima opened her eyes and gazed across the room. Lèke was there, chained on the other side, looking at her. He shrugged and did his best to smile.

Sakima looked away, then shifted her glance back down at the ground. To add insult to injury after injury, she thought, the one man I really care about is here to witness my humiliation, my downfall—and ultimately, my death.

She sighed and closed her eyes again.

Grandmother of the South, please see me. Please visit me, talk to me. Give me a sign.

I know I've failed miserably, but is there truly no way out? I feel that there isn't and that my life is over. The lives of these men with me, too. All of the Mannahatta people.

But still, I need hope. I crave it. Can I not get even one small sign that there might be light at the end of all this darkness?

The silence was overwhelming. Sakima realized she was completely alone now as tears rolled down her cheeks.

As the *Ästra Ån Ima* traversed through the multiverse, through black holes and wormholes, Sakima prayed for sleep, for unconsciousness, perhaps even for death, as the Taturåkee ship sped on. On its way back to the planet Taturåkis.

Back to a future unknown.

MANNAHATTA AND TATURÅKEE WORDS

MANNAHATTA WORDS

A

Achgindamen *(ah-gin-DA-men)*. One who has read and learned from many books.

aèsës *(aye-ah-sis)*. Animals (but not pets). Can also be used as an insult.

Ahi Manunsko *(AH-hee Mahn-ooks-su)*. The most senior Elder of the Mannahatta people. His name translates to "he is a very angry man."

ahoaltuwi *(ah-HO-ahl-tu-wee)*. Means "loving one." Aunt Ahoaltuwi is the wife of Takachsin's best friend, Lippoe Pahòke.

ahpòn'tëta *(ah-pahn-TEE-tah)*. Cookies.

aimalàxàmuk (*ay-mah-LAX-ah-mook*). Bitches (negative use); female dogs (normal use).

Alànëmëskat (*ah-lah-nuh-MISS-kaht*). The Star Walkers, the multiverse/wormhole traveling people. This word is a combination of *alànkok*, stars, and *pèhpëmëskat*, walkers. From the Mannahatta myth of the People Who Fell From the Sky.

Alànkok Luweyunk (*ah-LAHN-goke Loo-WAY-oonk*). The North Star.

Amimi (*AH-mee-mee*). Sakima's older sister. Her nickname is Mimi. Means, "little dove."

ànkùntëwakàn (*hank-oo-tah-WAH-kahn*). Blessings.

ansikëmès (*ahn-SEE-kah-mess*). The maple tree.

ansiptakàn (*ahn-SEE-top-kahn*). The female version of the male leader's headpiece. This headpiece for women also trailed down from the head to the back, but much farther down than the men's version, almost to the ground. Also known as *ansipëlaon*. See also: psikalu.

Apatschin (*ah-PAT-sheen*). The name of Sakima's childhood boyfriend; "Pat" for short. Means, "he who has gone."

awèninkahke: (*ah-wah-NINGA-hkay*). The departed people. Those who have walked on.

B - E

chesimus (*chess-see-muhs*). Means "little brother." Chessi (*chess-see*) is the name Sakima has given her favorite knife.

chitanësit sëkahsën mpàki (*cheet-tah-NAH-seet SHAH-kah-sahn moke-kay*). Mannahatta name for their tanks. Literally, "strong vehicle made from iron."

èchei (*uh-chay-YEE*). "Wow!" or "Gosh!" or "Cool!" Alternate spelling is "ekee ay," which is a phonetic spelling as well (for that alternate).

ehasuwichik (*eh-ha-sa-WEE-cheek*). Preaching, sermonizing, speaking to groups.

Eldëror (*el-door-roor*). Home planet of the Star Walkers; thus the beginning of the "Elder" council. Name is a tribute to Princess Leia's home planet, Alderaan, and the home planet of the Ewoks, Endor.

elgixin (*ale-gee-zin*). Simply means "field." The Elgixin Field is a large grass space that sits in the middle of the Mannahatta Technology & Research Center's campus.

F – I

gachpees (*gatch-pees*). Twins.

gischileu (*gee-she-loo*). Means "true". Leke Gischileu is Sakima's love interest in the series. His name means "Loyal and True"; in other words, one who is very faithful and real.

hè (*hay*). Hello; hi; hey, yo!

Hìtami (*hee-TAH-mee*). Sakima's older brother, whose nickname was Tommy. Means, "the first" or "the one who came before."

ila (*eee-LAH*). A single warrior.

ilaok (*eee-LOWK*). Warriors.

J – K

Kahèsëna Hàki (*kah-hee-sen-ah HAW-kee*). Mother Earth.

kèkayëmhès (*kay-kie-OOM-hess*). The government and the rule of law.

Kèkayëmhès Wikwahëmink (*kay-KIE-oom-hess week-hoomg*). The government building.

kèkwi këlamapisun (*kay-kwee lala-mahpee-soon*). A beautiful belt meant for formal occasions, it had tiny black, purple, and white beads made from seashell bits integrated in patterns across the entire belt.

këlulël (*kah-LOOL-lush*). An all-purpose curse word meaning something similar to "damn."

kèpchat (*kef-chaht*). A fool.

Kìkay Achimulsikaon (*kik-aye ah-chee-mule-see-COW*). The Elder Council Longhouse.

Kishelë (*key-shell-luh*). God. One of many names for the Creator, which also include Ketanëtuwit and Kishelëmùkònk.

kittakima (*kit-TAH-kem-ah*). Royalty; for example, the queen. See also: nikanixit xkwe.

kohètëta (*koe-hay-TOO-tah*). Aunt.

kpakuwe (*kuh-coo-wuh*). Chatter, also a chatterbox.

kwèn'shùkwënay (*wen-SHOOK-wen-nie-ah*). This is the name for mountain lion, bobcat, or cougar.

L

Lèke (*lay-kay*). The loyal one. Leke is an up and coming warrior and Sakima's love interest. Full name is Lèke Gischileu (*GEE-shah-loo*) which means, "he who has proven himself to be true."

Lenape (*len-AH-pay*). One of many tribes akin to the Algonquian nation along the northeastern seaboard of North American. The Lenape were the original people of the island of Manhattan on planet Earth.

lënu (*LEN-oo*). A man.

Lëpweichik Èlikhatink Mannahatta (*lep-wah-EE-cheek el-ee-KAH-tink Len-ah-pay*). The Mannahatta Technology & Research Center. Literally, the wise ones + the village + Mannahatta = Village of the Wise Ones.

lëpweokàn kèku (*lea-way-OH-kahn kay-too*). Artificial Intelligence (AI). Literally translates to "the intelligent thing."

M

Machto Pequonitto (*MAHCH-toe pay-quo-NEE-toe*). Sakima's brother-in-law. Means "evil spirit."

maluwe (*mah-LOW-way*). Damn it, or darn it. Means something similar to, "Dammit!" or "Curse it!"

manëtu (*mahn-AY-too*). Demon monsters.

Mannahatta (*man-nah-HAHT-tuh*). Mannahatta is the planet in an alternative universe where Sakima and her family live. It means, "beautiful land of many hills." Mannahatta is also the name of the people on the planet as well as their language.

Matanto (*mah-TAHN-toe*). The Mannahatta name for the devil.

màxkwi (*mahx-kwee*). A bear.

mechakgilik (*mek-ah-GEE-leek*). The mechanical/robotic super-suit designed by Sakima. The word means "great big suit." Often referred to as a "mechSuit."

mechkwèn'shùkwënay (*mekweh SHOOK-wen-nie-ah*). A part-machine, part-living creature lab-created lion. Also known as a mechMountain lion or mechCougar (used for both).

mechmàxkwi (*mek-MAHX-kwee*). A part-machine, part-living creature lab-created bear. Also known as a mechBear.

meechgalanne (*metch-gah-LAH-nay*). Means "hawk". The warrior and tactical technician, Mitch Galanney, is a homonym of this word.

Mënatink Ohëlëmi (*mah-NAH-ting OH-lay-may*). New York City, most specifically Manhattan. Literally, "the far away island" and means the Land Below.

Mhuwe (*muh-HOO-way*). A man-eating giant of Mannahatta folklore. A creature with horns and patchy fur that can grow twice as tall as a human.

Mimëntëta *(mee-mee-ahn-TAY-tah).* Sakima's niece and her sister Mimi's daughter. Literally means, "baby," but in this context, "Little Mimi."

mpoalonium *(bow-LONE-ee-um).* A powerful element from another world given from the Alànawènik. Literally translates as, "Power from the Gods." The element is written as Mp on the Periodic Table of Elements; atomic number 111, atomic weight of 333.

mwekane *(mm-WAY-cah-nay).* Mannahatta word for dog. The diminutive form, mwekanètët, means "puppy."

mwichti *(muh-WEECH-tee).* Feces, officially. But often used like the English swear word, "shit."

N

Na në lekèch *(nah nah LAY-kich).* Let it be so.

Nagatamen Mùxul Allanque *(nah-gah-TAH-men mah-HOO-lay ahl-LEN-kay).* The alien spacecraft driven by the Alànëmëskat, the Star Walkers. Typically referred to simply as NaMùxAll. It means, "the Trusted Starship."

nikanixit xkwe *(nee-kay-nee HUN-kwah).* Another word for queen; a female leader. See also: kittakima.

Nimàt *(NEE-mat).* Sakima's slightly younger brother. The word literally translates to brother.

Nink Shawi *(Ning -SHAW-wee).* The edge of the Mannahatta world, a magical location with clear views from Mannahatta to the Land Below.

nitis (*nee-tees*). Means companion or friend. Nitis Tschutti is one of the Elders on the Mannahatta Council.

Ntite Pìkchëlhe (*nee-tay pik-shell-AY-ah*). The Think & Draw 2000 (the number 2,000 is *tèlën txën nisha*). A talking, meeting-facilitating electronic whiteboard.

Nuhëma (*new-HEY-mah*). The Grandmother of the South. Her full name is Nuhëma Shaoneyunk.

nulakìl (*new-LAH-keel*). To jump. Literally, "I jump well."

nuwingi (*noo-WING-ee*). Means "the willing one". Second Lieutenant Nuwingi is a leader in the Mannahatta military.

nuxtët (*NO-wah-tut*). Uncle.

O – R

òhchu (*oh-choo*). Òhchu Peak, the tallest mountain top on Mannahatta. Means hill or mountain.

Pahòke (*pah-HO-kay*). Means friend or friendly. It is also the last name of Takachsin's best friend, Dr. Lippoe (meaning "wise one") Pahòke, PhD.

pahsahëman (*pah-sah-HAH-mahn*). Mannahatta football, played on a field about the size of a current-day soccer field and sometimes on a field miles long. Mannahatta football is both a game and a system to train warriors for battle.

pëmëtunhe (*pay-mah-TOO-ahn-heh*). Preacher. Preaching.

pèmitàn mpàki (*pay-MEE-tahn moke-kay*). Mannahatta word for their hovercar. Literally means "floating vehicle."

Puhùntèk Mahtakeyëwakàn (*poo-HOON-deck mah-tah-Kay-yoo-WAH-ken*). The Mannahatta War Room.

S

Sakima (*sah-KEE-muh*). The heroine of these tales, the first Mannahatta female warrior and a woman of legend. The daughter of Takachsin and a member of a family of great honor.

shaèk (*SHY-ak*). Measurement similar to yard or a meter; roughly three feet in length.

shèshkulhlëwès (*sheesh-kool-HAHL-la-wase*). School teacher. Dr. Lëwis Shèshkulh is a data scientist at the Mannahatta Technology & Research Center.

Shëwanahkòk (*shah-wah-NAH-coke*). White people, or people of European descent.

skattek (*SKAY-tayk*). Means "a zealous (devoted, diligent) one". Colonel Skattek is a high-ranking officer in the Mannahatta military structure.

Skontay Chìpilësu (*SKOON-day Chee-pee-LIS-su*). Name of the portal to the multiverse. Means the "dangerous doorway," the "exciting passageway." In common usage it means simply, "portal."

T

Takachsin (*tuh-KUH-shin*). Sakima's father. Means leader. His nickname is "TeeTee" (for T.T.) and his wife calls him "Taka."

Tamanend *(tuh-MUH-nend).* Sakima's family name. A well-established name in Mannahatta history.

Tangetta *(tan-JET-ah).* Sakima's younger sister, whom she affectionately calls "Tangerine." Her name means "short, small, and sweet."

taonkëlàxàm *(tone-GLAHK-um).* Bastard. Literally translates to "stray dog."

Tèkëne *(TAY-kun-nee).* The forest. This is the massive, ancient forest near where Sakima lives.

tëme *(TEM-may).* Coyote. Also written as *tëmetët.*

tèpahtu *(tay-pah-TOO).* Stupid.

tèpahtu lënu *(tay-pah-TOO len-oo).* Stupid man.

tëpinxkèpi *(tah—pinks-SKEP-ia).* Sakima's cuff.

tschikenum *(CHEE-can-um).* Turkey. The Turkey Clan is one of the influential groups of Mannahatta, it symbolizes good luck and fertility. Sometimes spelled *chikënëm,* pronounced the same.

tschutti *(chay-SHOO-tee).* Means "comrade" or "compatriot". Nitis Tschutti is one of the Elders on the Mannahatta Council.

tulpe *(TOOL-pay).* The turtle. The Turtle Clan. One of the influential clans of Mannahatta. It symbolizes wisdom and loyalty, as well as stubbornness.

U, V

There appears to be no Mannahatta words beginning with U or V.

W

wanìshi (*was-NEE-shee*). Thank you; thanks.

Wematëgunis (*wem-ay-tay-GOO-nees*). The little people of the forest. They are elf-like mythological people who help any Mannahatta individual who might find themselves lost or in trouble in the forest.

Wîkëwam Shawken Obroa (*WEE-ka-wahm Shaw-ken Oh-bro-wah*). The Mannahatta Science, Research & Technology building. Named using the Mannahatta word for house/building (*Wîkëwam*) plus nods to two Star Wars planets—*Shawken*, famed for science and tech, and *Obroa*, known for its vast libraries and medical centers.

Wikhakamik (*wee-kah-kah-MEE-kay*): Being there when the End of the World has arrived.

wulissa (*woo-LEE-sah*). The feminine of *wulisso*. Means "the best girl" or "pretty girl". Sakima named her puppy Wu' Lisa; Lisa for short.

wulit (*woo-leet*). Suffix or prefix that means "the best."

Wùnita (*woo-NEE-tuh*). Sakima's mother. It means, "she who knows," or "she who is able."

X, Y

xinkwtëme (*zing-TWAH-meh*). Wolf.

yakaon hakink (*yay-KAH-own HAW-kink*). Underground shelter.

Yakwahe (*yuh-KWAH-hay*). The giant hairless bear monster of Mannahatta legend that attacks New York City.

Z

There appears to be no Mannahatta words that begin with the letter Z.

TATURÅKEE WORDS

Taturåkee (*tat-ur-AH-key*). The people of the planet of Taturåkis.

Taturåkis (*tat-urr-AH-kes*). Home planet of the Taturåkee, the people led by Locus Mub. A desert planet whose name is a tribute to both Rakis from the *Dune* series and Tatooine from *Star Wars*.

Ziåd (*zee-ahd*). The god of the Taturåkee people.

ABOUT THE AUTHOR

THOMAS MORE developed a fascination with science fiction during his childhood years. This early passion evolved into a life-long love of both reading and writing, eventually leading him to an advanced degree in creative writing.

When not crafting stories, Thomas More enjoys playing guitar, piano, drums, and trumpet, and reading new and classic sci-fi books.

Born and raised in NYC, he lives in Manhattan.

———

FOLLOW THE AUTHOR

amazon.com/author/thomasmorewriter

goodreads.com/ThomasMoreWriter

instagram.com/thomasmorewriter

facebook.com/thomasmorebooks

x.com/thomasmorebooks

pinterest.com/thomasmorewriter

tiktok.com/@thomasmorewriter

ACKNOWLEDGMENTS

Special thanks to Matthew Turano for his wonderful, creative, and impactful developmental editing for this series. Thanks, too, to Lisa Hannan Fox for her perfect copyediting and proofreading. With gratitude to my online teachers including David Farland, Brandon Sanderson, Chris Fox, and most especially Holly Lisle. And finally, thank-you to Alex Newton for creating the amazing book description used on the back covers and book listings.